The Drowners

Jennie Finch

First published 2013
by Impress Books Ltd

Innovation Centre, Rennes Drive, University of Exeter Campus
Exeter EX4 4RN

Typeset in Sabon by Swales & Willis Ltd, Exeter, Devon

Printed and bound in England by imprintdigital.net

British Library Cataloging in Publication Data
A catalogue record for this book is available from the British Library

ISBN: 978-1-907605-38-3 (pbk)
ISBN: 978-1-907605-39-0 (ebk)

This book is dedicated to my parents,
Ben and Mavis Finch.
Because I promised.

Acknowledgements

No book is written in isolation and this one is no exception. Many people have taken the time to answer my questions or shared their knowledge with me and I am deeply grateful.

Special thanks to Jackie for her continuing and astonishing range of information about both the probation service and the social conditions and changes of the 1980s.

Thank you to my publishers, Impress Books, who took a chance on *Death of the Elver Man* and have let me continue to roam through the Levels, causing mayhem.

Thanks to Judy for the tandem, to Jack for the custard, to Kath and Derek for the cauliflower soup and to all the readers who took the time to comment and review *Death of the Elver Man*. It is a wonderful feeling, knowing there are people out there who enjoyed the first book. I hope this one does not disappoint.

A big hello to Arnold and Rita who provided the perfect place to finish this book.

Many thanks to the media people who have given me the chance to discuss and present my work, especially Phil and Amy from Radio Tees and all at Southside Broadcasting and Siren FM. A special thanks, also, to Michelle, my wonderful proofreader.

Prologue

It had been a fine evening, and Michael 'Sticky Micky' Franks was in a remarkably good mood considering he was several miles from home and there was no sign of anyone around to give him a lift. He stood on the doorstep of the pub peering hopefully out across the Somerset Levels for a few minutes, his swaying bulk steadied against the front wall, but the only light came from the pale moon glinting through the trees and after a short while he decided to just make his own way. Despite the late hour it was a mild night, the last of the day's warmth radiating thinly from the tarmac of the road and a soft breeze rustling the leaves on the overhanging trees. Micky ambled along, humming to himself in a particularly tuneless fashion, his eyes flickering in and out of focus as his brain struggled to keep him upright and moving. At a bend in the road he hesitated, turning his head from side to side as he considered his options. The road was longer but had a better surface than the footpath which cut off to his left and disappeared across the Levels. He'd need to pick his way through the occasional boggy patch, and there were some stretches where the nettles and brambles had grown over the path, but it was at least a mile shorter than the alternative and Micky wanted to get home. His head was buzzing and he knew from experience the buzzing would soon turn to an ache and then a pounding. In a rare flash of lucidity he cursed his weakness for 'natch' before hauling himself over the rickety stile and setting off down the narrow footpath. In his inebriated state he completely forgot this was the choice he made every time.

The air cooled rapidly as the night set in and wisps of mist began to form around his ankles as Micky toiled his way along. The moon was waning and there was only just enough light to make out the line of the footpath as it snaked through the water meadows and around the endless drainage ditches that bisected the land. He shivered, pulling his thin jacket around him as he wondered whether he might not have been better off on the main road. He might even have picked up a lift at some point. People were still friendly round about and would often stop for a lone pedestrian especially late at night. He stopped and glanced over his shoulder but the stile and the road were a long way behind him, already out of sight, and with a sigh he forged on.

He was past the old Roman brick works and heading for the bridge over Kings Sedgemoor when a flicker of light off to his left caught his attention. He stared into the darkness and was about to dismiss it as an illusion when he saw it again, a faint golden twinkling a little way off near a clump of willows. He hesitated but the mystery of the light won over his natural indolence and he changed direction, stepping carefully through the slightly muddy patches until he reached the edge of another rhyne, a wider channel cut through the peat and marsh to drain the land. The light danced before him enticingly as he stumbled along until he emerged from the undergrowth and found himself next to a small clearing, the flat black surface of the rhyne stretching away into the distance. The light flickered on the bank of the canal and next to it he saw what looked like his wallet, open on the ground.

He fumbled in his jacket pockets as he stepped forward, eyes fixed on the edge of the bank and the twenty pound note fluttering gently from the top of the worn leather. He couldn't remember the last time he'd had a twenty and greed overcame caution as he knelt down and reached out to grab the money. As the light went out he felt hands grab him by the shoulders and he was hauled head first into the murky waters of the canal. The shock of the cold made him gasp and the water burned through him as it rushed into his lungs. He barely had time to struggle before losing consciousness, his last thought that it couldn't have been his wallet because he'd left it on the kitchen table . . .

Chapter One

Alex flung herself up with a start, heart pounding and gasping for breath as she was blasted into wakefulness by an unexpected sound. After a moment she realized she was safe at home, in her own room, in her own bed and no-one was chasing her. Then she registered the noise echoing around the room, which sounded like Abba's latest pop song being played at teeth-rattling volume. She snatched up the clock and peered at the luminous dial – it was three in the morning.

'Oh bloody hell, what now?' she muttered, switching on her lamp and swinging her legs out from the warmth of the covers. She flinched as her feet hit the uncarpeted floor and she gritted her teeth as she rummaged around for some socks and a jumper. It was almost the end of October and despite the lingering warmth of the late autumn sun the nights were getting cold in her house by the river. She opened the door and the noise got louder. Above her she heard Sue stirring, the crash of angry feet on the ceiling heralding her arrival at the top of the stairs.

'What the fuck are you doing?' Sue demanded, sticking her head over the banister, her fury at odds with the angelic face and flowing hair.

'I was going to ask you the same thing,' Alex retorted.

Sue picked her way down the stairs, moving with the delicacy of an indignant cat whilst Alex flung open the door to the back room. Impossibly the noise was even louder in there and they peered through the window seeking the source of the racket. On the far side of the river the Iron Beehive, a pub of ever-decreasing repute, was lit up by a dazzling array of flashing multi-coloured lights. Dark figures scurried back and forth, climbing on to a massive double-decker trailer where outsized Monopoly-themed models rocked and twirled in time to the music. They could hear the faint thumping of the diesel generator as the music paused for a blissful second and then started all over again.

'God, is it that time of year again already,' Alex groaned.

Sue stared out of the window and shook her head. 'Will you please tell me what is going on? This is insane – is it even legal?'

Alex turned away from the window and walked back into the hallway, the noise level dropping slightly as they closed the door behind them.

'Don't you know?' said Alex with a hint of waspish glee in her voice. 'No one's going to do anything about it, so there's no point complaining. 'Tis Carnival.'

'You could have warned me,' said Sue the next morning as she hunched over her breakfast coffee.

Alex shrugged. 'I wasn't in town last year,' she said. 'I was out in that freezing cold cottage in the sticks. I had no idea there was a float at the Beehive and I guess I didn't expect that.' She gestured vaguely towards the back door.

'No one in their right mind would expect that,' muttered Sue. She was, by her own admission, not a morning person.

Privately, Alex was inclined to agree with her, but she was feeling pretty rough herself. She had not been sleeping well since the events of the last few months and had struggled to get back to sleep even after the Abba festival ended at the Iron Beehive and a blissful silence fell over the town. She could feel the beginnings of a headache in her left temple and the light seemed unnaturally bright in the normally shady dining room. She rubbed at her eyes but that just made it worse so she ducked her head and tried sipping her coffee. Suddenly the room seemed to lurch to one side and she realized she was going to be sick. She pushed herself up from the table and dashed for the kitchen, just reaching the sink in time. Black dots danced in front of her eyes and she felt her whole body turn hot, then cold and then hot again. There was a hand on her shoulder and Sue bent over and ran the tap before lifting her upright and guiding her gently to a chair in the dining room.

'I don't want to seem unsympathetic,' Sue said, 'but you look bloody awful.' She went back into the kitchen and returned with a damp towel and a glass of water.

'Here, try sipping this.' She wiped Alex's neck and face with the towel and then stared at her, head to one side.

'I'm sorry, I don't know what happened,' said Alex, trying to steady her hands. 'Look, I'm shaking all over.' She shook her head, trying to clear it but the room began to spin again and she leaned forwards, breathing deeply as she struggled for control over her wayward sense of balance.

'You keep screwing up your eyes,' said Sue. 'Does the light seem too bright or something?'

Alex gave a tiny nod. Sue vanished into the kitchen and returned with another glass.

'Roll your sleeves up,' she ordered.

Alex stared at her sullenly. 'What for?'

'Just do as you're told for once will you? Have you got a rash anywhere?'

Alex unbuttoned her sleeve and dragged at her jumper to reveal a scattering of small red blotches running up her arm from inside her elbow. She stared at them for a moment and blinked before looking up at her friend.

'Well, what do you know,' she said softly.

Sue grabbed her hand and pulled her arm out straight before rolling the glass across the inside of her elbow. The marks faded slightly but were still clearly visible.

'I think you've got meningitis,' she said. 'I'm getting the doctor – you get back to bed now.'

Alex wriggled in the chair and managed to haul herself to her feet, swaying slightly as she hung on to the table.

'Don't be daft,' she said. 'Meningitis is what kids get. I can't be ill today – I'm supposed to be starting my new job.' She let go of the table, stepped towards the door and fell flat on her face. Sue leant over and hauled her into a sitting position, back propped up against the stairs.

'I *so* hate Mondays,' she muttered as she hurried to the telephone.

The doctor arrived with disturbing speed and checked Alex's temperature and responses to light before helping Sue get her back upstairs.

'It is meningitis,' he said, 'but relatively mild. I don't want to take her into hospital unless I have to, but she must have someone here for the next few days. Monitor her temperature and keep an eye on the rash. If she starts to get a fever over about 101 call for an ambulance. She'll probably need something for the headache. I'll drop by in a couple of days but phone the surgery if you've any questions or worries.' And he was gone.

Sue was left staring at the door as it closed behind him, a plastic forehead thermometer, a prescription for something she couldn't decipher and a leaflet entitled, 'Meningitis – don't delay!' in her hands.

'Great,' she muttered, 'just wonderful. I could have done that without him.' There was a stirring from the room above and she hurried upstairs to check on her friend.

Sue's phone call to the Highpoint Probation Service offices caused total panic. Pauline, the chief administrator, took the call and relayed it upstairs to Garry, the senior probation officer, immediately. Garry was straight on the phone to the head office, sending Pauline back down to close the front door and make sure there were no clients in the day centre.

'Keep it calm, though,' he said as she headed for the door. 'We don't want to start an unnecessary panic. Just keep the building clear until I can establish any quarantine protocols.'

'Unnecessary panic,' she muttered, scurrying down the stairs. 'As if there's such a thing as necessary panic.'

The door was wide open when she reached the ground floor and the first officers were milling around in front of the reception desk sharing stories about their weekends and wrangling over the week's rota. Pauline pushed her way past and slammed the door just as the first clients reached the threshold.

'Oi! What's that for then?' demanded an angry voice from outside. Pauline leaned against the window and called back. 'Go home. Believe me, you'll thank me later on.'

There was a pause and some shuffling of feet before several voices called out, 'Is that all of 'un then? Can we all go?'

'What about our day's attendance? Is we gettin' marked in, 'cos I got up right early to get here?'

There were murmurs of agreement and then the first voice said, 'I need my bus fare. Can't afford to go back without it. What about that?'

There was renewed knocking on the door and more raised voices, but Pauline shot the bolts home and glared at the group on the doorstep.

'I said GO HOME. We'll be in touch and everyone'll get marked in for today. And you!' She pointed at a young man with a Mohican haircut wearing a rather battered leather jacket. 'Brian Morris, yes I'm talking to you. I'm sorry you can't come in to get your bus fare, but I'll make sure it's refunded next time.'

'Girt load of good that is,' muttered Brian, turning away in disgust. 'How'm I supposed to be gettin' home then, eh?'

Pauline sighed heavily and double locked the door. At the desk the entire staff was staring at her.

'Are we being held hostage or something?' asked Lauren from the counter. 'Only I've got a half day today on account of it being Dave's birthday.' She looked over the top, standing on her toes as she peered at her manager.

'Don't you start,' said Pauline. 'This is not my idea. We've had a call from Sue about Alex. Apparently she's gone down with meningitis and Garry's calling someone – haven't a clue who – about some sort of quarantine protocol.'

The probation officers stared at one another nonplussed for a moment before Eddie Smart, a middle-aged, middle-rank and slightly rotund man hissed through his teeth and shook his head.

'Meningitis – that's nasty. Especially for young people. They had an outbreak in the school a couple of years ago and it was closed for weeks. Still, I've got a load of paperwork to do so I'm off to the splendid isolation of my office'. He grabbed his post from the reception desk and hurried off up the stairs, moving considerably faster than his bulk would suggest possible.

Margaret Lorde, immaculately turned out as ever, shrugged and picked up her black leather bag before making her way majestically to the first floor.

Pauline raised her eyebrows at the remaining officer, James 'Gordon' Bennett, who was left alone leaning nonchalantly on the counter.

'Quarantine protocol?' he said.

'Don't,' snapped Pauline. 'I have no idea what he's up to. I'm just office staff and I do as I'm told.' She glanced uneasily at the entrance and said, 'Do you think we should put up a notice? There'll be a whole crowd of clients any minute and I really don't want to spend the day shouting through the door.'

Gordon grinned wickedly. 'Perhaps a big red cross and the word PLAGUE,' he suggested, 'or maybe "Abandon hope all ye who enter"?'

Pauline laughed in spite of herself. 'I think we should have that over the door anyway,' she said as she whisked Lauren away back into the office.

Gordon frowned at the locked door, pursing his lips in thought before pulling the telephone over to the front of the desk and dialling. He drummed his fingers impatiently as he waited for a reply. When Sue finally answered she sounded uncharacteristically flustered.

'What's happened?' he asked.

There was a pause as Sue identified him and then there was a heavy sigh down the phone.

'Gordon, I haven't a bloody clue. Alex just keeled over at breakfast and the doctor says she's got meningitis – but "only mildly", whatever that means. He rushed off before I could ask him anything and I don't even know who he was. He was a duty doctor from somewhere and as far as I can see from his signature he's called Dr Squiggle.'

Gordon pondered this for a moment.

'Are you all right?' he asked.

'I'm fine,' she said. 'No spots, no headache, nothing. I've got to stay here though because I'm not supposed to leave Alex on her own. Not that I want to at the moment – she looks pretty awful to be honest.'

There was the sound of voices from the stairwell and the door to the office opened, the office staff trooping out to head up to the meeting room.

'I've got to go,' said Gordon. 'I think Garry's called one of his meetings. I'll phone when it's over but don't worry about trying to get in to work. The door's locked and we're all inside away from any clients. Let me know if you need any shopping and I'll get it later.'

He put the phone down and hurried after the last of the admin people, a lanky, glum woman called Alison who had been Alex's assistant until a couple of weeks ago. He smiled at her encouragingly but she just stared back, the picture of self-pity.

'I'm probably going to get it now,' she said sulkily. 'I'm the one who was working in her office and dealing with all her files.' She sniffed, staring at him with pale watery eyes.

'Oh, I'm sure it has a shorter incubation period than that,' said Gordon untruthfully. Actually he realized he knew absolutely nothing about meningitis, except that it was a nasty illness and he really hoped it wasn't very contagious.

In the meeting room there was a lot of shuffling around as people looked at one another suspiciously and tried to avoid direct physical contact whilst still appearing calm and in control. The only person who really carried it off convincingly was Lauren, who trotted over to her usual low chair and settled back to watch the big people panic. She hoped they wouldn't be too long because in the rush she'd left her bag downstairs and there was particularly succulent doughnut inside. Lauren, for all her diminutive stature, had an extraordinary appetite and although it was barely ten o'clock she was already hungry.

Garry clapped his hands and tried to direct people to empty chairs.

'Can we sit down please?' he called over the buzz of conversation and the scraping of chairs being moved to slightly more isolated positions. 'People, come on, leave the damn chairs where they are and settle down!'

Lauren leaned over towards Eddie in the seat next to her and murmured, 'So how far do you reckon them meningitis germs can jump then?'

Eddie grinned as he looked around. 'Most people seem to think about two, three feet. I reckon it's too late if it's catching anyway.'

Some semblance of order had fallen on the gathering and Garry stepped forward into the limelight, a serious figure trying to project leadership and stoicism in the face of adversity.

'As you probably know,' he said, 'Sue has called in to say Alex Hastings has meningitis.' He held up a hand as if to quell a panic despite the fact no-one in the room moved or spoke. 'I understand this is a worrying development, but I am taking professional advice and have been assured there is nothing to cause us concern. Now, Alex has not been here for the last two weeks and so Sue is our only possible point of contact.

Some of you will have worked with her but some probably have nothing to do with her . . . Yes?'

Eddie stuck his hand up. 'All due respect, Garry, but if this is contagious it could have passed via any one of us. And look – we're all here now together.'

There was a general murmur and some shuffling of feet as the staff pondered this sobering thought.

'Perhaps with hindsight we should have remained – more isolated,' said Gordon.

Paul Malcolm, an energetic and idealistic young officer who dealt with the younger clients, joined in. 'Does it count as an industrial injury if we catch it?' He looked around and continued. 'Only I got scabies from a client once and that didn't, but meningitis is a bit more serious.'

Margaret, who was sitting next to him, leaned a little further away and screwed up her face in disgust. 'That's really not nice,' she said. 'I'm not sure we need to know things like that.'

'Yeah, a bit too much detail there Paul,' said Eddie.

'If we could get back to the matter in hand,' Garry shouted above the rising voices. The phone on the main table began to ring and after a moment Pauline rose to answer it. Silence fell as everyone tried to hear what was being said.

'Yes, yes, I see. Thank you,' she said, before replacing the receiver.

'Was that the county medical officer?' Garry asked. Pauline nodded. 'Well, that call was for me. You should not have taken it.'

Pauline blinked at him and shook her head. 'You seemed to be waiting for me to answer it,' she said finally, as an uncomfortable silence stretched between them. 'He seemed eager just to deliver his message and get off the line so I didn't have much choice.'

Garry's face twisted into a frown and his lips turned pale as he clenched his teeth together.

'I do not expect to be addressed like that in front of my staff,' he said. 'Perhaps you could remember that in future. Now, what did he say please?'

Pauline was almost white with anger but she took a deep breath as she controlled her temper.

'It would appear to be non-contagious if Alex has viral meningitis,' she said. 'However, if it is bacterial then there is a high risk of infection and we should all watch out for the warning signs.' Her voice was steady but her clipped tones would have been clear warning for any man more perceptive than Garry.

'Well that's not much help,' he said, ploughing on heedlessly. 'Do we know what sort it is?' He stared at Pauline as if she was concealing this information and she felt a rush of fury at the way he was behaving. Years of patience, restraint and diplomacy trembled and began to crumble, leaving only the desire to say exactly what she thought of him, in front of *his staff* and hopefully so loud anyone still outside in the car park heard her too.

'Perhaps I can help here,' said the ever-tactful and always reliable Gordon softly. 'We didn't know the questions to ask until now, did we Garry?'

He continued, reminding them all that Garry had made the call to the medical officer in the first place. 'So now I can have a word with Sue and see if she knows. In the meantime perhaps we should all return to our offices and erm, await our fate, so to speak.'

For a moment it looked as though their senior was going to ignore this way out of the confrontation but then he nodded and said, 'Yes, you should all go and wait until we have some more information. In the meantime the building will remain closed as a precaution.' He spun around and was gone before anyone could respond, leaving Pauline fuming – but still employed.

Sue spent a frustrating half hour on the telephone trying to speak to the doctor who had attended that morning. The call had gone to a central switchboard, she was informed, and taken by the 'duty professional' next in line. They could probably locate him but, really, they were very busy and it would take a while, so perhaps she would prefer to speak to her own surgery?

'Bloody HELL!' she yelled, slamming down the receiver. 'Of all the pompous, patronizing, self-opinionated, unhelpful bitches . . .' There was a groan from upstairs and she hurried to her friend's side. Alex was lying on her back, the bed covers in disarray.

'Say what you think,' she whispered. 'Don't hold back.'

'I'm sorry, I didn't mean to wake you. How are you feeling?' Sue fussed around the room, checking the curtains were closed to keep out the light and trying to straighten the bed.

Alex opened her eyes and flapped a hand at her. 'How the hell do you think I'm feeling? I feel like someone's come in and mugged me in the night and left me with hot nails in my eyes.' She licked her dry lips and added, 'Can I have something to drink? I'm so hot – look, leave the covers please. I just need some water.'

Sue laid her hand on Alex's forehead. She certainly felt as if she was running a temperature.

On the way back from the kitchen with a glass, Sue seized the forehead thermometer off the table. Alex had propped herself up in bed and grabbed the glass, sucking greedily and emptying it in a few seconds.

'More,' she said, holding it out with an unsteady hand.

'When I've done this,' said Sue, trying to get the plastic strip to lie flat on Alex's head. Alex flinched and turned away, dropping the glass as she burrowed into the pillow. At that moment the phone rang downstairs and Sue hurried to answer it muttering angrily to herself.

'Yes?' she snapped as she snatched the receiver from the holder.

'Sorry, have I caught you at a bad time?' asked Gordon.

Sue sighed and felt herself slump as she dropped into a chair by the front window.

'To be perfectly honest, Gordon, this whole day is turning into one of the worst I've had for a long while.'

'I'm afraid I've got some questions from "he who wants to be obeyed",' said Gordon.

'I don't expect I'll be much help,' said Sue. 'I can't even get hold of the doctor we saw this morning. Alex looks awful and seems to be developing a real fever and I can't leave her to get whatever I'm supposed to get with an illegible prescription!'

There was a pause as Gordon digested this information.

'Do we know if it's viral or bacterial?' he asked finally.

'Oh bloody hell, how am I supposed to know?' Sue snapped. 'I found a medical encyclopaedia in Alex's room with these flow chart things in it, but it keeps telling me to seek urgent medical attention – which I am trying to do, but with remarkably little success may I add."

There was another pause and Sue could almost hear Gordon nodding as he considered this.

'Your best option is probably to get her own surgery to call round and check on her,' he said. 'I'd write out the questions you need answering and you can get them to decipher the prescription too. Between you and me I'd spice it up a bit – not too much so they whisk her into hospital but say she's beginning to really suffer with the headache and is shaking a bit – something like that. They should come round straight away and hopefully we can sort out how to help you both. At the moment I'm stuck in here like the Prisoner of Zenda whilst Garry does his best to alienate the entire office.'

Sue took a deep breath to steady herself and thanked him before ringing off and trying their local surgery. She didn't like playing dumb but it seemed to get results, especially when dealing with the more arrogant members of the medical profession, and another doctor was at the door within the hour.

At her desk in the probation office Lauren slammed the phone down in disgust and was treated to a warning frown from Pauline.

'Sorry,' she said. 'It's just Dave's cancelled this afternoon. There's been some incident he says so he's got to work.' She clambered down from her special chair and headed for the tea room at the back of the main office. 'I was looking forward to that too. Anyone want a cup?'

Pauline held up a hand and gestured Lauren back to her desk.

'Enough everyone,' she said. 'Just because we've no clients in today doesn't mean there's nothing to do. We can all use a day catching up, so come on, get on with it please.' She turned back to the front door as there was a knocking followed by rattling of the handle. Sighing in frustration she crossed the lobby and peered through the narrow reinforced window.

'Go home,' she mouthed at a young man with thinning gingery hair who was staring back at her. The unfamiliar figure knocked again, more urgently this time, and twisted at the handle again. 'I said GO HOME!'

'I was told to report here today,' came a plaintive voice through the heavy door. 'I'm supposed to start at 9.30.'

'I don't care. Come back tomorrow and we'll log you in. Now go away and stop bothering us.' Pauline turned her back on the pleading face and marched into the office, the inner door slamming behind her.

'Never known anyone be so eager to meet their probation officer,' said the irrepressible Lauren.

Pauline snorted. 'Well, keep an eye on him will you? I don't like the look of him much. There's something a bit odd and we don't know who the hell he is. Just our luck, a new client today. It's not a good start and it looks so unprofessional.'

At these words the office transformed into a picture of industry. Heads down and fingers flying over their type-writers, the women focussed on the case notes and reports before them. Pauline was generally a good supervisor, strict but fair, but the one thing she hated was anything she deemed 'unprofessional'. Lauren risked a glance out of the window, her large brown eyes following the forlorn figure as it shuffled across to an exceptionally large and beat-up car parked in the corner of the staff car park.

'Well, the first thing we do tomorrow is put him straight about *that*,' came Pauline's voice from behind her. The figure opened the driver's door and slumped into the front seat. After consulting his watch he reached under the dashboard, pulled out a tin and proceeded to roll a very thin cigarette.

Pauline huffed impatiently. 'So now he's going to sit there and we can't even go out and tell him to move. This is ridiculous.' She glanced down and added, 'Well, we're stuck here so you might as well get on with your work Lauren.'

Reluctantly, Lauren clambered back on to her chair and began to thumb through the files beside her. It had started out as a half-day filled with promise but was going downhill rapidly.

Out on the Somerset Levels PC Dave Brown was too busy to regret his ruined birthday plans. A fast-track graduate, he had ploughed through his first two years as a beat officer as efficiently as he could. Older PCs with more years behind them had started off treating him with wariness. After all, how many supposed high fliers chose the Somerset force to launch their glittering careers, they joked. PC Brown just nodded and smiled and kept on doing the best job he could. He volunteered for the unpleasant shifts and dirty jobs just enough to be noticed, but not so often his colleagues would accuse him of sucking up to the seniors, and slowly his determined and intelligent approach earned him a measure of respect amongst his peers. His breakthrough had come just six weeks ago with the kidnapping of Lauren by Derek Johns, a dangerous and violent gang leader bent on avenging the suicide of his youngest son whilst in police custody.

It was Dave Brown who had correctly identified the murder weapon from a tiny clue at one of crime scenes and he who had put together a whole slew of different events to track down the killer. He had arrived at the cottage where Johns was hiding out in time to help Lauren's rescuers and had secured the scene, preserving the evidence that Derek Johns had been the victim of an accident and Lauren had acted in self-defence. Lauren had been terrified she would be charged over Johns' death and he had spent an increasing amount of his time off duty with her, offering reassurance and support as she came to terms with her ordeal.

Now, for the first time, he found himself at ease in the sometimes strange and insular world of Highpoint and the Levels, partly due to the growing acceptance of his peers and partly as a consequence of his new-found friendship with Lauren. Pausing for a moment he felt a flash of disappointment at letting her down, but a shout from the canal bank focussed his attention once more.

'Something over here Sarge,' called one of the search team.

The sergeant looked up and waved in acknowledgement before turning back to the rest of the men.

'Right, keep at it you lot. I want every inch of this area combed and marked off on the map. Don't touch anything now, just call me. You!' He beckoned Dave over. 'Come on, Constable. You're supposed to be good at this sort of thing. You're with me.'

Dave stood up gratefully easing his aching back as he stretched and hurried in the direction of the find. Behind him a couple of uniformed PCs exchanged glances before bending to their task once more.

'What have you got?' the sergeant demanded. An unfamiliar PC from the Taunton station was crouched beside the path running the length of the drainage ditch. In front of him was an old, battered leather wallet, its contents roughly stuffed into the main pocket. 'Any name or address? Don't touch it man!'

The PC jerked his hand back as the sergeant bent over and opened the wallet gingerly, using a stick. A bank note fluttered out and danced along the path in the freshening breeze. Dave was off after it as fast as he could go, feeling in his pocket for a clean handkerchief as he ran. The note lifted in the wind, turned over and wafted out over the water just as he grabbed one corner. Holding it away from his body he carried his prize back to the sergeant and together they eased it in to a clear plastic bag. Nodding his approval the sergeant held up the note, now sealed away from any more outside contamination, and whistled softly.

'It's a twenty,' he said. 'Now who would have a spare twenty out here on the Levels? And who would leave it behind if it belongs to our body?'

'If he was killed, Sarge,' said Dave. 'We don't know that yet, do we?'

The sergeant gave the twenty pound note a final, rather regretful look and placed it in his leather evidence pouch.

'Maybe not. He could be just another drunk who's wound up in the rhyne but I've got a strange feeling about this one. Come on, I want to do a proper check along the path before the detectives get wind of him and turn up. Bloody glory-grabbers.'

PC Brown looked at his retreating back quizzically. The sergeant hadn't struck him as particularly fanciful or even very imaginative and in the new climate of scientific investigation he was surprised to hear a superior officer admit to something as nebulous as a hunch. Strangely he felt his respect for the man increase as he began his own tramp down the path, eyes casting left and right as he searched for something – some anomaly, something out of place that might help them piece together what had happened to poor old Sticky Micky Franks.

Chapter Two

'Well, the good news is it's viral so you're not contagious,' said Sue cheerfully, plonking herself on the end of Alex's bed. 'The bad news is it is meningitis which is nasty, brutish and can be rather long drawn out.'

Alex was propped up on several pillows, her face white and strained. She opened one rather bloodshot eye and peered at her friend.

'So what can they give me?' she asked.

Sue sighed as she shook her head. 'Sadly they can only suggest painkillers and rest – lots and lots of rest. They say that although you've got some spots you won't be helped by antibiotics and there's nothing like an anti-viral thingy so we can only help with the symptoms.'

Alex groaned and closed her eye. 'I hate it when you get technical. I don't suppose you would consider just killing me now would you?'

Sue rose and headed for the door. 'Not yet but I'm sure I'll feel like it in a week or so,' she said over her shoulder.

The news came through mid-afternoon and it was with some relief Pauline unlocked the main door to the building.

'Is he still out there?' asked Lauren peering round her senior.

'Looks like it,' said Pauline. 'Oh, hang on, he's coming over. Lauren, can you phone up to Eddie and Gordon please. Ask them to come down.'

Lauren scooted back to the relative safety of the office and called the two men before taking up position at the front counter. After all, she thought, if there was going to be any fun in the office she wanted to be part of it. Her half-day was ruined and she had no idea when she'd see Dave. And she'd not even been able to give him his birthday present . . . Her attention switched back to the door as the strange man from the car park pushed it open and stepped inside. Eddie leaned on the counter looking as cordial as possible whilst Gordon wandered over to greet the newcomer.

'Ah, sorry about the wait,' he said. 'Bit of an emergency. All cleared up now though. So, who have you come to see?'

The stranger glanced around at them nervously and fished a slightly crumpled letter out of his pocket. He opened it.

'I'm supposed to meet Garry Nugent,' he said, 'but that was at ten. I was here but I couldn't get in.'

His voice was soft, a little high and with a slight London accent. Lauren watched as he looked around, his eyes glancing off them in turn until he came to her. She waited for the inevitable double-take as he registered her height, only partly disguised by the stepped stool she was using, and held his eyes when he turned back to her for a moment. He flushed a deep crimson and swallowed hard before focussing on Gordon, who was now grinning with enjoyment at his discomfort.

'Are you sure about that?' Gordon asked, putting on his 'seasoned professional' face. 'Mr Nugent is the senior here and as such does not have a direct case load.'

Bit of an understatement, thought Lauren. Garry spent considerable energy keeping as far away from the clients as possible, a good thing for all concerned in her opinion. She

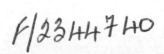

studied the new client carefully and decided she didn't like him very much. He was dressed in faded jeans, sneakers and a checked shirt and his clothes seemed to hang on his thin frame as if intended for someone just a size larger. He was very pale with washed-out eyes, and his hair, what there was of it, stuck out in little spikes where he had been running his fingers though it in frustration during his long wait. She glanced at his hands and noted the tell-tale smudge of nicotine between the index and second fingers of his left hand. He was a caricature of a newly released prisoner. The newcomer shifted from foot to foot, uncomfortable under their collective scrutiny.

'Here,' he said, offering the rather crumpled piece of paper to Gordon, who took it with some reluctance. There was a pause as Gordon scanned the letter and then he cleared his throat and raised his eyebrows in surprise.

'Ah, I see. Well, I think perhaps an explanation is in order,' he said, and he held out his hand. 'Welcome to Highpoint Probation. Sorry about the mix-up but it has been rather an odd day.'

Gordon turned to the assembled company and said, 'This is Richard Peddlar. He's our new officer, coming in to take over from Alex.'

There was a moment of deeply embarrassed silence as they stared at Garry's latest recruit, the awkwardness stretching out until Eddie recovered himself and stepped forward to shake hands.

'Well, hey, welcome. Come on up and we'll let Garry know you're here.'

Lauren struggled to contain a giggle that bubbled up inside and threatened to undo all of Gordon's diplomacy, but she felt Pauline's eyes on her and slipped hurriedly down from her stool and stood hidden behind the counter as the men left the room, a much relieved Richard Peddlar in tow.

Pauline stalked round and fixed her with a glare. Nothing was said, but Lauren ducked her head and hurried back to her desk much chastened. This was, she decided as she sorted through Sue's Part B notes, one of the worst Mondays she could remember.

PC Brown missed it on his first sweep as he was focussing on the bank of the canal. Reaching a tree that marked the hundred-yard limit from the spot where the wallet had been found, he turned and retraced his steps, eyes scanning the grass verging the old tow path. The wind was getting up again and it was cold out on the bank. He glanced sideways at the dark water rolling slowly past, thick and brown with mud from the early winter storms and suppressed a shudder at the thought of drowning in that foul soup. As he turned his attention back to the path he saw something glint in the last fragments of sunlight. Just a flash but enough to reveal a metal object lying in the longer grass a few yards from his starting point. Stepping carefully so he didn't damage any of the immediate area he peered down at the object, parting the surrounding growth with a stick.

'Sarge,' he called, 'come and have a look at this.'

The two men stood and stared at it for a moment. 'Well, what do you make of that then?' said the sergeant finally.

PC Brown shook his head. 'Damned if I know, Sir,' he said.

The sergeant moved away down the path towards the main search area and signalled to the photographer who was hanging around looking bored.

'What the hell is that doing here?' he muttered as he began to record the scene, working hurriedly as the light faded.

'No footprints so maybe it was thrown here,' commented PC Brown.

'Reckon you may be right,' said the sergeant, 'but what the hell is an old brass candlestick doing all the way out here?'

Although it had been a week since the onset of her illness, Sue didn't like leaving Alex on her own. The office was only five minutes' walk away and once her temperature came down there was nothing she could do to make her friend more comfortable or speed her recovery, and Garry, who had been half-way decent about the whole thing, as she had to admit, had decided he could no longer spare her.

'I'll be back around lunch time,' she said, fussing around the room and tweaking curtains and pillows. 'You just stay in bed and bloody behave yourself all right?'

Alex was reaching the bored and impatient stage of illness, the time where she really felt she should be getting better and was confounded by her own weakness when she tried to do the slightest thing.

'I'll be fine,' she muttered. 'Just go will you? Stop mucking about with stuff. At least the Carnival's moved off to Glastonbury so I might get some sleep at night.'

Sue pulled a face at Alex's back and went downstairs. She had some sympathy with the last sentiment. The Carnival carts based in town went out to the surrounding towns and villages at night to replay the whole thing over several weeks. Despite the lateness of the hour they returned with lights on and music blaring deep into the night, especially if they'd emerged winners in one of the smaller regional shows. The Iron Beehive seemed to have been particularly successful this year and the whole thing was beginning to seriously get on her nerves. Stepping out of the house she hesitated, then pulled the front door shut behind her. It would be fine, she thought. Of course it would.

PC Brown stood at the side of the autopsy room, hands behind him and back straight as he watched the pathologist begin work on Michael Franks. From the outside he was the picture of professionalism. Inside he wanted to bolt from the room and hang over the nearest available sink, but one of the younger sergeants had already left at the first sign of intestines and he felt the eyes of the Taunton police on him, appraising, measuring, testing his resolve. Dave Brown was ambitious as well as clever and he clenched his teeth, tightened the muscles around his stomach and refused to show the slightest dis-comfort. He recalled the words of his mentor at Hendon, a tough and often foul-mouthed sergeant with a full twenty-five years experience behind him. He'd pushed Dave hard, testing his determination, questioning his choice of career and coming close on occasions to driving him from the course. As his time at the college was coming to a close, the man changed from enemy to valued teacher and Police Cadet Brown understood he had been preparing him for the next few tough years ahead.

'There'll always be those who are jealous,' the sergeant had said. 'Those not as able or those not as willing to put the work in. Don't listen to them. You keep your head down, do the best you can and you should make sergeant in record time. Just remember, you'll be younger and less experienced than half the men you're leading so you need to be better than them – smarter, quicker and tougher all round. Good luck.'

They had shaken hands and that was the end of his training. He'd caught the train to Somerset the next day and had scarcely had time to stop and muse on life since. One thing he did know for sure, however, was that if he ran away from the autopsy he'd ruin two years of the hardest work he'd ever done. So he stood in his allotted place and tried to concentrate on the voice of the pathologist. Suddenly he heard his name being called.

'Ah yes, you're Constable . . . Constable Brown isn't it?' The pathologist was staring at him and gesturing with one red-gloved hand. 'Come over here where you can see properly. You won't learn anything over there. Come on.'
He waved several students aside and Dave Brown found himself up close and personal with his first post-mortem. Over the next twenty minutes or so he discovered some smells don't fade with time, that the average human brain weighs about a kilo and a half, and Sticky Micky's last meal had been some sort of meat hotpot washed down with an excessive amount of natural cider. As he left the hospital he was gratified to receive a nod of acknowledgement from the detective sergeant in charge of the case. It was almost worth it, he thought, as he clambered into the car and made his way back to the station in Highpoint. Despite the chill in the air he

wound down the window, convinced the smell of Michael Franks was still clinging to his uniform.

Alex woke from her post-lunch nap feeling better – surprisingly better. She raised her head from the pillow, ready to surrender again at the first sign of the monstrous headache's return, but apart from a slight humming in her ears all seemed well. She slid her legs over the side of the bed and sat up, waiting again, but her vision stayed clear and the room, so recently a spinning nightmare, was still. She was bored, she realized. Bored almost to the point of madness. What first – a book perhaps? There was a small television in the spare room – maybe she could get that and set it up next to the bed. Then she thought of the kitchen. Coffee! Oh, she was so sick of water, fruit juice, more water mixed with juice – it had to be coffee. She took a deep breath and rose to her feet, grabbing for the doorframe as her weakened body trembled. After a moment she felt better again and began to make her unsteady way downstairs.

The open staircase loomed before her, tempting and terrifying in equal measure and she clung to the banister rail, taking one step at a time, both feet safe before trying the next. Shaking all over by the time she reached the safety of the ground floor, she dropped into the armchair nearest the stairs and closed her eyes for a moment. The cold woke her twenty minutes later. Her eyes were sticky and the sickness she'd suffered over the past week threatened to return as she wriggled her way out of the chair and lurched over towards the kitchen door.

'Pathetic,' she muttered to herself through gritted teeth. 'This is just ridiculous. A few days in bed and I'm reduced to crawling like a baby!' Somewhere deep inside a little voice was telling her to get back upstairs whilst she could still manage it but ahead of her, just on the front of the shelf in the kitchen, she could see the coffee tin. A souvenir of happier times, it was decorated with stylized designs from continental railway posters. She'd loved it the moment she'd seen it in the shop and it was one of the few items to survive the great purge of memories that preceded her sudden and unexpected move to Somerset. She closed her eyes for a moment, imagining the rich, heavy aroma, anticipating the dark, almost buttery taste of that first sip. She felt herself wobble and opened her eyes hurriedly. Damn, she was weak. Physically weak and – admit it – a coffee junkie too.

With shaking hands she filled the kettle and rummaged through the cupboards for a beaker, spoon, sugar and her precious little French cafetiere. The smell when the hot water hit the ground coffee was intoxicating and it was hard to wait until the water turned dark, deep brown and the last of the beans nestled up at the top. Finally it was ready and she pushed down, so carefully and slowly in one smooth movement, watching as the scalding liquid cleared and the grounds were trapped below the metal filter. Two sugars first, then the coffee and only then a dash of milk . . . as important a ritual as any addict getting a fix, she thought, putting the used cafetiere in the sink and lifting the beaker carefully. Now, if she could just get back upstairs before Sue arrived home again.

The journey up the staircase took twice as long as the trip down and she was exhausted by the time she sank into her bed. Greedily she sucked at the hot, bitter drink, relishing the rush of caffeine through her system but even this could not keep her awake long. She had time to regret the fact she'd forgotten to grab a book before she fell into a deep sleep.

Out on the Levels a group of men converged on the village of Woolavington, arriving by car at intervals until all six of them were settled in a private room at the back of the Royal Arms pub. The landlord served them in person before retiring discreetly to make sure he was seen by his more regular customers in the bar. Times were hard, he reflected, and he needed the money, but he was not entirely happy about the arrangement. Pulling himself a half he tried to put it out of his mind and began a round of greeting and jokes in an attempt to lighten the sombre mood in the bar. The death of

Micky had cast gloom over customers and staff alike and rumours his drowning was being investigated by the police had done nothing to help business, as the more nervous drinkers (or those with nervous and vocal wives, he thought) were staying away. Add in the damn Carnival dragging people from one end of the county to another and he'd be lucky to make the wages bill this month. He nodded to his wife, on standby near the kitchen just in case there was a call for food from his guests. Responding with a scowl she retreated from view wiping her hands on her apron as she went. Another problem, he thought glumly. Somehow he had to tell her there was likely to be more 'bookings' for the top room and he'd already agreed to them.

Upstairs an arrangement was being hammered out by representatives of five groups, all from different areas but with common interests.

'Tis no point us all fighting each other,' said a man at the head of the long table. 'We got a great opportunity here, not likely to be coming again soon. With Derek gone and young Newt banged up they is like headless chickens and all that business is open for the taking.'

A tall, blond man in his early thirties rose and addressed the group. 'I agree. Tom here knows the Levels far better than we do but we all know how useful this area can be. With the Johns gang out of the way we can open it up and use our contacts, make a safe base for operations. I'm in and I suggest you all join us. What about you Mark?'

His companion, an older man with thin brown hair and piercing green eyes nodded slowly. 'Reckon you may be right,' he said. 'We got to sort out a few things first though. I'm not so sure about this new stuff.'

Several heads bobbed in agreement, mainly from the older men around the table. 'Right,' said a heavy-set man with a short, grey beard and a crooked nose. 'There's plenty of return from baccy and such. Don't see we need to be branching out into this new stuff. What's in it that's worth the risk then, Geoff?'

The blond man nodded at the speaker. 'We all respect Walter's experience,' he said smoothly. 'He's been operating in Exeter longer than some of us have been born and no-one knows the business better.'

There was an appreciative murmur around the table and Walter dipped his head in acknowledgement.

'Still,' Geoff continued, 'things change and if we want to keep ahead we need to change with them. There was a time when you could only take about twenty quid abroad with you and there was a market for anything fancy and foreign but now with this Common Market it's only worth bothering with smokes and booze. And booze is a problem what with the weight and breakages. Lot of breakages we seem to be getting round about Christmas Jimmy.' He gave the man opposite him a hard stare.

Jimmy shrugged, affecting indifference. He was middling height, average build and with mousy hair. There wasn't one single distinguishing characteristic about him which made his life very easy. No-one gave him a second look, not even the police hunting for the transport boss who was running trucks loaded with a fortune in smuggled alcohol and perfume.

'Stuff gets knocked around,' he said softly. 'Sometimes we need to take a bit of an off-road path so a few bottles might get damaged. I hope you're not suggesting my lads are on the dip?'

When he turned his head to stare back at Geoff there was nothing ordinary about his face. Suddenly it had hardened, his pale hazel eyes gleaming as he radiated anger at his opposite number in the ports. Geoff met his gaze and for a moment the table fell silent as the two men squared up to each other. The tension was broken by Tom at the other end of the table, his voice calm as he said, 'Now then lads, we'm all businessmen here and I hope we can all respect each other. See the problems from our colleagues' point of view. En't no need for none of that.'

Despite his soft words there was a ring of authority in his voice and the two men shifted in their chairs. The last member of the group leaned forwards and raised his hand. He was the youngest of the six men, short and stocky with a brawler's build and crude tattoos on his knuckles. The group looked at him curiously as the only stranger amongst them.

'Yes Max,' said Tom, nodding in his direction.

'I'm runnin' Bristol now,' said Max, his eyes darting from one to another as if expecting a challenge to this boast. When none came he hurried on. 'Seems we got most of what we need here – what with the ports,' a nod to Geoff, 'decent transport network,' another to Jimmy, 'and all of us in good places for sellin' on and such like. Just, I reckon we forgot one thing. Maybe they Johns gang is out of the way but that don't mean we got a free run at it. All the baccy, that weren't never run by the Johns lads. That's them didicoys an' I don't see them lettin' us walk in and take it off 'un.'

Tom stared at the little punk, his face still and expressionless, though inside he was seething. He'd not wanted to include Max Long but the new gang lord had expanded his range of interests and field of operations too fast for him to be ignored. After a lot of thought he'd decided to trust to the old adage, 'Keep your friends close but your enemies closer'. The brat had put his finger right on the one flaw in the whole scheme, a difficulty he hoped to deal with if and when it arose. He became aware of the other men watching him, wondering how he was going to deal with this. There was a grin on Max's face, a sneery, mocking look and the man tilted his head to one side and raised his eyebrows, challenging him for an answer. Keeping his voice soft and his tone light he looked straight back and said, 'Just leave that to me. 'Tis on my patch an' I'll fix it.'

Max gave a short, harsh laugh. 'That so is it? An' we just accept it?' He looked around the group, an expression of disbelief on his face. 'Now why should we all do that?'

Walter was on his feet before Tom could open his mouth. 'Because his word is enough,' he said, leaning forward over the table. 'Tom Monarch was running goods through the

Levels before you learned to piss in a pot and if he says it's fixed then 'tis fixed.'

The two men glared at one another, eyes locked as neither dared back down and risk losing face before the rest of them. They were similar in build and height but next to Walter's grizzled menace Max's gang tattoos and prison muscle looked as convincing as a fake tan. After an agonizing minute during which several of the group tried to cast around looking for a weapon without seeming to move, Max gave his laugh again and shrugged as he turned away.

'Well, if you say so, old man,' he said. 'Come on, let's get out of here.' He gestured to the other young men and Jimmy rose to join him, followed after a moment by Geoff.

Mark let out his breath in a heavy sigh as the door swung closed behind the trio.

'I hope I didn't speak out of turn,' Walter said, and Tom shook his head.

'No, no and thank you for the support.' He gazed at the closed door for a moment. 'Reckon we might have our work cut out with them lads. Times is changing but I don't know I care for it sometimes.'

'Young Geoff en't so bad,' said Mark. 'I worked with him last year, and his Dad afore that. They's sound. Young Jimmy, he's a bit of a hot-head but knows his business. 'Tis Max Long I en't so happy about.'

'Well, he's got the market right? Up there in Bristol, they's mad for stuff. Not so much call down my way, 'cept maybe at the university in Exeter,' said Walter.

'Well,' said Tom, pouring the last of the beer from a bottle into his glass, 'was not such a bad start. We got the route in.' He nodded to Mark. 'We got the means with Geoff and Jimmy, and we ship north with bloody Max Long and south with you.' He nodded to Walter. 'So let's just see how it goes eh?'

They raised their glasses and toasted the new enterprise, each one smiling and nodding as they hid their private reservations.

'Reckon this is alright for meeting though,' said Mark, glancing approvingly around the room. 'Nice and private, side door so we don't have to go through the rabble downstairs and old Phil Watson, I've known him years and he understands business. Not likely to be bubblin' away to the wrong person.'

After a series of warm farewells and hearty handshakes they slipped through the side door into the night, leaving the landlord to face his wife's disapproval. Hidden eyes followed them as they drove off in their cars, each heading in a different direction but each with a home to go to, somewhere familiar and sheltered and warm. As the last of the taillights disappeared into the night the watcher stepped out from the shadows of the overhanging trees and stared at the bright lights of the pub spilling forth from the lead-paned windows. Behind the glass, figures moved in easy companionship from one table to another and the flickering of a log fire could be seen in the background.

He watched as the lights went off in the top room, then flashed to signal 'last orders' in the bar. Stepping back into the gloom, he waited until the last customers were ushered out and bolts were pushed home on the main doors. Only then could he slip out into the last of the moonlight and cross the road in safety to seek shelter in the cold dampness of the beer cellar. He'd need to move on soon, he thought, curling up on a low table in the centre of the room. Wouldn't be long before Phil discovered the hasp on the latch had been tampered with and he didn't want to be around when that happened. Tomorrow he would resume his search for somewhere more permanent, at least for the coldest part of the winter. Breathing in the smell of the beer as it mingled with the dampness of the earthen floor, he slept.

Chapter Three

Iris Johns looked in the mirror and frowned, tucking a stray strand of hair neatly behind one ear. She was dressed soberly, as befitted one so recently widowed, and she was struck by how old she looked. Her roots needed doing again, she thought, but then she paused to reconsider. For years, all the long years since her eldest son's birth, she'd added a touch of auburn to her hair. Just a hint of brightness at first but over the years she'd grown used to the routine of colouring and shading. Now she was free of the whole messy business if she chose. She could go back to her natural colour, for Derek was gone and there was no-one to pass comment or, more importantly, ask awkward questions. She bent her head forwards and pulled at the parting across the crown of her head. For the first time she saw the tell-tale signs of grey streaks and she snapped her head up again, feeling a flash of anger. It was too late. Derek had taken her innocence, her youth and one of her sons. Now it seemed he'd taken her looks too. Her beautiful golden hair was gone and she was damned if she was going to turn into a bottle-blonde. All her life it seemed she'd had to swap one lie for another – well, not any more. She picked up her bag and gave her reflection one final glare before heading out into the early morning light to catch the bus into town. She had a long difficult journey ahead of her and there would be plenty of time for brooding on the train down to Newton Abbot.

'This is just bloody stupid,' muttered Alex through gritted teeth.

Sue fixed her with a steely glare then turned her back and opened the door to call down the stairs. 'She's in bed and she's to stay there.' She turned back with a deceptively sweet smile and added, 'I've told her not to listen, however hard you plead and whine. Like that film about the gremlins – you're not getting up, you're not going out and you're not having any more coffee until the doctor says so.'

She swept from the room leaving Alex torn between resentment and exhaustion. Sue had been furious when, on her return from work, she had found Alex collapsed half in and half out of bed, coffee spilling over the bedside table. She had also been rather less than sympathetic when the caffeine rush from even the little Alex had managed to drink brought on a migraine headache of monstrous proportions. Alex had spent the weekend flopped like a broken doll in bed with the curtains closed. She had also had to suffer her friend's cooking – or what passed for cooking. Sue was not interested in food unless it arrived fully prepared and garnished on a plate in front of her. Privately, Alex was surprised she even knew how to turn the cooker on and was half expecting the house to go up in a gas explosion by Sunday. She had comforted herself with the thought that at least Sue had to go back to work on Monday and she could drag herself down to the kitchen and find something edible, but she had underestimated her flat mate.

At half past eight that morning, the doorbell had rung and there had been the sound of voices from the hall below. Alex was feeling well enough to be bored but not really well enough to do anything about it, so she lay with her eyes closed dreaming of the rare delicacies awaiting her – crisps, bread and jam, even cornflakes were beginning to seem appealing. Then the bedroom door had opened and Sue had stepped in to announce she had set up a rota and Alex would have someone in the house at all times until the evening.

Alex leaned back on her pillows, closed her eyes and wished, not for the first time in the past week, she was dead.

The train to Newton Abbot was stuffy and crowded and Iris sat in a corner seat, book held before her like a shield. Despite all her efforts she could not concentrate on the deathless prose of her popular novel and finally she stopped trying and spent the time tuning in to the conversations around her. She wondered how many others were going to Dartmoor, making the long and difficult journey to the prison that floated, adrift in the middle of the bleak moors. Doubtless she'd find out when they all queued up for the bus to Princetown, the village that had grown up around the jail, hugging its walls like a fungus. Gradually the voices faded from her consciousness as she gazed out of the window at the flickering scenery and wondered just what she was going to say to her son.

She felt a tremendous weariness as she lined up to present her visiting order, to be searched and to hear the same tedious litany of rules and regulations standing between her and the only family she had left. Finally the door was unlocked and she was hustled through to the visiting room in the company of a dozen other nervous, anxious and, in several cases, downright tearful people. The women – they were overwhelmingly women with a sprinkling of small children – scattered around the room and seated themselves at the tables, all facing the barred door at the far end. She selected a seat as far away from the women with children as possible and sank into a chair, her heart sinking at the horrid familiarity of the whole routine. How often had she sat in rooms like this waiting to see her husband, she wondered. First him and now her son – would it never end? She closed her eyes for an instant, opening them at the sound of the prison door being unlocked. There was a rush of male bodies, all clad in blue trousers, striped shirts and grey jumpers, all smelling of that unmistakable prison odour compounded from sweat, testosterone and cheap tobacco smoke overlaid with the scent from prison-issue soap.

As she smelt that she was transported back to an earlier time, a time before Derek Johns and her life as a person in her own right. On leaving school she had been sent to the local DHSS office to work as a filing clerk. 'The Misery of Stealth and Total Obscurity', they had called it, but it was her only real job and for a few short months she had revelled in the freedom, the feeling of having her own money and the heady idea that she might have a future in the Civil Service. The Ministry had some strange ways and one of the strangest was the regular issue of a clean towel and a bar of soap to each employee. The same soap used in prisons, but then she didn't know that at the time.

There was a rattle as the chair in front of her was pulled out and her remaining son dropped into it. She studied his face, searching for the boy she had lost on the day he was sentenced, her heart squeezing inside her as she saw the tightness around his mouth, the lines already forming at the corners of his eyes. He was harder than she remembered, shaped by anger and grief and the necessity of survival in this grim, horrible place.

'Got any fags, Mum?' he said by way of greeting. She rummaged in her bag and pulled out a packet, passing him one and lighting it for him under the watchful eyes of the warder who had stationed himself by the wall next to them. Iris looked at him, puzzled for a moment by his presence, but Newt shrugged and tapped his jumper, a vivid red and yellow garment that stood out like a flag amongst the uniform blue and grey of his fellows.

'Escaper,' he said shortly before leaning over the table and smiling at her. 'Good to see you,' he said softly. 'Was it bad, the journey down?'

Iris shook her head and smiled in return, touched by his concern. Derek would never have thought to ask. It would not have occurred to him that the visits could be hard – expensive, long and so lonely sometimes. He was a much better man, her Billy, and she was going to do everything she could to keep that spark of goodness alive, to nurture it and protect him until finally he had the chance to grow into the man his father never became.

'I was wondering,' began Newt awkwardly, 'about Dad – about a funeral or something. Did they . . . I mean, has there been any news or anything?'

This was the moment Iris had been dreading. For an instant her mind went totally blank as she struggled to decide whether to tell her son the truth or not. Weeks of indecision roiled around in her head as she sought the right words. Then in a moment of clarity she realized this was not the time. Not here, in this heartless place surrounded by hard, watchful eyes and listening ears. Keeping her voice low she said, 'They's not yet found a body. Not surprising though, what with the flood water behind the gates and the tide pulling out to sea . . .'

She stopped, surprised at her own emotions. Derek had rarely been kind and in the last year of his life he had acted like a madman, killing and mutilating those he saw as his enemies, yet there was still a trace of sorrow for the brash, good looking young man who had swept her off her feet so many years ago. She recovered her composure and continued.

'I was thinking of arranging a service though. Like a memorial for all those as knew him. Reckon we need something to mark his passing, set it all to rest.'

Newt nodded, his face solemn. 'Would be fitting,' he said. 'Maybe they'd let me out for that, so I can pay my respects. Though . . .' his voice trailed off and he tugged absently at the jumper, '. . . maybe they won't. Don't know till we ask.' He gave her another of his smiles and held out his hand. 'Any chance of another fag?'

Sue struggled to concentrate in the Monday morning meeting. True, she often found it hard to focus as Garry dragged and mumbled his way through the ever-increasing flood of directives, bulletins and regulations that threatened to engulf the service – what she and Alex privately referred to as the 'rising tide of idiocy'. In fact she was well on her way to developing the ability to doze with her eyes open, a bright, attentive smile on her face. This morning, however, things went a little differently. First there was the formal introduction of the new officer, Ricky Peddlar, who was taking over from Alex. Even leaving aside the fact Alex was very popular amongst most of the officers and staff, the newcomer had not made a good impression. He seemed eager to please, almost too eager as he trotted forward to join in conversations, add his point of view or make a silly remark, always accompanied by a slightly self-conscious little laugh or a self-deprecating shrug. He hung around in the staff room at break times, his pale eyes flicking from one speaker to the next, nodding along in agreement to everything said. Sue decided to ignore him and simply treated him as if he was not there, but Lauren had taken an active dislike to him.

'Weasley,' she said, summing up all his bad qualities in one short, sharp word. 'Something not trustworthy I reckon.' Out of Pauline's earshot she added, 'Don't know what Garry's thinking of, though I suspects maybe he's not at the moment.'

Privately, Sue agreed with her on both counts. Her first impressions of Ricky had been clouded by the unfortunate circumstances of his arrival, relayed with some relish by Lauren. It was difficult to get the image of his thin, rumpled figure tapping persistently but ineffectually at the door and she instinctively felt he was grubby, dirty around the edges. She watched Ricky from behind her stack of memos, trying to separate her professional judgement from the resentment she felt on behalf of her friend. After all the ridiculing of Alex as an incomer, all the bullying and sneering at her coming from London, which he persisted in doing, Garry had appointed this scruffy, inexperienced and weak-looking specimen. Ricky sensed her gaze and looked up, catching her eye with a slightly arch smile and she looked away hurriedly.

She was startled into attention by Garry slamming his folder down on the table. The sound was like a slap and all heads turned in his direction. Opposite him Eddie was getting quite agitated, his face flushed and his normal good humour entirely absent.

'Due respect Garry but . . .'

Garry leapt to his feet, pounding the table with his fists and shouting across at Eddie. 'But it's not is it? Due respect – every time you say that you mean the exact opposite. No respect! I have no respect from any of you. Well, you can think again because times are changing and you are all going to have to change with them. I've seen some of new ideas arriving at headquarters and there is a big shake-up coming. So you can all make your minds up – you can get on board or you can *go* somewhere else and *do* something else.'

Shoving the table aside as he went, Garry slammed his way out of the room leaving the entire team staring after him in astonishment.

'Bit over the top, if you ask me,' said Eddie.

Sue was a little more forthright. 'What the fuck was that about?' she asked blinking as she looked around the room.

A few tight smiles accompanied this remark as people shifted uncomfortably in their seats.

Gordon cleared his throat and stood, holding up his hand to attract attention. 'Perhaps in the interim we could decide on the new court rota?' he suggested in his calm, soft voice. 'No.' He gestured as Eddie made to stand up, 'I think I will go to see Garry on my own. Could you organize the next few weeks ready for his approval? And our new colleague here,' he nodded towards Ricky Peddlar, who was sitting back in his chair looking distinctly alarmed by events, 'could undoubtedly benefit from some constructive advice on local ways.'

There was silence for a moment after he'd left the room and then Sue said, 'Seriously – what's going on?'

Eddie shook his head in disgust. 'Don't you ever pay attention,' he snapped, scowling at her.

Sue looked at him in surprise. 'Not if I can possibly help it,' she said. 'Does anybody?'

Margaret sniffed disapprovingly. 'Well, perhaps we could have some of your valuable attention now to help sort out matters for the next few months. There is rather a large gap in our provision, in case you haven't noticed, especially due to the loss of Alex. We've the day centre to run with more and more orders coming through and, no offence,' – she gave Ricky a vague smile – 'but we are an experienced officer short.'

Eddie shrugged his shoulders. 'Well I can carry on with the workshop until Alex gets back,' he said. 'Do we know how long that is likely to be?'

He raised his eyebrows at Sue who shrugged back. 'For ever if she doesn't do as she's told,' she said. 'I'm trying to make sure there's someone with her during the day, to make her rest, but it's not easy finding people who are willing to give up some leave to baby-sit her. Let's face it, she's not the easiest person to help at the best of times.'

Pauline tilted her head to one side and gave her one of the looks that froze the office staff in their tracks. 'So who have you got looking after her today?'

Sue smiled at her, 'I thought she needed a bit of a lesson after last Friday,' she said. 'Alison said she'd be happy to do it.'

Phil Watson, landlord of the Royal Arms tiptoed around the kitchen at the back of his pub putting on coffee for the reduced staff due in for the lunch shift. Not that there was much of a lunch shift at the moment he thought gloomily. No-one had much money even if they were lucky enough to have a job. Prices kept rising and rising, his costs were going through the roof and wages were going down as ordinary folk found themselves pushed into part-time and short-term work by the Jobcentres, which were desperate to keep the official unemployment figures down. Phil hated laying off his workers, many of whom had been with him since he took over ten years ago, but with the average wage of a farm worker stuck at less than a hundred quid a week and the threat to the Wages Board still hanging over them, most were foregoing their lunchtime 'pint and plate' in favour of something in bread from home. Maybe he should buy shares in plastic lunch boxes, he reflected gloomily. A door slammed overhead and the sound of footsteps on the stairs told him he could not put off the confrontation with his wife any longer.

'Morning Marie,' he said brightly as she pushed the door open and stepped into the dimly lit kitchen. She gave him a hard stare before brushing past him to the range where the coffee bubbled in its pot.

'You is up bright and early this morning,' she said, pouring herself a cup. 'Busy day ahead then?' She rummaged in the cupboard over the work surface, slamming the door shut as she came out empty handed.

'Ah, yes – sugar,' said Phil, beating a hasty retreat into the bar where the tables were set ready for lunch. He grabbed some sugar in paper packets and slid behind the bar, taking a deep breath before steeling himself for the looming argument.

'Thanks,' said Marie, stirring her coffee energetically. Phil kept his eyes lowered as he picked up the spoon and rinsed it under the tap. The silence stretched between them, accentuated by the stillness of the empty pub. A fly buzzed against the window, hurling itself at the glass in a desperate bid for freedom. Phil knew exactly how it felt. He glanced up and saw his wife was watching him over the rim of her coffee beaker.

'So when was you planning on telling me then?' she asked and gave an amused snort at his startled look. 'Oh for goodness sake man, I ain't stupid. Anyways, that Tom Monarch, he put his head round the door to thank me for their supper. Made a point of it, in fact. Said he was looking forward to next week. Least he's got some manners, not like some of 'em.'

Phil opened his mouth but couldn't think of a single word to say.

'Look, I know times is hard and likely to get no better, far as we can see ahead, but I don't like this. There was Micky, drinking here all night, only night them lot was here, right?

41

He's hanging around and muttering and grinning at them and suddenly he's dead, drowned in the canal on his way home. I think that's a bit of a coincidence and so do you if you was honest about it. Well, you've made an agreement now and it don't matter how good his manners is, you don't go back on your word with Tom Monarch, so we must just get on with it. Mark my words though,' she flung over her shoulder as she headed out to the bar, 'ain't no good coming from this. No good at all.'

The atmosphere in the probation office at Highpoint was strained as the officers went back to work and the clerical staff settled down in their office. Pauline unlocked the main door and they prepared for the inevitable influx of queries, excuses and hostility that comprised a normal day, but strangely there was no rush for the desk. The waiting room was empty, the dust flickering in the last pale sunlight of autumn as it drifted, undisturbed, in the hush. In the main office, however, there was some fierce wrangling going on.

'I reckon is your turn anyway,' said Lauren, glaring at Mavin, a tall, willowy woman with a shock of auburn hair. 'I had the last two newbies and Alison took over Alex early, so is someone else's job this time.'

Mavin sighed as she folded her long frame into her typing chair. 'I've spent months getting Eddie's records in order,' she said. 'I'm not handing that over and starting again from scratch. It's not fair to ask me and I won't do it. What about you Sam?' She nodded towards a small, plump woman sitting at her typewriter and pointedly ignoring the whole conversation.

'Me? What?' Sam blinked at her from behind her large, blue-tinted glasses and shook her head in mock sympathy. 'Oh, I've got Paul's brood and they come through so fast I've got twice the number of reports to do compared to the rest of you. I'm not in any position to nurse a new starter I'm afraid.' She bent her head over her work and refused to be drawn any further into the discussion.

Mavin turned back to Lauren and shrugged. 'Well, I heard they've decided you should take him, so it doesn't matter what we say, does it?' Pauline swept in through the lockable safety door and looked around at the bent heads, a picture of industry. She suppressed a smile as she noted the flushed faces and lack of paper in Lauren's typewriter.

'Yes,' she said, 'we did not get around to allocating the new officer in all this morning's excitement. Up to now we have been trying to operate on a rota basis, in fairness to everyone. After all, there may be a lighter case load for a first year officer but there is a lot more hands-on work for the support person. Now Lauren, you have been very successful in this role over the past year or so and I am wondering whether you might like to take on responsibility for nurturing our new colleagues on a regular basis.'

There was a long silence as Lauren stared at her desk, at a loss how to answer. This was a tremendous compliment from Pauline who was notoriously difficult to please and in any other circumstance she would have jumped at the chance to take a role that offered more variety, more interest and relief from the seemingly endless grind of preparing court reports, but there was a downside. Finally, she raised her eyes and looked miserably at Pauline who was watching her closely.

'Well, it's a big decision, so perhaps you would like to think about it and come to see me later,' said her senior with surprising gentleness.

Lauren took a deep breath and nodded. 'Yes.' Her voice was strangely high. 'Thank you, I'll do that.'

'Right then, back to work.' Pauline turned back towards the window, frowning at the empty yard. 'I wonder where they all are?' she added. 'Last week we were virtually under siege but today – I don't know what's happening.'

Upstairs, Sue was also at the window, tapping her foot impatiently as the clock ticked away the minutes past the hour. 'Where the hell has he got to?' she fumed. Patience exhausted, she tugged her door open and headed for the stairs, narrowly missing Gordon who was coming back from his meeting with Garry.

'Whoa! Slow down – you're getting as bad as Alex,' he said, steering her gently round by the shoulders.

'Sorry Gordon, I just didn't see you there. Oh, how did it go with Garry then?' She flicked her chin upwards to indicate the top floor.

Gordon sighed. 'I'm not sure to be honest,' he said. 'When I got there he was sitting at his desk and he acted as if nothing had happened. He listened to me and made some notes and then said to go ahead and organize things as I thought best. I'm really not sure he heard much of what I said.'

For almost the first time since she'd known him, Gordon looked genuinely worried and Sue hesitated, wanting to give him some of the support he showed to everyone else in the office, but there was a sudden bang downstairs, the sound of the front door being slammed, followed by loud voices, and instead she gave him a quick smile and took off down the stairs. Gordon gazed after her and shook his head before resuming his trek to the room at the far end of the corridor where his own problems waited.

In the reception area all was chaos. Pauline had come to the counter as soon as she heard the door slam and was remonstrating with an all-too familiar figure as a group of youths shoved one another and made mock wrestling moves before flinging themselves onto the chairs. Sue glided across the room, seized one young man by his ear and hauled him to his feet. There was a sudden hush as the rest of them saw her, and several pairs of feet slid down from the coffee table and came to rest on the floor as their owners sat up straight and tried to look away without appearing too obvious.

'Shut up Brian,' she said without turning her head, and the argument at the counter ceased mid-sentence. For a moment the only sound was a low moaning from the youth she had by the ear, now bent over, his head on one side, greasy hair flopping over one eye.

Sue let go, stepping back and flicking her fingers as if shaking something noxious from them. 'And you can sit down properly too, Darren,' she said. Darren folded himself into the nearest chair, clutching his ear and glaring at her.

'Now, just what is going on,' Sue demanded, 'and why are you all late? Your day centre orders are for 9.30 and if you're not here on time we can count you absent and report you. So, go on, give me a good reason not to.'

There was a round of shuffling and a bit of mumbling from the group as they glanced at one another, no-one willing to speak up and risk Sue's wrath.

'Come on,' she said, tapping her gold-sandalled foot impatiently. 'You were making enough noise a minute ago. What about you Brian?' She swung round and fixed him with a piercing look. 'You look like a leadership sort of person. Why don't you tell me what's been going on?'

At that moment the door creaked open a few inches and one eye peeked through the gap. At the sight of Brian it vanished and there was the sound of footsteps hurrying away down the steps and across the yard.

Before Sue could react, Pauline was at the door and off after the fleeing figure. 'Simon,' she called. 'SIMON!'

'Oh, I should have guessed,' said Sue. 'You should all be thoroughly ashamed of yourselves. Stand up. Now!'

The group shambled to their feet, arms flopping at their sides, eyes firmly fixed on the worn carpet as if seeking a dropped fag-end. Sue gestured Brian over to stand with the others.

'Well, what a bunch of brave lads you are,' she continued, her voice dripping scorn. 'How many of you are there – five? And not one brain between you. Five big tough lads picking on someone all on his own. Oh yes, really something to boast about. Well, it is something to go on your records and if there is ever the slightest hint of anything like this again you are all going back to court. Do you hear me?'

There was a slight shuffle, a shrug or two from the group and she shouted, 'Do you hear me?'

'Yes Miss,' muttered Darren followed by a few sullen "Yeah"s'.

'Right, well don't you forget it. Now bugger off into the day centre and wait until someone comes for you. And no using the pool table either. You can just stand and wait.'

The door into the centre slammed behind them and Sue took a deep breath as a voice from behind said, 'We can't actually breach them for that you know.'

Sue sighed as she turned to face Gordon, who was leaning on the counter watching her. 'I know that,' she said, 'but those little dumb bunnies don't'.

Gordon grinned at her, raising one eyebrow in admiration. 'You are a bad woman,' he said.

'Maybe, but I think I'm a decent probation officer,' she countered. Gordon nodded. 'You are certainly turning into one,' he said. 'Still, be careful, Sue. Things are changing round here. The job is turning into something . . . different and we will need to change with it. Just watch your step, okay?'

Sue stared after him as he made his way back up the stairs. He looked tired, she thought. Tired and worried. And if Gordon was worried then something was definitely wrong.

Sue caught up with Pauline in the office after lunch. 'It didn't take Brian long to revert to type,' she said.

Pauline shrugged. 'Well, he's back with his family,' she said. 'There's a distinct lack of moral fibre in that particular gene pool. He's drinking again and of course all his old friends are around him egging him on, so I suppose it's only a matter of time . . .' Her voice trailed off and she stared sadly at the desk for a moment.

Pauline was very fond of Brian, Sue recalled. She'd known him for years and watched him grow up, a credit to the local Boys Brigade with a real chance of making something of himself before he slipped slowly into the ooze of petty crime and substance abuse that surrounded so many young people in the area. She'd hauled him out on several occasions, the last only a few months ago when he had been part of the probation team in the Raft Race, but it looked as if he was going under for the third time and even Pauline had little hope they could rescue him again.

'What was all that racket anyway?' Sue asked.

Pauline snorted impatiently. 'Well, for goodness' sake! Simon was out there trying to park his lorry. You know the way he moves backwards and forwards and makes all those beeping noises?'

Sue nodded. Like half of the town she was familiar with young Simon Adams and his imaginary lorry. The lad ran everywhere, normally on bare feet and along the roads, 'driving' a truck that existed only in his mind. It was a miracle he'd not been run down and seriously injured, if not killed, but no-one had yet been able to persuade him away from his fantasy.

'Well,' Pauline continued, 'that bunch of half-wits,' she jerked her head towards the workshop where the day's arrivals were now labouring under the eagle-eyes of Eddie, 'they decided to ride imaginary motorbikes around him and box him in. Simon found he couldn't move his lorry without hitting one of the 'bikes' and he was in tears before they left him to come inside.'

Back upstairs in her room, Sue laid her head on her desk and closed her eyes. She was suddenly very, very tired, almost overwhelmed by a sense of the futility of her actions. Nothing seemed to change, or it took so long to change it was often too late, and for every one she helped out of a life of crime there were two more at the door. It was hard to remember that although she saw the same old problems time and again, they were embodied in different people. She tried to keep in mind that it was this lad's big brother or older cousin she had helped last time and this problem was a new experience for a new offender. A young lad who maybe felt no-one could possibly have felt like this before, so there was no way out of this situation and no way anyone could help. With their hard eyes and crude letters tattooed on their knuckles, their suspicions and the scorn with which they treated this, their

last chance, they were becoming interchangeable, indistin-
guishable one from another except for the occasional lost,
gentle soul like Simon. Some days she wondered why she
bothered.

Alex spent the morning sulking in bed and when she wasn't
sulking she was dozing. Despite all her protestations she was
still desperately tired and her whole body had been weakened
by the ferocity of the virus and the effects of the roaring
temperature she had endured for two days. Her eyes hurt
when she tried to open the curtains and it was too dark to
read in the dimness of the shaded room, so she lay, helpless
and fractious, with boredom her only companion. Life really
sucked, she thought. She was supposed to take up her new
post several weeks ago and she was becoming increasingly
concerned they might decide to forego her skills and experience and appoint someone else – and then where would she
be? Truly everything that could go wrong had gone wrong.

Then she opened her eyes as the door creaked open and
Alison peered round the frame. They blinked at one another
for a moment and Alex re-evaluated her level of misery.
Alison had never failed to irritate, infuriate and generally piss
her off the whole time they had been forced to work together.

Alison gave one of her trademark sniffs and smiled feebly.
'Oh hi, are you awake?'

Alex grunted, biting down on the obvious. 'Well I am now.'
It was nearly midday and to her surprise she felt hungry, the
first time in days.

'I can get you some lunch.' Alison suggested.

Alex forced a smile. 'That would be great. Thank you.'

Alison nodded and drifted off down the hall, leaving the
door ajar. 'I'll get some soup,' she said as she went down the
stairs.

Alex groaned and laid her head back on the pillow. One
reason she had lost her appetite was the impact of Sue's
cooking. Sue was not, by her own assertion, a domesticated
sort of woman and for the first few months as Alex's lodger

had managed to avoid preparing anything more complicated than tea and toast. Alex didn't mind the arrangement in the least. For her, cooking was a way of relaxing after the stresses of the day. She loved to prepare and serve food and Sue had developed into a handy kitchen helper, quite happy to clear away and wash up afterwards. Faced with having to make a meal for them both, however, Sue's meagre culinary skills were stretched beyond bearing. She had started by preparing relatively simple café staples – sausage, egg and toast, beans on toast, soggy bacon and toast.

Even in the best of health Alex would have struggled with some of these offerings, as Sue found it almost impossible to get her timing right. Invariably, one element would be charred and another stone cold, if not half-raw. Then Sue discovered soup and for several days had produced dishes of highly coloured, over-salted liquid, often cold, with the inevitable burnt toast. Recently, she had been getting bolder and several nights ago she had conjured up a supermarket cauliflower cheese with a very pink chop on top.

Alex tried to be appreciative. After all, she knew how hard her friend was trying, but when the left-overs appeared boiled up as 'soup' the next day, she abandoned all pretence and flatly refused to even have the tray on the bed. Sue was deeply hurt and they spent the evening in separate rooms, barely wishing one another 'goodnight'. Still, Alex thought, setting Alison on her was going too far.

There was a scuffling outside and Alex braced herself as the door swung back and Alison shuffled sideways into the room lugging a tray.

'Are you comfortable or do you need to be propped up a bit?' she asked, juggling her burden.

Alex sat up straight hoping she managed to at least get the tray down safely – she had no desire to be 'wearing' whatever Alison had unearthed in the kitchen. As her lunch appeared before her Alex widened her eyes in surprise. Soup, yes, but nothing resembling Sue's efforts. A serving of fresh vegetables with bits of chicken and noodles steamed in a large white beaker, golden croutons bobbing in the fragrant liquid. Several slices of crusty bread spread with butter were fanned out invitingly on a small plate and the spoon was wrapped in a crisp napkin. She blinked and glanced up at Alison who was eyeing the tray critically.

'I thought it would be easier to manage a mug in bed,' she said. 'There's more bread if you want it and I've made some vanilla pudding to follow. Sue said no coffee but I could get you some tea if you like.'

Alex stared at her and then nodded eagerly. 'Wow,' she said, picking up the spoon. 'Hey, this is really great. Where did you get the soup – it's marvellous?'

Alison stopped at the door. 'I made it,' she said in a voice that suggested she'd just missed off 'of course'. 'My Gran always made us chicken soup when we were ill and she showed me how before she died. She called it "Jewish penicillin". You have one sugar, right?'

Alex nodded again, her mouth full as she tried not to bolt the first decent meal she'd had in over a week.

'Okay. I'll bring a pudding up shall I?' said Alison, disappearing down the stairs again.

Later that afternoon, Alex lay, drowsy and pleasantly full, contemplating the puzzle that was other people. Take Alison, for example. She seemed equally satisfied with herself however she did something. Good or bad, well done or shoddily, Alison wandered through life seemingly untouched by other people's expectations. The only time she reacted was in the face of criticism and then she was fierce, denying any slight whether real or imagined and indulging in sulks out of all proportion to the perceived injury. Yet she could conjure up the perfect lunch for an invalid, deliver it with the minimum of fuss and act as if it were nothing special.

She sighed, shifting in the bed that was now getting too warm and a bit rumpled. She decided to try the television Sue had lugged into the bedroom and set up on a small table at the end of the bed. The flickering from the old black and white screen triggered her headache if she watched for too long, but a few minutes were not too bad and she was desperately bored. She wriggled out of bed, turned the switch and slid back under the covers as the picture gradually appeared. The early evening news was beginning and she was just in time to see her mother, in handcuffs, being bundled into a police van.

Chapter Four

Ada Mallory stood in her back garden watching the winter sky in all its golden, pearl-bright splendour. Despite the shorter days and the ever-encroaching winter that seemed to cut into her joints more and more with each year she was still captivated by the beauty of the Levels as autumn shaded into hard winter. Above her the light from the setting sun flung itself across the sky in reckless shades of orange and red, the few high clouds turning purple where the light cast their shadows across one another. Then in the distance there was a shrill sound, faint but gathering strength and she flung her head back, grinning with delight as the strangest of sights formed in the distance. A great, grey cloud seemed to boil out of the land, rising and falling in waves as it roiled back and forth. From behind her came a rush of wings and another smaller flight of birds soared overhead, the two groups meeting and melding into one great pulsating mass. She watched, captivated by the sight as the starlings wove their way over the Levels, swooping down as if to examine an area before rising again and moving off in another direction.

Suddenly, the cloud fractured, breaking in two as if torn down the middle, and a larger, black silhouette rose in their midst. A kestrel, she thought, or perhaps a sparrow hawk. She watched the drama unfolding in the distance as the raptor swerved and dived towards the great cloud of birds only to have it melt away at the last moment until, though surrounded by prey, it retired defeated, leaving the starlings to continue their dance in peace. Finally, a handful of birds dropped from the sky and then they were plummeting in their hundreds, a storm of dark droplets pouring from the sky as the colony found a resting place for the night.

Ada watched until the last of the sun's colour faded from the sky and with a shiver against the encroaching cold roused herself from her reverie. She walked to the end of the path to check her plants were covered and the shed was firmly closed against the chill air. As she turned back to the house she caught a glimpse of something way off to the left, out near the Shapwick Rhyne. Screwing up her eyes she stared into the darkness and was rewarded by a brief flash of light, a mere twinkle that was gone as she blinked. For a moment she considered investigating, but it was cold and none of her business anyway, and with Kevin gone there was only her to light the fire of an evening so she'd better get on with it. In the distance the light shone out again, unseen by Ada or anyone else before it gutted out.

'What were you *thinking*?' said Alex, propped up in an armchair in the downstairs room as she talked to her newly released mother on the telephone. There was a sigh down the line, a very familiar sound for Alex who had heard that soft, long-suffering sound most of her childhood and a lot of her adult life.

'Don't be like that dear. You sound just like your father. And your brother, come to that.'

'Hector or Archie?' Alex asked. Sue glanced up in surprise and Alex frowned at her and shook her head impatiently. Sue shrugged and went back to her book, wriggling further into her armchair as she tried to look as if she was not listening.

'Hector of course. He and your father have been quite – well, I thought at least you would be a bit more understanding . . .' Her voice trailed off, the disappointment echoing down the empty phone line.

Alex tried not to grit her teeth as she strove to match her mother's calm tones.

'Perhaps if you explained a bit more – what were you doing there in the first place. Did you just get caught up in it all and ended up arrested by mistake?'

She couldn't quite erase the hopeful tone to her voice. Please let it all be a silly misunderstanding, she thought. Please don't let my mother be turning into a hooligan at this time of life.

'It is just so heartless,' her mother said. 'Those poor farm animals, crammed together in horrible, smelly trucks, piled on top of one another. You can hear them as they drive by you know, crying and calling out. I think it's disgraceful, the way they are treated and I don't see why we should carry on doing it just to please the *French*!'

Alex struggled to keep a straight face at the scorn pouring forth from the last sentence. 'So – you were . . .?' she said hopefully.

'Really Alex, don't you follow the news? Some young people turned up a few weeks ago, just to highlight this horrible trade and the police were quite heavy handed, rounding them up and pushing them around for no reason. Well, that just made things worse once they'd dragged them into court – and what a waste of time and money that was too. Honestly, I despair of this country sometimes, I really do.'

Alex was rapidly becoming overwhelmed by this flood of information from her usually reserved mother, especially as none of it seemed to make much sense, let alone answer her question. She tried again. 'And you were there because . . .?'

'Well, I was walking past the court building on Thursday – you know how your father likes to shop at the market

54

during the week – and there was a group of them coming down the steps. I was going to just carry on past but then I heard someone call out, "Hello Brown Owl!" and it was Rebecca. Rebecca White, who was one of my little brownies from the village. She seemed so pleased to see me after all these years and I got talking to some of them. They are such nice young people and really committed, despite the way they've been treated.'

There was a pause and Alex tried to frame her next question, but it was answered before she could find the right words.

'Of course, I sent your father off on his own to do the shopping. I didn't think he'd be interested.'

Despite her concern, Alex felt her admiration for her mother growing by the minute.

'So you went along because of Rebecca?' she asked.

'Well, yes at first. But you should have seen the way the police behaved. I was horrified – they were quite brutal and I'm sure they were acting unlawfully. After all, everyone was on the pavement, it is a public highway and no-one from the town was complaining. They seem to hate all these trucks roaring past every hour of the day and night just as much as we do.'

Alex reflected on the implications surrounding the use of 'we' for a moment.

'Anyway,' her mother finished, 'I was only asking one of the officers what right they had to stop ordinary citizens from travelling along the road. We hadn't even got to the main protest because they had put out barricades and things. He got quite nasty and pushed me to one side before telling me to go home. The cheek of it, a cocky young lad with no manners behaving like that! I wish I had had him in *my* class. I would soon have taught him some basic politeness. The next thing I knew he'd called some of his friends and I found I'd been arrested.'

Alex took a deep breath and cut across the narrative. 'Did they say what for?' she asked. There was a scuffling sound and the phone went down with a loud clunk. Alex pulled the receiver away from her ear, pulling a face as a jolt of pain shot through her head. She tried to avoid Sue's anxious look and focus on her mother who was back on the line.

'Let me see, it says I've been arrested and cautioned, well yes I know that. How patronizing this all is . . . Ah yes, it says something about the Public Order Act 1986. Does that make any sense to you?' There was a pause as Alex digested this information, then her mother added, 'I don't suppose you could come home for a few days could you? It would be a comfort to have you here. To be honest, your father's not much use at the moment. He's spent most of the day out in that shed of his, smoking that dreadful pipe.'

'Don't even think about it,' muttered Sue, eyes fixed on her book.

Alex flapped her hand at her and searched for the right words. 'Actually I can't at the moment,' she said. 'I've been a bit ill . . .'

Sue snorted, abandoning all pretence of reading. 'A bit ill? You've been very ill and you still are,' she said loud enough to be heard down the phone.

'Is that Sue? Hello dear, how are you?' called Alex's mother.

'Fine, thank you, Mrs Hastings!' Sue replied.

Alex held the receiver out towards her but Sue waved it away, turning her attention to the fire that was beginning to burn down in the grate.

'Why does she always call me Mrs Hastings?' asked Alex's mother. Alex scowled at Sue's startled look and covered the receiver with her hand for a moment.

'And don't you even think about asking!' she hissed.

As Sue went out to the yard to get more coal, Alex explained about the meningitis, trying to avoid emotive words like 'fever', 'hospital' or even 'meningitis' itself. The whole business left her exhausted and she put up little resistance when Sue hustled her back to bed.

'I'm so sick of this,' she grumbled as she sank back into her pillows.

'Think yourself lucky,' said Sue. 'I'd love a chance to stay off work for a week or two. It's all getting very odd and rather strained at times. I think Garry is finally losing it, the day centre's almost ground to a halt and the new bloke is as much use as a chocolate teapot. I'd make the most of it if I was you.' She turned to leave and then said, 'Oh, I forgot – I thought you might like a copy of this.'

She reached into her pocket and pulled out a rather crumpled photocopy of a letter on County Hall paper. Alex peered at it in the dim light, struggling to make sense of what it said, then suddenly burst out laughing.

'That is wonderful,' she said. 'I'm going to have it framed and stuck up by my desk when I get back.' She grinned broadly as she put the letter on her bedside table. 'There can't be many people who have an official notice saying they're not a health hazard to their co-workers!'

Going out with a policeman wasn't quite what Lauren had expected. She had visions of evenings spent by the fire whilst he shared stories of the dark secrets at the heart of life on the Levels. She'd thought she would have someone to take to parties or go out for a meal with, but actually, nice as Dave Brown was, he worked ridiculous hours. She'd been worried he maybe had another girlfriend, someone a bit more conventional tucked away, but she was beginning to realize he put his job before everything else. He didn't have time for one girlfriend let alone two. So, once more she found herself stuck at home staring at the television after a hurried apology delivered over the phone. Something important had come up, he said, and he had to work overtime again. He was genuinely sorry but still there was that quiver of excitement in his voice, a sense that he was rather looking forward to whatever it was that was so important. Not that she'd find out from him what it was, Lauren reflected as she gazed into the fire. He never talked about his work. He was far too professional for that and she sensed how ambitious he was. He wasn't going to do anything stupid, anything that might keep him in uniform for the rest of his working life.

She sighed, wriggled back in the armchair and resigned herself to another lonely evening, but her mind kept drifting to the problem of Pauline's offer. On the one hand it was very tempting and there might even be a bit of a promotion in it. Sort of a half-promotion, she thought, but even that was better than nothing. She was very glad of the job at the probation office and felt she was lucky to have it. Not many people were willing to take a chance on her when she left college, looking at her in surprise when she rattled through their pathetic little typing tests or turned out a perfect shorthand transcription. As if her height affected her brain, she thought. Still, she liked the probation office where no-one treated her as an idiot or some sort of pet animal and she was expected to do pretty much the same as everyone else. She was unlikely to get anything as interesting or challenging anywhere else and so the chance to take on another role was extremely welcome. But – there was always a 'but' – she would have to start with the new boy and she had a basic, primitive dislike of Ricky Peddlar. She didn't want anything to do with him and she certainly didn't want to be responsible for helping him shape up into a decent officer. If she were honest about it she rather hoped he'd crash and burn – and the sooner the better. She found herself missing Dave more than ever. She could talk to him and know he wouldn't go off telling anyone else and he really listened, thought things through and then offered great advice. She needed all of that before she committed herself one way or the other.

The police station at Highpoint was in a state of uproar. For years, life had ambled on with nothing more serious than the odd burglary mixed up with an inordinate amount of drunken disorder, fighting outside pubs and occasional petty theft. Now, whilst the area was still coming to terms with Derek Johns' killing spree, there were two suspicious deaths in a month out on the Levels. The younger officers were fired up, many of them eager to tackle this unprecedented rise in serious crime. The older hands shook their heads sadly and muttered in the tea room about the impact of television, films and the number of 'incomers' moving in to the area bringing their unpleasant ways with them. They cited the rise in crime over the summer months when tourists, 'grockles' in local slang, and seasonal workers arrived in large numbers, often bringing traffic problems, litter and a fine disregard for local feelings with them.

'I dunno,' grumbled the desk sergeant, 'seems as how they come on holiday and think they don't have to obey no laws no more. Like they ain't never going to have no accidents neither, way some of 'em drive.'

There was a general nodding of heads as the old guard reflected on the changing world around them.

'All kinds of stuff they bring with 'un,' said a career Constable. 'Mind you, I was in court last month and ol' Peterson was on the bench. He was really tearing a strip off some lad from Bristol. Know what he said?' He raised his voice a few notes and added a slight shake to produce the familiar, querulous tones of Somerset's oldest serving magistrate. "You come to our town, snoo-gliffing and think you can just get away with it!"'

There was an appreciative ripple of laughter, hastily quelled as the Inspector looked around the door and frowned.

'That's enough of that now,' he said. 'There's nothing funny about all this. Briefing in the main room – five minutes, all of you.'

There was a general move towards the door as the evening shift followed him in to the large central office, several of them ruing their choice of assignment. Normally the night shift was quiet apart from closing time at weekends and Carnival. The younger lads went out on the beat whilst the old guard looked after the cells, handled queries about missing cats and caught up with the paperwork. It was undemanding, safe and generally warm in the station and the perfect place to see out the last few years before retirement.

Suddenly, however, there was an outbreak of violence and this time it was happening at night. They shuffled around the room looking for seats away from the eye of the Inspector. The lucky few would get to man the police station. Anyone unfortunate enough to catch his eye was likely to find himself freezing out on the Levels for the next eight hours – not the first choice for anyone in the room. The room fell silent as the Inspector positioned himself in front of a large map, pointer in hand.

'Right, we've got another body,' he said, pointing to the area around Shapwick Rhyne.

There was a soft groan from the assembled company. Shapwick was an area of exceptional natural beauty with stretches of ancient marshland, scrub and habitat for a host of endangered and rare species of birds and animals. Sadly for the searchers that meant it was boggy, wet and cold out on that exposed part of the Levels. The winter rains had already set in and parts of the marsh were flooded, and to complete their joy there was no road nearby. They would be walking to the site in the dark.

Ignoring his team's reaction the Inspector continued, 'It's a strange one, this. You will all remember the body of Michael Franks was found out near Cossington last month.' There was a nodding of heads around the room. 'Well, there are similarities between the two scenes, quite apart from their relative geographical proximity.'

PC Dave Brown felt a nudge from a colleague sitting next to him and tilted his head a little towards him.

'What the hell does all that mean?'

Dave grinned and whispered, 'They were found close to each other.' The policeman grunted. 'Can see that from just looking at the map,' he muttered, earning himself a glare from the sergeant sitting at the end of the row of chairs. The Inspector carried on, oblivious to the shuffling and anxious glances around him.

'First we need to secure the area and this means a large team of officers. Some interesting finds were made a significant distance from the actual body last time and so we are looking at the preservation of a radius up to a quarter of a mile. The search of this area will go ahead tomorrow, in daylight, but the pathologist and related specialists will need to begin work on the site at once, especially in light of the somewhat inclement conditions. I don't need to remind you to watch where you are putting your feet and to make sure you don't contaminate the scene. I want all the officers who have completed the new training days in preserving a crime scene to raise their hands.' Half a dozen men, including PC Brown complied. 'Right, you are with me. The rest of you will be with Sergeant Billings, further out on the perimeter.'

As the men got to their feet and moved to join their respective groups, PC Brown's companion said, 'Don't need all that translated though. We is heading for a long night in a muddy field – and it's raining.'

Dave shook his head at him. 'Told you to go on the training,' he said. 'Sometimes you get stuck with extra duties but on a night like tonight I've got a better chance of at least being in a tent!'

His companion pulled a face. 'What do I want to be doing, mucking around with a load of dead bodies this late on. Besides, you is always going to be called out for this now.'

He was interrupted by the Inspector, who called out, 'Oh, yes I need several volunteers to remain behind, to man the station.' There was a surge from the perimeter group and the Inspector stepped back, startled by the response. Pointing at three men he said, 'Right, get back to the desk then. Tell the duty sergeant I sent you.'

Dave's reluctant friend picked up his jacket and grinned. 'Well, seems as how I'll get to spend the night next to a nice hot cup of tea. Worth playing the odds sometimes eh, college boy?'

There were moments when Dave's calm, affable exterior came close to cracking and this was one of those times. He felt a surge of fury course through him and he wanted nothing more than to reach out and strangle the man with his own tie.

Biting down on his anger, literally as he clenched his teeth, he nodded and turned away so he wouldn't have to look at that smug face any longer.

There was a voice from behind him. 'Everything okay Constable?' He turned back and saw the Inspector watching him, head slightly on one side. He took a deep breath, 'Yes Sir, fine thank you'.

The Inspector looked at him for a second and then nodded, 'Good, good. Well, you're with me for this one.'

PC Brown grabbed his waterproof jacket and headed for the door wondering what the night had in store for him.

Tom Monarch shifted slightly in his seat but was careful to keep his face calm and attentive as the man opposite gazed out of the window, pulling one ear-lobe as he considered Tom's proposition. Both men had a glass of tea in front of them, strong, bitter tea, that had been served hot but was now stone cold. It was hot in the crowded space and Tom felt a bead of sweat begin to trickle down the side of his face. He blinked one eye, resisting the temptation to wipe it away. Finally the owner of the caravan turned back to face him, addressing him by his Roma name.

'Tell me, Tamas,' he said, 'why should we do this?'

Tom had thought long and hard about this meeting, from the moment he had made his promise to Max Long and his cronies. He knew he only had one chance to persuade the Gypsy Chief and when he replied he spoke carefully and slowly, to emphasis the importance of the matter.

'There's a power gap out on the Levels now,' he said. 'Since Derek Johns is gone and his lads is not around seems there's a good opportunity to step in and set up some stuff we've all been wanting. But 'tis tempting to those outside see – I reckon we should move now and make sure of our place afore the rest of the Johns gang gets their heads together.'

'You say "we", Tamas, but you are not one of us. You're a *gadjo* now. You chose that and you knew what it meant. Why should I listen to you after you walked away and broke your mother's heart?'

Tom blinked and felt a lump rise to his throat at the mention of his mother. It had been the hardest thing he had ever done, leaving to be with his sweetheart. Bella was part gypsy – what some of the Roma called a *'didicoy'* – and in a lot of families that wouldn't have been insurmountable, but not in his. They kept to the old ways, with the lineage passing through the mother's line. Tom's children would have been didicoys too and that was not acceptable. Not in the family of the Chief anyway.

Struggling to keep his voice steady Tom said, 'You are right but I'm not banished. I left but I keep my family in my heart. I only want to prevent trouble for us all, my people and the *kumpania*. If we work together you can keep your routes open and secure and I will make sure my people stay away from your areas. Together we will keep out the outsiders and make the Levels safe once more.'

'You may term yourself "Monarch", Tamas but I am Chief here. Do not forget that! There were many who wanted to name you *marime* and in reality you are as good as banished. You have no say in this and no status in the *kumpania*. Now, you come to me with nothing but veiled threats. Do you have anything to offer in exchange for my consideration?'

Tom bowed his head slightly. 'Forgive me Milosh. I intend no insult to you or the *kumpania*. I was thinking of the seasons, the way every year spring comes after the cold of winter and the rivers and streams flow with life. Rich pickings that rightly belong to the Roma. The loss of Pitivo must have caused his mother much grief but it is time for another harvest and another man to take control of the elver fishing.'

There was a long, long pause as Milosh stared at him and Tom held his gaze, determined not to back down. Suddenly Milosh laughed and reached over the table to slap him on the shoulder.

'Well, little brother, you were always rash but no-one ever doubted your courage. Here, this is too cold to drink now.'

He gestured towards the tea glasses. 'Let us have something a bit more warming to seal our agreement.' He stood and called to the back of the caravan. 'Dika! Bring out fresh glasses and a proper drink. It is thirsty work, this bargaining,' he added as he sat back in his chair.

His wife appeared at the door suspiciously fast and she nodded at Tom as she set the clean glasses and a bottle on the table, taking the cold, scummy tea with her as she turned back to the other room. The brothers raised their glasses in a toast and drank together for the first time in many years.

'Now Tamas,' said Milosh, reaching over to pour them both another tot. 'Tell me how you can guarantee us the elvers. I hear there are new people on the Levels. Strangers from the towns and outsiders thinking to move in. Would you know anything about that then?'

Tom sipped appreciatively and set his glass on the table before answering.

'Don't worry about them incomers,' he said. 'They'll be staying around Avalon, keeping to the marsh roads and they's just passing through, most of them. They'll not be going near the river and I'm hoping there'll not be that many venturing out on to the Levels for a while neither.'

Milosh nodded thoughtfully. 'So maybe you know something about this music too?' He glanced at Tom's startled face. 'Or maybe not. Strange sounds being heard, out at night. Like pipes playing or a flute maybe so folks say. Almost a tune but somehow never seems right and if you try to find who it is playing it goes quiet again.'

Tom shook his head. 'Don't know nothing about that,' he said. 'You sure it was not just the drink playing?' He raised his glass again and smiled. Milosh watched his face for a moment and then shrugged. 'Well, there's more things can harm than a bit of music and probably is nothing more than that.'

They raised their glasses again, both smiling but both secretly determined to find the source of the ghostly sounds.

Outside the rain was falling steadily, drumming on the roof and windows as the wind gusted across the Levels.

PC Brown hunched his shoulders and turned up his collar only to turn it down again as the rain funnelled down his neck and trickled on to his back.

'Hold that torch still can't you?' snapped the sergeant as he wrestled with a tent pole. 'Little help over here!' he yelled, and several miserable-looking policemen sloshed their way across the stretch of marshy ground and grabbed hold of the canvas flapping in the wind.

Dave glanced over at the lucky few left in the warmth of vans and had a quick grin as they were hustled out to secure the perimeter.

'Constable – if you can't do a simple thing like keep the light steady you can go and help mark out the boundary!' snapped the sergeant, and Dave turned his attention back to the task in hand.

'Sorry, Sir,' he said as he focussed the light on the tent, which was finally taking shape over the sodden heap lying on the ground.

The tent seemed very flimsy, swaying in the wind and already sagging from the weight of the water collecting on the top. The policemen struggled to set the poles in the ground, hampered by the slick mud that sent them slithering whenever they tried to force the pegs into the marsh.

PC Brown watched for a few minutes before finally stepping forward and saying, 'Get some flat bits of wood – bark even – and if we stand the poles on them it'll stay steady while we get the pegs in, Sir.'

The sergeant looked at him for a moment, then back at the mess the group were making of the job.

'Go on, then – you try it. Here.' He grabbed the nearest man and pushed another torch into his hands. 'Stand there and give us some light will you?'

Dave slid and sloshed his way across to the nearby stand of willows and hacked off a few thick strips from the trunk using his pocket knife. With the somewhat reluctant help of another Constable he lodged the tent poles on these, adjusting the tension on the ropes as each settled, partly floating on the mud. Just in time, the tent settled over the body and the soaked policemen huddled around its meagre shelter as the doctor's car pulled up. It didn't take him long to pronounce the death and in a few minutes he was off down the muddy track again, the envious eyes of the assembled police force following him as he headed for his warm, dry home.

No sooner had he left than the Inspector's car drew up and stopped with its engine idling on the far side of the area. There was a crackling of radios as he attempted to communicate with the sergeant, but the weather was against them and finally the Inspector wound the window down and beckoned him over. There was a brief conference, the sergeant leaning close to the car window whilst the Inspector sat inside issuing instructions and trying to avoid the rain running off the man's hat. Dave watched as the sergeant made his way back across the sodden ground and the car reversed away towards the track that passed for a road this far from civilization.

'Right, there's not much we can do in these conditions without risking more contamination of the site,' said the sergeant. 'I need a couple of men watching the perimeter – make that four, one for each corner. And I need a volunteer to stay here with the body to make sure there's no mistakes.'

He looked straight at Dave as he said this and not for the first time Dave wondered why he had not chosen banking or politics or even teaching when he left university. Somehow the whole team was looking at him even though no-one had turned their head in his direction. He raised his hand wearily. 'I will if you like.'

There was a feeling of relief in the group as the rest relaxed, knowing they would be heading back to the Station to finish their shifts in relative comfort. The sergeant nodded. 'Right, I'll go and tell the others and let the lucky four know they're staying here.'

Dave watched his colleagues shuffle off towards the van, then stepped back into the minimal shelter offered by the entrance to the tent. As the vans loaded up and drove off down the track, the darkness and stillness returned, the only sound the steady falling of the rain and random flapping of the canvas covering the grim scene at his back. PC Brown walked round the tent carefully adjusting the ropes until it was secured to his satisfaction. A few dozen yards away his fellow policemen shuffled and muttered in the cold and wet, stamping their feet and shifting their weight in an effort to keep warm. 'Everyone all right out there?' he called.

''Tis okay for you. You'm in the tent,' retorted one.

'I'm not – I'm outside like the rest of you,' he called back.

'Reckon we could take turns out of the rain though,' suggested another.

Dave sighed. 'We can't go inside,' he answered. 'It's a crime scene and we can't go trampling all over it. Sorry guys, but I'm not standing inside either.'

There was a deep, sullen silence and he thought he heard one of them muttering '. . . college boy'. Then all was still apart from the rain that just kept falling.

Chapter Five

'What the bloody hell were you thinking!' roared Tom, smashing his fist on the table. At the opposite end sat Max, hunched forwards wearing his usual scowl.

'What? You think 'tis only you can decide what we do then? Was not planned anyway so you've no call to be getting worried about your authority or nothing. Was just luck really – too good a chance to miss.'

He leaned back in his chair, arms folded and stared at Tom defiantly. Around the table the rest of the group shuffled their feet, several of them looking down at the floor.

Walter glanced from one to another and cleared his throat. 'Maybe we need to see how we can turn this to our advantage,' he ventured.

Tom rounded on him furiously. 'Our advantage? This stupid little punk decides to implicate himself in some suspicious death out on the Levels, out on *our* patch and you think we is going to find some benefit do you?'

Max flushed at Tom's unflattering description and rose to his feet slowly, fists clenched as he leaned over the table.

'You mind your mouth,' he growled. 'Times has changed and you gotta change too or you'll find we is all moved on and left you behind.'

He made to move round the table towards Tom and it was Geoff Bund who reached out to stop him.

'Now then, Max,' he said pleasantly, 'let's have none of that. We got a good set-up here, everyone with their place and all making one right strong operation. Seems to me we should be looking to the next few weeks, trying out stuff and making the most of these dark nights.'

Max and Tom glared at one another for a few seconds and then, like a pair of wary cats, backed away and sat down.

'Is coming up to Christmas,' Geoff continued, ignoring the tension in the room. 'Lots of demand this time of year. People wanting a bottle or two, maybe some nice cigars, perfume for the wife – and all them parties. Reckon there's a decent opening in livening up them parties, don't you think? I know a few likely lads would fancy a bit of stuff for over the festive season – know what I mean?'

There was a nodding of heads around the table. 'Mind you,' said Walter, 'I'm not so sure about this new stuff. I'll maybe stick to booze 'n' baccy. 'Tis what I know and I'm thinking there's not so much demand down my way for branching out.'

Max snorted in disgust. 'You got that big university slap in the middle of your patch,' he said. 'Nothing they students like more than a bit of whiz of an evening. I seen 'um, dancing all night, up my way. And I got news of something even better. Look here.'

He reached into his pocket and pulled out a small, clear plastic bag. Inside was what appeared to be a sheet of paper crudely printed and divided up with dotted lines into squares a bit bigger than a postage stamp. The men leaned over and peered at this strange offering, exchanging puzzled glances as they passed it from one to another. Finally, Tom picked up the bag, flipped it over a couple of times and flicked it back up the table.

'So?' he said, unimpressed.

Max leaned over and retrieved the package. 'This,' he said, waving it in front of him, 'this is worth over fifty quid.'

There was stunned silence before Tom gave a harsh laugh. 'You'm dreaming boy. Fifty quid for a tatty bit of paper like that? What's it supposed to be anyway – is all smudged.'

Max grinned, a feral grin that showed his broken front tooth. 'Called "key wings", they is. There's twenty-five of 'um on this little bit of blotting paper and kids'll pay two, three quid for each.'

Jimmy Earl reached out and took the bag, turning it over and twisting it round as he peered at the contents.

'I see them now,' he said finally. 'Look, they's keys with feathery bits behind. Key wings, like you say. Still, how come they's worth so much?'

Max grabbed for the bag and laid it on the table in front of him. 'They's printed up with the name first,' he said. 'Then you puts a drop of LSD on each one. Kids buy a tab, eat it and – there you go, instant high. Key wings is the best 'cos is powerful, almost neat. Not like some as gets cut with all sorts of stuff. This's got a good kick to it but don't poison them nor nothing.'

''Cept what it does to they heads,' said Walter. 'I don't hold with this, you know. Bit of weed, that's one thing, but this,' he flapped his hand at the offending bag, 'can be evil. Makes them think they can fly and all sorts of rubbish. I don't know as how we should be handling this.'

He folded his arms and looked round the table, trying to establish how much support he had. Tom looked worried, frowning at the bag and its dangerous contents. Mark had moved his chair a way out from the table, distancing himself from Max. Well, that was to be expected really – the older men looking at it one way and the young lads seeing only profit and not broken lives. In Walter's eyes there was a world of difference between sneaking a bit of tax from the Revenue and selling a life-time of misery and addiction. To his surprise, young Jimmy Earl didn't seem too eager either. He poked a finger at the bag and slid it away across the table.

'Don't know about this,' he said. 'Seems you can just drop this in your pocket, carry it in a car, even on a bus. Where's my lads come in, then?'

'I was thinking we had this as an extra, like,' said Max, eager to reassure him. 'Course, most of what we is handlin' is more *traditional*. This is just a bit of a bonus on top.'

Jimmy grunted, unconvinced but willing to be persuaded.

'I'll need to ask my lads,' he said. 'See how many is willing to carry them things. Is a bit of a step up, a couple of cases of booze or a few fags to stuff like this. Penalties is much steeper so is much more of a risk. They'll need to agree before we touch it, right?'

Max scowled and pushed the bag back into his pocket.

'Just tell 'em how much more they is going to get without having to lift no heavy boxes and slog around all them back doors at pubs,' he said. 'Just one drop often, that's all. Rest of the distribution gets done down the line and they's no way of linking us to it once is out in the hands of the sellers. No marks, no identification, nothin'. You tell 'em, is the easiest money they is ever going to make.' He pushed his chair back and stood. 'We done here then?'

The rest of the group looked at Tom, who nodded and waved him out. There was a collective sigh of relief when Max and his dubious merchandise left the room and for the first time they became aware of how the others felt about the way things were going. As Geoff and Mark turned towards him, mouths open to speak, he held up a warning hand.

'We need him,' he said flatly. 'He's young, he's ambitious and he's got his eyes on the Levels. Bristol's a big patch and it makes him mighty powerful, specially for a lad that new to the business. Better he's in with us here than outside and plannin' his moves.'

Mark gave a sigh and rested his elbows on the table, reaching for another bottle of beer. 'I know, you is right but

I don't like it. Don't like the cargo, don't like his ways – hell, don't like him.'

The men around the table nodded and muttered their agreement as the meeting began to break up.

'You was very quiet,' said Jimmy, looking at Geoff.

The man in charge of the ports shrugged. 'Don't really affect us,' he said. 'Don't come in from abroad, most of it. Folks cook it up all over – hell, in pots and stuff in kitchens. No need to risk bringing it in from overseas, so my lads don't need to be touching it. Reckon you could get out of it too if you wanted. Don't need no lorry, like you said.'

Jimmy frowned and glanced towards the door as if expecting a furious Max to burst back in and confront them all.

'Maybe,' he said, 'but is likely to be the most profitable part of the operation. Reckon my lads want a piece of that.'

Tom leaned across the table abruptly, interrupting them with a sharp gesture. 'No opt-outs,' he said fiercely. 'Don't want to give him the idea he can manage without us. Next thing we know there'll be more like him swarming over the Levels and there'll be open war out there. This is *our* patch and *we* say what travels and who carries it. Understand?'

The two young men flinched before his anger. It was easy to underestimate old Tom, to write him off as a throw-back, but as they looked at his hard, bold stare they remembered all the whispered rumours about the King of the Levels and his powerful contacts. Like two insolent boys they nodded and were rewarded by Tom's slow, warm smile.

'Good lads,' he said, grasping each by the shoulder before turning away.

Jimmy and Geoff exchanged looks. They knew who they'd rather back if it came to a showdown with Max and it wasn't the boy from Bristol.

It was a rather shaky Alex who arrived at work the week before Christmas. Bored out of her head with the inactivity and desperate to secure her new post, she had put on a brave show for the doctor and persuaded him to sign her off as fit. Her first Monday back and she was already regretting her actions. The welcome from downstairs was warm and sincere, and even Alison seemed pleased to see her. Lauren clambered on to her stepped stool, leaned over the front desk and gave her a hug before leaning back, staring at her hard for a moment and saying, 'You sure about this? You is looking a bit pale still.'

Alex forced a smile and laughed rather shakily. 'I'm fine,' she said. 'Just the effect of being indoors for so long.'

Pauline looked round the door and said, 'Sorry to break up this reunion but Garry wants a word as soon as you get in.'

Alex sighed and picked up her briefcase. 'Back in the jug again,' she called over her shoulder as she set off upstairs.

Garry was standing at his window staring down into the yard when she pushed open the door to his office. For a moment, Alex had to screw up her eyes against the light as he turned and, still silhouetted against the morning sunlight, gestured her towards a chair by his desk. She blinked a couple of times and her eyes adjusted once more to the dimmer light in the room.

'Is anything wrong?' Garry asked, watching her keenly.

Alex shook her head and forced a little laugh. 'No, no, nothing at all. I'm out of practice, getting up in the mornings,' she said, trying to keep her tone casual.

Garry frowned as he sat down behind his desk, never taking his eyes off her face. 'As long as you are fully recovered?' he said, making the statement into a question before continuing. 'We need someone to take control of the day centre as a matter of urgency and that person needs to be completely capable of fulfilling the role to the highest standards. It is a crucial part of our provision and we cannot afford any more delays.'

She'd been back less than an hour and already Alex was getting a headache. She wondered if he expected her to apologize for her illness – 'I'm so sorry I got meningitis at such an inconvenient time Garry. I'll try to be more careful in future.' Instead, she managed a sickly grin and reached into her case, pulling out the final doctor's note.

'I'm all signed off as fit to return,' she said, proffering the evidence.

Garry glanced at it with distaste and waved it away. 'Good,' he said, insincerely. 'Give it to Pauline to go in your file.'

She replaced the certificate wondering if he thought he might still catch something from it.

'Now, we have a growing list of clients assigned to the day centre – the magistrates have finally caught on to the fact it exists and is a sensible and viable alternative to a custodial sentence.'

Garry was in full flow now, rehashing the speech he gave to the Probation Committee and groups of interested lay people. She sat up, tried to look impressed and hoped someone would give her something useful to work with some time soon – like a budget or some helpers or even a list of these clients who were now, technically, her responsibility.

'There is, of course, still some discussion on the pattern of primary responsibility,' Garry continued. 'Whilst ideally the officer in charge of the day centre will hold the probation orders for all clients this may not prove possible in all cases. It has been decided, therefore, that these will remain with their original officers for the interim and part of your role will be liasing with them on appropriate activities.'

That meant he had decided she wasn't up to managing all the clients yet, Alex thought, and this dog's breakfast of a system was in place so something could be salvaged if she messed it all up. Great, that was just great. Welcome back Alex.

'Well, we are glad to have you back, of course,' Garry said. There was a pause before Alex realized she was supposed to get up, make some meaningless reply and leave.

'Ah, I'm glad to be back,' she managed, struggling out of the chair as she juggled with her briefcase and coat. Garry watched her struggle for a moment and nodded as she disentangled herself and headed for the door.

Outside she stopped for a moment and took a deep breath, letting it out slowly as she sought to regain her composure. On the stairs down to her office she spied Alison heading towards her, arms full of files.

'Glad I caught you in time,' said her assistant. 'Come on, I'll show you where you are now.'

Alex glanced down the corridor towards her comfortable, familiar room and realized she was no longer based in the main building. With mixed feelings she followed Alison down to the main reception area, left through the day centre doors and past the recreational area to the back of the building.

'Here you are,' said Alison, pushing a door open and stepping back to let Alex enter.

Someone had tried to make the place presentable and as she looked around the room she saw her possessions placed on the desk, her plants perched precariously on the narrow windowsill. It was dim in the small amount of light that trickled through the thick meshed glass window, oozing past the security bars before seeming to collapse, defeated, in a yellow swathe across the desk. Alison reached around the door and flicked a switch, illuminating the scene with harsh neon. Alex blinked in the bright light and felt tears form in her eyes. She scrubbed at them angrily, muttering, 'Sorry – I'm still a bit photophobic. Takes me a while to adjust to the light.'

Alison dumped the pile of files on the desk and turned to look at her anxiously. 'I know it's a bit of a step down from your old office,' she said with her habitual lack of tact, 'but they needed that for the new officer. Have you met him yet?'

Alex shook her head and sidled past her to get to the desk. Dropping gratefully into her chair she sighed heavily. 'No, not yet. What's he called again? I know Sue mentioned him but I can't remember . . .' She cast around and spotted her desk lamp in a box shoved under a spare chair.

'There's only one plug,' said Alison, pointing to a single, outdated socket across the room by the door.

'Great,' muttered Alex. 'So what am I supposed to do until I can get some more fitted?'

''Um, well we did the best we could,' said Alison.

Alex felt fresh tears begin to form in her eyes and this time they were nothing to do with the light. 'I'm sorry,' she said. 'It's just—.' She gestured at the cramped space, not much more than a modified cupboard really, and felt just how much she was worth to the service.

'Don't be worrying,' said a familiar voice, and Lauren's head popped round the corner. 'I spoke to Bert and he's going to come down later when he gets in, sort out what you need and where you want stuff. We just rescued it all and set it out so you'd not come back and have nowhere to sit down and get away from all the lads. Speaking of which, they's arriving so I told 'em to play quiet on the pool table for a bit. Hope that's all right?'

Despite her headache, despite the angry lump in her throat, Alex felt herself smiling at her indomitable friend. It was a measure of Lauren's forceful personality that the peace of the day centre was still undisturbed following the arrival of the clients.

'The new bloke, he was right eager to get in and take over,' Lauren continued.

'So what's he like?' Alex asked again.

Alison glanced at Lauren and said, 'Okay I suppose. Bit young, bit callow – typical first year officer I guess.'

Lauren pulled a face and slid around the doorframe, pushing the door shut behind her. 'I don't know,' she said. 'It's not like he's done nothin' but he makes me a bit uneasy. I'm not sure I want to work for him, even if it is a promotion.'

Alex looked at her, surprised by this bit of news. 'What? This is new – tell me.'

Lauren opened her mouth, but at that moment there was a muffled crash from the direction of the day centre's main room, followed by shouts of laughter. Alex was round the desk and had the door open in a second.

'Later,' she said to Lauren. 'I think it's time I started work.'

She strode down the corridor, flung the main door wide and roared into the sudden silence. 'Well gentlemen, it seems you have some tidying up to do.'

Alison and Lauren eyed one another warily, before Lauren jerked her head in the direction of the main room. 'Reckon she's got it all under control. I'll be off then,' and she was gone, leaving Alison to sort the files on the desk in the buzzing, flickering neon light.

For the second time in a month PC Dave Brown found himself too close to an autopsy table for comfort. As he entered the cold, white room with its shining metallic surfaces and almost imperceptible smell of blood and ripe meat, the other officers stepped aside and he was once more standing at the front of the group, a few uncomfortable feet away from the victim from the Avalon Marsh.

'Ah, Constable Brown, good to see you,' said Dr Higgins, nodding in his direction. Dave Brown managed a slightly lop-sided smile in reply. 'I believe we have you to thank for the preservation of the subject,' continued the pathologist as he wriggled into his surgical gloves and turned towards the table.

Dave cleared his throat and shifted uncomfortably from one foot to another. 'Well, no, not really,' he said. 'There was a whole team involved and everyone does their bit you know . . .' His voice trailed off as Higgins lifted a scalpel from the tray next to his elbow and held it up to the light, squinting at the blade critically.

An attendant stepped forward to draw the sheet down, exposing the grey, bloated body to the harsh light. There was a general intake of breath as the pathologist leaned forward as if to make the first incision. Dave felt his head begin to swim and realized he was holding his breath. Forcing himself to watch as the knife hovered over the waxy flesh, he tried to focus on Higgins' voice reeling off the known details for the benefit of the tape recorder that whirred away softly in the corner.

'Middle aged man, well built, medium height,' he said. 'No visible trauma to the front of the body, extensive discoloration of soft tissue due to prolonged exposure to water.' He nodded to the attendants, who lifted the corpse and rolled it over. 'Ah, now here we have signs of lividity along the back, buttocks and shoulders. Not, you notice, the usual pattern which is . . .?' He glanced around the room, one eyebrow raised whilst the police glanced away or shuffled their feet nervously. Dave glanced towards the body and looked up as he felt all eyes in the room on him.

''Um, normally in the head and neck,' he said.

Higgins beamed at him approvingly. 'Indeed, yes – and this is because . . .?'

'Most bodies float head down, on their front,' Dave finished miserably.

Higgins nodded briskly and signalled to the attendants to turn the body over again.

'Right. So here we have a drowned man who shows signs of being left on his back for some time after death. And now,' he put the scalpel back on the tray and leaned over the head, prising the eyelids open, 'sadly, I think we have lost our other clear indicator. The eyes will dry out if a victim dies on land leaving a distinct horizontal line.' He twisted the head around, peering at the exposed eyeball. 'Alas, the evidence is transient and the signs are now inconclusive. So we must probe a little further.'

He lifted the scalpel and began to cut, making a deep incision from one shoulder to the breast bone. Dave tried to breath through his mouth and as little as possible, as the body on the table was systematically filleted, gutted and hollowed out leaving just a shell. By the time it was over, Dave felt as if he could easily swap places with the remains on the table. His head was aching, his vision was blurred and every tiny muscle in his back and around his chest was screaming with pain from tension. All he wanted was to get out of there with his pride intact, but Dr Higgins had one last test for him.

'Constable Brown,' he called, just as Dave reached the safety of the door.

Dave turned back, reluctant but determined, as the remaining policemen gathered outside the room and watched him with malicious eyes. Higgins was rinsing his hands and arms off in a sink and smiled pleasantly at him as he towelled off.

'Could you please take that bag back with you?'

He indicated a brown paper sack on the side, sealed with chain of evidence labels. Dave lifted it and was surprised by how light it was. There was a faint rustling from inside, the only indication it wasn't empty.

'I took the liberty of stripping the hands,' continued the pathologist. 'The skin was starting to detach so I removed it to preserve the fingerprints and any evidence from under the nails. If you could sign for it on the way out and drop it off at the main lab I'd be most grateful.'

Dave risked a glance at the body, now covered with a stained sheet, and waiting for the porter to wheel it into the freezer. The hands, he recalled, had been encased in paper bags. He walked out of the autopsy room with the evidence bag clutched in his pale fingers and just made it to the Gents before he succumbed to the acid roiling in his stomach.

At the end of her first day in charge of the day centre Alex collapsed, exhausted, into her office chair. The neon light was as brutal as ever and the buzzing sound seemed louder with every passing minute. Bert had arrived earlier, shaken his head and pulled that face workmen seem so fond of, the one that means 'I can do it but it's a really difficult, long and expensive job', when he saw the single socket. She had half decided she would get by, but more than a few minutes under the light made her realize that was not going to work.

There was a tap on the door and Sue stuck her head round. 'All done?' she asked.

Alex rubbed her eyes and tried to stretch some of the tension out of her neck. 'I guess,' she said.

There was a pause as Sue took in the tiny, cramped space with piles of books on the floor, pictures propped up in one corner and the angry, hissing neon light casting its baleful glare over everything.

'Don't think you are,' said Sue, and she looked back down the corridor, beckoning to someone.

There was a scuffling of feet and suddenly the room was filled with people. Pauline and Lauren were first, then Alison wearing what Alex mentally dubbed her 'virtuous' face. Gordon and Eddie brought up the rear. 'Paul's sorry he can't help,' said Gordon, 'but he's out with Ricky, the new bloke, and probably won't get back before Bert locks up.'

Alex was pushed gently into her chair and wheeled out of the doorway where she gave directions and felt the smile spreading across her face for the first time since her return to work. In half an hour the space was transformed from a muddled cupboard with a desk shoved inside to something resembling a comfortable working environment. Bert appeared half way through and sniffed disapprovingly at the sight of a multisocket board running around the edge of the room, but a hard look from Pauline sent him scurrying off to find some off-cuts of carpet to cover the offending cables. As her friends stepped back to admire their handiwork, Alex struggled with a lump in her throat.

'Maybe them upstairs don't seem to care,' whispered Lauren, 'but that don't mean you isn't valued by everyone that really matters.'

'Right,' said Eddie, rubbing his hands together, 'who's for a drink then?' Alex was exhausted but she felt she really should accompany her colleagues after their show of solidarity.

She was saved by Pauline, who tapped her sharply on the shoulder and said, 'I don't think you should push it on your first day back. We'll raise a glass to you but you go off home now. Will you be all right until Sue gets back or do you want someone to come with you?'

Alex smiled, trying not to look relieved. 'I'll be fine,' she said. 'It's only five minutes away.'

'I'll pick up something for dinner on the way back,' said Sue, and then glared at the look of alarm flitting over Alex's face. 'Like fish and chips! God, one dodgy recipe and the world thinks I'm trying to poison you.'

Alex waited until Sue had flounced out down the corridor before saying to Lauren, 'Actually poison would be merciful compared to some of the stuff she's produced these last six weeks.'

Chapter Six

Iris found herself making excuses for the delay in arranging a memorial service for her late husband. Not that many people asked her about arrangements, but she was aware of curious glances as she walked through the village of Middlezoy on her way to the post office or to pick up milk from the shop. Her life was so mundane suddenly, a life like every other now her husband was gone. She wasn't sure whether to be relieved or disappointed that his friends, the collection of villains and supporters who had tramped through her house all her adult life, failed to offer their help at her time of loss, but on reflection she was happier without them around. The only one of them worth anything had been Bill, she thought, as she sat before her gas fire one evening. Big Bill Boyd, her husband's faithful deputy and best friend, who had been murdered last spring out on the Levels. Big Bill, the only man who had treated her with kindness, who showed her respect, who saw her as a person in her own right and not just 'Derek's wife'.

'Enough of this, girl,' she said sternly. 'Nothing you can do now – is all over and finished with and you've to carry on with how it is, not how you want it to be.'

Above all, she thought, she had to look out for Newt. Her one surviving son would be released from Dartmoor some time in the next year and she was determined he was not following Derek's path into a life of crime. She'd lost her younger boy, nicknamed Biff, to the 'family business', but Newt was another matter. He was smart, a quick, clever young man with charm and a ready smile. Despite his constant truanting whilst at school he had developed a liking for books and had been equally happy tearing across the Levels on a beat-up motorbike or lying on the couch, reading. Newt, she decided, was going to make something of himself but first she had to get him over the loss of his father, get him to move past what had happened the last year and willing to look to the future.

She sighed heavily as she picked up the letter that had arrived in the morning's post. Clearly labelled from Dartmoor prison, for the whole world to see, it looked as if the envelope had been passed around half the village before it landed on her door mat. She'd read it three times already but unfolded the crisp, white paper, unable to resist reading it again. Slow, harsh anger boiled up inside of her as she scanned the same callous, pompous words.

We regret to inform you that given the history of prisoner 1174: Johns, William, we are unable to recommend a temporary release on compassionate grounds to enable him to attend the funeral of his late father, Mr Derek Johns.

They hadn't even got that right, she thought furiously. It's a memorial service, not a funeral. And it wasn't as if she expected him to be able to stay. She just wanted him to be there, to lay the memory and image of Derek to rest so he could start to move on. That was not going to happen if he just sat there, brooding about events inside the walls of Dartmoor. There were too many people in Dartmoor who had known Derek, who might expect Newt to step into his shoes.

She sat for some time, twisting the letter around in her hands before finally, reluctantly, she reached for the telephone.

The Gang of Six were in a fine mood when, a few days before Christmas, they met up to assess their ongoing operations across the region. Phil Watson had laid on a bit of food to go with the drinks and the men sat around the table in the room upstairs, picking at Marie Watson's famous mincemeat pie and sampling the mulled wine.

'This is right bloody horrid,' said Max, screwing up his face as he spat the wine back into his glass.

'Traditional, that is,' retorted Walter, pouring himself another glass. ''Tis a festive welcome that, from the landlord, so show some appreciation.'

'Rather have a decent pint,' muttered the young man from Bristol. 'Reckon I'll go down and get something proper to drink.'

'You sit down and wait,' said Tom Monarch sternly. 'Phil'll be up shortly. We don't want no curious eyes peeking at you and wondering what you is doing so far from your patch. Not when things is starting to go our way.'

Max scowled but took his seat again, pushing the offending wine away angrily as he did so. 'Don't see the point of meetin' in a pub if'n can't even get a drink,' he muttered, but further complaints were cut short when the door opened and Phil Watson slipped in to the room with a loaded tray.

'Well now gents,' he said, 'I reckon mulled wine is all right and good but maybe you'm wanting a proper drink.' He set the tray down in the centre of the table and stepped back as Max reached for a pint of bitter, a grunt his only thanks.

'Mighty thoughtful of you,' said Tom, followed by murmurs of agreement from around the table. 'Perhaps if we got all we's wanting, now we can have a bit of time – private like?'

Phil kept his 'jovial landlord' smile on his face until he was outside at the top of the stairs where he stopped and took a deep breath. He glanced back at the door, firmly closed now, and wished, not for the first time, he had never started all this.

Around the table the group was taking stock of their first few months' work. Overall, it had been highly successful, despite a few minor organizational hiccups. Cargoes from across the Channel were cut out of the loading process by Geoff's men and stacked away, out of sight, ready for Jimmy's special drivers. Once on the road they found their way through the region, watched over by Mark's men from Cheddar, who used some of the more isolated nooks and crannies around the Gorge to store them, assembling orders ready for moving on to the shops, businesses and less orthodox outlets in Bristol, Somerset and Exeter. At the far end of this operational chain, Max took delivery of goods for the eastern area whilst Walter used his long-established contacts to keep Exeter supplied and happy. In the centre, controlling and overseeing the whole thing, was Tom, who ran the orders through the Levels and surrounding region. It was, without doubt, the most sophisticated operation the south-west had ever seen and the combined profits already exceeded their expectations.

The only problems they had encountered in the past few months were on the Levels themselves. Although large areas were sparsely inhabited, there were relatively few decent roads and even fewer suitable for a lorry. Too great a rise in heavy traffic was likely to draw unwanted attention and there were few 'safe' routes into Highpoint itself. Glastonbury, the other focal point for Tom's trade, was even more of a problem, with all traffic funnelled on to two viable roads, one from the east and Shepton Mallet and the other coming in from the west and Taunton. The west route was the busiest and a few more lorries would probably pass unnoticed despite the recent decline in local commerce, but it was coming in from the wrong direction. Tom had studied the problem with his usual thoroughness and thought he had a solution, but he wanted to sound out the group first.

'I'm thinking we need a secure store for some of our goods,' he said. 'Cargoes come in, and they's big some of 'em. Now you Max,' he nodded to the man from Bristol, 'you got some decent lock-ups, safe places for sorting and organizing. Walter here,' he indicated the man opposite him, 'he's been doing this so long now, got his whole network in place but we'm just setting up out here. Can't see the Johns boys lettin' us use none of their places, . . .'

This brought a round of sniggering from the assembled company.

'So I'm thinking we should try something different. Police, they's rolling up the last of Derek Johns' sorry crew, so we need to keep away from them and their ways.'

There was a general nodding of heads.

'So I'm thinking of usin' the Levels to our advantage. Seems more and more is being set aside what with they Greenies up on their hind legs and the old peat workings gettin' closed off.'

'I heard they was shutting off a whole slice of the Avalon,' said Jimmy, 'just on account of some old toad they found.'

'Was a salamander, I think,' said Mark, helping himself to another bottle of beer. 'Right rare, it is. Peat cutting's finished I reckon, out here anyways. Can't make a living off the marsh no more without big machines and they's all being taken down. Will be a wilderness in ten years, mark my words.'

'All the better for us then,' said Tom. 'Out past Shapwick, all the way to Wedmore nearly and inland to Glastonbury is empty land most of it.'

''Tis no wonder is empty,' grumbled Geoff. ''Ent no roads, nor no land neither to speak of. Lethal, a lot of it. Salamanders or whatever, they's welcome to it, I reckon.'

'So all we need,' said Tom, 'is a safe way across. Could hide a year's cargo out there, tucked away all snug, and no-one ever coming within sight of it.'

The rest of the group looked at him as if he had lost his mind.

'Yeah, right, like *all we need*,' said Max, waving his hand dismissively. 'Suppose you got that all worked out then?'

A slow grin spread across Tom's face. 'Well, just so happens I have,' he said.

Tom was the last to leave that evening and he made a point of looking in to the kitchen and thanking Maria for her hospitality. She responded with distant politeness, a brittle smile on her face, but Tom was not offended by her attitude. He knew how she felt about the arrangement, even sympathized with her reluctance, but as long as she kept to the terms he'd agreed with her husband he had no quarrel with either of them. Whistling softly to himself he opened the back door and stepped out into the dark yard behind the pub. The wind was getting up and he pulled his coat collar around his ears against the chill. Softly in the breeze came a line of music, almost familiar, tantalizing in its incompleteness, but before he could identify it, it was gone. He stood for an instant, listening to the wind as it gusted around the cars and rustled the last of the fallen leaves. Just as he was convinced he'd imagined it, the sound came again. Only a couple of bars played on a flute or something similar – and it was gone again. Tom walked across the yard, out of the splashes of light from the windows, and leaned against the wire fence, straining to hear.

'Hello? Anyone there?'

There was a moment's silence before a few mocking notes floated past him on the wind. Without thinking, Tom tightened his grip on the fence and felt the rusting barbs cut into his palm.

'Bloody hell!' He let go hurriedly, turning back towards the light to examine his hand. The door opened and Maria looked out.

'Everything all right?' she asked. 'Oh, what you done there?'

She wiped her hands on her apron and reached out, lifting his hand to examine the palm in the dim light.

'You come in now and I'll dress that for you,' she said, tugging him towards the pub. 'Don't argue – can be right dangerous, them rusty fences. Better check you's up to date with your tetanus in the morning too,' she added, as she pulled him into the kitchen and took down the first aid kit from the cupboard.

Tom stood obediently by the sink as she washed and cleaned the wound, only flinching a little as she dabbed it liberally with antiseptic.

'Keep still now,' she scolded, taping the gash together with plaster before letting go. 'So what was you doing then, trying to climb out over our fence?'

She seemed to have forgotten her nervousness around him, Tom thought. Close up she looked tired, tired and worried, but she was still a fine-looking woman. As if she sensed his thoughts, Maria stepped back, dropping her eyes to the floor and wiping her hands on her apron again.

'Strangest thing,' Tom said, ignoring her withdrawal. 'There was – like music outside. Pipes or something, playing in the open – maybe just over the hill. Didn't see no-one, though. Don't suppose you ever heard 'un?'

Maria shook her head. 'No, but then I'm not out much. Got too much to do round here to be swanning around, listening to music. Mind you, a couple of regulars mentioned something like that, last week I think it was. Sort of eerie flute music, no real tune but almost like something . . .' Her voice tailed off as Phil's imposing bulk loomed in the doorway.

'Now then Tom,' he said. 'This 'ent in our agreement.'

His voice was jovial but his stare was hard and the message clear. He was tolerated, but within strict limits and standing in the kitchen with Maria was beyond them.

Tom nodded and turned to go. 'Well, thank you for this,' he said, holding up his bandaged hand.

'You see about that tetanus injection,' said Maria as he stepped out into the darkness once more. Behind her Phil let out his breath in a long sigh.

'You be careful now,' he said gruffly. 'Don't want to be getting' too friendly with the likes of Tom Monarch.'

Marie sniffed in disgust, 'Well maybe I should'a just left him bellowing out there? Is all we need, Tom Monarch getting lock-jaw off our back fence. What with him and Micky, people'll start saying we's cursed or something.'

She swept off into the bar and began clearing the counter with a clanking of glasses and banging of ashtrays whilst Phil stood by the kitchen window, staring out into the darkness and wondering what exactly he'd got them both mixed up in.

Alex was putting the finishing touches to her workshop proposals and trying to prepare herself for a meeting with Garry later in the day when her phone rang.

'Hello?' she said absently, her mind still on how to justify her ideas in the light of the new, punitive guidelines that were seeping through the system.

She paused as she tried to identify her caller and then her mouth went dry as she struggled to reconcile her conflicting emotions. Struggling for a professional tone she focussed on the more positive feelings whilst a shiver of dread pushed itself deep into her mind.

'Mrs Johns – yes, sorry. This is Alex Hastings – Newt's – I mean William's probation officer.'

For an instant she wondered if this were true. Did she still have any of her old case-load left? Garry had been remarkably unenlightening about the whole subject on her return and she had simply carried on with the files Alison had transferred into her new office, most of which had clients on day centre orders anyway. Newt, she realized, was probably the sole exception.

'I'm sorry to bother you,' said Iris Johns, 'it's just I don't know who else to ask, and Billy, he always speaks well of you, so I was hoping you might be able to help.'

Poor old Newt was seriously short of friends if he 'spoke well' of her, Alex thought. She was still feeling guilty about the way she had neglected him during the past year. Somehow he seemed less – urgent – than the clients who appeared in reception dripping blood on the carpet or full of woe having been thrown out of home again. Newt was safe in prison and at least fed and housed for the next year. And there was the small matter of his father's murderous rampage across the Levels, culminating in his attempt to lure her to a deserted cottage where, presumably, he intended to kill *her*.

'If I can, of course I will,' she said.

At the other end of the phone Iris was finding the conversation just as strained. She hoped desperately Alex might be able to persuade the authorities at Dartmoor to let Newt attend the memorial service but asking Alex to help after what her husband had put her through just seemed wrong. Screwing up her courage she hurried on with her prepared explanation, ending with, 'I don't want my boy carrying on like this and I reckon if I can stop him brooding on Derek, get him past all this, perhaps he can start again when he's out. Maybe get a proper job and do something useful.'

Despite her fairly horrible recent experiences of the Johns family, Alex felt the beginnings of admiration for Iris. She had lost her husband, she had lost her youngest son and her other boy was incarcerated seventy-five miles away in one of the toughest prisons in the country but she still believed something could be salvaged out of such a terrible time. Even as her inner voices clamoured for her not to get involved she reached for her diary to make an appointment for a home visit.

'I hope you had the sense to make it in the evening,' said Sue, when Alex confessed her folly over lunch.

Alex nodded, her mouth full of egg and cress from the new sandwich bar in the square. 'Mmm, yes, don't really know if I'm supposed to go see parents . . . especially seeing as Newt's over 18.' She took a swig of tea, pulled a face and pushed the beaker away.

'Yes,' said Sue with sympathy, 'I think the milk's off again.'

'Why the bloody hell didn't you warn me then? Oh yuck, I feel sick.' Alex left the second sandwich untouched and got up to leave the table. As if summoned, Lauren materialized beside her and eyed the abandoned food.

'Knock yourself out,' said Alex, and headed back to the day centre.

Lauren hopped up on to the vacated chair and picked up the sandwich.

'So what's eating her then?' she said between bites.

Sue explained about the phone call, keeping a wary eye on her own lunch as she did so. She had a packet of Jaffa Cakes with her and these were, she knew, a particular favourite of her admin assistant. Lauren screwed up her eyes thoughtfully as she chewed.

'Not sure as how she's supposed to still have Newt anyway,' she said. 'Most of 'em was passed over to . . .' she jerked her head in the direction of Ricky Peddlar, who had just entered and was hovering by the kettle, hoping to be invited over to join someone. 'Reckon Alex'd do better by Newt than he would though. Even considering – all as is past now.'

Sue watched Lauren's face closely. Lauren had also suffered at the hands of Derek Johns and it was only Alex's quick thinking that had saved her from being swept away down the canal along with her kidnapper. Lauren met her eyes with a steady gaze.

'Just 'cos Derek Johns was a bad 'un don't mean Newt is, nor Iris neither. I heard she threw the old bastard out – changed the locks and everything. He was on the doorstep crying like a baby but she never let him in. What my cousin says anyway and she lives opposite.'

'I'm not sure Alex should start stirring up all those memories, especially after her illness,' said Sue. 'She's not well again yet – most nights she just collapses on the sofa and doesn't even want to eat.'

Privately Lauren thought this might have more to do with Sue's cooking than any residual illness. Lauren had an extraordinary appetite but even she baulked at most of Sue's offerings.

'Maybe she can just write a letter or something,' she said. 'You tell her to bring it to me rather than Alison. I'll do it after work.'

Sue nodded gratefully. 'Thanks. By the way, I heard about Pauline offering you that job to mentor the new officers. Do you know if you're going to take it? Just, well, I rather like having you as my assistant. I don't think I'd have got this far without you.'

Lauren, the so-tough, don't-give-a-damn Lauren, caught her breath at the unexpected compliment. She looked down at the table, overcome with embarrassment, before managing a gruff reply.

'Well, I'm not – you know – not sure yet. Seems a good opportunity but I'm not sure about – some stuff.'

Sue sneaked a look at Ricky who was still stranded by the sink, trying to look as if he was busy with making his tea. She wasn't too sure about some stuff either.

Pushing open the door to the day centre, Alex was brought up short by the sight of Brian and several of his little friends running round the main room brandishing the pool cues.

'Hey – stop that now!' she yelled. Two of the culprits pulled up short, dropping the cues on to the pool table guiltily but Brian and his other friend – damn little Darren, she realized – carried on flailing at one another, giggling and giving whoops of delight as they narrowly avoided hitting one another.

Without thinking, Alex stepped between them, arms raised to protect her head. There was a resounding thud as Darren's pool cue made contact with her left wrist and her whole hand went numb. She cried out as a fierce pain shot up her arm and curled over the injured wrist instinctively. The movement saved her from a blow in the face, as Brian's cue whistled past her bent head. There was sudden silence, broken only by the sound of the two cues landing on the floor as the two young men stepped away in horror at what had happened.

Fighting the wave of dizziness that threatened to over-whelm her, Alex straightened up and faced the group, now standing up against the wall, their heads down. Alex gritted her teeth against the pain now flooding through her whole arm and said, 'What the BLOODY HELL do you think you're doing? Stand up straight you stupid little idiots! Well? Can't I leave you for a second without this sort of reckless, dangerous behaviour breaking out? Come on – you're all just this far away from being breached.'

She held up her good hand, finger and thumb barely apart. There was silence from the group apart from the odd shuffling of feet. On the floor behind her one of the pool cues rolled noisily into a corner, bouncing a couple of times off the wall before coming to rest.

Taking a deep breath, Alex glared at the ringleader. 'Brian – over here. NOW!', she added, as the object of her fury tried to slide behind Darren. Brian shuffled over towards her, eyes flicking from side to side. With his lank, greasy hair and jerky movements he resembled a cornered animal, she thought. A dangerous cornered animal. Finally, he stood in front of her, but the twitching didn't stop, even when he lifted his head to stare at her sullenly. He'd lost weight again, she realized. He had been lean and fit a few months ago when he took part in the raft race, the weeks of living in a secure and caring environment with Pauline working their magic as an enthusiastic and cheerful boy emerged from the husk of the Brian she knew only too well. There was something wrong again – something serious. She glanced across at the other three who were still huddling together on the far side of the room. There was a lot of trembling going on and although she hoped she commanded some respect she didn't think they were that scared of her.

'Right, clear up this stuff,' she said. 'You are all out of here today. I'll be logging this in your records and expect you back here tomorrow morning – on time. You're not getting credited with today either.' Darren opened his mouth to protest. 'Don't say a word, just think yourselves lucky no-one was more seriously hurt. I'll see each of you tomorrow and decide then whether I want you in my day centre, so I suggest you spend some time thinking of reasons why you should stay.'

Brian fixed her with a glassy stare. He was sweating, she noticed, his face turning pink and with a sheen across his forehead. For a moment she thought he was going to throw up as he burped and then swallowed a couple of times but then he turned on his heel and stormed out, the door slamming shut behind him. She waited until the other three had finished putting the pool table to rights and followed Brian out of the room before allowing herself to sink into one of the dilapidated armchairs in the corner, hunched over her arm in agony.

'Well, that solves a few problems for me,' said Alex that evening as she and Sue sat in front of the fire.

Sue looked over her wine glass at her friend. 'So no driving?' she said.

'Not for a while anyway,' Alex confirmed. 'The bone's chipped, they said. Not broken but actually worse in some ways.' She flexed her fingers experimentally and winced as the movement sent the pain throbbing through her whole arm. 'Well, at least I can still work – I was dreading having to tell Garry I'd be off again. I don't feel exactly secure as it is. I just get the feeling he would love to get rid of me.'

Sue refilled their glasses, in defiance of the instructions from the hospital about mixing pain killers and alcohol, and settled back in her chair.

'I think you should talk to the Union,' she said. 'Don't give me that look – you know he's trying to bully you. He *is* bullying you, otherwise you wouldn't be thinking about going to work with that arm.'

Alex was saved from having to answer by a knock on the door. Sue disappeared for a moment, returning with Lauren, a rather sheepish PC Dave Brown in tow. Lauren jumped on to a sofa and accepted a drink but Dave declined on the grounds he was driving and really should set a good example.

Sue went in to the kitchen to make tea, leaving their guests with Alex. Lauren looked around in frank curiosity.

'Is even more books than I remember,' she said. 'How many you got now then?'

Alex grinned and shook her head, 'I don't count them,' she said, 'I just read them.'

'And hardly ever dust them,' said Sue, returning with a mug of tea for Dave.

Alex laughed. 'I remember when I was training in London, I had quite a reasonable little flat – a bedsit with a separate kitchen, but there was a bath in the kitchen! No, really, under a lift-up counter. It was wonderful, having my own bath up there in the eaves. Anyway, my landlady was a fascinating but eccentric Polish woman and she came round one day to have a chat. She said she was worried about all the books.' Alex took a slug of wine, set down her glass and continued. 'I thought perhaps she thought they were too heavy for the floor so I tried to reassure her they were mainly paperbacks and not all that heavy but she sighed and threw her hands up in the air. "It is not good", she said, "Not healthy". I couldn't work out what was the matter until she leaned over, grabbed my arm and said, "Dust Alex, so much dust they attract. Not healthy at all".'

The laughter was cut short by another knock on the front door. Alex and Sue looked at one another in surprise. One set of visitors in the evening was unusual. Two lots were completely unheard of. Dave saw their anxious looks and got to his feet.

'I'll go,' he said. 'Might be someone from the station anyway. I have to leave my contact details seeing as I'm working on this big case at the moment.'

There was a hush in the back room as the three women strained to hear what was happening at the door. There was a rumble of male voices, then the sound of the door being closed again and Dave walked back into the room.

'It's your brother, Alex,' he said. 'He's just taking off his coat.'

'Alex stared at him is astonishment, her shock showing on her face. In her mind she offered a silent prayer, 'Let it be Archie, let it be Archie, please let it be Archie . . .'

A tall, blond man in his late 30s appeared in the doorway just behind Dave.

'Hello, Sis,' he said cheerily. 'You in the wars again? What is it this time then?' He beamed at the assembled company. 'Hello everyone. I'm Hector – Hector Hastings Norman. Jolly nice to meet you all.'

He flung himself down on the sofa, his weight bouncing Lauren up in the air and sending the rest of her drink spilling over them both.

'You girt stupid bugger!' she yelped, pulling away from him and brushing ineffectually at her stained jumper.

'I'm so sorry,' said Hector rummaging in his pocket and pulling out a clean, white handkerchief. 'Here, let me help'. He reached over to her but Lauren sprang off the couch and turned away from him.

'Reckon we'd better be going,' she said, her eyes bright with anger. Alex heaved herself to her feet, awkward with one arm in a sling. 'I'm really sorry about this Lauren. Please, don't go yet. I can find you something clean and we can wash that, get the stain out straight away.'

Lauren's expression softened for a moment. 'No, is all right – will come out easy enough. We just dropped by to see you was all right. Don't you worry – is not your fault.'

She delivered this last comment over her shoulder at Hector, who had risen from the sofa and now stood, towering over her. He looked, Alex thought, like a mournful giraffe. She followed Lauren and Dave out into the front room, pulling the connecting door to behind her.

'Actually Dave, I'm really glad you called round. I wanted to ask you about something.'

Dave shrugged on his heavy coat and held Lauren's jacket for her.

'Fire away. I'll help if I can. Something professional is it?'

Alex nodded. 'Yes. Is there any talk of something new doing the rounds?' Dave looked up sharply and she hurried on. 'I was with the lads today and I'm sure they'd taken something. One of them was sweating – I thought he was running a temperature at first. And they were all jumpy; on edge but loud, and – not aggressive, but uncontrolled. More so than usual.'

Dave narrowed his eyes thoughtfully. 'Any signs of breathing fast?' he asked. Alex nodded. 'Attention span?'

Lauren laughed mockingly, 'That lot got no attention span to start with,' she said. Certainly true, Alex acknowledged silently, but come to think of it she had spent most of the morning trying to get them to focus on a routine clean-up of the local playground.

Dave hesitated before saying, 'Could be "whiz" – amphetamines – used to be known as 'uppers' sometimes. There's never been much of a problem until recently but we've been getting reports of groups running round, acting a bit crazy, yelling and just keeping on half the night. One of the local doctors reported a probable overdose last week too. Lad of sixteen. Took some pills his mates gave him. He had a heart attack.'

'That's awful,' said Lauren.

'It's unusual,' said Dave. 'He had a heart problem no-one knew about and the damn things sent his heart rate up too high. Still, it's dangerous stuff and a class B drug so this is a serious matter.'

'Reckon that's how you did that then?' asked Lauren nodded towards Alex's arm.

Alex shook her head. 'That was me being stupid,' she said. 'They were larking around and I just stepped in between a couple of them. It was a daft thing to do and my own fault. I should know better by now.'

Dave gave her a hard look. 'Maybe, but that's still technically assault if not GBH and if they were under the influence that makes it worse.'

'No, really, it was an accident,' Alex insisted. 'We're dealing with it at probation. It's fine.'

'Do you have any evidence they were on something?' he pressed.

'Just a suspicion,' said Alex firmly.

Reluctantly, Dave let the matter go and he and Lauren slipped out into the night where the clouds were gathering and a mean little wind was getting up. Alex gave a shiver as she closed the front door against the cold and checked the curtains at the front window for the third time, just in case they had moved in the draught. She knew it was bordering on obsessive behaviour but she didn't care.

Back in the living room, Sue and Hector were eyeing one another warily. Alex flopped back into her chair and sighed heavily as she contemplated her older brother.

'Well done Hector. Thanks for that. So, to what do we owe the pleasure of your company?'

Hector shifted on the couch, still dabbing at his wine-stained trousers as he avoided his sister's eyes. 'Oh, you know, down here on a bit of business and thought I'd drop in.' It was a remarkably unconvincing performance.

'Seriously Hector – why are you here?'

Her brother cleared his throat and stared into the fire for a moment. 'A couple of things actually. We were wondering if you were coming home for Christmas. Really hoping you were – maybe you could talk some sense into Mater over this animal protest thing. Dad doesn't know what to do and she won't listen to me or Archie.'

Sue raised an eyebrow, her eyes twinkling as she struggled not to giggle. 'Mater?' she whispered. Alex frowned at her but Sue would not be silenced. 'Hector *Hastings Norman*? Don't you mean Hector Norman Hastings?' she asked Hector sweetly.

'No, no – family name,' said Hector. 'Dad was a classics scholar so we all ended up with Greek names but Mater insisted we have both surnames.'

'So you are really Alex Hastings Norman?' said Sue barely able to contain her amusement. 'Wow that must have been great at school. What's Alex short for – Alexandra? Is that Greek?'

'Shut up, Hector,' snapped Alex. 'Don't you dare say another bloody word!' She reached for the bottle and poured herself another drink. 'Oh, go and get yourself a glass from the kitchen. Through there,' she waved in the direction of the off-shot. 'I presume you don't intend to drive back home tonight?'

Hector got to his feet and shambled towards the door. 'I rather hoped I could crash here overnight,' he said. There was the sound of cupboards opening and closing as he rummaged through the contents.

'On the left, second shelf,' Alex called without moving. There was a clinking sound and he re-emerged clutching a large tumbler.

'Very sensible,' said Sue, pouring him a generous measure. 'You get lots more in one of those. No – I'm only joking, sit down.'

Hector returned to the sofa, sipping his wine and looking rather sheepish. Alex waited for a moment and then said, 'So, why do you need my help with mother?'

'You know about all this nonsense over the lorries out at Brightlingsea?' Hector said. Alex nodded, refraining from adding she didn't necessarily see it as nonsense. 'Well, she was sent a fine. All she had to do was pay it in the time limit and that would have been that. She'd made her views known, stood up for her principles or whatever she thought she was doing – but she won't pay it. So we decided we would.'

Alex jerked her head up and stared at him. 'Are you mad? You can't do that – she'll go crazy.'

Hector looked as if he were going to cry. 'Well, yes, she did actually. She was absolutely furious when she found out. You remember that set of picture plates she had on the wall?' Alex nodded. 'Well, she pulled them all down and threw them at us. I don't know what's got in to her. She was like a woman possessed. And then she said she was cancelling Christmas because she was sick of cooking and clearing up after us all and wanted some time to herself.'

'Wow! When you say "us", who exactly do you mean?' asked Alex.

'Oh, me and Pater. Archie too, though he didn't think it was such a good idea even before the plate thing.'

'No, really?' murmured Sue, captivated by this unfolding domestic drama.

'Well, I couldn't get home even if I wanted to,' said Alex, raising her broken wrist in its sling. 'Personally I think you are all a load of idiots but I'll call her if you like and see what she says.'

She reached for the phone but Hector coughed again and shook his head. 'Well, that's the thing,' he said. 'We don't know where she is. She stormed out last week and no-one seems to know where she has gone.'

Outside the little terraced house, he watched as the copper and his weird little girlfriend left. He smiled with satisfaction as the curtains twitched under Alex's fussing, but it was too cold to hang about. Pulling a knitted hat low over his face, he turned up his coat collar. The wind was getting up again and he needed to get under shelter before the threatening snow began to fall. Damn the festive season, he thought, as he tramped along the footpath by the river. He'd sussed out a nice little bolt-hole just last week, up at the holiday camp near Brean Sands. It was warm, it was furnished and there was a big communal kitchen, largely unattended for much of the day. He had been able to help himself, eating when he wanted, sheltering safe in his own space for the first time in several months and then suddenly the whole place seemed to spring into life. He had been lucky, though – if he'd been asleep then he'd have been caught, as the cleaners had rolled by and started opening up the chalets and making them ready for the expected Christmas visitors. Fortunately, he'd been out on one of his scavenging missions and returned, his arms full of biscuits, a big block of cheese tucked under his arm, to see the door wide open and complaints from the two women inside audible from across the road. He'd slunk away, glad he had his coat and hat with him. That was all he'd been able to salvage, though that evening, after waiting in the bushes on the perimeter all day, he'd broken into one of the unfinished chalets and helped himself to a few bits and pieces.

Now he was back by the canal, bunking down in one of the abandoned pill boxes left over from the war. It was shelter but little more. He stuffed the gun slits with the blankets he'd purloined and hunted along the bank until he found some old doors left over from an abandoned fisherman's hut. The hut itself was rotten, little more than a rickety roof balanced on walls that were falling to pieces. After he'd hauled the few solid bits back to block the doorway to the pill box he kicked and smashed the rest into kindling and used it to set a fire on the scarred concrete floor. The damp wood gave off a solid bank of acrid smoke and so little heat he finally stamped it out in disgust.

The next morning he woke early from his broken, cold sleep and set off down the towpath, ever wary of other walkers or the hated river wardens. He was almost down to Standards Lock before he saw some small sheds on a patch of semi-legal allotments off to his left. He hopped over the small ditches cut into the boggy land and examined the buildings. Several had strong padlocks on their doors and although they were likely to contain more valuable items he was aware of the handful of farm buildings within earshot and decided to try the older, more dilapidated ones first.

The first building was obviously abandoned, offering a couple of rusty trowels, a rake handle and a litter of crisp packets and empty cider bottles, evidence of a cheap and dirty night out for some local youths. The other was much more rewarding. The door creaked as he pulled it open and the air was musty, smelling of damp earth and the sharp tang of rusty metal, but inside, layered in cobwebs and covered with a blanket of dust, was a collection of items he craved. As he rummaged through the hut he realized he would need several trips to carry everything he wanted – not such a good idea as, despite the air of neglect around him, there was always the danger someone might choose this exact day to look in on the shed. There was also the possibility he had been seen and after a moment's regret he decided coming back was too risky. Reluctantly, he passed over a battered folding chair, a large toolbox and most of the pots and mugs. He made a pile of the chosen items – a mug, bowl, spoon and kitchen knife, a medium sized saucepan, some fish hooks and line he thrust into one pocket and an old penknife into another. He wrapped the whole lot in a worn but serviceable blanket and lifted the main prize – a paraffin stove which appeared to have some fuel in it. One last look around and he was gone, out of the door and across the allotments, still deserted in the weak, early morning light.

He made his way back to his temporary home without being seen and stashed his loot in the far corner. Sitting in the dim, cold space he considered his options. Painfully limited though they were, he needed to keep himself out of sight, fed and warm enough to stay alive for the next few weeks. Once the long Christmas holiday was over, he reasoned, he could return to the relative comfort of the holiday park up on the coast, waiting out the rest of the winter in a chalet at the far end where few ventured in the closed season. Until then he had to hang on to his purloined possessions, which involved keeping nosy walkers and adventurous children away from his pill box. Couldn't trust anyone these days, he thought. Thieving bastards was everywhere.

Chapter Seven

Hector left the next morning, heading back up the motorway for a cosy weekend with his family, but it was not until that evening that Sue was able to confront Alex about the family revelations.

'So – Hastings Norman?' she said sweetly over the dinner table. 'Is that double barrelled then?'

Alex stared at her. 'I should have known you wouldn't let it go,' she grumbled. 'No, it's just my mother wanting to keep her family name so we got it too. Of course, the pay-off was the bloody awful names Dad inflicted on us.'

Sue leaned forward eagerly. 'So go on – what is "Alex" short for – tell please.'

Alex pushed her plate aside, the meal half finished. She was too proud to let Sue cut her food up for her or even butter her toast but despite her best efforts couldn't manage on her own. Once again she was thwarted by her own stubbornness . . .

'If you ever tell anyone, anyone at all, I will hunt you down and personally beat you to death – understand?'

'What, even Lauren?' Sue asked innocently.

'*Especially* Lauren,' said Alex. 'Okay, this was going to come out anyway with bloody Ricky Peddlar turning up, so I might as well tell you.'

This was another surprise for Sue but she knew better than to interrupt now Alex was in a talking mood.

'I've got two brothers,' said Alex. 'Archie who's the oldest, then Hector, then there's me and finally a little sister. Dad lumbered us all with names from the *Iliad* – Archie is actually Agamemnon. He decided really early he could put up with people thinking he was Achilles – it's a bit more butch, I think. I'm Cassandra and if you think that's bad can you imagine what my little sister suffered at school? She got Clytemnestra. I leave it to your imagination, the nicknames *she* had to put up with. Hector got off pretty lightly.'

Sue waited but that seemed to be all Alex was going to tell her. 'So where does Ricky Peddlar fit in to all this?' she asked.

Alex twirled her empty beaker and stared at the table, a scowl on her face. 'He was at university with me,' she said finally. 'I don't know how the hell he got in because he's thick as pig-shit but he turned up a year after I began. I can't believe Garry appointed him – he's the laziest, most spineless, odious little weasel I've ever come across. And he's a racist, sexist, homophobic pig'.

'Maybe that's why Garry appointed him,' said Sue. 'In his eyes that's an impressive list of qualities.'

Despite herself, Alex smiled.

'One thing from last night though,' said Sue. 'You both seemed more worried about Christmas than your mother disappearing.'

'She does that,' said Alex getting up from the table. 'When we were younger we'd come downstairs in the morning and Dad would be trying to make breakfast and shoving any old rubbish into our lunch boxes and we knew mother was off again. Often only overnight but a couple of times she was gone for more than a week.'

'Where did she go?' asked Sue. Alex shook her head as she gathered up her half-finished plate and headed for the kitchen.

'No-one knows. We never asked – in fact we never mentioned it, not even between ourselves. I think we all wondered but no-one dared say anything in case it made matters worse.'

'Pity. You might have an idea where she is now,' said Sue, clearing the rest of the dishes and following Alex into the narrow kitchen. 'Leave that. You can't wash up or you'll get your cast wet and you're not drying up either. We're already dangerously close to a "nil wine glass" situation.'

Alex pulled out a stool from under the worktop and perched herself by the bench. 'Did your family act like that?' she asked. 'Only, I wondered all the time if we were the only ones. I used to look at other mothers and couldn't imagine them just disappearing like that. Though when she was back home, my mother didn't look like she'd disappear either.'

Sue scrubbed at the dirty pans, piling the clean dishes on to the draining board. 'I think there are strange goings-on in every family,' she said. 'You never know what people will do under pressure and there's nothing like a family to generate all sorts of emotions.'

They went back into the living room and settled in front of the fire. Sue never talked about her family either, Alex thought, sneaking a glance at her friend.

'What about you,' she said casually. Will you be going home for Christmas?' Sue shook her head but said nothing.

'Well, if we're both going to be here I suppose we ought to brighten the place up a bit.'

Dr Higgins rarely worked on a weekend. It was one of the advantages of a rural appointment and one he appreciated greatly, especially in the summer when he was able to indulge his passion for rambling. The job was changing though. New tests were being developed, everything from more accurate chemicals for gunshot residue to this new idea that everyone's unique genetic makeup could be read and used to identify them. That was a bit away still, much to his relief, but the whole business of forensics was becoming increasingly complex and specialized. He was a brilliant man, highly trained and always willing to add to his knowledge through reading but he could feel the whole field pulling away from him. It wouldn't be long, he thought, before there were eager graduates with shiny new degrees in crime scene work pushing through the doors and making him feel like an old, tired amateur. He sighed and rubbed his eyes before replacing his glasses and returning to the latest puzzle.

The second body from the Levels, unlike poor old Micky Franks, had not died by drowning. The man had been identified the day before, by a distraught wife in her late thirties, clutching the hands of two teenage children as she struggled for composure. Identifications were always grim without the added ravages of water damage. The second victim had been a River Warden, one of the small band of intrepid men who walked the Levels, guarding the fragile waterlands from poachers, illegal peat cutters, egg collectors and stupid little hooligans who thought it funny to set fires in the dry, golden grasses of summer. Robert Donnoley, he said to himself as he turned on the lamp and settled to the backlog of reports and requests. He was called Robert Donnoley. He had a wife and a son and a daughter and someone hit him over the head and left him to die, alone on the marsh. And then someone else came along and tried to make it look as if he had drowned. Now why would they have done that?

Christmas in Highpoint was a jovial affair on the surface. The pubs did a roaring trade despite the dire financial situation that was affecting so many people. The days before Christmas Eve saw huge crowds flocking to the supermarket, panic buying as the shops were to be closed for three days, and the shelves of the butcher's shop were empty by early afternoon every day. Alex and Sue spent a chaotic half hour in the Woolworths by the quayside rummaging through crates of decorations and boxes of tinsel before emerging, somewhat battered but triumphant, with arms full of decorations and a ridiculous amount of 'pick & mix' sweets.

'Just need some decent wine and we're all set,' huffed Sue as she shouldered the heavy shopping bag.

'What about dinner?' asked Alex. 'We have to have something decent for Christmas dinner.'

Sue shrugged as she set off down the High Street. 'We've got wine, we've got sweets – what more do you want?'

Alex trotted after her and tugged at her sleeve, pulling her towards the Cornhill building where the market was held. Every Wednesday and Saturday there was an auction of local produce in the covered square at the rear and Alex had spent many happy hours wandering around the tables and watching the auctioneer, an elderly woman with her hair in a stern grey bun and the rest of her swathed in even sterner tweeds, dispose of fish, fowl, game and vegetables. The square was full, this Saturday before Christmas, and proceedings were going with a swing. The auctioneer strode between the tables, selecting the next lot at random and inviting bids whilst waving a rambler's cleft stick at anyone foolish enough to pass comment out of turn.

'Now, what am I bid for this fine brace of coneys?' she said, lifting a pair of rabbits, still in their skins. 'Come on now, a lovely plump pair here. Do I hear a pound?' There was a shuffling of feet from the crowd. 'All right, seeing as it's Christmas hows about seventeen and six then?'

Sue stared at the auctioneer in amazement. 'Seventeen and six?' she hissed to Alex. 'What's she on about?'

'Shush!' said Alex as she held her hand up to bid, 'Fifteen shillings!'

'Now I hear fifteen shillings – fifteen – is there sixteen anywhere? Thank you sir, sixteen shillings – lovely brace, meaty little critters these, surely worth more than that,' she said, glancing at Alex, who nodded. Sue watched, open mouthed as Alex swiftly sealed the deal and handed over the money to the auctioneer's clerk, a dusty, faded looking woman sitting at a table in the corner. Alex took her sales slip, stuffed it into her pocket and grasped Sue firmly by the elbow as she hustled her out of the market.

'I'll go back and collect them this afternoon,' she said. 'Now, let's look in at the butchers and see if there's a chicken left.'

'*How* long have we had decimal currency?' Sue asked as she was dragged somewhat reluctantly out into the frosty air.

'Oh, almost sixteen years,' said Alex, keeping a firm hold on her friend's arm.

'So why is she . . .?'

'It's just the way she does things, okay? Everyone knows about it and everyone can work out the price so it really doesn't matter. Just don't – ever – say anything when she's around. She's a bit touchy about that sort of criticism.'

'A bit touchy? She's barmy!' said Sue. 'And why did you buy those rabbits? They've still got their skins on.'

'I thought we could both make nice Davy Crockett hats over the holidays,' said Alex as she hurried down the road. 'And if you don't shut up, all you're getting is a lucky rabbit's foot for Christmas.'

Amidst the meetings and greetings, the buying of presents and treating of children there was another trade in Highpoint that festive season. In the corners and alleyways of the town's dark heart, small groups of youths gathered to mutter a request, exchange money and receive their goods secreted in a furtive handshake. The routes across the Levels carrying goods from Bristol and beyond were running well and the trickle of new cargoes was becoming a steady stream. Some buyers were curious, some egged on to false bravado by their peers and a few, overwhelmed by a sense of futility and despair, by the endless poverty and lack of any other prospects, were willing to try anything to gain a few hours of oblivion. Inexperienced, sometimes experimenting in isolation, this was the last Christmas for several of them. The big, bad world had arrived in Highpoint and by the time anyone noticed it was already too late.

The Gang of Six celebrated their business success with a noisy and boisterous party to celebrate the New Year in the Royal

Arms. Profits were up in all areas, due in part to the high taxes on alcoholic drinks and tobacco as well as the much-hated VAT levied on all legitimate sales. Importing from the continent and selling through their own network avoided both these costs and demand for their 'special offers' was running at an all-time high. In addition, Max Long's new goods were finding favour with a widening circle of young people, something he was quick to point out in the early, business part of their meeting.

'They loves it,' he gloated. 'Them kids in town, they can't get enough of the whiz and the wings is doing good too. Told you – easy money all round, this is.'

Around the table there were shrugs and a few grunts but no-one wanted to say much. Tom, seated at the end as usual, eyed his band of followers and was both disturbed and relieved by their reaction. He had serious doubts about expanding into the new goods and he was pleased to see most of the group seemed to share his concerns. It was dangerous, dabbling in drugs. Penalties were very high for anyone caught distributing and he knew his network of contacts in useful places were less likely to turn a blind eye to this sort of thing. Besides, this stuff could be dangerous. He was not a sentimental man and years of law-breaking had hardened him to most things but he didn't agree with selling to children and in his eyes most of Max's 'customers' were still just kids.

He was beginning to suspect they had made a grave error getting involved with Max in the first place but he was damned if he could see how it could have been avoided. Through any number of sleepless nights he'd lain awake wrestling with the problem. Max was well connected, with powerful friends and allies up Bristol way and he was determined to move into the West Country, bringing his drug culture with him. Better, surely, to bring him in to the group where he had some chance of controlling his activities – even if he was putting himself and his companions in danger. If only there were some way of getting rid of him, he thought, watching Max preen and crow at his success.

'Well now, I reckon we's all had a very good Christmas,' he said, cutting across Max's flood of self-congratulation. 'Will be midnight soon and I thought we deserves something special so there's champagne coming and food. Let's drink to a prosperous New Year.'

The gathering cheered up at once and the men pushed the tables to one side, relaxing and talking about their plans for the next few months. Only Jimmy Earl seemed that friendly with Max, he noted. Of course Jimmy needed to keep on his good side if he wanted to be included in the deal. Max didn't need Jimmy and his fleet of lorries. He could easily cut the young man out and arrange his own transport. Geoff Bund kept a good distance between himself and Max, chatting to Mark about hiding places in Cheddar. Tom listened to that conversation with half an ear whilst considering the group dynamics. Geoff didn't want to be drawn in to any of this. His workers were too vulnerable to detection, what with the sudden checks with dogs and such. The last thing Geoff and the dock workers needed was a load of really heavy stuff arriving for 'special handling'. No, Geoff wouldn't have anything to do with it, whatever any of them said.

The champagne arrived, a bottle each, and the group had a fine time wrestling with the caps and firing the corks at one another. Tom smiled and nodded to each of them as they raised their drinks, Max and Jimmy swigging the foaming wine direct from the bottle. Tom kept smiling, kept nodding and wondered how long he could hold it all together.

Alex's mother, who went by the relatively restrained name of Dorothy Elizabeth Hastings Norman (when she wasn't being addressed as 'Brown Owl'), arrived on the doorstep on New Year's Eve. Alex greeted her appearance with a mixture of exasperation and relief – whilst she was utterly sick of the stupid fuss the whole 'Brightlingsea' business had stirred up amongst the family, she was beginning to worry about her mother's lengthy absence. Dorothy had often made threats about cancelling Christmas in the past but never actually followed it through, but from the miserable phone calls she had endured from the rest of the family on a daily basis since the Christmas Eve it seemed her mother had really meant it this time. The boys had looked hopefully at their youngest sister, but Clytemnestra, or Nesta as she was now called, was slightly less acquainted with the kitchen than Sue and the scratch meal of sausage sandwiches, crisps and shop-bought mince pies had not gone down well with the rest of the family. In contrast, Alex and Sue had been quite festive with a chicken dinner, some excellent wine and friends dropping in over the holiday, a very different time to Alex's self-imposed misery of the previous year. Still, she was increasingly worried by nagging concerns about her mother's whereabouts and had become quite sharp with Hector and Archie when they rang to complain about the prolonged absence. Opening the door and finding her standing there, looking a bit tired but obviously in good health, was the best present she could have received.

'Don't ask where I've been,' Dorothy warned as she stepped through into the warm back room and dropped a small bag into an empty chair.

'Wouldn't dream of it,' said Alex, trying to be cool and adult but in reality grinning like a little girl. 'Is that all you've got with you?' She gestured towards the bag.

'My, that fire is lovely,' said her mother, holding out her hands and sighing happily. 'Now Alex, surely you offer your guests a cup of tea when they arrive?'

'I'll get it,' said Sue, springing to her feet.

'Thank you dear, so kind. And a belated Happy Christmas to you, by the way.'

Sue threw a smile over her shoulder and called, 'You too. Back in a moment.'

There was a pause as mother and daughter eyed one another, wondering how their relationship developed from this strange moment.

'I suppose they made a perfect pig's ear out of Christmas?' said Dorothy, finally folding herself into the corner of the sofa.

Alex snorted in amusement. 'They expected Nesta to cook,' she said. 'Of course I don't think anyone thought to go shopping or look in the freezer in time either.'

Dorothy nodded, her eyes fixed on the flames in the grate. 'Well, I'm not sorry. I was just – so – angry!' She punctuated each word with a sharp gesture with her right hand. 'I had to get away. How dare they behave like that. They had no right . . .'

Alex realized her mother was close to tears and leaned forwards but Dorothy waved her away impatiently.

'Don't fuss. I've had more than enough of that this last month.'

Sue returned with the tea and they sipped their drinks and nibbled at the last of the chocolate biscuits, contemplating the fire and searching for a way to restart the conversation. Finally, after slurping the last of her tea and plonking the mug down on the coffee table, Sue dived right in.

'So you were at this protest,' she said, 'and you were fined for a Public Order offence. Why didn't you want to pay it?'

Alex opened her mouth to apologize for her friend's bluntness but Dorothy seemed happy to talk.

'Well, I thought that was a bit cowardly. After all, so many young people – and some not so young may I add – are standing up and not being bullied into going away. Just because I can pay the fine doesn't mean I should get off with nothing more than a slap on the wrist.' She tilted her head and gave Sue a little smile. 'Some of the protesters have gone to prison and there is a lot of publicity now. The public are waking up and starting to see just how horrible this sort of trade is and I want to help with that.'

'If you hadn't paid it . . .,' began Alex.

'I didn't pay it,' her mother snapped. 'I refused to pay it and someone else decided they knew better.'

Alex kept a tight grip on her temper and continued.

'If it hadn't been paid you would have been back in court. Then you would have had a further fine and a proper criminal record. I don't see what that would have achieved.'

'I would have had a chance to speak for myself,' retorted her mother. 'All my life I've sat by and nodded and agreed with people – well what is happening is just plain wrong. And not just what's going on out at the port either.'

Alex looked at her mother in amazement, shocked at her vehemence.

'All over the place, even in all those nice affluent little villages out in the country, we have more and more people losing their jobs and then their homes. We are supposed to all be better off but most of the people I know are worse off and what's more they are miserable. I know I am.'

Alex opened her mouth to reply but Dorothy started again.

'I don't mean to be disloyal but I don't agree with people like your brother getting paid an obscene amount of money whilst someone who works stupid hours nursing in a hospital has to struggle to get by. I never did agree with "greed is good" anyway. I think greed is despicable and we should share things out a bit more equally.'

Her ire expended, Dorothy flopped back into her corner and closed her eyes leaving Alex searching for a response.

'So, what are you going to do now?' she asked finally.

Dorothy sighed and shifted on the sofa.

'I don't know,' she said quietly. 'I'll go back home in a few days – if you don't mind me staying here for a while?'

'No, that's fine. It'll be nice to spend some time together. I'll make a bed up in the back room for you.'

'Thank you dear,' said Dorothy. The fire crackled, flaring briefly before settling in the grate. 'I was ready to go to court you know,' she added. 'I wanted to stand up and make a difference.'

'You might have ended up in prison,' said Sue bluntly. 'They're taking the Public Order Act very seriously and using it for all sorts of stupid things. They can ban pop festivals using it, stop people picketing – it's a real catch-all and my advice would be not to get caught up in it at all if you can avoid it.'

'Well, how are decent people supposed to stage a protest then?' demanded Dorothy.

'I think that's rather the point,' said Sue. 'You can't.'

Ada Mallory greeted the New Year alone, standing on her back step watching the stars slide gently across the deep, soft sky. She had dug out a bottle of her best home-made blackberry cordial, an interesting beverage that sat in the bottle fermenting with the natural yeast in its seeds until released, often with an accompanying explosion. Ada rarely drank nowadays, memories of her father and Frank, her late, ex-husband too vivid for her to succumb to that weakness, but she was feeling sad. With her son away in the travelling fair the loneliness nibbled away at her, sapping her strength and draining her energy until some days she wondered why she bothered getting out of bed. There was a scuffling behind her and she felt the soft touch of a cold nose on her arm. She sighed and leaned towards the rough warmth of Mickey, one of her two lurchers. The dog huffed at the cold and gave a soft bark.

'What's that then boy?' she asked, ruffling his ears. Mickey stiffened and raised his head, a growl forming deep in his chest. Ada stepped back into the doorway, wary and alert at the faintest possibility of danger. Like Alex and Lauren, she had suffered at the hands of Derek Johns and it had undermined her belief in her own strength. She no longer felt invincible out in her own home. In the long dark nights she was glad to have the dogs around her, even if Mouse lived up to his name and Mickey was getting on a bit, his muzzle greying and one hip causing him to limp in the cold mornings. She shushed the dog, stroking his head and straining to hear what had disturbed him. All was still apart from a light breeze rustling the branches of the willows overhanging the stream at the back of her garden.

'Get off you girt daft thing,' she said affectionately and turned to go back inside. A soft, plaintive sound drifted on the breeze and she momentarily froze before turning very,

very slowly back to the open door. Her eyes were blinded by the light in the kitchen and she pulled the door to behind her, blinking and looking away into the distance to clear her vision. There was a pause and then the sound came again, floating past her ears and into her mind, a half-recalled fragment of music, teasing and tantalizing and threatening to pull her towards the unseen source. In the distance, on the edge of the Avalon Marsh, there was a spark of light and Ada stepped back through the door, closing and locking it swiftly behind her.

'Get in the front now,' she said to Mickey and gave him a nudge in the direction of her cosy little parlour. She followed the dogs through and closed the middle door as well. Despite the warm fire she was shivering as she poured herself another glass of blackberry cordial and it was a long time before her hands stopped shaking.

Chapter Eight

January, always a dismal month after the outburst of self-indulgence surrounding the end of the year, was particularly gloomy at the probation office. Alex and Sue arrived back to work to find everyone in a state of shock. Someone had broken in over the holidays, tearing through the main office and trying to break into the locked record cabinets. Several drawers had been forced open and the files were strewn around, in some cases with pages ripped out and screwed up. Several typewriters had been pushed off the desks and the office holiday and duty calendar had been altered so the coloured dots and squares now spelt out a series of rude words. Lauren was standing in front of it, reading the multi-coloured result with some interest.

You know what's got me?' she said to Alex later in the day. 'All of them words was spelt right, even the posh ones.'

'I didn't know there were any posh swear words,' said Sue.

'Well, even the long ones then. Don't know of no client could spell well enough to do that. And how come they never triggered the alarm then?'

'Better ask that boyfriend of yours,' said Sue. 'Isn't that his job?'

Lauren blushed and turned her attention to a particularly lush egg and cress sandwich.

'Seriously though Lauren, you don't think it's an inside job do you?' pressed Alex. 'Why would anyone want to break in the office? Most of us can't wait to get out.'

Lauren put her sandwich down and looked around the room before speaking. 'I don't reckon it's one of us,' she said, 'except maybe someone new. Someone we don't know so well.'

'Oh come on,' said Sue. 'I know you don't like him much but that's really stretching it a bit.'

Lauren scowled and picked up her lunch again, taking a large bite. 'Don't know about that,' she said somewhat indistinctly. 'Looks like it was a man 'cos they typewriters is beastly heavy. Tall too, 'cos the calendar's right up on the wall. And nothing like this ever happened before did it?' She glared at Sue and Alex defiantly but they were spared her wrath by Pauline who stuck her head round the door and called Lauren back to the office.

'She's got a point though,' said Sue after Lauren had left, muttering furiously about her lost lunch hour. 'You do wonder how anyone got in without setting off the alarms.'

The day only got worse as Alex was called in to see Garry that afternoon. She climbed the stairs, searching her memory to recall what she had done now to upset him, but stopped in the doorway, shocked to find Lauren's PC Brown and Sgt Willis from the Highpoint station already in the room.

'Come in Alex,' said Garry, who was seated, as usual, behind his desk. He used the damn desk like a weapon, she thought, as she closed the door and made for the chair in the middle of the room. The 'naughty girl' chair, she called it in her head. Settling herself in front of the men, she folded her hands in front of her and turned a perfectly polite, neutral expression to the two policemen.

'Gentlemen,' she nodded, before looking at Garry. 'What can I do for you?' Garry shook his head and frowned as he gestured towards Sgt Willis. I hope he doesn't think *I* broke in to the damn office, Alex thought. Her cast, now grey and fraying around the edges, was itching abominably and she gritted her teeth as she fought the urge to poke at it. Sgt Willis shifted in his seat and cleared his throat, obviously uncomfortable about something.

'I'm afraid I have some rather bad news,' he said softly.

Alex felt a flash of panic run through her. Not her mother – oh please, let her wretched, difficult, wonderful mother be alright.

'I believe you have a young man, a Darren Foyle, attending the day centre.' It was a statement not a question. Alex tried not to let her relief show as her heartbeat slowed to a more reasonable rate and she fought a tremendous desire to let her breath out in a sigh. Nodding cautiously she sneaked a glance at Dave Brown but he was staring at the floor. This was more than a routine arrest, she thought.

'I'm sorry to have to tell you Darren died over the Christmas period,' Sgt Willis continued in his soft, slow West Country burr.

Alex stared at him, not sure she had heard correctly. 'What?'

PC Brown raised his head and said, 'We believe he was experimenting with some form of hallucinogenic. He is reported to have woken up screaming on Boxing Day night and assaulted his father before running out into the street. Several neighbours heard the noise and saw him leave but no one knows where he went then.'

'So – so how do you know . . .'

'His body was washed up on the beach at Brean Sands last night,' said Sgt Willis. 'It seems as he was in the sea for some considerable time but we don't know how he got to the coast in the first place. He was only wearing a light shirt and he had bare feet. Is a long way to the coast from Highpoint and it's not likely he got a lift, undressed like that.'

This was too much detail for Alex, too vivid a picture in her head and she stared at PC Brown for a moment, horrified by what she had heard.

'You spoke to me, the week before Christmas,' said Dave, leaning forwards in his hard chair. 'You said something about thinking maybe some of the lads in the day centre were on drugs.' He nodded towards her plastered wrist and continued, 'And they caused that, didn't they.'

Sgt Willis added, 'We need you to tell us what you know. We believe Darren took something that affected his mental state. He ran off, still screaming and seemed to think he was being chased by something. Several neighbours recall him shouting about heat, fire and such like. If he had taken something nasty we'll find it in the toxicology tests but we really want to uncover the supply lines. This is new, round here, and we want to stop it before it takes a hold.'

There was a pause as the three men looked at Alex, a silence broken by PC Brown. 'Please, Alex, help us out here. We really need to know – anything you can give us might help. Don't let this stuff get a hold. We don't want anyone else to die.'

Alex realized she was about to cry. Darren had been a royal pain in the arse, if the truth were told. He'd been sly, difficult, defiant and rude yet still – he was one of hers. A young life, given into her care and now lost. She wanted to be anywhere but here, under the eyes of these men, judging her every action. She wanted to be back in the workshop with Darren's friends, recalling his best moments, his rare triumphs, making his life worth something. She began to rise and Garry's voice cut through the ever-expanding silence.

'Sit down please.' There was a pause and then he addressed the police. 'I am sure we will have some useful information to help you soon.' He rose and they followed, somewhat reluctantly, shaking hands as they left.

When the door closed he returned to his place behind the desk and for a moment contemplated Alex, seated before him in utter misery.

'So,' he said. 'Your injury is due to an assault by a client. An unreported assault.'

'I slipped,' said Alex. There was silence in the room as both sat, waiting for the other to speak.

Finally, Garry said, 'Slipped?'

'I slipped in between them to stop them fencing with the pool cues. It was stupid and it's my own fault.' She sat upright in the chair, her eyes focussed on a spot just behind Garry's right ear. She might have to listen to him but she didn't have to look at him as well.

'Am I to understand you suspected they were under the influence of an illegal substance at the time?' Garry asked, his voice deceptively calm.

'I had no proof of that,' said Alex. 'They were a bit lively but that's nothing new. Their eyes looked all right and they'd not been drinking. It's not that easy to tell sometimes.' She stopped as she realized she was slipping into defensive mode. Garry had that effect on her and she was increasingly determined not to fall into the trap of explaining her every action. As it was, she needn't have worried because Garry was not in a listening mood.

'So, you decided to ignore the warning signs despite receiving a serious injury,' he said. 'You thought you knew better and once again you went your own way without any consultation or consideration for the consequences. Well, the direct result of that is the untimely death of a young man. A young man we were supposed to be helping and who we have failed.'

'That is grossly inaccurate!' Alex said, fury bringing tears to her eyes.

'If you had taken some action at the time, Darren Foyle would probably not be dead,' snapped Garry. 'We have a duty of care towards our clients and that does not mean we should tolerate law-breaking or ignore dangerous behaviour just for our own convenience!'

Alex was stunned by the force of his anger. There had been differences of opinion with Garry before but nothing like this.

The sound of loud, angry voices floated into the room from the courtyard below and Garry flicked his fingers at her in a dismissive gesture.

'Go on, take some control over your clients. I can hear they have arrived.' He turned his attention to the folders on his desk, ignoring her as she got to her feet and walked to the door. Outside in the corridor she leaned against the wall for a moment trying to catch her breath. There was a faint red mist floating across her vision and her heart was hammering in her chest. Her progress down the stairs was slow and careful, hand tight on the rail as she struggled to keep her balance. She could not recall ever feeling as upset, hurt or humiliated as she did at that moment.

The afternoon was supposed to be given over to literacy, a weekly struggle to get something readable (or even legible) out of her group. Alex had felt reservations about the class from the beginning and her inexperience as a teacher became increasingly apparent as the sessions dragged on. They needed a proper tutor, she thought, not someone like me who doesn't know what they're doing. She shouldered the door open and walked into the main hall, drawn to the smaller classroom off to one side. From the sound of it the class had made their own way in and were moving the tables around again. Striding across the room, she flung the door wide and was greeted by the sight of Brian balancing on the back of a chair, arms out and laughing whilst the rest of the group stood on the tables clapping and cheering him on.

'Five, six, seven . . .' They noticed her in the doorway and hurriedly scrambled down on to the floor. Brian's head jerked round and he lost his balance, crashing to the ground and narrowly missing the corner of a table.

'Oh hey, fuck – that were girt close', he said, rolling to his feet completely unabashed.

Something snapped inside Alex, some final thread of self-control. Ignoring all protocols and legal restraints she seized Brian by his ear, hauled him to his feet and dragged him towards the new whiteboard in the corner. Brian shrieked, a high-pitched sound reminiscent of a small, trapped animal and Alex finally let him go, to slump on to the floor clutching at the side of his head.

'Shit, shit, you'm crazy!' he shouted. 'You can't do that you mad bitch. I 'ent puttin' up with it neither . . .' He shut up the moment Alex stepped towards him and levered himself in to a chair.

'And the rest of you,' snapped Alex, and the youths scrambled for places as far away from her as possible, seating themselves in a loose semi-circle around the whiteboard.

'I have had enough of this,' she continued, prowling back and forth and stopping occasionally to stare one of them in the eyes. 'From now on there will be respect shown in this centre. Shut up and put your hand down,' she added without turning her head. The youth at the far end lowered his hand and glanced uneasily at his next-door companion who shrugged, a 'Who knows?' gesture.

'This will be a two-way process,' Alex continued, working her way down the line of chairs. 'I will show you as much respect as you deserve – which is precious little at the moment. You will behave with respect towards me, towards the staff in the office and towards one another. Is that clear?' There was a faint scuffling from the group that she chose to interpret as assent.

'This will be demonstrated through your behaviour, your appearance and your language,' she continued. There was some surreptitious eye-rolling behind her back and without turning she added, 'I mean it so there is no point in pulling faces.' She swung round and glared at the culprits. 'Understood?'

Shocked by her apparent ability to see through the back of her head several lads sat up a bit more, nodding like a couple of donkeys.

'Right. You will behave in a safe and polite manner at all times. You will arrive on time, wait quietly if your supervisor is not ready for you and you will *sit up properly* on the chairs.' She swivelled round and slapped the back of one chair, startling the occupant upright from his slumped position.

'You will keep your feet on the floor and not put them up on the tables or other chairs.' There was a muffled stamping as several young men complied before she could get to them. Denied her prey she resumed prowling, stalking behind them and watching as they swivelled their heads like a row of baby owls, trying to keep her in sight. She was just beginning to wind down and feel a little calmer when someone muttered a remark to his neighbour and there was a hastily smothered laugh from the bunch within earshot.

'In particular,' she said, storming round to the front and glaring at the sniggering youths, 'you will moderate your language! You!' She pointed to one lad at the end of the line.

'Wasn't me, honest,' he protested.

'I don't care if you said it – you obviously thought it funny and sadly half of us missed the joke so go on, share it with us.'

'Don't remember, Miss,' said the youth, staring down at his dirty boots.

Alex crossed over to the pristine white board and picked up the nearest pen.

'Well, I would figure it a safe bet that it contained this word,' she said and wrote 'FUCK' on the board in large, red letters.

There was a collective gasp and a voice said, 'You can't write that!'

'Oh yes I bloody well can,' said Alex calmly, and added 'BLOODY' to the board. 'Well, gentlemen, I think we will explore this fascination you have with certain words and see if we can perhaps learn something. Now, what can you contribute to this list?' She looked at the row of stunned faces in front of her and quashed a desire to grin at their shocked expressions. 'Anyone? Well, it is strangely silent in here. Let me help you get started.' She turned back to the board and wrote 'SHIT' in large letters. 'There, everyone's second favourite word at the moment I think.'

The silence lengthened until finally Brian cracked and held up his hand. 'Bum!' he said defiantly.

Alex nodded. 'Good, "bum" will do for a start. Here you go.' She held out the pen and he recoiled as if she had offered him a live snake.

'Oh no, I 'ent writing nothing on no board.' He shook his head and hunched back in his chair.

'What did I say about sitting properly?' said Alex and Brian straightened a little but still made no move to get up.

'I'm left handed,' said Alex, 'and this wrist makes it very hard for me to write anything, especially on an upright surface like this.' She gestured towards the board. 'So you will just have to do it yourselves. Anyway, you're happy enough to scrawl on other people's walls so you can damn well do it here. And there's another – come on Brian, no-one goes home until we've finished, which means you will miss the free bus and have to spend your travel expenses on what they're intended for, just for once.'

Brian slid out of his chair and lumbered over to take the pen. Then, with a sigh that was almost theatrical, he wrote the word on the board, in tiny letters down in the right-hand corner.

'Awright?' he said, staring at Alex angrily. There was a collective snigger from the rest of the group.

'Pathetic,' said Alex dismissively. 'Totally feeble. Is that the best you can do? Anyone would think you were scared of a word.'

She turned her back to him and walked away to the other end of the line leaving him holding the pen. This time the sniggering was aimed at Brian and he flushed, furious at the insult. Scrubbing the corner clear with his sleeve, he wrote the word in large red letters in the middle of the board, dropped the pen on to the rack underneath it and flung himself back into his seat.

'Where's Darren anyway?' came a voice and the group looked around, searching for their partner in crime.

'Yeah,' said Brian, 'He's got girt neat writin' has Darren. Reckon he should be here to do this.'

Alex froze on the spot, mouth dry and her pulse racing. They didn't know, she thought. None of them knew about Darren. What, she wondered, was the protocol for telling a group their friend had died and none of them had realized until – oh, maybe a week had passed? She made a snap decision. She would tell them – but later, when the session was over. They were still too wrought up to take it calmly and she couldn't dismiss them half way through this particular exercise. It wasn't ideal but it was the best she could come up with.

'Darren's not here so we'll have to make do with your efforts,' she said, her voice sounding even and calm. There was some grumbling at this but several of the group were beginning to get rather intrigued by what she was doing and almost immediately several suggestions for new words were called out. As the board began to fill with an interesting and imaginative selection of words they grew bolder, delving deeper into their vocabularies, but whatever they came up with, Alex calmly handed them the pen and stood by as they wrote it out. As the afternoon wore on they became restless, especially when they realized she was not going to be shocked or react in any way except to show mild interest. Then some bickering broke out between Brian and Timmy, a young man who showed some promise but was too easily led to do anything with it.

'Is not swearin'. Is different,' said Timmy.

'I reckon 'tis though. If it en't swearing then what is it then?' Brian retorted.

Alex hastened to intervene. 'What isn't swearing?' she asked Timmy, who scowled at Brian as he answered.

'Spas,' he said. 'If I calls him "Spas" he's likely to go mental, same as if I call him a . . .' He stopped abruptly, actually blushing at the word he did not utter. Alex hid a grin. They had finally got to the point where she could move on to the next stage.

'Right, so now we look at what these words actually mean and why many people find them so offensive,' she said, flipping the board over and ruling three columns on the blank surface.

'What's that then?' Brian asked pointing to the centre column.

'Scatological,' said Alex.

There was a long pause before Timmy finally plucked up the courage to ask, 'Where's that to, then?'

'It means having an obsession with excrement,' she said.

There was a longer pause before Brian ventured, 'Like shit then?'

Alex nodded, 'Yes, exactly like shit.'

The group pondered the board for a moment before one of them asked, 'So we've got relig . . . religious, sexual and scat . . . scat . . . shit, right?'

'And we will find most swear words fall into one of these three categories,' Alex continued. 'But first I need a whole lot more words from you.' She copied the first offerings into their appropriate column, spun the board again and raised her eyebrows expectantly.

It was a very subdued class that trailed out into the drizzle of the late afternoon. After forcing them to say, write and define a wide range of bad language they were wretched and exhausted and she was reconsidering her earlier decision to delay telling them about Darren but it was too late. She could not send them away and have them find out on their own, realizing she must have known all along and hadn't even bothered to mention it. Quietly, calmly she told them a body had been found on the beach up the coast and the police were waiting for formal identification but it looked like Darren. There was a long silence as the lads gazed at the floor, several with their hands clasped together as if in prayer, a couple with their eyes shut as if, by not seeing her deliver this news, it might not be true. Finally, they stood and shambled out, a dispirited group with a great deal to think about, or so she hoped.

'Brian,' she called, as he moved towards the door, 'may I have a word?'

He crossed the floor, tall and sullen with wary eyes watching her.

'What?'

'I wondered if you had any information you could share with me, to help stop this happening again to someone else.'

'Was not I,' he said, but she grabbed at his arm to stop him leaving.

'I didn't think it was,' she said. 'The police think he'd taken something – maybe something new, stronger than he was expecting, and it gave him hallucinations. I don't think you gave it to him but I wondered if you might have any idea where we could look to find who did.'

Brian stared at her, his eyes flat and bright in the neon lighting. His tongue flicked across his lips and for a moment she was reminded of a snake about to strike.

Finally, he said, 'Reckon you should ask Simon the *Spas*. Yer favourite, he is. Maybe you should be askin' him, not me.'

He turned away, slamming the door back and leaving a dent in the nice new plasterboard from the door handle. Simon? Strange, quiet Simon Adams with his imaginary lorry? Alex felt her remaining faith in rehabilitation drain away. If Simon were involved in this then her ability to judge another's character was nonexistent. She had experienced too many shocks in the past few days. Her mother had shown strength of will previously unknown, Darren's death, horrible as it was, could well lead to the end of her career if Garry had his way, and now Simon had been fingered as a drug dealer. Her head was pounding and she realized her vision was starting to blur. With watering eyes she looked around the room and focussed on the white board, still bearing the evidence of the afternoon's session. Grimly she wiped it clean of every insult and obscenity before turning off the lights and closing the door behind her. She was in the main reception area, signing out to go home and lie down when she remembered her office was still unlocked.

'You look right awful,' remarked Lauren.

'Migraine,' said Alex, trying not to screw her eyes up against the light. 'I've forgotten my office. I'll just go back and lock up and I'm off.'

'Give that key here,' said Lauren, holding out her hand. 'You get off now. I'll make sure is all closed up proper.'

Alex handed over her keys and gave a deep sigh. 'Thank you,' she said.

'You going to be alright walking home?' Lauren asked, studying Alex's chalk-white face. Alex nodded and winced as a bolt of pain shot through her head. 'Well, you give me a call, soon as you's there.' She watched as Alex walked slowly to the front door and made her way down the steps, one hand on the side rail to steady herself.

'What was that about?' said Pauline's voice behind her.

Lauren held up the keys and said, 'Alex has been taken ill. I said I'd lock up for her.'

Pauline nodded. 'She's still not over the meningitis,' she said anxiously. 'I'll have a word with Sue and see if she can get her to rest up for a few more days. By the way, would you pop in to see me when you've finished please? I'd like to discuss the allocation of officers with you if you have a minute.'

Lauren managed a sickly smile as she climbed down and hurried past her senior to the entrance to the day centre. Time was up, she thought with a sinking feeling. She had to decide about the new job, and despite all the evenings she had spent worrying about the problem she still didn't know what to choose.

With the return to work in the New Year he was able to take up residence in the holiday park once more. The pill box had served its purpose, keeping him dry and fairly sheltered through the bitterly cold nights but he was glad to be back in a proper bed, even without any bedding. The chalet was cold and there was no power but that didn't bother him too much and it was too risky, using a light at night despite the fact he had chosen a small chalet tucked away at the very back of the site. There was only a skeleton staff to cover the entire site as the management tried to keep their costs to a minimum by hiring seasonal workers, even for management positions. The security men were mainly clustered around the front of the site watching the main buildings and manning the entrance and even then they displayed a distinct reluctance to leave the warmth of the centrally heated administration block, let alone wander the vast, empty park. Still, one light out in the darkness would be enough to bring the whole staff in their big, clumsy boots round to his temporary home. He spent the first few days resting and watching the security men from a safe distance to establish their routines.

Once he felt reasonably secure he began his foraging and quickly replaced the items he had been forced to abandon before Christmas, kitting himself out nicely at the expense of the holiday camp but he was soon restless again. His whole life lacked purpose. For years he had worked to accumulate wealth and power, running a profitable if somewhat shady business empire and enjoying the fruits of his labours. Now he was reduced to skulking in the dark corners of the world he had once ruled, afraid to show his face and without a friend to share his sorrows. He reflected bitterly on his old companions, the men who had followed his orders without question and who had paid him the respect he was due without hesitation. All that was gone and he was forced to live like a hunted animal, running from all who might recognize him, afraid to show his face in daylight. He sat in front of the dusty mirror in the bedroom of the chalet and stared at his reflection in the dim light that trickled through the thin curtains.

Once he had been handsome in a rough, wild sort of way but now his face was scarred, a great livid weal running from below one eye to the remains of his ear. He tilted his head to one side and squinted at the bald patch where the hair no longer grew over a wide indentation. Looking at the dent in his skull made him shiver with remembered pain, the ghastly sickness that had overcome him when he regained consciousness on the broad mud bank of the River Parrett. His teachers had always said he had a thick skull. Well, they had been right on that score. He supposed the blow to his head would have killed a lesser man, but Derek Johns thought he was no ordinary man. He forced himself to confront the nightmare in the glass once more. It was no ordinary man staring back. He had become the Bogey Man.

Chapter Nine

The next morning Sue wandered into the kitchen and switched on the light, jerking awake by the sight of Alex hunched over the sink and eating mandarin oranges straight from the tin.

'Shit, you startled me! What are you doing, lurking in the dark like that?'

Alex screwed up her eyes and mumbled. 'Turn that bloody light out will you? That's better. I've got a bit of a headache still.'

Sue heard the spoon hit the bottom of the tin and then both clattered into the sink.

'You should go back to bed,' she said.

'I'm fine,' said Alex.

'No, you're not. You've got photophobia again and the only time I've ever known you to eat mandarin oranges is when you've got migraine, when you eat little else. Now unless you want me to switch all the lights on, go back to bed!'

'My damn office is so gloomy it won't be a problem if I can just get in to work,' Alex muttered. 'Besides, I'm sure I've got an important meeting today. I just can't remember what it is . . .' Still grumbling, she nonetheless allowed Sue to steer her back up the stairs and collapsed on to her bed with a sigh.

'I'll check your diary and make sure we phone to cancel any appointments,' said Sue firmly. 'I'm in the office all day so I'll pop back at lunchtime.'

Alex groaned and put the pillow over her head.

'Don't be so mean,' said Sue. 'I'll pick you up a sandwich, okay?'

When Sue got to the probation offices Lauren was leaning on the counter, eyes bright with mischief and a sly grin on her face.

'Alex not well then?' she asked.

Sue shook her head. 'No, I sent her back to bed. What's with you anyway? You look mighty amused by something.'

Lauren nodded towards the day centre door that was propped open. There was the sound of voices interspersed by the noise of cups being clattered on to saucers. 'Magistrates training day,' she said. 'Garry's all lined up to show off the day centre. I don't know if he'll be upset or glad Alex 'ent here.'

Sue grinned appreciatively and then leaned over to ask her about the new job.

'I took it,' said Lauren. She tilted her head up and looked at Sue defiantly. 'Maybe I don't feel too happy 'bout my next new officer but is only for a year. Then I know I get to pass him over to someone else and I get more of a say in who I works with. I figured I could keep you on for a bit, if you want?'

The relief on Sue's face made Lauren's day and she smiled back at her, happy she had finally made a choice. At that moment Garry stuck his head around the door and frowned at Sue.

'Where the hell is Alex?' he hissed. 'I'm stalling them but there's only so much tea they can drink, you know.' He glared at her as if the magistrates' limited capacity for hospitality were her fault.

'I'm sorry, Garry, I was just coming to look for you,' Sue said sweetly. 'I'm afraid Alex is ill and won't be in today.'

A look of panic swept over the senior's face as he realized he was going to have to deal with the magistrates and the court clerks all on his own.

'Perhaps Eddie might show them the workshops?' Lauren suggested. 'And Gordon knows a lot about the whole system. He went on the training days with Alex. He could probably do a question and answer session.'

'Yes, thank you, Lauren. I am perfectly capable of dealing with this myself,' Garry blustered.

Lauren scowled and stepped down below the counter muttering, 'Liar', though fortunately so softly only Sue could hear.

'Perhaps you could inform Eddie and Gordon they will be required,' said Garry. 'Really, this is most inconvenient and thoughtless.'

The door slammed behind him, leaving Sue wanting to make rude gestures at his departing back. Gordon, she recalled, was out in the yard cleaning his car again. She strolled outside and watched as he pulled the contents of the boot out followed by the interior lining. A strong smell of alcohol washed over the car park and Sue wrinkled her nose in disgust.

'Who was it this time?' she called from a safe distance. Gordon jumped and looked around before he spotted her.

'Alas,' he said with a shrug, 'I found Rosie outside one of the farm gates last night on my way home. She was rather – incapacitated – and it was getting very cold. I couldn't just leave her there so I gave her a lift back to town.' He stared at the ruined carpet and shrugged. 'She had a gallon of "natch" with her and she absolutely refused to leave it behind so I put it in the boot. Unfortunately I think it might have sprung a leak on the way home.'

Sue shook her head at him. 'Gordon, do you learn nothing from history? "Cider" Rosie spends her life propped up on farm gates. And the last time you gave her a lift she was so drunk you almost had to scrap the car it was such a mess. You're the only person in the whole world who would give her a lift!'

Gordon smiled sadly and picked through the damp boxes and bags on the ground.

'Someone has to,' he said. 'In spite of all her problems, she's a fellow human being and she needs a hand just like anyone else.'

Secretly, Sue rather doubted 'Cider' Rosie qualified as a human being any longer. She had drunk so much poisonous natural cider she was pickled and wrinkled like an old raisin, her voice was a harsh croak and her personal hygiene non-existent. Her primary method of communication seemed to be shouting incoherently and then hitting someone, and everyone who knew her gave her a very wide berth. Gordon was the only person she would listen to, and then only very rarely, but still he persisted. There was something almost saint-like about his patience, she thought, though he was no fool. It was a very sorry probationer who tried to take advantage of Gordon, and his knowledge and experience made him the most valued and respected member of the Highpoint team. She remembered her errand and crossed the yard to deliver her message privately.

'Alex is ill again,' she said, 'and Garry's got all the magistrates and half the court staff in there.' She jerked her thumb towards the day centre building. 'He wants you to do a session with them – maybe answer questions a bit later on today.'

Gordon nodded absently. 'Of course,' he said. 'I'm free most of the afternoon so I'll see him over lunch and arrange it. How is Alex by the way? I do think she came back too soon.'

Sue pulled a face. 'I don't think she's fully recovered and the last few weeks have been really hard on her but she's convinced Garry will take it as an excuse to get rid of her. I've told her she should talk to the Union, to be honest. I think

Garry is a bully and he's getting worse. Someone needs to step in and stop all this.'

They were interrupted by Pauline, who hurried down the front steps looking uncharacteristically flustered.

'Gordon, come quickly,' she said. 'It's Garry – he's having a fit.'

Gordon dropped the ruined carpet back into the boot, slammed the lid and loped towards the stairs, Sue and Pauline in pursuit.

'What kind of a fit?' Sue asked. 'Falling down or raving?'

'Both,' said Pauline, following Gordon through the day centre door.

In the teaching room Garry was standing in front of the white board, swaying and shouting incoherently. As Sue came through the door he stabbed an accusing finger in her direction.

'You,' he cried, 'you, hypocrite, spawn, witch! You and your evil friend! I'll see you out of the probation service, you hear me?'

'Now then, Garry, let's not make a scene here,' said Gordon as he tried to calm the hysterical man. Garry lashed out and hit him in the face.

'Get away from me,' he yelled. 'You're just as bad. All of you, scheming and plotting, trying to make me look bad . . .'

Gordon stepped inside his flailing arms and grabbed him from behind, forcing Garry's arms out and away from his sides.

'Go and get Eddie, for goodness sake,' he panted as Garry slumped forwards, all the aggression gone in an instant.

Sue watched from a safe distance as Gordon manoeuvred the now-silent senior in to a chair in the corner with the help of John, the court clerk. Most of the magistrates were either still in their seats, transfixed with horror, or crowded at the back, watching fearfully. As her eyes roamed the room she focussed on the white board. Alex had cleaned the lists off but forgotten the original jumble of words on the flip side. It was,

Sue thought, a remarkably inventive selection of invective. Almost an exhaustive study of English swearing.

'So which one of us is your "evil friend", do you think?' Pauline murmured.

'Oh, almost certainly Alex,' said Sue, nodding towards the offending white board.

Pauline glanced across and tried to hide a smile. 'Witch?' she whispered.

Sue snorted and flounced towards the door. 'I wish,' she said, and headed upstairs to get the ever-dependable Eddie.

'Not the most successful Magistrates' Day,' said Gordon later in the day. After Garry had been taken off in an ambulance, "for a check-up," according to the paramedic who had attended the scene and administered a tranquillizer, Gordon and Pauline had taken over, smoothing the ruffled feathers of the magistrates, walking them around the new facilities and generally trying to make them feel positive about the possibilities opening up in rehabilitation and training. It had been exhausting and probably futile but, as Gordon said, they had to try. And at least it wasn't a client who had thrown a fit in front of them. Privately, Sue wasn't sure the meltdown of their senior officer was better publicity than a couple of gobby teenagers but she wisely kept her views to herself.

Gordon developed a rather spectacular black eye over the course of the morning and looked decidedly rakish as he addressed the staff meeting that had been arranged for the middle of the afternoon.

'I am sure you have all heard about the unfortunate incident this morning,' he said with magnificent understatement. 'I have been in touch with headquarters and they have asked me to take over the running of the office for a few days until we have a clearer idea of what it happening.'

'It would help if we had someone in the day centre,' said Ricky Peddlar from the back of the room.

Sue rounded on him in fury. 'Alex is doing a great job with the day centre. She's just not recovered fully from a very serious illness – okay?'

'Yeah, right. It was her stuff left on the board for the magistrates to see, wasn't it? No wonder Garry went over the edge,' sneered Ricky.

Gordon jumped in hastily, his voice cutting across the babble of protest from Alex's colleagues. 'That is enough! We do not know exactly what happened – or what is wrong with our senior officer.' Here he glared at Ricky who sank down in his chair scowling. 'I would suggest we avoid idle speculation and concentrate on our jobs. Margaret, will you take charge of the court rota please?' Margaret nodded and scribbled a note in her diary as Gordon moved on to Eddie. 'We have had an offer of unclaimed bikes from the police,' he said. 'I wondered if you could set up some workshop time and see if we can provide some of the lads with their own transport.'

Eddie grinned broadly. 'I've been hoping they'd come through,' he said happily. 'Any chance of taking on someone to help with the workshop then, Gordon?'

Gordon held up his hand. 'One thing at a time,' he said wearily. 'Let's just get things moving again and see how long Garry is going to be away.'

Ricky was leaning back on his chair and rocking back and forth. Margaret gave him an annoyed look. Ignoring her, he chipped in to the conversation.

'Well, why is Alex in the day centre when she can't do the practical stuff?'

A shocked silence fell across the room.

'Look, all this psychological mumbo-jumbo is all very well when you're a student but surely she can't just experiment on the clients like this, can she? They deserve some proper help. Real skills, you know.' He sat back and folded his arms, a smug look on his face.

Sue recovered first and launched herself at him with a scathing verbal assault.

'What are you talking about?' she demanded. 'Firstly, Alex is an experienced officer and you have no right to talk about her like that. And the management decides who works in each section and who does what job. Just who the *fuck* do you think you are, questioning her ability like that?'

'What do you mean, "psychological"?' demanded Lauren. 'And "experiment". What's that about then?'

'Well, surely you know that as a psychologist she has certain ideas about reforming character,' said Ricky. 'It's a whole different approach to the work and I'm not sure it is suited to such a practical environment as the day centre.'

Gordon stepped into the centre of the group and shouted, the first time Sue could recall ever hearing him raise his voice in anger. It was an impressive sound and she drew back into her chair immediately.

'That is quite enough! This meeting is over. I will inform you of developments as and when I hear any news. Ricky, perhaps you would be so kind as to accompany me to my office.' He strode out of the room without a backward glance leaving Ricky to scurry after him.

'Bloody good job an' all,' Lauren muttered. She was already regretting her decision of this morning and wondering if it were possible to wriggle out of it but she felt Pauline's eyes on her and decided she'd better wait a while. She tapped Sue on the arm as the somewhat disconsolate group of staff trooped back to their offices.

'I never knew Alex was a psychologist,' she said. 'She never said nothing, did she?'

Sue scowled at the doorway, still spoiling for a fight.

'He doesn't know what he's talking about,' she said fiercely. 'Thick idiot – she did philosophy at university. She told me so and, anyway, she's got hundreds of really heavy, boring books by dead Greeks and crazy Germans in the house. No-one but a philosophy graduate keeps their books after they finish, believe me.'

Ada wasn't sure of the protocol surrounding Kevin's probation officer any longer. She had been quite happy contacting Alex and stepping in to force the investigation that had led to his release from Bristol prison after he had been accused of murdering the Elver Man last year. That was just her business too, looking after her son. But Kevin was gone now, off with the fair and who knew when he would be back. He was technically still on probation but she was fairly sure that was an unofficial arrangement and she had picked up enough gossip around town at Christmas to realize Alex was not faring well at Highpoint. The last thing she wanted to do was get her in to trouble but she was worried, very worried and more than a bit afraid. Ada was not a superstitious person but she had grown up on stories of the Levels, of the spirits that haunted the ditches and marshes and the strange people who roamed at night. On one hand, she knew they were only stories but she also knew what she had seen at night and was sure of what she'd heard – and she didn't like the pattern that was emerging.

After some reflection she decided to take the free supermarket bus in to town and see if she could spot Alex at the market. If that didn't work she'd try Lauren or, as a last resort, one of the other officers. Ada had a deep mistrust of the law and all its minions, including probation officers, and Alex was the first she thought had treated her and her son as people rather than just 'clients'. An innocent in the ways of the creeping managerial culture, Ada didn't realize it was exactly this behaviour that was causing Alex so much trouble now. As she stood at the end of the road waiting for the bus to arrive, Ada watched a low-slung lorry heave its way across the rough track to her left. It was just too wide to keep all its wheels on the gravelled surface and kept lurching to one side as it slipped on the surrounding mud. It drew level and the driver stopped, rolling down the window and greeting her cheerfully.

'Ada, well now, is you wantin' a lift then?' he called down.

'Is that you, Stevie Yeo? What's you doin', dragging that big old thing round these parts then?'

Stevie grinned at her and rolled his eyes. 'Is some girt fool from the ministry,' he said. 'You know they's stopped cutting out on Avalon, since turn of the year? Well, they says is to be all fenced off, see. Now, we says to them, just wait a few months and get some decent withies, make something as looks like it belongs here. But no, they's got to have they fences up now, so I'm lugging all this ugly old iron around.' He jerked his thumb towards the back of the truck where several rows of black metal railing sections were tied loosely in place.

'Is a fool job,' Stevie continued. 'All just fixes with a few bolts so any bugger with a spanner could get in anyway. Still, is a couple of weeks' work and keeps us off that bloody community programme a bit longer. Might even turn in to something more settled, what with all they changes goin' on around here. Oh, here's the bus then. You take care now Ada,' and with a wave he was off again, the lorry slipping and sliding along the side road off towards Avalon Marsh, the ugly square railings rattling and clanging on the back.

Ada stuck out her hand and the bus, only a single-decker this morning she noted, pulled up beside her. Clambering aboard, she nodded to the driver, glancing down the length of the bus at the other passengers. Half a dozen people were scattered around the vehicle, most of them clutching baskets and shopping bags, though one woman was sitting at the back holding on to a wriggling child.

'Morning Pete. Bit quiet today 'ent it.'

Pete closed the door behind her and pulled out on to the narrow road without bothering to look. There was so little traffic across the Levels that no-one ever bothered to look.

'Mornin' Ada. 'Tis no more quiet than for the last few months. Reckon they'll be taking the bus off soon. We is already running this little thing 'cos they says the big'un's a waste'.

Ada took a seat several rows back and watched as the empty landscape slipped past, turning slowly from peat and reeds to the occasional farm or house with a cottage garden. With a grinding of gears and a series of judders Pete manoeuvred the bus round a sharp bend, up over a sudden hump in the road and on to the main road. The scenery changed as houses began to fill the fields on each side of the road. The town was growing ever outwards, creeping towards the wilderness that surrounded Ada's home. The houses stood in small groups, huddled together as if for safety under the wide, cold sky. Most were built from brick, a shocking orange colour against the shiny black of the new tarmac that wove around them in narrow ribbons. Ada glimpsed a large sign promising 'New, luxury homes for families – easy terms – no deposit'. The arrow at the bottom pointed out into a muddy field where a huge board shouted 'Join us at the Coppice!' As there was not a tree in sight on the whole muddy mess, Ada could only assume the name was a coy attempt at fake rural living, probably dreamed up by a team of advertising experts who thought 'the countryside' was, indeed, another country. She spotted Pete watching her in the bus's rear-view mirror.

'Is all changing now,' he shouted above the rattle of the engine. 'Don't know the place half the time.'

Ignoring the signs stuck up around the driver's cab, Ada rose and walked over to lean on the ticket counter.

'I remember working there,' she said. 'Was old Wilson's place. All trees it was, for cider when the factory was still going, out near Westhay.' She gazed out of the window sadly, swaying in time to the rocking of the bus. 'Don't seem right somehow,' she said finally.

Pete grunted in reply, his attention focused on the run in to town. The road turned abruptly to the left, snaking past a couple of roundabouts and then on to the riverside. The noise of the bus was much louder, reverberating off the grey stone wall that acted as a flood barrier during the twice-yearly equinox tides. Ada retrieved her bag from the seat and stood by the exit, her eyes flicking over the shop fronts as the bus made its way past the High Street, now pedestrian-only, and round to the shopping centre. Lots of buildings closed up, she noted. A fair number of charity shops too, as well as a sprinkling of what she mentally termed 'fly-by-night merchants'. Anyone who opened up a shop for a few weeks, sold stuff at a big discount and was gone the next month was only worthy of suspicion and avoidance in her opinion. Ada watched her money very carefully and she was not easily parted from it.

After checking the time of the return service, Ada made her way to the Cornhill where the Wednesday market was just getting underway. There was a thin straggle of onlookers mixed in with a few customers interested in buying, but most lots went to the first and only bidder. Standing in the corner, she watched critically, appraising the merchandise before deciding on a decent sized stewing cockerel. Opening the bidding at 'seven and sixpence', she was startled to hear a counter offer, so much so she missed her chance to raise the stakes to twelve shillings and lost her supper. Turning away crossly she bumped into Alex who seemed as startled as she was.

'Ada, hey – hello. How are you?' said Alex as she smiled at her old acquaintance.

'I was comin' to find you,' said Ada, relieved she did not need to brave the probation office after all. 'I wanted to talk to you 'bout something, quiet like.'

Alex's heart sank. Not a problem with Kevin, she thought. Please don't let him be in trouble. Kevin was off with the travelling fair and she had pulled strings and renewed contacts with old friends from college to set up a network of places he could report for the remainder of his probation order. Her unofficial arrangement with a series of offices around the country seemed to be holding up but it relied on Kevin behaving himself. One arrest and they were both in deep trouble.

'Hang on a minute while I pay for this and we'll go and have a coffee or something,' she said, and headed for the cash desk. Ada trailed along behind her and scowled as she saw the lot number.

'Was you bought my cockerel!' she said. 'I thought I recognized that voice.'

142

'Gosh, I'm sorry. I wouldn't have bid if I'd realized it was you,' said Alex. 'I'd only just arrived and I saw her holding it up – I just jumped in.'

'What you want with a tough old bird like that anyway,' grumbled Ada.

'You know they have best, tastiest meat,' said Alex. 'They need long, slow cooking but turn in to amazingly good casseroles. And the carcass is great for soup.'

Ada grunted, hiding her surprise at Alex's knowledge of peasant cookery. Alex watched her face and grinned, guessing her thoughts.

'I've been a poor student a very long time,' she said. 'I decided early on I'd better learn to cook unless I was going to live on "Smash" and baked beans.'

They left the Cornhill, walking into the warm sunshine from the chill of the old market hall. Even though it was only late January, it was comfortable as long as they kept out of the shade. Perhaps there would be an early spring, thought Alex and she smiled at the thought. A little way down the High Street was a long-established and venerable café called The Golden Egg and at Alex's suggestion the two women opened the door and went inside. They were greeted by a rush of steam, the smell of bacon frying and the clatter of china and cutlery. Spotting a table near the counter, Ada manoeuvred her ample bulk around tables and diners, coming to rest on one of the wire and plywood chairs. Alex followed her, brushing past a couple of disgruntled youths who had been heading for the same empty table. One of them seemed about to challenge Ada's right to the last spaces in the café but a closer look at her determined expression caused him to turn away hastily.

'I'll have tea,' said Ada firmly. 'I don't like all this frothy stuff they chuck on coffee nowadays.' Alex wriggled her way to the counter, ordered two teas and edged gingerly back to the table, tea spilling over in to the saucers as she juggled the cups with her broken wrist before finally sitting down.

'So, how are you managing out on the Levels without Kevin?' she asked, looking around for something to mop up the table. Ada shrugged, dealing with the problem by lifting her cup off the saucer and pouring the tea back in before rubbing the saucer on the tablecloth.

'Wasn't like he was there much last year anyway,' she said, ignoring Alex's scandalized look. 'Got used to being on my own an' he sends money – he's a good lad like that. Fer goodness sake!' Ada reached over and swiftly repeated the trick with Alex's cup and saucer. 'Anyway, that's not what I want to talk about. There's something going on. Something nasty, out my way, and I didn't know who else I could talk to.'

Alex felt a rush of relief, swiftly followed by apprehension. She had been drawn into Ada's problems before and she still had nightmares about her experiences. Although very fond of Ada, she was not keen on getting involved a second time. Wondering how to wriggle out of whatever was coming her way she took a sip of her tea and immediately regretted it.

'Ugh,' she said pulling a face and putting the cup down hastily.

Ada slurped at her drink, sloshing a mouthful round and wrinkling her nose before swallowing.

'Used to be much worse,' she said. 'Least they wash the cups now.' She sighed and replaced her half empty cup on the saucer before leaning forwards over the table.

'I was wanting to tell you about they strange sounds and stuff.' She glanced around the busy café but the buzz of conversation effectively drowned out her voice and made sure they were not overheard. Still, Ada beckoned Alex forward until they were bent over the table, as blatantly conspiratorial as it was possible to be in such a crowded space.

'There's a story, see,' Ada continued. 'Was told to me by my uncle when I was little an' scared the life out of us, I can tell you.' She nodded a couple of times and waited until Alex finally gave in.

'What story is that Ada?' she said reluctantly.

'Out on the Levels, in them big rhynes and canals, there lives these people,' said Ada. 'Much of the time they minds their own business, keeps themselves to themselves so to speak. Sometimes though they is bored, or lonely. Then they goes looking, spying on us folk. Sometimes they follows people they see passing by, on the banks and sometimes they creep up on houses and peer through the windows.'

Alex listened nervously, knowing it was only a story meant to frighten children but finding the references to spying through windows chimed with her own obsessions.

'When they find someone they like, someone they really like now, they wait and they wait and then they take something precious.' Ada's voice was falling into the cadence of a storyteller and Alex felt herself being drawn into this shadowy world of malevolent and supernatural beings.

'Don't matter what it is,' said Ada, her eyes unfocussed as she related her story. 'Could be an animal, or a child or maybe just a thing – so long as it's precious to you. That's what matters. And then they wait some more whilst you look. You hunt around, calling and liftin' things, searching for what it is you've lost, until finally you give up 'cos it's gone but the hurt of it never leaves you. It pulls at you, the grievin' and so one night you's walking home alone and you see this little light, all twinkling in the distance. So you follow it even if your parents always told you not to go out on the Levels at night because when they took your most precious thing they bewitched you too. And when you reach this light, right there on the river bank, there's what you lost. What they stole from you. So you goes over and kneels down to take it back and that's when they grab you, rising up from the water and seizing you and pulling you under. And they have you then. You belong to them.'

There was a moment's silence between the two women before Ada raised her cup and took another slurp of tea.

'Reckon you'm right,' she said pulling a face. 'Is not up to much, is it.'

Alex blinked at her, still absorbed in the darkness of Ada's story.

'Now, I know 'tis a fairy tale, made up to keep kids away from the rivers and such but there's something going on at night and two people is dead already. I know one was ol' Mickey Franks, and is a miracle he never fell into the canal before, but there was them rumours I heard about his wallet and the lights and now I'm hearing that there music. Right creeped me out, I can tell you.'

As so often happened with Ada, Alex was struggling to make much sense of the conversation.

'What music?' she asked.

'Why, New Year it was. I seen the lights dancing on the marsh and then it was like a flute or something. All soft and strange, never quite made a tune but it sounded like something I almost knew. I could feel it, tugging at me like it was calling. So I locked the door. 'Ent no Drowners getting me.' She nodded her head firmly and settled back in the chair making it creak gently in protest.

'Drowners?' asked Alex.

'That's what they called 'em,' said Ada. 'Drowners.'

'Oh!' Alex searched for a polite way to suggest the whole thing was perhaps just imagination but Ada leaned forwards again, tapping the table with an impatient finger.

'I know is only a story! I know is not real, but what I'm saying is I think someone's making it *seem* real. Someone, mebbe, as wants folk to keep away from the marsh and they don't care what they does to make sure.'

'So perhaps someone is actually killing people, just to frighten the rest of you away? It's a bit drastic,' said Alex.

'Well, is not like it's never happened before,' Ada pointed out. 'Nothing like the threat of mortality to keep folks indoors of a night.'

Not for the first time, Alex reminded herself not to underestimate Ada. She might sound like a postcard caricature sometimes but beneath her eccentric exterior was a fierce, proud woman who had educated herself and probably had a better vocabulary than many of Alex's peers. People didn't always conform to society's expectations she thought, remembering her mother's recent misadventures. They could always surprise – and sometimes disappoint. Especially disappoint where many of her clients were concerned.

'I don't know what to suggest,' she said finally. 'Maybe you should talk to the police . . .'

Ada cut her short with a curt wave of her hand. 'Police!' she said scathingly. 'What do they know? They never come out our way 'less they's dragged out. None of 'em knows their way around and most of us Levellers, we can run rings around 'em. I was tellin' you because of that lad of your'n anyway. Don't know as he's right in the head but he's always polite, says hello and stuff as he goes by, so I'd not want him hurt.'

Alex opened her mouth to ask, then took a deep breath. Simon, she thought. Ada was talking about Simon.

Chapter Ten

Tom wasn't sure his brother would turn up and it was with some relief he recognized the lean, dark figure emerging from behind a stand of trees and crossing the road towards him.

'*Sastimos*,' said Milosh in greeting, climbing into the front seat of the car.

'*Sastimos* – to your health,' replied Tom. Milosh looked tired, he thought. His brother was five years younger than him but his face was drawn and there were grey hairs showing in his black hair.

'So, are we going to sit here until your *gadje* friends see us or do I get to ride in your fancy new car?' said Milosh.

Tom grinned, thinking, as he put the car in gear and moved off down the road, how much he missed his brother.

'Perhaps you are more anxious to avoid any passing *Rom*,' he said.

Milosh stared out of the window at the soft evening as it withdrew across the Levels. A gentle mist was rising from the banks of the rhynes; narrow drainage canals cut in parallel lines crossing and criss-crossing the land. Occasional footpaths and cart tracks appeared, running in straight lines between the rare metalled roads and marked by hedges of hawthorn or withies. In the distance, over Shapwick, the evening murmuration was beginning as a cloud of starlings formed, growing darker as more joined from every corner of the marshy land. He turned back to his brother.

'Spring will be here soon,' he said. 'The people are ready to name the new Elver Man. I have your word he will not run in to any . . . problems?'

Tom glanced up from the road. It was tricky, driving with the sun in his eyes and the car moved constantly from light to deep shadow cast by trees on the other side of the hedgerow.

'Of course,' he said. 'I've given orders to my men and they all know to stay away. Are you changing the site for collection?'

Milosh stared at him for a moment. 'Why do you ask?'

Tom sighed, keeping his temper and striving to sound casual. 'It would seem a good thing to do,' he said. 'The police know the last site, after Pitivo was killed there. I will keep my men away – but I need to know where 'tis they should avoid looking.'

Milosh considered this for a moment, fidgeting in the soft leather seat. He reached in to his pocket and pulled out a worn pouch containing tobacco and some thin papers but Tom lifted a warning hand so he shoved it back in his pocket with a loud sigh.

'You are a real *gadjo* now, Tamas,' he said. 'You are so concerned with things – this car, your nice clothes, a house to weigh you down. Look out there,' he gestured through the wide windscreen at the land around them. 'See the colours? If we were outside we could smell the air and hear the wind and the birds. Not sealed in this – thing – of yours.'

Tom braked sharply, swung the heavy car round and set off up a narrow, unmade track.

'Enough, slow down!' said Milosh through gritted teeth. The car slowed a fraction. 'My back will be broken with all this rattling around.'

Tom brought the car to a halt just in the shelter of a small hillock, a slight rise in the universal flatness surrounding them. Opening the driver's door he got out and stretched, waiting for his brother to join him. Together they stood, looking out over the old peat works, across an uninterrupted landscape of water and marsh that stretched away in the distance until it reached the foot of the Mendip Hills. It was very quiet in the still air of dusk and had it not been for the first of the lights from farms and occasional houses embedded in the soft purple haze of the foothills they might have imagined they were alone in the world. Tom kept his eyes on the distant lights when he spoke.

'I need to use the bridges,' he said.

Milosh stood next to him, hands hung loosely at his side.

'You cannot,' he said softly.

'I must,' said Tom.

Milosh rounded on his brother.

'The bridges are our secret!' he said. 'You cannot allow the *gadje* to use them. I forbid it.'

Tom turned slowly and looked at Milosh.

'You can't have it both ways,' he said. 'I'm no longer *Rom*, remember? You can't forbid me to do anything. I wanted to tell you out of courtesy, of family and friendship. I *will* use the bridges but I promise only a few of my most trusted men will know of them and I'll only use them near the centre of the marsh. I'll not be letting them wander around and all the others will remain a secret.'

Milosh was silent for a minute, staring across the plain, now in deep shadow as the sun set behind them. Tom waited. It was important his brother spoke first, for his pride.

'Why must you use them?' asked Milosh finally. 'You have vans and lorries – why use the marsh roads?'

'The traffic would be noticed,' Tom explained. 'I need a safe place to store my goods and send them out in smaller amounts. There's an area near the centre, where the peat cutting has been stopped. Is deep – about four feet, so it's hidden from the paths. Has got sheds and best of all the council have just fenced it all off. One of my men was working on the fences and knows how we can get in.'

'What has this to do with the bridges?' demanded Milosh impatiently.

'We cannot have vans going along the roads and then just turning back,' said Tom. 'They'd leave tyre prints along the tracks, leading to our store. We'd get away with it for a while maybe, but after a week or so people would notice and ask questions . This way we can move our stuff in from off the road and no-one'll know.'

'I may not be able to stop you,' said Milosh, 'but I want your word you alone will use the bridges. And they must not be used to bring in the drugs!' He turned his head and stared at Tom. 'I want you to swear. There are evil things moving through the towns and we have nothing to do with it. If you had any sense left neither would you.'

Tom shifted uneasily from one foot to another.

'I swear,' he said. 'I don't want anything to do with that stuff either. Ain't right, selling it to kids.'

Milosh spat in his palm and held his hand out for Tom to shake.

'Well brother, now you owe me a favour, perhaps you can tell me something about these strange stories I'm hearing. They say the Drowners are back and hunting on the Levels. Would you know anything about that?'

Tom shook his head thoughtfully before answering.

'Was a warning,' he said. 'There was this man, always hanging round, listening in where he's no business. I spoke to him and then I had several of my lads make the point a bit more forcefully. I thought he'd got the message but seems not. Couple of the younger gang bosses, they spotted him and followed him out onto the Levels. Reckon he was so drunk, he was seein' things and tipped hisself into the big canal. One of 'um, smart lad from the ports, he decided to send a message, maybe scare a few people off from round there so they made it look like he was drowned.'

Milosh listened, nodding occasionally and stared out into the darkness thoughtfully.

'I'm glad you had no hand in that,' he said. 'It is a pity the man died, but at least I know my brother is not a murderer. But the music, Tamas – what about the music?'

Tom shrugged his broad shoulders and turned back to the car.

'I will be honest with you, I have no idea 'bout that. Folks keep hearin' it but I'm damned if I know where is coming from. Promise you, Milosh, is none of my doing.'

The Highpoint office seemed very calm with Garry gone. The women in the office smiled and seemed particularly patient with even the most difficult client, and the probationers responded with some rudimentary politeness. There were fewer missed appointments and even the court days seemed less arduous.

For the first time in many months, Alex woke one morning without a feeling of dread in her heart. She was beginning to enjoy her work again, she realized. There were still the daily bumps along the road, especially where certain people were concerned, but generally she felt more capable and optimistic than she had since arriving at Highpoint.

One of the bumps in her road was Alison who had reverted to her usual stubborn, sulky self, a lank streak of self-righteousness whose role as Alex's support seemed to be a source of perpetual discontent. Despite all her efforts and a couple of late nights tidying and filing the paperwork herself, Alex could not match up all the forms she needed to the cases she supervised. Some notes were incomplete, some files were full of the wrong information and some stuff was just plain missing.

'I know I've done most of this,' she moaned to Lauren at the end of one particularly stressful day. 'I remember filling in the referrals and the plans for all the attendees because that led to a massive row with Garry about what şort of provision we were offering. Now half of them are gone. I don't know what's happened to the system to be honest.'

'Maybe Alison's got them?' Lauren suggested. 'Typing them up perhaps?'

Alex shook her head. 'I asked and she insisted she'd not touched them. You'd have thought I was accusing her of something – actually thinking about it, if she hasn't been near my files recently just what the bloody hell *has* she been doing?'

'Pauline gave her a load of Social Enquiry Reports to do,' said Lauren. 'Just while you was away. I've been busy with "Wonderboy" and so we was a bit pushed.'

Alex frowned at the mention of Ricky.

'What is it between you two then?' Lauren asked. She sat in Alex's chair in the tiny office, swinging herself backwards and forwards with every sign of enjoyment. It was making Alex feel sick just looking at her.

'Just stop will you?' she snapped. Lauren grabbed the desk to steady the chair and looked hurt.

'Was only asking,' she said. 'No need to snap like that.'

'No, I meant please don't spin around like that. You're making me giddy. It's a bit hard to explain, about Ricky . . .' She paused, considering all the implications of the conversation. Alex was an intensely private person and she had found it hard even to share her house with Sue at first. She gave little of herself away and rarely talked about her past. The arrival of her family in her carefully guarded Somerset world had shaken her more than she liked to admit. She was very fond of Lauren but was aware that she was now Ricky's support assistant and she didn't want to do anything to influence that relationship. Sharing her past experiences of Ricky, tempting as it seemed at the moment, was just asking for trouble.

'Oh, you know,' she said vaguely. 'Things are different at university and sometimes people get tangled up in stuff that's not important.'

Lauren gave her a withering look.

'I think he's still "tangled up", the way he's been talking,' she said. 'And what's this about you bein' a psychologist?'

Alex was startled but recovered quickly.

'I did philosophy at university,' she said firmly. 'You know that. I bet you've sneaked a look at the personnel files.'

Lauren grinned. 'Well, I did, just after you came,' she admitted. 'Mind you, they've been moved since, so that was the only time.'

'What do you mean?' asked Alex. 'Do you know where they are?'

Lauren shook her head. 'Nope. An' neither does Pauline I reckon 'cos she was swearing about it earlier today.'

'You don't think they've disappeared too, do you?' Alex asked, trying not to appear too anxious. 'If it was a client in there that night, well there are addresses and all kinds of personal details in the files. Phone numbers – everything.'

'That cabinet weren't touched,' said Lauren. 'Was the case files someone went for, with some of the court stuff an' a load of boring new protocols from regional at Taunton. Is just, Pauline was goin' to update the rota for everyone, this bein' the end of January, and they was gone. Officers and us clerical too. Whole cabinet was wiped clean, she said.'

Despite the disturbing nature of this development Alex was glad she had succeeded in sidetracking Lauren, moving her away from the sticky area surrounding Ricky Peddlar and his 'revelations'. She would have to talk to her friends soon, she thought. She just needed a bit more time.

The chalet had served him well after his grim time sleeping rough over Christmas but Derek Johns was feeling the need to move on. Spring was coming early to the West Country with the first snowdrops mingling with gold and purple crocuses in the flowerbeds around the camp. There were more birds in the morning and the sound of their singing was a reminder that the seasons were moving on and fine weather was on its way. Oblivious to this outbreak of nature's joy, Derek was more concerned about the imminent arrival of very early visitors, holidaymakers looking for a cheap break out of season and more concerned with the location than the lack of traditional amenities. He was awakened to the danger when the tractor hauling the little 'train' began to worm its way around the adjacent sector, the carriages filled with fresh linen and the first teams of cleaners preparing for the extended season. It was time to move on and he packed up his belongings whilst considering his next move. The holiday camp had been too far away from the Levels anyway, he thought. There was a lot of stirring and plotting going on out there and he needed to get back and sort it out. He might have to disappear for good but he intended to make sure things were set fair for Newt on his release. The Levels belonged to his son and properly run would provide a decent income so Derek could go somewhere warm and live a quiet life, free and happy, away from the law and the threat of arrest for his murderous little rampage. Yes, Newt would have to see him right.

It was a long trudge back inland, avoiding the main roads and skirting round the villages that littered the back roads. It had been a dry winter with only a scattering of snow and now the sun was out, drying the land and keeping the fringes of the great marshes firm enough for a nimble and experienced traveller to pass without danger. Derek had grown up on the Levels and he knew the areas to avoid and how to identify a safe path. For all his disdain for nature, he used the clues left by the natural world instinctively and so arrived, tired and hungry but both unscathed and unseen, on the banks of the River Brue.

The water was high but not flooding and there was no sign of the mud normally left by winter overspill so Derek headed upstream, skirting Westhay and ploughing doggedly on as the sun sank behind him and the Tor of Glastonbury rose against the orange sky, guiding him home. As the light faded he decided he'd better find somewhere to spend the night. Despite his long day walking he was still too far north for most of the abandoned pill boxes, the majority of which were strung along the old defensive line known as the "Taunton Stop Line". He cursed quietly as he realized he would need to trek several miles to find shelter if he relied on the fortifications. Despite the rising moon it was getting very dark and Derek was only too aware of the dangers surrounding him, both natural and man-made. Picking a safe route around the rhynes, over ever-shifting marsh subject to sudden floods and unexpected enclosure was almost impossible. He cast around, peering into the gathering gloom. He had wanted to get to the Wastes, an area that was perfectly summed up by its name, consisting of treacherous stretches of liquid mud, a maze of narrow channels and a few forgotten drover roads. Dotted around this area were a few old machine gun posts and the remains of several failed farms. Derek had expected to find shelter and a base for his campaign in this forgotten patch of the Levels. Now he faced an extremely uncomfortable night in the open unless he sneaked into a barn or risked venturing in to Westhay or Meare in search of an open outbuilding.

Suddenly he saw a single flash of light in the distance, over the river and towards Shapwick. Immediately, Derek was rooted to the spot, his whole body still as he waited for some further sign. Around him the air was still as though the Levels were holding their breath and waiting with him. In the distance was the sound of an animal, an otter perhaps, sliding into the water of the river to his left. Ignoring the tiny rustles and ripples as they rose around him, Derek held still until, away in the distance, came the mutter of voices, hastily stilled. Like a predatory animal, Derek moved swiftly but silently towards the river, crossing on a tiny footbridge made from a concrete post laid across from one bank to another. Once safely across, he placed his bag of belongings on the ground, slipping a carving knife out of the side pocket and into his belt so that it was within easy reach. He checked the position of the bridge and his belongings Then, keeping his head low, he skirted a solitary farm and headed towards the source of the voices. Someone was out on his patch and he wanted to know who – and why.

He slowed even further as he approached the old peat works, keeping off the ancient tracks that still ran from the cuttings to newer paths and eventually on to the roads used to transport bags of rich earth to the stations and ports of the area. The area boasted a few, rare wooded patches and Derek slipped under the cover of the stunted trees, wincing as the willow branches whipped at his face and legs. Sinking down on to his knees he waited and finally his patience was rewarded. Voices floated towards him, startlingly close in the night air, and he froze in his hiding place as he heard footsteps coming his way. Moving very slowly he eased his knife out from his belt, feeling a twinge of regret at the loss of his beautiful and versatile Normark, lost on the canal bank when he had almost drowned last year.

Two shadowy figures passed just in front of his hiding place, closely followed by a third. The leading figure turned and in the pale moonlight Derek recognized the craggy features of Tom Monarch, self-styled 'King of Somerset'. His eyes glittering with anger and his heart full of hatred, Derek forced himself to stay where he was. He wanted nothing more than to plunge his knife into his old rival's throat but Tom had his henchmen around him and Derek had not come so far and suffered so much to commit suicide through a moment's rashness.

'Now then, you got them tools you was talkin' about?' said Tom softly, and the last man in line grunted, swinging a small workman's bag from his shoulder.

'No problem,' he said softly. 'Is right here. Where is it you'm wanting this entrance then?'

A light shone out from a torch and Derek blinked in surprise. Outlined in the glow was a metal fence, matt black in colour and about three feet high, sealing off the peat excavations. Now what the bloody hell was that all about, he wondered. He leaned forwards hoping to get a better look and there was a rustling of leaves as his heavy frame disturbed the overhanging branches. Tom's head whipped round and Derek froze as those hard, dark eyes hunted through the darkness. Finally, Tom relaxed and turned back to the fence.

'Just the breeze,' he said. 'How's it coming then?'

'Nearly there,' the workman said, and at that moment there was a clank and a section of the fence swung free, tipping in to the deep trench on the inside of the enclosure. The noise seemed shockingly loud, echoing off the rusting iron sheets of the remaining buildings to the left. It landed with a splash, disappearing from Derek's view.

'Watch what you'm doing!' Tom hissed as the workman leaned forwards and tried to haul the section up out of the water.

'Sorry,' gasped the man. 'I wasn't expecting it to just go like that.' He was panting with the effort as he fished for the railings.

'Just get in there and lift it up will you,' snapped Tom. He looked around anxiously. 'Reckon that'll bring anyone on the Levels out, the racket you's making.'

'Is all full of water!' protested the workman. 'Look, 'tis all flooded and 'ent no idea how deep it is. We was told to keep clear, not set foot off this here path when we was fittin' this here fence.'

'Keep your voice down!' hissed Tom. 'I'll not be telling you again. Get in there and pass that out – now.'

The workman slid over the edge and gradually lowered himself in to the mud at the bottom of the cutting, his breath coming in short, ragged gasps. Tom and his associate leaned over to watch as the man's legs disappeared up to his knees before he hit the bottom.

'Ah – is bloody freezing!' he complained, but Tom snapped his fingers impatiently, gesturing to his henchman to grab the end of the fence as it slid up over the edge. Derek watched as the man struggled out onto the bank, thick mud plastering his legs.

''Bout time – now fix it back using these,' ordered Tom, ignoring the man's discomfort. He held out a small box that rattled as the workman opened it and tipped out fresh bolts and a tube of lampblack. Swiftly the barrier was repaired and the bright steel of the new fixings were smeared with the blacking to blend them in with the framework. Tom stepped forwards and examined the section carefully, leaning over to inspect the back before nodding.

'Right, get that bit cleaned off,' he said grinning broadly. 'Looks right mucky compared to the rest. Don't want to be too obvious now, do we?' Derek stayed motionless, his legs beginning to cramp and his back aching, as the men finished up and checked around to make sure they had not left anything lying around.

'Hurry up, damn you,' Derek muttered as the pain in his cramped body built up until he felt he had to move – or shout in agony. At last, Tom was satisfied and the group moved off through the night leaving Derek alone. He waited until they were out of sight before allowing himself the luxury of tilting over slowly on to his hands, a soft groan the only sound he made. As his cramped knees began to spasm he rolled over on to his side and lay there, panting softly. After a few minutes the pain began to ease a little and he was able to sit up, looking around to make sure he was still alone, before hauling himself to his feet. He moved out from the shelter of the trees, pins and needles in his feet making him clumsy. The iron railings were now clearly visible in the moonlight and he examined them carefully. Most sections were fixed with smooth-headed bolts, the backs firmly locked into place by some sort of covered fastening. Unless he had seen Tom Monarch's men in action he would not have noticed one section was secured by traditional bolts, so well were they camouflaged. Derek leaned over the fence and peered into the darkness beneath. Water, mud, more water – what was Tom up to, he wondered. Why go to all this trouble for an old, deserted peat working?

There was a scuffling sound behind him and Derek spun round, poised and ready for any danger. Suddenly a torch shone through the darkness, dazzling him as a voice called out.

'Oih – you there – what you'm doing then?'

Instinctively, Derek turned away, raising his arm to shield his eyes from the glare. There was the sound of footsteps and the voice was closer this time.

'Yeah, you – this is private property. Is dangerous too. How did you get over here anyway?'

It was too late to flee. The intruder had probably seen his face by now and although he might not have been recognized yet, Derek knew the scars on his face were too distinctive. If this clown reported him to the police, someone would identify him and that could not happen. Who would have expected a watchman out this far anyway? He hesitated for a second, his back turned to the light whilst he felt with his left hand, checking the carving knife was still in his belt. Then he leaned a little way over the rail and made gurgling noises, spitting in to the water below.

'Oh bloody hell, stop that now,' said the watchman. He shifted his torch to his left hand and moved closer.

Just a little more, Derek thought. People were so stupid, so easily fooled. Just dying to help, without a thought for the consequences. He let his body slump a little further, struggling to suppress a giggle. Just dying to help . . .

As the watchman reached out for him, Derek swung round and smashed a fist into his face. The man staggered backwards and Derek grabbed the heavy torch, twisting it out of his grasp. The watchman raised his hands to ward off the blow, trying to escape from his assailant. He got in one desperate hit before Derek brought the torch down on his head. The watchman collapsed with a groan, the air leaving his body as he tumbled to the ground. Derek waited for a moment, standing back and listening but there was no sign of life. The light had gone off in the struggle and Derek shook it, knocking the front impatiently. He felt a sharp pain in his hand as a sliver of glass from the broken lens cut into his palm.

He cursed and shook his injured hand before turning his attention to his victim. Leaning over he grabbed the man by his collar, trying to haul him up off the ground. Suddenly the body came to life, striking out wildly and clawing frantically at his face as the watchman fought for his life. Derek stumbled backwards, hitting the fence before recovering from the shock.

'You bastard!' he hissed as he felt the watchman's fingers make contact with an eye socket. He swung the torch, bringing it down on the man's head once more. There was a crunching sound and the watchman collapsed like an empty sack. Derek stepped back and waited but this time it was all over. Derek felt around his eye gingerly, flinching as he touched the swollen flesh.

'Bastard!' he said again, and vented some of his fury on the corpse at his feet, kicking and stamping on the dead man's chest. After a moment he came to his senses and stopped, panting from the exertion. 'Is your own fault,' he muttered, looking down at the body. 'What the bloody hell is you doin' out here anyway?'

Desperately tired, he leaned against the railings for support and waited until his breathing returned to normal before casting around for a place to dispose of the body. Eyeing the rusty buildings surrounding the peat cutting, he considered leaving the man inside one of them. The idea had its merits – Tom Monarch was obviously planning to use the site for something criminal and the presence of a dead body would seriously inconvenience him. Still, Derek had his eyes on the abandoned cider factory down the road about half a mile. It was well placed, off the main road and with a number of separate buildings round a paved courtyard. He had used it in the past as a hideout for colleagues wanted by the police as well as a handy base for smuggling tobacco, and he didn't want to attract too much attention to the immediate area. There was nothing for it, the watchman was going in the river.

For a skinny bloke the guard was heavy and Derek was sweating and trembling by the time he got him down the track and away from the peat factory. Dropping his burden onto the soft ground, he bent over, hands on his knees as he tried to calm his pounding heart. When he straightened up, his head began to swim and he realized he hadn't eaten anything all day. For a moment he was tempted to walk away, leaving the dead watchman by the side of the track, but the thought of the cider factory and the security it offered spurred him on again. The torch was digging into his back where he'd shoved it into his belt and Derek considered discarding it but decided it was too useful to abandon and so, with gritted teeth, he resumed his long, slow trek to the banks of the Brue.

Just as he prepared to roll the body into the slow-flowing water he had a thought. Exactly what *was* a night watchman doing out on the Levels? He opened the man's jacket and rifled through the pockets, pulling out a small notebook and a wallet containing several pound notes and a fiver. Derek stuffed the money in his own pocket and, shielding the torch with his body, opened the notebook. Names, addresses and – bingo – dates and shifts worked. According to the list, he was watching the half-built nature reserve at Shapwick. Thieves came out at night and building materials were always popular – a bit heavy and difficult to move sometimes but very easy to sell on, in Derek's experience. There was a glint of reflected light from the watchman's chest and Derek peered at it in the torch light. A metal badge with a barred gate and 'Tor Security' stamped on it was pinned to his pullover. Derek removed it and held it in his hand for a moment, wondering if he might be able to use it to his advantage, but the memory of his ruined face made him drop it in disgust. He was never going to pass in a crowd again so the stupid thing was of no use to him.

Hunting through the trouser pockets Derek unearthed a handful of coins that joined the notes in his pocket and a large iron key. He took the key as well – very useful things, keys. You never knew when they might just open a door in a time of crisis. He felt in the back pocket and came up with a small photo album, pictures of a rather tired, dusty looking woman and two teenage children with identical crooked smiles. Derek thought of his own boys, the talented, handsome Newt and his burly younger brother, Biff. He dropped the pictures into the mud next to the badge, turned off the torch and knelt beside the body, tucking the arms together to minimize the noise as it rolled in to the river. There was a splash and for an instant he thought the man moved, one arm rising to the surface as if appealing for mercy before the river took the body and it began to drift downstream. Derek stood up, picked up the torch and walked away without a backwards look. His bag was still where he had left it and he shoved the torch inside, pulled out a broken biscuit and resumed his tramp to the cider factory, munching away as he stepped out along the tiny footpath.

Lauren was starting to dread the sound of the phone ringing on Dave's days off. Not that he had any at the moment, she thought bitterly as she replaced the receiver and flung herself onto the sofa. Every time they planned something together he was called back in to work. Every single time – and he always agreed. She was feeling decidedly unappreciated after four months of coming second to his job and there were moments when she wanted to tell him not to bother any more. But then, on the rare evenings they spent together he was wonderful. Dave never made a big thing of their difference in size but he didn't try to ignore it either. He was just easy and natural as well as great fun to be with. He treated her like an adult and sometimes he could make her feel like a princess.

Lauren twisted round and stared out of the window where a steady drizzle was falling, running down the windows in slow, fat drops. The door to the front room opened suddenly and Jonny, her younger brother, stuck his head round, his dark hair tousled and his brown eyes full of mischief.

'Hey Sis,' he said. 'What you brooding for? No Dave again today?'

Lauren scowled at him and turned back to the window.

'Come on, you can't sit here sulking all day. You know he's got to work all them extra shifts if he wants to get promoted so why don't you and me go out. We can take the car, maybe go up onto the Quantocks. What do you say?'

Lauren gestured at the rain, which was beginning to fall more heavily.

'Not in this,' she snapped. 'Look at it. Is horrible out there.'

'Well then, how about we go to Glastonbury? I'll spring for a pub lunch an' we can come back via Street. Maybe pick up some nice new shoes for us both.'

Lauren was tempted. She liked Glastonbury, as long as it was out of season. She had made the mistake of going to the town last June and found herself caught up in the wave of revellers attending the new 'festival' a local farmer had arranged. It had been a frightening experience and she had not been back since. And she loved Street – a town dominated by shoe making, with a dozen factory shops to browse. She slid off the sofa and grinned at her brother.

'Reckon that's the best offer I'm goin' to get today so you're on.'

Chapter Eleven

At Highpoint police station PC Dave Brown was attending an emergency briefing, but he still felt a twinge of regret at letting Lauren down yet again. For two and a bit years he had dedicated every waking moment to his job but now he felt himself pulled in another direction. He was damn lucky she was so understanding, he thought. A look around the room showed how many men were not so fortunate. A number of his older colleagues were divorced or separated from their partners and most of the younger men were either settling in to life as community PCs or, in a few rare cases, had postponed any idea of a serious relationship whilst aiming for a position a bit higher up the food chain. The Inspector's voice cut through his musing and he forced himself to pay attention.

'I know this unusual, but these are unusual and disturbing events and I want every one of you to be aware of what we are faced with. That is why I've asked Dr Higgins to come here today and share the results of the latest post-mortem with us.'

'Thank you Inspector,' said the pathologist, stepping up to the large crime board and gazing at the photographs for a moment. He looked very tired, Dave thought. Standing in front of the room with shoulders slumped and a grim expression, Dr Higgins looked more than ready for retirement.

'We have another murder,' said the pathologist, his soft voice carrying through the stillness in the incident room. In the pause following this statement there was a shuffling of feet as the assembled police squad shifted uncomfortably in their hard plastic chairs and exchanged glances.

'In all my many years of service in the county I have rarely had to deal with a violent death, yet now we have three suspicious incidents in the space of a few months. I believe there are links between the killings but there are also some important differences I would like to explain.'

He turned to the board where three photographs headed up the display.

'First we have Michael Franks,' he said, pointing to the first image.

'Sticky Micky,' someone muttered, drawing a glare from the Inspector.

'Mr Franks,' continued the pathologist firmly, 'died from drowning. There was water in his lungs matching that of the canal in which he was found. There were a few bruises along one shoulder and arm but nothing serious and certainly nothing that could have contributed to his death.'

'Probably fell over when he was pissed,' came a mutter from the back.

'Several personal items of Mr Franks were found on the bank next to where we believe he went in to the water, in particular, a leather wallet with a twenty pound note tucked inside.' There was a general stirring at this news. Twenty pounds was a lot of money to be fluttering around on the river bank.

Higgins turned back to the board and pointed.

'Our next victim is Robert Donnoley. He was a River Warden, out on his rounds just before Christmas. Mr

Donnoley was also found in the canal and the immediate assumption was he, too, had drowned. However, forensic examination of the remains indicates he was dead *before* he entered the water. The actual cause of death was a single blow to the head.' Here he indicated a close up of the back of Donnoley's skull. 'As you can see, the trauma was extensive, suggesting a very powerful blow. So powerful, in fact, that several fragments of bone were forced into the brain – here,' he pointed, 'and here.'

Ignoring the reaction from several of the more squeamish officers he continued his talk.

'Despite careful analysis we have been unable to recover any useful trace elements from the hands or under the fingernails and so we assume he was surprised by his assailant and had no opportunity to defend himself. He was probably dead for several hours before being placed in the river as there was no water in the lungs and the lividity marks on his back and buttocks indicate he was on his back for some time immediately after death.'

Dr Higgins added two further photographs to the board to illustrate these points. A muttering arose from the officers as the gruesome details were displayed in front of them.

'Bloody hell, bit too much detail there,' whispered one PC sitting next to Dave, who gave a vague smile and kept his eyes on the pathologist. Waste of time, him dragging those hands across town, he thought grimly. Thank you very much. None of this showed on his face as he maintained a cool, professional exterior and waited for the new information on their third victim.

'Finally we come to our most recent case.' Dr Higgins tapped the third photograph. 'This is Andrew Cairns. Mid-forties, married, two children, working as a security man for a firm based in Glastonbury and patrolling the nature reserve at Shapwick. As you doubtless are aware, there has been a spate of thefts from building sites recently and Mr Cairns was on duty at night to prevent any further loss. His body was recovered from the north bank of the Brue, just below where the Bounds Rhyne enters, here.' He indicated the place on a map pinned up next to the photo board.

'Interestingly, whilst Mr Cairns does appear to have drowned, he had also suffered considerable head trauma and the pattern of bleeding internally suggests this was pre rather than post mortem. In addition, the water from his lungs contains numerous microscopic larvae, specifically *Centroptilum luteolum*.'

Here he looked pointedly at his audience who stared at him with blank faces.

'English Mayfly. Very common but only, please note, found in slow moving streams and rivers. And so,' here he turned back to the map and tapped on the place where the body had been found, 'we can presume that Mr Cairns entered the river somewhere else. From the condition of the body he had not been in the water for more than, say, twelve hours.'

PC Brown swallowed discreetly, hoping they would be spared a close-up of the corpse. He still had bad dreams about the hands, rustling in the brown paper bag.

Someone behind him asked 'How do we know that then?'

There was some sighing and nudging from the older officers surrounding the questioner.

'Is fast water, up by Bounds Rhyne, specially when has been raining. So them larvae, they won't be there, right?'

Dr Higgins nodded encouragingly at the speaker.

'Certainly, that would be the case. So we need to establish where the body might have been dropped in. There was considerable detritus on the clothing, specifically leaves from willows, moss and peat.'

'Well, is all peat round there,' muttered someone from the back. 'And all willows too.'

'Ah, but this peat was old, from a reasonable depth – say three or four feet. This peat came from a recent working.' He turned back to the board, ran his finger along the map and pointed to a stretch upriver from Westhay.

'This is our nearest candidate and, given the weight of the body and the fact there are minimal signs of dragging, unless

Mr Cairns was spending his evenings bog-snorkelling, he was either killed beside the river or carried there along some sort of path or track. My guess would be here.' He indicated the remains of a footpath.

The Inspector stepped forwards and nodded his thanks as the pathologist took a seat in the front row.

'Right now, we need to start a search as soon as possible of this area,' he indicated the Westhay Level from the peat works to Catcott Farm, 'and down to the river bank. Then along here towards Westhay Bridge—'

Dr Higgins interrupted him. 'It is unlikely he was dropped from the bridge. That type of immersion would have left some marks, signs of trauma. He was almost certainly rolled in to the water.'

Trying to hide his annoyance, the Inspector nodded in acknowledgement and continued. 'Westhay is unlikely partly for that reason but also that's the main road. Much too risky, even pushing him in from the bank. Downstream from there, though, there's nothing between the two farms. Now, we've maybe a mile and a half of river bank to search, concentrating on the south bank first on account of the peat on his clothes and him being based at Shapwick. One team will cover the Reserve, see if there's any sign of an intruder on the site. The rest of you will suit up and work the river bank.'

Dave Brown put his hand up. 'Do we know if there are, er – any other matching indicators?'

The Inspector stared at him for a moment before answering.

'Well, that's what we are looking for, lad. Right, the sergeant's got the teams worked out. Collect your gear and report to the car park for transport.'

Dave waited until the room cleared a bit before going up to the board, staring at the photographs and the map. There was a movement behind him and he turned to face Dr Higgins, who was studying the display.

'An unusual case, I think,' said the pathologist.

'You say we have one man who was drowned,' ventured Dave. 'Then one who was bludgeoned but made to look as if he'd drowned and then one who was bludgeoned and drowned as well?'

'Yes,' said Dr Higgins thoughtfully. 'Interesting, isn't it.'

Lauren's mood lifted as she bowled along the flat road across the countryside in Jonny's car. The rain had eased and the sun was forcing its way through the clouds scudding across the pale blue sky. The road was almost empty as they turned right on to the Levels and drove along between the water meadows and occasional hamlet or farm. She opened the window a fraction and breathed the fresh, green-scented air, relishing the sound of birds singing of the joys of imminent spring.

She was grinning by the time they turned into Glastonbury, the town buzzing gently with the usual influx of local shoppers and the handful of first visitors of the season. These were mainly older couples, lively pensioners with grown-up children and the freedom to roam purchased through the dividends from shares in the newly privatized industries and extra years of the company pension scheme. Untouched by ever-rising unemployment and benefiting from spiralling interest rates, they were the only thing standing between a lot of rural communities and economic disaster. She watched them through the big bay window of the pub that Jonny had suggested they eat in, as she and her brother waited for their food.

'Reckon most of the tea shops 'ud be struggling without them oldies,' she said.

Jonny nodded and took a pull at his pint. 'Reckon a lot of the West Country would,' he said. He'd recently got a job working as a hospitality manager at one of the local hotels and had been shocked at how close the line between 'getting by' and 'going under' had become. 'Seems we need the Grockles, at least for a bit longer, till things look up.'

Lauren snorted in disgust. 'Can't see things looking up for a while,' she said. 'Not until they sort themselves out and do something for us ordinary folk. And that 'ent happening any time soon I reckon. Too busy helping a bunch of greedy rich boys get richer, they is.'

At that moment their main courses arrived and put an end to Lauren's political tirade, at least for as long as it took her to clear her plate.

'Fancy a pudding, Sis?' Jonny asked as the sweet trolley trundled past them heading for the main dining room.

'Well, I might squeeze something more in,' said Lauren. At that moment she glanced out of the window at the High Street and froze.

'Jonny, look, 'tis Iris. Iris Johns, over there by the chemist.'

Jonny leaned forwards and peered out. Iris, dressed simply in a dark coat, turned and realized she was being watched. There was an uncomfortable few seconds as her eyes met Lauren's gaze and then she nodded an acknowledgement and turned away. Lauren watched her walk away down the street, shifting in her seat to keep her in sight until the abrupt arrival of the sweet trolley snapped her back to the business in hand. A nervous young man hovered next to their table, plate and serving spoons in his hands. Jonny gave him a wide, welcoming smile and the waiter swallowed hard, sneaking a glance over his shoulder before smiling back.

'Hello Kirk,' said Jonny. 'Nice to see you again.'

Kirk chuckled, his eyes darting to and fro anxiously.

'Hello, Jonny. Fancy you turning up here then. I thought you were in Highpoint.'

'Oh, you know, I like to get around a bit. Seemed like a nice day for a run out.'

The manager materialized at their table, his hard eyes taking in the scene. Kirk ducked his head slightly and his ears turned bright red. Lauren, who was used to Jonny and his many friends, leapt in to save the situation.

'I don't know, there's just so much is so nice. What do you reckon is your best pudding then?' She smiled up at Kirk, the picture of innocence.

'It depends if you want something fruit based or maybe perhaps a bit more substantial,' said Kirk, the relief showing on his face.

'I 'ent so sure you can serve a proper pudding on them plates mind,' Lauren went on, seemingly engrossed in the sweet trolley. 'Is not a *pudding* if you can see it through the custard. Is only a dessert otherwise.'

The manager blinked rapidly as he digested this novel interpretation of his menu.

'Perhaps you would prefer a bowl?' he suggested.

Lauren threw him a glittering smile. 'That's perfect,' she said. 'Thank you.'

There was the briefest of pauses before the manager realized he had somehow been manoeuvred into fetching the bowl himself and turned away, seeking someone appropriately menial for the job. Before he could delegate Kirk, Lauren launched in to a series of questions about the pies, puddings and fruit plates on offer.

'Thank you,' the young waiter whispered, the instant the manager was out of earshot.

'Sorry,' Jonny muttered. 'I didn't expect to make trouble. When are you off?'

'Not till seven,' Kirk muttered, bending over the trolley and lifting a particularly succulent chocolate cake out for Lauren's inspection.

'Meet you behind the Rifleman then?' Jonny suggested.

Kirk had time for a nod before the manager returned bearing a bowl and followed by a girl from the kitchen with a white jug.

'Here we go, my dear,' said the manager. 'And I thought you would need a little more custard to make it a *real* pudding.' He gestured towards the serving girl, looking as pleased as if he'd conjured her up as well as the custard.

'Why thanks,' said Lauren, beaming at him. 'Is lovely to get such good service.' She watched as Kirk served her pudding under the watchful eyes of the manager, who finally nodded his approval and moved off to micro-manage someone else. They all exchanged relieved smiles and Jonny lit a cigarette whilst Lauren finished off her meal. After demolishing her chocolate cake, custard and 'little splash' of cream, Lauren was ready to face the shops in Street and hurried out into the warm afternoon.

To her surprise she spotted Iris, still hovering down the High Street. Jonny was inside paying the bill and for a moment Lauren contemplated going back inside to wait for him but her hesitation was her undoing. Iris was walking towards her, a determined look on her face, and Lauren resigned herself to the encounter. Iris stopped a few feet away and hesitated before speaking.

'Hello Lauren,' she said softly. 'I'm sorry to intrude but I wondered if you could spare a minute?'

She looked nervously over Lauren's shoulder just as Jonny stepped out of the pub and started across the road towards them.

'Hey!' he called. 'What do you want?'

He moved across to stand in front of his sister protectively but Lauren laid her hand on his arm to stop him.

'It's all right,' she said. 'Iris just wants a word. Why don't you go and check the car.' It was an order rather than a question.

Looking decidedly unhappy, Jonny walked off to the side-street where his new Nova was parked and Lauren nodded to Iris to come closer.

'Is a bit delicate,' said the woman, and now Lauren got a good look at her and realized that Iris had been crying.

'Let's sit down, over there, look, by the flower beds,' said Lauren guiding her towards an empty wooden bench. 'Now, what's this you want to talk about then?'

Iris blew her nose, dabbed at her eyes and took a deep breath before she answered.

'I'm so worried about my Billy,' she said. 'He's getting himself all wrought up about Derek and I don't know as how he came to terms with losing his brother either.'

Lauren nodded sympathetically and waited for Iris to get to the point. She could see Jonny hovering on the corner, watching her anxiously and was mildly irritated by his overly protective attitude. Iris had done her no wrong. Her husband, Derek, was another matter and Lauren was exceedingly glad Derek was dead and gone, but Iris had turned away from her violent husband and his mad quest for revenge. She had thrown him out of the house, changed the locks and refused to see him, which made her all right in Lauren's reckoning. She realized Iris was speaking again and decided to let Jonny stew for a bit longer.

'Now he's on about Derek's funeral, though we can't have a real one – not a proper funeral on account of there's no body ever been recovered. I was hoping to do some sort of memorial service maybe, though I'm not sure many folks would want to come.' She dropped her head and gazed at her clasped hand for a moment before fixing Lauren with a defiant look.

'Still, he wasn't always so bad. Once he was half-way decent, just a bit wild and used to getting what he wanted the whole time. If it helps Billy, I'll stand up and say I miss Derek, that I'm sorry he's gone, but the prison, they won't let him out for the day. Because of that silly running away thing he did. They say he's an escaper and he's not entitled to any release until his sentence is up.'

Lauren digested this for a moment.

'So when is he out then?' she asked.

Iris sighed and shook her head. 'Well, should have been round June but they took half his remission off him so now is probably not until end of September,' she said.

'Bit late, waiting nearly a year,' said Lauren thoughtfully and Iris nodded.

'Well there's some,' she said acidly, 'some folks as think I'm not properly respectful, waiting this long with nothing to mark his passing. Mainly Derek's cousins that is. Bunch of inbred half-wits without a brain cell to share between 'em.'

Despite herself Lauren laughed aloud.

'Why don't you say what you think, Iris. Don't mind me.'

'Ah, I know, but really – what a collection of losers they is! I been fobbing 'em off, saying maybe they might find the body and we'll be able to give him a proper funeral and then I was trying to make 'em wait until Billy could be there, but they's getting right pushy now. Saying I don't care and I'm disrespectful to Derek's memory. Seeing as how he got hisself drowned trying to kill you and all, I 'ent so sure is possible to disrespect it, mind.'

Lauren had always been told not to speak ill of the dead but she was finding it hard not to agree with Iris on just about every point.

'So, what is it you're wanting from me then?' she asked.

Iris looked down at her hands before answering.

'I was wondering if Alex Hastings might have a word on Billy's behalf. I know it's asking a lot, specially as Derek behaved so badly towards her . . .'

Privately, Lauren thought this was something of an understatement. Derek had, after all, stalked Alex for most of the last year, breaking into her house, slashing her car tyres and finally trying to kill her. Had she been in Alex's place, Lauren would have been tempted to walk away from the whole family and leave young Billy 'Newt' Johns to rot in Dartmoor but she had known Alex long enough now to realize her friend was more forgiving and, on occasions, infinitely more professional.

'I thought she did send that letter,' said Lauren, stalling for time whilst she tried to see a way out of the problem. She might not be Alex's official assistant any more but she still felt a strong obligation to protect her, especially from the memories and emotions generated by the Johns family.

'She did, yes, and that was very kind of her,' said Iris. 'It's just – they didn't seem to take anything into consideration when they turned him down. I thought maybe – if she could – perhaps speak to them? Billy's not going to try and escape. That's just daft, and they know it. They's punishing him for what Derek made him do and I don't think that's fair – do you?'

'Hang on, what do you mean, Derek made him do?' Lauren asked.

Iris's face hardened, her eyes glittering in the weak sunlight.

'Was Derek's idea, that stupid "escape" of Billy's,' she said. 'He'd heard something around the Levels about a "grass" in Dartmoor, so he told Billy to keep his ears open an' call him if he heard anything. Course, he said to keep it secret so Billy, he wasn't going to risk using the phones inside the prison in case someone heard so he did that run into the village. That's how Derek found out about poor old Frank Mallory.'

Lauren was aghast. 'Does he know?' she asked. 'I mean, I suppose technically that could make him an accessory to Frank Mallory's murder!'

'I never told him,' said Iris. 'I'll maybe talk to him when he's out but I reckon he's got enough problems at the moment. Though there's times I'm so tempted, hearing him talking about Derek and thinking the man was worth looking up to!'

Iris looked about to burst in to tears again and despite everything Lauren found herself moved by the woman's courage and the devotion she showed towards her son. Lauren had gone to school with the Johns brothers, at least on the rare occasions they deigned to attend, and the younger lad, Biff, had been one of the kids who had made her life miserable. Newt, on the other hand, had never bothered her and actually called Biff and his little gang of nasties off a couple of times. She guessed she owed Newt too.

'All right,' she agreed. 'I'll talk to her for you. I don't know if she can do anything more, mind, and she's still got her arm all plastered up so I don't think she can drive very far at the moment.'

Iris gave her a glittering smile and for an instant Lauren could see the beauty and charm that had broken hearts across the Levels.

'Thank you. Thank you so much.'

Iris gathered herself, taking a deep breath and putting her handkerchief back in her bag.

'You know,' she said as she stood up, 'I just want it all over. I want to say goodbye and walk away from the whole damn lot of 'um.'

'Except Newt,' said Lauren.

Iris fixed her with a steady gaze and smiled very slightly. 'Yes, except for Newt.'

It was muddy down on the banks of the River Brue and the Highpoint police officers were grateful for their waders and waterproof jackets. It began as a cold, wet morning and there was the usual round of grumbling but gradually the rain turned to drizzle, the clouds lifted and the sun fought its way through to bring sparkle and colour to the water meadows and reed beds. There were worse ways to spend a bright, spring day's overtime, Dave Brown thought as he plodded slowly and carefully along the edge of the water, stick in hand. He examined the ground carefully before taking each step, looking for footprints or signs of recent disturbance. There were a few areas of disturbed leaves and damaged grass but these proved to be caused by the local wildlife: otters and newly arrived migratory birds searching for food and material for their nests. Undeterred, Dave worked his way along the bank, parting the reeds and tall grasses with the stick as he went.

As the sun rose it began to feel pleasantly warm and he realized he was rather enjoying himself. There was something both undemanding and satisfying about a detailed search. He wondered for a moment if he were doing the right thing, pushing for promotion and trying to fast-track his career. The majority of his colleagues were perfectly happy as ordinary PCs, their lives the perfect mix of comfortable routine and an occasional burst of wild excitement at the rare, more serious, crimes. They talked a lot about their homes, their gardens and their pensions and certainly in these uncertain economic times they were exceedingly fortunate. Then he thought of the years ahead, long, slow years of the same thing, the same petty offences culminating perhaps in the much coveted position of desk sergeant. The day might be pleasant but such a future was not for him.

He turned his attention back to the task, moving methodically along his allotted patch. Suddenly there was a shout up ahead and when he rounded a clump of willows he could see Sergeant Willis leaning over, peering in to a reed bed. The men who had been close enough to hear the call began to emerge from the surrounding greenery and the sergeant stood up and waved at them angrily.

'Get back now! We don't need your great big feet all over the scene. Stand up there, on the top of that path and wait!'

Dave hurried forward, sticking close to the river bank as he called out.

'Sarge, should we get on the side of the path? Maybe under those trees, on the grass?'

Sergeant Willis looked at him for a moment and then nodded.

'Right, of course that's what I meant. Over there, you lot, and wait whilst we check the track for footprints. Brown, you get the photographer out of the car. Time he earned his overtime, I think. I'll keep an eye on the scene down here.'

There were a few boot marks on the path but nothing very much, except they seemed to be heavy prints. A couple of them leaned over with a scuffed edge as if the maker's foot had slipped a little.

'Could be carrying something,' said Dave hopefully.

The photographer grunted and snapped away, head down and coat collar turned up against the breeze. Once he'd finished, he tramped over to the riverbank where Sergeant Willis was waiting for him. Dave Brown considered the footprints for a minute. Whoever had walked along here had come from inland, along the old track from some disused peat workings. There were no return prints, he noted. And the scuffing on one side did look like the mark of someone struggling with a heavy load. He moved back up the track, keeping to one side and scanning the ground as he went.

'What you looking for then?' asked one of the waiting PCs. Dave shook his head and kept walking. He'd know it when he saw it.

Alex and Sue decided to take advantage of Garry's absence and treated themselves to a rare day off. Although her wrist was still plastered, Alex offered to drive, leaving Sue torn between indulging in a decent glass of wine at lunchtime and putting up with Alex's awful old car. In the end the wine won, but half-way to Street she was regretting her choice.

'Bloody hell, can't you take the bends a bit slower?' she growled as she was thrown against the door and then bounced up and down over a short gravelled patch of road. Alex glanced at her in surprise.

'Sorry, I'd not realized it was bumpy,' she said and slowed down slightly. The aging Citroën wallowed over the irregular surface, bobbing and rolling slightly from side to side.

'I'm getting sea-sick,' Sue complained, grabbing for the dashboard in an attempt to steady herself.

Alex frowned, concentrating on the narrow road.

'It's not that bad. What a fuss.'

'It's all right for you,' snapped Sue. 'You've got the steering wheel to hang on to.'

Her mood improved as they pulled into the large car park behind the factory shop and the sun came out, driving away the last of the drizzle.

'Shop first,' said Alex firmly. 'I've seen you in here after a few glasses of wine. On our budgets we need to be a bit more selective in our purchases.'

They spent a happy hour and a half browsing through the huge store, opening boxes and trying on new and unusual shoes. The factory shop was a source of constant delight, though mixed equally with disappointment. Some of the more interesting items were only available in one size – inevitably the wrong one. There were even some shoes only offered in one pair, prototypes or ends of run priced to recover cost. Glancing at her watch, Alex realized she was hungry and it was creeping past lunchtime. Reluctant to leave such a treasure-house, Sue was eventually lured away by the promise of a pub meal and they retired to the Bull's Arms to gloat over their purchases.

'I don't know how you can resist,' said Sue, eyeing Alex's one shoe box. 'And they're not exactly exotic are they?'

Alex put her desert boots on the floor, hurt by her friend's remarks.

'Well, at least I'll have warm feet,' she said sulkily. 'How many pairs of tiny, shiny sandals do you need anyway?'

'One more than I've already got,' said Sue firmly. 'Always one more. Can we have pudding?'

They emerged from the pub's dim interior into a perfect spring afternoon and Alex felt a sudden rush of optimism.

'I know,' she said, 'Let's go to the seaside!'

'But there are all these other shoe shops,' Sue objected. 'We've only been in one so far.'

Loath to spend the rest of the day staring at endless (in her eyes identical) pairs of shoes, Alex decided on a compromise. One more shop, it was agreed. Sue could decide which one, and she had half an hour to browse as she wished.

'Take it,' said Alex. 'It's the only deal on the table and you know what the buses are like round here.'

Sitting outside on a metal bench, she closed her eyes, enjoying the speckles of gold and red that floated in to her vision. The sounds of the busy road faded away and she felt warm and drowsy, and really quite content.

'You can't sleep there,' came a scandalized voice and she jumped, almost falling off the bench. Lauren was standing in front of her, a wicked grin on her face.

'Bloody hell, you startled me!' said Alex. 'What are you doing here anyway? I thought you were going out somewhere with Dave.'

A scowl flitted over Lauren's face and she shook her head angrily.

'He's off again, working,' she said. Somehow she made it sound as if poor old Dave was spending the day cavorting in a sauna with scantily clad ladies of dubious morals.

''Um,' said Alex, as she tried to keep a straight face. 'Well, he is trying for promotion.'

Lauren gave her a hard stare before turning round and looking back up the road for her brother.

'Well, Jonny promised we could go get some new shoes,' she said. 'There he is,' and she waved at the figure hurrying towards them from the car park.

'Try in there,' suggested Alex, pointing towards the largest shop on the street. 'Sue's inside, probably driving all the assistants mad.'

'That's Lauren's speciality,' said Jonny, puffing slightly as he came to a halt next to them. He flashed her a smile and, not for the first time, Alex was struck by his charm. His easy way and good looks had many of the younger staff in the office sighing over him, much to Lauren's amusement.

'Reckon they's all too dumb to see they is wasting their time,' she commented one afternoon after watching several juniors on YTS 'work experience' flutter around him like anxious butterflies. Now she was tapping her foot with impatience, eager to start spending Jonny's money again.

'You coming?' she asked Alex, who shook her head and settled back on to the bench.

'I've already got some new shoes,' she said, tapping the box beside her.

Lauren reached out and lifted the lid, peered inside and closed it again without comment.

'What?' asked Alex.

Lauren shrugged. 'Well, at least they're not boring brown,' she said. 'Though I'm not sure Garry's going to take to that shade of blue.'

'I knew I should have got the lavender pair,' said Alex thoughtfully, tucking the box back under her elbow.

Jonny laughed and raised his eyebrows at her. 'You,' he said, 'are turning into a bad woman!'

In the end Sue had to be prised out of the shop and Alex eyed the sky anxiously. Although the clouds had gone, the light was already changing as the sun moved towards the horizon and the short early spring day began to draw to a close.

'I really wanted to go to the sea,' she said a little sadly.

'Why not,' said Lauren cheerily. 'Let's go to Brean – is beautiful, the sunset off the sands. Magical to see.'

She turned to Jonny, looking up at him hopefully. Jonny glanced at his watch and she said, 'Plenty of time for you to get back. You'm not wanted anywhere else until seven. Come on.'

'I'll need to get you back home before I head back to Glastonbury,' he said, looking markedly unenthusiastic.

'Tell you what,' said Alex. 'I'll run Lauren back if you need to get off. It's only a few miles past Highpoint – easy.'

'I don't know as I should,' said Jonny, eyeing Alex's plastered wrist. 'Are you sure you're okay to drive with that?'

Alex glared at him and wriggled her fingers through the grey, fraying remains of the plaster.

'I think is a great idea!' said Lauren. Come on, you go off ahead and we'll follow, right Jonny?' She was off down the street towards the car before anyone could react. With a heavy sigh, Jonny set off after her wondering what he had done to deserve such a stubborn older sister.

Over the rise and down the narrow path, PC Dave Brown was walking slowly and carefully, observing every mark and sign of recent activity. One of the photographers trotted along with him, keeping to one side to avoid damaging any evidence. Occasionally, Dave stopped and indicated a boot print or some bruised grass but the path revealed very little after the overnight rain. The light was beginning to dim with the setting of the sun when they finally reached the entrance to the old peat works. The two men stopped and looked around them, hesitating before entering.

After a few moments Dave moved in to the deserted yard, keeping to the right of the main path that led to the grass surrounding the fenced-off workings. Suddenly he spotted an area of flattened grass, off to the left and near to a clump of willows. Beckoning to the photographer he picked his way over whilst the cameraman adjusted the aperture and focus.

'Can you get this with and without the flash?' Dave asked, pointing to the area where the grass was clearly torn up near the railings. 'Gives a better idea of the colours and such without, if you can manage it.'

The photographer nodded and leaned over the damaged turf, snapping and adjusting the settings as the sun dropped lower in the sky. Finally he stopped and shook his head regretfully.

'Sorry, I'll need to use the flash for the last few. Is too dark now.'

As the flash went off there was a sparkling in the grass, a reflection throwing the light back at them. Dave blinked to clear his sight and gestured to the photographer, then leaned forwards and parted the remaining foliage. Embedded in the mud were pieces of glass and as Dave lifted the largest segment with a gloved hand he realized it looked as if there was blood along one edge. He turned to the photographer and grinned in triumph.

'Got him!' he said softly.

Chapter Twelve

Derek Johns had always kept different parts of his life separate. Only his long-time confidant, 'Big' Bill Boyd, had been privy to all his business secrets and Bill, sadly, had ultimately proved to be unreliable. With his usual ruthlessness, Derek had disposed of Bill, cutting his throat and leaving the body out on the Levels last summer. Now, back in his safe house in the old cider factory, Derek felt his loss and for the first time experienced a twinge of remorse. Bill had served him well and faithfully for thirty years – from the time they first met at school – and there was no-one Derek had trusted as much as Bill. Derek wandered around the small room that was hidden at the back of the storehouse, once a repository for cartloads of apples, fresh picked and destined for the huge presses on the main factory floor. The air was still faintly scented, even after ten years of abandonment. The ghosts of several generations of workers, those who had dedicated their lives to the perfection of the cider-maker's art, seemed to wander, aimless, at night, driven by the wind as it whistled through the gaps in the slowly rotting timber walls.

Derek was not a superstitious man but he was beginning to regret his choice of hidey-hole. Apart from the cold, the damp, the draughts and the illusion of movement produced by moonlight shining through the branches of the surrounding trees, he was too close to the peat works for comfort now the coppers had descended in force. Expecting to be able to spy on his rivals and disrupt their operations, he found himself confined to the concealed room with a limited view out over the land behind the building. The outlook over the heath to the emerging nature reserve at Shapwick was stunningly beautiful at dawn and dusk but Derek Johns stared through the grimy slats that concealed the glass from outside, unmoved by the starlings as they swarmed and pirouetted across the golden sky.

His supplies were running low and he contemplated a quick trip out to hunt for something to eat but the cold was starting to affect him, making him lethargic and slowing his responses. He'd cut his hand on the glass from the torch and after a few days it showed no signs of healing. In fact it was still red and very painful. In the dim light he could not see clearly enough to detect the signs of infection and he was so inured to the smell of his own unwashed body he failed to detect the tell-tale scent of decay as the wound began to suppurate. Like a wounded animal, he went to ground. For all his violent temper, Derek Johns could be a patient man and now he waited, still and poised, for the fuss to die down, the coppers to clear out and Tom Monarch to come calling at the peat works down the road.

Alex and Sue rolled in to work on the Monday after their shopping trip feeling remarkably happy and relaxed. The absence of their senior was having a positive effect all round, with smiling faces on the reception desk, short but highly efficient meetings led by Gordon and a new willingness to volunteer for unpopular duties such as the Family Court.

'All we need now,' said Sue, standing in front of the glass door leading to the upper corridor and admiring her shoes in the reflection, 'is for some of this to rub off on the clients.'

'I wish,' said Alex ruefully. 'Still, it's nice while it lasts. Oh, by the way, I meant to ask you about Simon.'

Sue frowned. 'What about Simon? Shy, weird, drives that imaginary lorry everywhere – what?'

Alex glanced out of the window and spotted several of her workshop group arriving. They filed in to the hut on the far side of the car park and she was relieved to see Eddie was already there, giving instructions and ushering in the late-comers. She had a few minutes to spare, she decided.

'Well, how on earth did he end up on probation in the first place?'

Sue dragged her attention away from her new shoes and sighed theatrically. 'It is one of the most ridiculous stories I've ever come across,' she said, leading the way down the corridor. 'Honestly, it's like some stupid farce.'

In her office she rummaged through her filing cabinet and hauled out a large, exceedingly battered manila file. Alex took it gingerly – it looked as if it might fall apart if opened.

'Do you mind if I have a quick look through?'

'Knock yourself out,' said Sue as she floated across to the desk and sank gracefully in to her chair. Pulling a diary out of the top drawer, she lit a cigarette and began flipping through the pages, making a list with her free hand.

Alex sat in the 'client' chair opposite and began to sort through the mass of papers. Simon's fascination with trans-port in general, and lorries in particular, had started early, she discovered. Social Services had been called in when he was only four. He'd been spotted inside a junk yard, clambering in and out of old, wrecked vehicles. Despite the best efforts of his mother, Simon kept getting out and was repeatedly returned to her care by the owner, a neighbour or, increas-ingly, the social worker. Things came to a head when he had to be rescued by the Fire Brigade from the top car in a stack of seven precariously balanced vehicles. Simon was removed from his family and placed in a care home for evaluation.

Whatever the authorities had hoped to achieve, it probably wasn't the terrified, traumatized young man that was the result of several years intensive therapy, foster homes and clinical intervention. Simon stopped speaking and developed a number of autistic patterns of behaviour, especially an aversion to being touched. It was this that finally landed him in court, when he was 'driving' his imaginary lorry around an apple orchard, supposedly helping with the harvest. Despite repeated requests to leave (that was the polite version), he continued running round the trees and demanding the pickers move the ladders so he could reverse his trailer into position. Eventually a couple of casual labourers grabbed him by the arms and tried to bundle him out of the gate. In the resulting chaos, Simon managed to break someone's nose and left several men with black eyes. When the police arrived to arrest the screaming boy he hit one of them too. Bloody hell, thought Alex. Assault, trespass, GBH and resisting arrest. Not to mention hitting a police officer. Simon was lucky he'd not ended up in prison with that lot. Yet there was nothing wilful about any of it.

She slapped the folder down on the desk and stared at Sue.

'Farce hardly covers it,' she said. 'He sounds like some hardened nut-job if you read the offences but actually he was trying to get away because he doesn't like being touched. He panicked, right?'

Sue nodded but made no comment.

'He doesn't understand,' Alex mused. 'He's got no real idea of private land and I think he forgets most of what he's told almost as soon as he's heard it. Just runs around in a world of his own, safe inside his lorry. I've never had any problems with him. What about you?'

Sue put down her pen and fixed Alex with a bright, hard stare.

'Just what, exactly, are you after?' she asked.

Reluctantly, Alex related her run-in with Brian in the day centre, repeating his accusation towards Simon. Sue snorted in disgust.

'Brian?' she said. 'Brian Morris? The toe-rag of the town – that Brian Morris? Why on earth would you believe one word that little shit utters?'

'He was really angry,' said Alex. 'Darren was his friend and he'd just learned he was dead. I don't think he was lying but I suspect he was telling what he saw as the truth. Simon's very – suggestible. He has virtually no friends and if someone's kind to him he'll do just about anything they want.'

'Is that what you really think or what you're hoping?' Sue asked as she took the file and tried to cram it back in to the cabinet.

'Bit of both I guess. You've got an awful lot of paperwork in there. How many cases are you carrying at the moment?'

Sue pulled the drawer right out and forced the folder back into place with a grunt.

'Oh, about thirty something – thirty three I think. You're right though – there does seem to be more in here than usual.'

She closed the top drawer and pulled open the next one down, flicking through the contents.

'What the hell is all this?' she said, pulling out a pile of very old, battered folders. Opening one at random, she stared for a moment and then slapped it shut again. 'Shit.'

'What?' Alex asked, reaching for the file. Sue pulled it out of range and shook her head.

'Oh no, believe me you don't want to see.'

Alex grabbed the next folder from the pile and opened it, staring at the photograph on the top for a moment before closing it again, putting it on the desk and rubbing her hands on her legs in disgust.

'Why are you keeping pornography in your filing cabinet?' she asked.

Driving down unexpectedly from Bristol that week, Max dropped into the Royal Arms for a bite to eat and to see if he could pick up anything interesting from his local contacts. When he walked in through the front door, Marie, who was serving a couple of likely lads with more money than most folk seemed to have at the moment, left by the kitchen door, scooting around the back to alert her husband.

Phil emerged from the cellar where he had been changing a keg and peered over the bar before hurrying out to join her by the cooking range.

''Ent a meeting day is it?' she asked.

Phil shook his head but checked on the calendar hung up by the old fashioned fridge, just in case. Mindful of the need for secrecy, Phil had avoided writing down anything in the least incriminating but Marie, with a rather macabre sense of humour, had drawn a black star next to the relevant days. According to the calendar, the next one was not for a week.

'So what's *he* doing here then?'

Phil stepped back to the doorway and risked another glance over to the bar.

'Waiting for some service, I reckon,' he said. 'Better get out there. Is not like we can afford to turn paying customers away now, is it.'

Marie shook her head. 'Oh no, I'm not going. You invited them in, so you go and serve him. Tom Monarch's one thing – least he's got some manners. That little punk though, I don't trust'un and I don't want nothing to do with'un.' She wiped her hands on her apron and glared up at her husband.

Phil knew that look. He'd seen it before, very occasionally mind, and he recognized the futility of argument. Still, a man had to try, he thought.

'Might be better if you go,' he said casually. 'Wouldn't want him thinking he was someone important, having the landlord see to him.'

Marie's eyes narrowed suspiciously before she smiled and gave a laugh.

'Get away with yer, you old faker!' she said, punching him playfully on the arm. 'Seriously, though, he gives me the creeps, that one. And I reckon he's more likely to talk to you than me. Maybe find out what he's doin' round these parts. Please?'

Phil sighed and shook his head, but he was smiling too. He never could resist his wife, something of which she was well aware. It was a sign of how good their relationship was that she did not play on his affection. When she did ask a favour it was usually for a good reason.

'Well, pub is almost empty now. You wait here, in case he wants to eat. Then you go and have a lie down. I'll clear up, don't worry.'

Marie watched him exit the kitchen and head for Max, who was seated at a table near the back door with the two likely lads. They stopped talking as soon as Phil appeared, she noticed. Not much chance of getting any information out of them, then. She waited until Max picked up the bar menu, glanced at his watch and then pointed to his choice, before slipping back out of sight, ready for the order to arrive.

At the pub table Max was involved in a fierce wrangle with his two companions. Initially only too happy to earn a bit of extra money for very little work, they were now trying to back out the deal. Rob and Charlie were known to the police as petty offenders, occasional shoplifters who tended to drink their ill-gotten gains and were a bit too unrestrained in their subsequent behaviour. It was an all-too familiar pattern and one many young men grew out of. They hadn't expected any trouble – and they certainly hadn't expected any of their customers to wind up dead on the beach.

''Ent what we was expecting,' said Rob, the leader of the two. 'Seems there was something wrong with that lot of stuff. I 'ent touching no more.'

Charlie looked up over his pint, took a gulp and fixed his eyes on the table, more than happy to let Rob speak for them both. Max fumed inside but kept the illusion of calm as he fought to keep them under control. They were a sorry pair, but both of them were already in too deep to be allowed an easy exit.

'Now lads,' he said easily, 'was just an error – bit of a mix-up. Is a bit unfortunate but these things happen.'

Rob scowled over the table. 'Was more than *unfortunate* for poor bloody Darren,' he muttered.

'No-one made him take the stuff,' Max pointed out. 'He wanted to and he took too much. Didn't tell no-one, didn't have no-one with him neither. Just daft that.'

'You'm making out was his own fault?' said an incredulous Charlie, shocked into speech.

Max shrugged and drank from his glass.

'Look, is not an exact science, making the stuff. Sometimes is so weak you need a couple to get going an' sometimes there's a big hit straight off. Only sensible, having someone with you, just in case. Any road, I hear you's got a right good way of getting the stuff out to them villages and places. Clever that, usin' some half-wit runner.' He nodded his approval and drained his glass. 'Another round?'

Charlie waited for Rob, sitting with his shoulders hunched and his eyes fixed to a spot on the table. Rob was engaged in scratching at the flaking varnish beside his empty glass. Max waited, knowing they would crack, and once they did they would do as he wanted. Finally, Rob looked up and opened his mouth to speak, but at that exact moment Phil materialized at the table bearing Max's hot-pot.

'Here you go then,' said the landlord as he set it down, deftly placing cutlery and producing salt and pepper from his pocket. 'Everything okay here?' He glanced at the less than happy group and added, 'Anyone for another drink?'

Rob seized his chance and rose, the chair scraping loudly in the deserted bar.

'I got to be off,' he muttered and headed for the door.

Phil had been a pub landlord for most of his adult life and he'd not survived all those years without an instinctive knowledge of body language and an almost uncanny ability to read a situation.

'I'll leave you to eat,' he said, keeping his voice as jovial as he could. 'You just call if you want anything else,' he added over his shoulder as he disappeared behind the bar and hurried into the kitchen.

Across the table Charlie began to rise from his place but Max was too fast for him. Seizing him by the arm, he hauled the lad back down and then pulled his hand across the table until it was barely an inch from the dish containing the hot-pot. Charlie struggled as he felt the heat from the casserole but Max was too strong and held him down with ease.

'In a bit of a hurry suddenly 'ent you?' said Max, picking up his fork whilst keeping Charlie's hand clamped in place. Max speared a piece of meat, blew on it for a minute and popped it into his mouth, chewing thoughtfully.

'Is good this,' he said. 'You should try it.' The fork snaked in to the pot and a scalding lump of meat landed on Charlie's arm. Tugging frantically at his trapped hand, the young man gave a cry, tears springing to his eyes with the pain.

'Oops, sorry about that,' said Max easily. 'Let's try again shall we?' Again the fork darted towards the dish.

'No, please . . .,' gasped Charlie. Max stopped, his hand poised above the still-bubbling stew.

'Not hungry then?' he said, raising an eyebrow and smiling calmly.

Charlie shook his head, trying to keep calm as the pain from his burnt arm began to intensify. Max nodded thought-fully, dipped into the stew and held a piece up for inspection. Charlie was shaking, the tears beginning to trickle down his face. Max waited, drawing out the tension before blowing on the meat to cool it and taking a bite.

'So,' he said, 'You got something you want to say about our little business arrangement?'

Not trusting his own voice, Charlie shook his head. He was finding it hard to breath and Max had his hand in a grip so tight he thought the bones would crack. All he wanted was to get out of that room, as far away from this nutcase as possi-ble. At that moment he would have offered up his granny as a victim in his place, and he was very fond of his granny. She had raised him, took him in when he had nowhere to go and had spent most of the last two years warning him about people like Max. If only, a tiny voice inside whispered, if only he had listened to her.

'So I take it is business as usual then?' Max went on smoothly.

Charlie nodded frantically.

'Good,' said Max, exploring his lunch and selecting a large piece of carrot. He munched on it for a moment before adding, 'You won't be forgetting this conversation will you?'

Charlie shook his head, still unable to speak.

Max smiled again, looking at him almost kindly.

'Well, just to make sure, reckon this should remind you.' He tugged at Charlie's hand, pressing the back of it against the cooking pot for a second. The boy gave a high-pitched scream, the cry of a trapped animal. As Max released his hand and pushed him away, Charlie hunched over gasping, saliva dribbling from his chin and mixing with the tears that rolled freely down his face.

'Off you go then,' said Max, turning his attention to his lunch. He didn't look up as the young man staggered to the door, arm cradled against his chest. In the kitchen Marie stared at Phil, horrified by the ghastly cry. Phil closed the door to the bar softly and gestured to her to go upstairs.

'I'll finish up here,' he said gently. 'Go on.'

Marie stumbled to the back door, turning back to look at him, her distress clear on her face.

Phil met her gaze and nodded slowly. 'I know,' he said. 'You was right. Now is up to me to sort this out.'

A quick review of all the officers' filing cabinets revealed a rather unpleasant selection of dubious material secreted amongst the case reviews, social enquiry reports and Part Bs. As acting senior it fell to Gordon to collect this and examine it, something he did with marked reluctance.

'I feel I should be wearing rubber gloves to touch some of this,' he confided to Pauline. She disappeared into the store-room, returning with several large black plastic sacks and a pair of bright yellow marigolds which she presented to him with a flourish.

'I've got an apron too,' she said, 'but it's got pictures of fluffy kittens on it – don't know if that's any use?'

Gordon took the bags and gloves with thanks but decided the kittens were probably a step too far.

'Gordon,' Pauline called after him as he made his way towards the day centre office, 'what's happening around here? It just seems everything's – well, falling apart. What with Garry going so strange and the officers being moved around. And some of that stuff coming out of head office – I'm not sure I recognize the job sometimes.'

Privately Gordon agreed with her but it was his job to keep the office running and get them all working as a team again. He couldn't start undermining their belief in the service, despite his misgivings about the way things were going and he was too professional to show what he really thought of the new emphasis on 'control' rather than 'rehabilitate'. With a heavy heart, he set about his task.

At the meeting he called after hours he went through his findings briefly, not wanted to give too many details of some of his discoveries. Whilst the female officers had all been graced with a variety of images and advertisements from 'male' magazines, the men had a varied selection of pictures and articles, some from the same sources but others from hunting journals, war comics and a disturbing number from the far right fringe. The appearance of what was essentially fascist propaganda struck Gordon as particularly sinister and he glossed over this in his summary. The offending items were already packaged up securely and awaiting collection by the police. His joke about the rubber gloves, he thought, had been unexpectedly timely. If there were any prints on the paper he had avoided contaminating them.

Even more worrying from his point of view was what had been removed from the cabinets. Every officer had several files that were missing pages and a number of them had substantial parts of some files missing. Alex and Sue were particularly badly affected and Alex, who had been struggling to make sense of the mess in her records for a while, had some folders with nothing official in them at all. If they were hit by an inspection, Gordon thought, they would all be in serious trouble but Alex would probably be facing dismissal. The first task was to get the mess sorted out and he instructed the assembled company to go through everything – every folder, file and 'dead' case still in their rooms.

'Some of the missing forms are in the wrong place,' he explained. 'I found a couple of Sue's Part Bs in Eddie's stuff . . .'

'Not guilty!' said Eddie.

'I didn't say you were,' said Gordon wearily. 'I don't think anyone here has anything to do with this but we have to get it sorted, and quick. I just hope we can find most of what's missing before someone asks for it.'

There was general nodding around the room, apart from Ricky who was leaning back on his chair, a bored expression on his face.

'I know it is asking a lot,' Gordon continued, 'but if and when we identify items that really are missing they need to be replaced.' He looked over at Pauline and gave a little shrug of apology. 'I'm afraid this may put a lot of extra work on you and the rest of the admins,' he finished.

'Surely the most important thing is to find out who did this,' said Ricky.

There was a moment's silence and everyone in the room turned to look at him.

'That is in hand,' said Gordon softly. 'The police are now involved and will be making a full investigation. I know I don't have to ask you all for your full co-operation.'

Ricky sniffed and resumed the study of his fingernails, swinging one foot back and forth. Alex risked a glance in Lauren's direction and stifled a grin at the look on her face. Her friend might as well have been holding up a sign that said 'I reckon you did it, Ricky', she thought.

Not many of the old families remained on the more remote parts of the Levels. Some had moved away in search of work, some went to nearby towns to be closer to schools or shops and some simply died out as the young ones married and moved away or were forced out by rising rents. Only a few hardy souls were left, clinging stubbornly to their homes, their gardens and their way of life. Ada Mallory was one such, a formidable character who defied land owners, councils and occasionally the police in defence of her right to live where she chose, on her own terms. She had few neighbours closer than a couple of miles, and few friends left in the area, so when Lily Dodds came calling she was greeted with smiles and an invitation into the kitchen.

'I'm sorry has been so long,' said Lily. 'Only, 'tis a long walk, with the bus bein' not running most times now. I bin meaning to drop by and now I is here askin' for yer help.'

Ada sat her down, brewed some tea and settled herself at the table.

'You ask away,' she said, pouring them both a large cup of exceedingly strong tea. Lily took a sip, screwed up her eyes with pleasure and set her cup down again with a sigh.

'Now that's proper tea,' she said. 'These young'uns, they don't know how to make a decent brew, what with them bags and funny twigs and *fruit* for goodness sakes! Tea is tea not some pink water.' She had another taste, nodded and took a deep breath.

'Is my grandson,' she said, finally coming to the point of her visit.

Ada nodded. She knew all about Charlie Dodds, who had been at school a few years below Kevin. He had been a decent enough young lad, she recalled. One summer he and Kevin had been quite friendly and spent the long, hot days paddling in the stream at the bottom of her garden, fishing for tiddlers and catching frogs. They had drifted apart when September rolled round and Kevin began to truant more often than he attended, but she remembered that summer as one of the happiest of her son's childhood. Kevin had been a late baby, born when Ada was almost forty and taking everyone by surprise. Lily, one the other hand, had started young and had three children by the time she was out of her teens. They were neither of them in the first flush of youth – or even of middle age – but looking at her friend's face Ada reckoned she'd been the more fortunate of the two. Poverty, physical work and anxiety had aged Lily beyond her years.

Unaware of Ada's wandering attention, Lily was still talking.

'He's got hisself in to some bother, mixing with the wrong sort. Now, I know that's what lads do at his age.' Ada nodded again, remembering Kevin and his seemingly endless run of petty offences. 'But these is really the wrong type. Serious trouble they is, and Charlie was out this morning and comes back around three, crying and such. In a terrible state, he was. Took ages to get 'un to tell what 'tis all about, and he's got this girt burn on his hand, see. I tried to get him to the doctors but he won't go. Says 'tis nothing, but it looks pretty bad.'

Ada nodded and waited, knowing there was more to come.

'I wondered if perhaps you had something, could suggest for it maybe?' Lily finished.

Ada considered for a moment. 'Burns is tricky,' she said finally. 'Depends how bad, how long it was afore he got it cooled down – all kinds of things make a big difference. Can't be sure I'd be doing the right thing, see.'

'Mebbe if you saw him?' said Lily hopefully.

Ada put down her cup, worried at the implications of this.

'I'm happy to help,' she said, 'but I don't reckon I've time to walk all the way to your'n and back this evening.'

'Oh no, course not,' said Lily hurriedly. 'Wouldn't dream of asking. I told Charlie to come along a bit after me, just in case. I hope you don't mind?'

At that moment there was a knock on the door, followed in seconds by the frantic barking of the dogs. Well, thought Ada, bit late if I do.

Charlie sat on the stool at Ada's kitchen table, his arm on some clean newspaper as she examined his hand. It was a nasty burn – blistered and cracked in places and covering a large area. She considered her options before going to the window-sill and breaking a few leaves off her aloe plant. Slicing them lengthways, she applied the sticky flesh to the burn before binding the whole hand firmly with strips of cloth torn from an old sheet.

'Ow – that stings,' Charlie protested earning himself a swift clip round the head from his granny.

'Show some gratitude,' she said sternly.

'Thank you Mrs Mallory,' muttered the youth, his head down.

Ada smiled at him. She still had a soft spot for the lad and if the truth be told, she missed having someone to look after, with Kevin gone.

'That'll settle down soon,' she said reassuringly. 'Will take all the sting out and start to heal it. There's antiseptic in them leaves too so you'll not get any infection in there. Now, 'twill need to be changed every day or so for the first week.' She frowned as she tried to work out the logistics of the problem.

'That's all right,' said Lily. 'If you want, he can cycle over to see you. What you say, Charlie?'

He was sitting up straighter now and flexing his fingers experimentally. He gave a wide, slightly gap-toothed grin and nodded.

'You'm right – is hardly hurting at all. What's that called, you said?'

'Is aloe. From Mexico or some such place. Lots of cooks, they keep it in the kitchen to rub on burns. Works like magic, it does.' Then, abruptly changing the subject, 'Where's you getting a bike from? Only I can't have you coming here if it's a bit . . . dodgy. Can't take no chances, with Kevin still being on probation, even if he is away.'

Lily laughed, 'I reckon that probation officer's the best thing as happened for some of the lads round here,' she said. 'They get to go to the workshop, pick a bike and do it up and then is registered with the police and they gets to keep it. Means they can go looking for work, get in for appointments, all kind of stuff. Is a life-saver for those out here on the Levels.'

198

Ada was suitably impressed.

'So what officer is that then?' she asked.

'Oh, Alex Hastings,' said Lily. 'She as got Kevin out of Bristol. They's most of 'em good, up there in Highpoint, but seems she really does care.'

Ada smiled to herself, knowing what Alex continued to do for Kevin, stretching the rules as far as she could to enable him to travel with the fair and still report in to offices along the way, to meet the conditions of his order. She turned her attention back to Charlie.

'Well, you come over every afternoon and I'll dress that for you and keep an eye on it. Off you go now.'

He scuttled out of the door, setting the dogs off again as he ran down the path and out on to the road.

'And close my gate behind you!' Ada called after him. 'Now Lily, exactly how did he get a burn like that?'

Lily dropped her eyes and shuffled her feet under the table. Ada waited, fixing her with a hard look until finally her friend told her about the meeting in the pub. Charlie hadn't given her many details but Lily was no fool. She could spot a lie as easily as breathing and had pressed her grandson until he admitted some of his recent activity, a confession that earned him the dressing down of his life.

'So, let me get this straight,' said Ada thoughtfully. 'These two little idiots is buying drugs from some character called Max, out of Bristol. They's getting that poor crazy boy to carry them out to drop-off points on the Levels and some more idiots is collecting them and selling them on, right?'

Lily nodded, adding, 'Not no more though. Charlie might be scared of this Max but when I finished with 'un he was a sight more scared of me. There'll be no more of that on his part, believe me.' She took a deep breath and finished, 'Just wish I could get my hands on this Max. I'd teach him to hurt my lad like that.'

With the discovery of a third body on the Levels, all leave was cancelled and the hunt for the killer intensified. Reluctantly the Inspector bowed to pressure from his Assistant Chief Constable and contacted the Special Action Group based in Taunton. The 'Saggers', as they were called by most of the ranking officers, were universally unpopular, partly due to their elevated status and priority funding but mainly due to the arrogance with which they approached the rest of the force. Several days after the discovery of Andrew Cairns' body they swaggered in to the incident room at Highpoint, talking loudly and seating themselves on the front row, throwing amused glances at the resident team.

'Don't you worry boys,' said one sergeant. 'We'll get you out of this mess, just you watch.'

The rest of the Saggers nudged and sniggered amongst themselves until the station Inspector entered the room. Nodding to the newcomers, he called his team to the remaining seats and began his briefing. After running through the first two incidents he turned to their most recent victim.

'There are several interesting developments,' he said, as he began adding photographs to the already crowded incident board.

'Firstly we have recovered items at the scene which suggest this may be linked to our two previous victims, specifically a leather case with photographs of Mr Cairns' family and a badge from his employers. We understand from his widow these reflect important areas of his life. He had been unemployed for some time and was extremely pleased when Tor Security offered him a job just before Christmas.' The Inspector tapped the pictures before continuing. 'Similar items were discovered at the sites of the other murders and suggests they are some kind of trophy or statement from the killer.'

PC Brown was unable to keep silent any longer. Raising his hand he said, 'Surely if they were trophies the killer would have taken them with him?'

The Inspector paused and fixed him with a long, hard stare.

'That is one theory, yes – I was coming to that. To continue, there are some flaws in this idea as PC Brown has so kindly pointed out.'

There was more sniggering from the front row and Dave slid down in his chair, arms folded.

'One very important discovery is a blood trace, taken from broken glass near the scene of the last killing. It is likely the glass comes from a torch lens, very possibly the same torch used to bludgeon Mr Cairns, and in the absence of any matching marks on the victim it is very possible it comes from the killer. The forensic lab is checking for matches as we speak and hopefully can rule out the victim as a source very shortly.'

Dave tried not to feel aggrieved that the Inspector hadn't credited him with this discovery. After all, the senior officer had been quick enough to slap him down over the trophy claims. Trying to calm his irritation he took several deep breaths and forced his attention back to the front.

'Finally, we have some questions over method,' continued the Inspector. 'The first victim, Mr Franks, was drowned and there is no evidence of a struggle and no sign of other injuries. Mr Donnoley, on the other hand, suffered a fatal blow to the head delivered at close quarters from behind.' He drew the audience's attention to the gory close-up on Robert Donnoley's skull. 'He was then submerged in the canal and left, probably some hours after death. Finally, Mr Cairns was hit twice on the head, again at fairly close range. He also suffered some injuries to his ribs and thorax, almost certainly pre-mortem, before being thrown into the river at Brue to drown.'

There was a long silence as the room digested this information.

'Bloody hell,' muttered one of the Saggers.

Sergeant Willis raised his hand and, on a nod from the Inspector, rose to his feet.

'I know there's this stuff left around near the sites,' he said slowly, 'but strikes me, is maybe two killers.'

There was a babble of argument, cut short by a gesture from the Inspector.

'Well, maybe Donnoley and Cairns, they was targeted seeing as they's both patrolling the Levels. Donnoley, he was a River Warden and Cairns was watchin' that new build at Shapwick. Could be they was just in the wrong place and saw something they shouldn't have.'

'What about the first one?' asked a voice from the front row.

'Oh, poor old Micky, he was half-cut afore breakfast most days. Could be he just fell in and drowned on his way home from the pub.'

'Well, what about the wallet,' demanded another Sagger.

Sergeant Willis shook his head. 'I wondered about that,' he said thoughtfully. 'There was a note in it – big note too. Not like Micky to leave off drinking with that amount of money still in his pocket. Anyway, is we that sure it really is his wallet?'

The Inspector glanced around for confirmation but received only shrugs from the assembled company.

'Has no-one checked?' he demanded.

There was silence in the room.

'Well, sergeant,' he said, 'I think you'd better get over to Mr Franks place and see if you can find out, don't you?'

Chapter Thirteen

Alex knew she had to speak to Simon but she approached the task with reluctance. Although convinced he was an innocent dupe in the whole sorry business, she still had to face the possibility – however small – that he was more actively involved. Clinging to her new-found sense of optimism, she feared the disillusionment that would bring. Finally, she ran out of excuses and called him over to her office after his workshop session with Eddie.

Simon looked nervous, fidgeting and fiddling, eyes darting around to take in the pictures on the office walls and the growing clutter on her desk. With a flash of empathy Alex realized he was uncomfortable in such a small space and led him out into the teaching room. Sounds of raucous laughter and the stamping and clattering of feet floated in through the thin wall, evidence of the regular post-Friday pool match in the main room. Closing the door to minimize the disruption, Alex gestured to the chairs, inviting Simon to sit. He chose a place as close to the door as possible, facing the windows, and waited, his fingers twitching and feet shuffling, whilst all the time he avoided meeting her eyes.

Speaking softly and calmly, Alex talked about his 'lorry' and where he was 'driving' at the moment. This drew nothing but a shake of the head as Simon began to hunch over in his seat. Persisting, Alex moved on to talking about the Levels in general – how lovely the skies were in spring and how nice the weather had been for the past month, despite the rain in the last week.

'Don't bother I,' said Simon unexpectedly. 'I just drive, specially if I got a job on.'

Alex blinked with surprise. Simon rarely offered any comment on anything said to him and here he was, handing her the perfect opening for her questions.

'Of course,' she said smoothly. 'Are there many jobs around at the moment? Just, there seems to be less and less so any job must be good.'

Simon gazed out of the window and the silence stretched out, the sounds of the pool match getting increasingly rowdy. Just as she resigned herself to failure Simon spoke again.

'Is not much around so you's got to take what is. Even if is for someone you 'ent too sure of.' He turned his head and looked at Alex, straight in the eyes for the first time. 'Mum, she can't afford to be keeping us all, specially as they's cut the Social.'

'Do you remember some of your – deliveries?' Alex asked.

Simon nodded.

'Are you – booked – to do any more?'

Simon resumed his staring out of the window, shrugging his shoulders.

'Simon, I don't think it's a good idea, these – deliveries. I didn't realize you were having problems with the dole office and I promise I'll look into it and see what I can do to help. Just promise me you'll stop doing the deliveries, will you?'

'I'll need to see 'un, let 'un know,' said Simon. 'Can't be letting them down, can I?'

Them, thought Alex, them – so there were at least two others involved.

'Perhaps if you tell me their names, I can drive out and speak to them for you,' she suggested.

Simon shook his head firmly. 'Oh no, can't be doin' that,' he said. 'Any road, I've got plenty of petrol in the lorry so might as well go myself.'

He stood up to leave and was out of the door before Alex could react. Cursing herself for a clumsy fool, she stood, stretched and looked out into the main room. The noise level was rising all the time and there was a fair bit of jostling and poking with the cues.

'All right, that's enough,' she said, heading for the table. 'If you can't play nicely I'm going to lock up and no-one gets to play.'

'Don't be such a spoil-sport,' said Eddie, as he lined up a tricky shot to take the last of the stripes. Leaning over behind him, Paul Malcolm gave him a nudge and the shot went wide. 'You bugger!'

Paul grinned and picked up his cue.

'Reckon you're on Family Court next week,' he said. 'Best of three, you said and I'm about to send this – down!' He slapped the final spot so hard it flew off the cushion, bounced on the floor and rolled out of sight under the cupboards in the far corner.

'Forfeit!' Eddie crowed. 'My turn,' and he sank his last shot with a flourish.

Alex shook her head in mock despair. 'Sometimes you are worse than the lads,' she said.

The door into reception opened and Sue floated in, cigarette in hand and a gleam in her eyes.

'Challenge,' she said, seizing a spare cue. 'I'm sick of you men monopolizing the table every Friday.'

Eddie and Paul exchanged looks, reluctant to humiliate a colleague.

'Come on, don't tell me you're scared?' said Sue, dropping the balls deftly into the triangle and sliding the set towards the centre mark. 'Where's seven spot?'

Eddie sighed and lifted his cue.

'You dropped it, you get it,' he said to Paul. 'All right Sue, you're on. You can break first if you like.'

'Where the hell did you learn to play like that?' asked Alex as Eddie and Paul left the day centre, utterly humiliated and, in Eddie's case, five pounds the poorer. Sue smiled – the picture of innocence as she held the fiver aloft before stuffing it into her pocket.

'Just how long do you think I would have lasted running Intermediate Treatment groups unless I could play pool? I used to be reasonable but I got one of the real whizzes to teach me the last few weeks before I left to come here. Now, I think we should take this lovely bonus down to the supermarket and get something nice for dinner, don't you?'

When Sergeant Willis returned to the Highpoint police station with Micky Franks' wallet in an evidence bag, the fall-out reached every member of the team. The Saggers could scarcely conceal their delight at this show of ineptitude and their leading Inspector began to push for control over the entire operation. PC Brown escaped the immediate aftermath as he was on his way over to the forensic lab, the wallet sealed and tagged ready for testing. There was little doubt over its ownership however. Willis had spotted it as soon as he opened the door. Lying open on the kitchen table, surrounded by the mouldy remains of Micky's last meal, it mocked the sergeant and the constable accompanying him. There was no money in it, of course. Micky lived very much on the edge and he had died only a couple of days before his giro arrived. The policemen collected the meagre post from the door mat – bill, giro, note from the benefits office probably suspending his payments for non-attendance – the remains of a life turned sad by poverty and unemployment.

'Well, this puts rather a different perspective on events,' said Dr Higgins as he lifted the bag and peered at the contents. He glanced over at Dave and raised one eyebrow. 'Any theories?'

The constable had been puzzling over the problem the whole way over to Taunton.

'I don't know,' he said slowly. 'If it wasn't for the wallet we'd be marking this one down as an accident. And the candlestick of course.'

Dr Higgins's head shot up and he leaned over the desk. 'Candlestick? What candlestick?' he demanded.

Dave was surprised by his reaction.

'Surely you got that at the same time as the wallet,' he said.

Muttering angrily to himself, Dr Higgins hunted through the piles of paperwork on his desk. Files and folders were lifted and cast aside as he hunted for the evidence list from the Franks case.

'Let me see,' he said when he finally located the correct file. 'Clothing, wallet, twenty pound note ... candlestick, candlestick, nope.' He stopped at the bottom of the page, shaking his head. 'No candlestick listed here.'

Dave stepped forwards and took the page, turning it round to show the back where a single item was listed.

'Well I'll be damned!'

He blinked at the page and shouted over his shoulder to the technician in the next room.

'Fetch me box 15F will you? The Franks case, any time now please.'

The young man slid off his stool and disappeared into the evidence room on the far side of his workspace, reappearing a few minutes later with a small cardboard box which he placed none too gently on the desk in front of his boss. He had headphones round his neck, Dave noticed, and an irritating tinkling sound accompanied him as he walked back to his bench.

'You just can't get the staff,' said Higgins, only half in jest. 'I can't get a word out of that one. He just sits there listening to that awful noise they call music.' Dave watched as the assistant settled himself back on his chair, replaced his headphones and began nodding in time to the sound filling his head. He'd tried a walkman on several occasions himself but just couldn't concentrate whilst listening to music as well.

Dr Higgins meanwhile had pulled on a pair of thin latex gloves and was lifting items out of the evidence box.

'Clothes – rather rank I'm afraid, even without immersion in the canal, a few coins and a door key from his pocket, watch – stopped but probably no clue there. The spring is gone so it was not working when he went into the water. Let me see – ah, here's the original wallet.' He held up the bagged item and placed it next to the one Dave had provided.

'Yes, yours is much older. Thinking about it, this one is a bit smart for an old lush like Michael Franks. Now, where is that – candlestick you say?'

Dave nodded.

'How extraordinary.' He fished around in the box and pulled out the object in question, a rather battered brass saucer with a stub of white candle still wedged in the holder. They both looked at it for a moment.

'It's like something out of a children's story,' said Dave finally.

'That's because it *is* something out of a child's story,' replied Dr Higgins. 'Tell me, have you ever heard of the Drowners?'

All the way back to Highpoint police station Dave Brown wondered how he was going to explain Higgins' theory to the Inspector – even worse, to the Saggers. An old, old folk tale designed to frighten children, come to life in the 1980s. It was ridiculous, yet it did make some kind of sense. Dave knew a bit of psychology and he understood that although people might reject the tale as literal truth they were still likely to avoid the area as their subconscious warned them away from danger. If you wanted to keep people off the Levels, it was a very clever way of going about it.

Apart from the fairytale elements, however, there were a couple of problems with the idea. All three victims had personal possessions left at the scene, but Micky's wallet had been planted – and it was the only one with any money in it.

He pulled into the car park, turned off the engine and thought for a moment. He was fairly sure there had been no money on the other victims at all. Now, everyone had a bit of change in their pockets, even a spent-up loser like Micky – so the others had been robbed as well as killed. Dave opened the car door and made his way to the Inspector's office, trying to order his thoughts. There was no doubt in his mind any more. They were looking for two killers.

The day she finally got her cast off, Alex spent the first half-hour in the Ladies at the hospital, scratching and peeling the debris from her shockingly thin arm. She barely recognized the twig-like appendage, a horrible maggoty white thing due to the layers of skin and debris that had lodged under the plaster. The nurse passed her over to the care of the physiotherapy department, a group of people for whom Alex had enormous respect whilst still viewing them as a bunch of licensed sadists. After a lecture on not over-using her hand for the first few weeks (weeks, she thought – weeks?), she left the hospital with a series of follow-up appointments and a stiff rubber ball to squeeze in the affected hand. This was, apparently, the best way to build up the muscles in the lower arm and regain the flexibility in her fingers.

Alex flung the ball into the back of her car in disgust, not caring that it sank beneath the growing pile of debris on the back seat. She had taken to carrying a lot of her reference books and non-confidential items around with her, partly as she had so little space in her new office, partly as she no longer had confidence in the security of the probation office following the recent incidents with the files. There was an added bonus in that no probationer ever asked her for a lift – the car was too scruffy and cluttered for all but the most intoxicated clients to consider. Alex had watched Gordon struggle to keep his car usable for the past year and decided she was just not the cleaning type.

Deprived of the support, her whole arm was aching abominably by the time she got back to Highpoint and she could barely manoeuvre into the remaining space in the car park. Narrowly avoiding a close encounter with the bins, she locked her vehicle and headed for the workshop, where loud voices and the clattering of tools warned her all was not as it should be.

'What the bloody hell is going on here?' she demanded, throwing the door back on its hinges so it banged against the wall. There was a shocked silence and six pairs of eyes swivelled round towards her before six young men bent over their workbenches, the picture of industry. Alex nodded as she walked around the space, looking at each one in turn.

'Better,' she said finally. 'Much better. Would anyone care to tell me where your instructor has gone?'

There was a silence, broken finally as one lad accidentally nudged a spanner that tumbled to the floor, bouncing and clanging in the stillness.

'Pick it up,' Alex said without looking. 'Anyone – where is he?'

Amidst a shuffling of feet and exchange of glances one hand rose tentatively at the back of the group.

'Charlie – well, come on,' said Alex, noting the bandage on his hand with some surprise.

'He's gone for a fag,' muttered Charlie. 'Said to just carry on, so we did.'

Alex digested this news for a moment. Not happy, she thought. Not happy at all.

'Any problems with the bikes while I was away?' she asked finally. There was a universal shaking of heads. 'Right, well it's almost lunch time so clear up, all of you. I want every tool wiped clean and put back in the right place.' She raised her voice above the noise, as the group suddenly developed an astonishing amount of energy, working with speed and enthusiasm to earn their release. 'No-one goes until I've checked everything is tidy and put away! That means you, Brian.'

Brian Morris stopped at the threshold and looked over his shoulder at her, his eyes dark with resentment.

'Mine is all done,' he said.

Alex walked over to the workbench, which was, indeed, clear, clean and seemingly untouched by anything remotely like work.

'Show me your bike,' she said, smiling at him to take the sting out of any perceived reprimand. Brian scowled, returning reluctantly to the back room where the bicycles, all unclaimed and unwanted models donated by the police, were packed.

'That 'un,' he said, pointing towards the far corner.

Brian's bike, if it was his bike, was lodged under several others, seemingly untouched and certainly unloved. Inside, Alex sighed. Eddie's idea for the bike project had seemed perfect at the time – a chance to teach some practical skills, the opportunity to engage this most disaffected of groups and a way to provide free transport at the end of it. They had visions of young men riding their bikes around town, proud of their own work. Brian's rusty hulk, on the other hand, suggested not all were taking to the idea with quite as much enthusiasm.

'Are you finding this a bit difficult?' she asked him, keeping her voice down in the hope of avoiding attention from the rest of the bunch.

Brian shrugged, his attention already wandering to the door and freedom.

'Brian,' Alex persisted. His eyes turned back towards her. 'You get to keep the bike so you can choose any of them, you know. It means you can get around a bit on your own.' She felt like an aunt, wheedling a grown up nephew into taking her out for the day. Brian shrugged again.

'Don't matter,' he said finally. 'Can't ride no bike. Never learned.'

'It never occurred to me, some of the lads might not be able to ride a bike,' said Alex, exasperated by her own assumptions.

'We could arrange to teach them,' suggested Sue. 'Or maybe get someone in. They could do something like the cycling proficiency test.'

Alex groaned and rolled her eyes in disgust. 'I can't see a hulking great hooligan like Brian Morris doing the cycling proficiency test. Riding round cones, giving hand signals – and it's run by the police.'

'Umm . . .' Sue wrinkled her nose thoughtfully. 'Yes, I suppose you're right. I dread to think what sort of hand signals he would give under those circumstances. It's a bit of a shame though, makes it a bit pointless if he can't ride the bike at the end of it. Couldn't you teach him, in the evening when everyone's gone?'

Alex shook her head firmly. 'There's no way I'm spending my evenings in the yard teaching Brian to ride a bike. Anyway,' she held up her newly liberated arm for inspection, 'what the hell do you think would happen if I tried riding a bike with this?'

'You is lucky,' came Lauren's voice from behind them. 'At least you got the choice. I can't ride no bike, no matter how I try. Bikes 'ent made for people my shape.'

Alex was surprised by this. Lauren rarely referred to her diminutive stature and even more rarely admitted it stopped her doing anything. She was actually one of the most positive and capable people Alex had ever met.

'You've never ridden a bike?' Sue asked.

Lauren shook her head and settled herself on a spare chair at their table.

'Always wanted to,' she admitted, as she unpacked her lunch. 'I tried a couple of times but first I couldn't reach the pedals and when I tried standing up, I just kept falling off. And them levers on the bars . . .'

'The brakes?' suggested Sue.

'Yeah, them. Couldn't get my hands round 'em to pull properly.' She held one hand up, looking at the short, stubby fingers sadly. 'So was one of them things I never got to do. Seemed wonderful, to be able to just get on a bike and go off somewhere on your own. 'Course, Mum wasn't too keen on that anyway, so I think she was pleased, secretly like, I never managed it. Anyway,' she continued, changing the subject entirely, 'what do you reckon on Garry then?'

'Garry? What about Garry?' asked Alex, who was still musing over the problem of Brian and the bikes.

'Well, we's got a little competition going. Five to one, he comes back in a month, three to one he comes back in a few weeks but cracks up again, ten to one he goes somewhere else, fifty to one he gets sacked.'

Sue shook her head, torn between amusement and shock. 'That is unbelievably callous,' she said. Then after a moment, 'Put me down for back in a month.' She fished in her pocket and pulled out a crumpled pound note.

'What about you Alex?' asked Lauren, taking Sue's money.

'I really don't think we should bet on something like that,' Alex protested. 'The man's ill – it seems wrong somehow.'

'Come on, he's done nothing but pick on you since you started here last year,' Sue pointed out. 'What do you care – he's a bully, he's stupid and he's totally lost it as far as the work is concerned. Honestly, Alex, sometimes you are just too forgiving for your own good.'

Despite her reservations, Alex was tempted.

'All right, I'll go for several weeks and then off again. Probably because that's what I'm hoping will happen, if I'm honest.'

'Now who's being callous,' muttered Lauren as she scribbled their bets in a small notebook.

On her way back to the day centre Alex bumped in to a surprise visitor – two visitors, to be exact.

'I'm wondering if you can spare a moment,' came the unexpected and rather unwelcome voice of Ada Mallory from the corner. Alex jumped, lost in her own thoughts and oblivious to her surroundings as she pondered the Brian Morris problem.

'Oh, hi Ada,' she said, forcing her face into something resembling a smile. Her eyes darted towards a second figure sitting in the gloom, a diminutive woman who looked older than Ada, though there was something familiar about her, as when she stood and walked forward she seemed to radiate the same determination.

'Lily Dodds,' said the woman. 'Charlie's grandma.' With unexpected formality she held out her hand and Alex shook it, wondering what she had done to deserve this deputation.

'Look, I'm sorry,' said Alex, 'but I'm a bit busy at the moment – can this wait?'

'Would appreciate a few minutes,' said Ada firmly. 'We come in on the bus, special to see you. Got to be off soon or is a long walk home. Bus leaves at three and 'ent another till Friday.'

Alex knew better than to argue with Ada when she was in a determined mood. With a shrug of resignation she led the women through the main room and into her tiny office. Ada looked around and sniffed.

'This don't look much,' she said disparagingly. 'Why 'ent you in that nice room upstairs?'

'I need to be on hand,' Alex muttered, annoyed and embarrassed in equal amount. 'Here.' She pulled out a folding chair and set it by the desk next to the others. 'Please, sit down. How can I help?'

Ada settled herself on the 'client' chair with Lily depositing her bulk rather gingerly on the other.

'We got some information as might be helpful,' said Ada. Alex looked at her blankly as she continued, 'About these drownings and such. All them strange goings-on out round Shapwick.' Nodding with satisfaction, Ada sat back looking very pleased with herself.

Alex sighed heavily and raised a hand in protest. 'Look, I appreciate you coming all this way to see me but it's really nothing to do with me,' she said wearily. 'I think you should talk to the police if you have anything to help them. They are investigating this – that's their job.'

Ada glared at her across the desk and leaned forward, tapping one finger on the desk between them.

'Well, firstly I don't know as I want to talk to no police, after the way they treated my Kevin, and secondly we figured you would want to know, seeing as is a couple of your young lads is mixed up in it all. Still,' she sat up and folded her arms, 'if you think I should go tattle to the police afore you've had a chance to talk to them, well 'tis up to you.'

Alex gave Ada a hard stare, but she was hooked and her visitors knew it.

'I suppose this has something to do with Charlie?' she said turning to Lily Dodds.

Lily had the grace to look a little uncomfortable, shifting in her seat and clutching her handbag more tightly to her bosom.

'He's a good boy,' she said with a touch of defiance. 'He means well but – well, he's too easily led and – a bit idle really. If there's a chance of making a few bob without having to put hisself out he'll take it. He don't mean no harm.'

Alex considered this statement for a moment.

'Would this be related to his hand?' she asked. 'I saw it was bandaged up this morning, in the workshop. What happened?'

Lily Dodds made a hissing sound, sucking the breath in through her teeth. The transformation was startling as in an instant she changed from doting grandmother to avenging fury.

'Don't know who it was,' she said. 'Just some bloke from Bristol called Max. Charlie wanted to stop, see. This Max, he seems to have taken offence at that. Rob, he left sharpish but Charlie, well he was stuck there.'

'And if they 'ent stopped, is possible there'll be more people hurt, maybe killed,' added Ada.

Once more Alex found herself adrift in the strange, illogical world of half-truth, rumour and assumptions that always seemed to surround her encounters with Ada and the other Levellers. Some of her confusion must have showed on her face for it was Ada's turn to sigh impatiently.

'Was them as gave your lad the stuff to bring in to town. You know, that poor boy, thinks he's a lorry.'

'Simon?' said Alex. 'I spoke to him, just last week. I think he knew he shouldn't have anything to do with it but he said he needed the money.'

'Well, we all need the money,' snapped Lily. 'The way things is, 'ent nobody got nothing no more.'

'Right,' said Ada. 'Everyone needs the money but there's some things you don't do. Don't matter how much you needs the money, some things is not worth it. 'Cos they's just wrong.'

'And no good'll come from 'em either,' finished Lily.

The women stood in unison and nodded their thanks to Alex. It was like being confronted by two Russian dolls.

'So you'll sort it then?' said Ada, standing in the doorway.

Alex managed a rather sickly smile before flopping behind her desk. She hadn't a clue what she'd agreed to. Suddenly Ada's head popped back round the door.

'So you'll let us know what we'm should do, yes?' and she was gone again.

Not for the first time, Alex wished she had a stiff drink secreted somewhere in her desk.

Derek Johns woke, cold and stiff, to the sound of footsteps outside his hidey-hole. Moving very slowly, he got up out of his camp-bed and slid across to the slatted window, peering out into the early morning. A mist was rising from the surrounding marsh, drawn by the warmth of the rising sun. The light fractured in the moist air, sending miniature rainbows glittering across the landscape, and outside in the surrounding trees the birds lifted their heads and sang for joy. Scowling with anger at this interruption, Derek stepped over to the false wall, leaning his head against the boards that covered the entrance to his hidden room. Several voices and the sound of heavy items being moved around seeped through the partition. Police, he wondered, or someone looking to make use of the abandoned factory? Could even be thieves after anything saleable – metal scrap or old tools maybe. The scraping stopped and then he heard knocking on the wall, up at the far end he reckoned but moving in his direction. Time to leave. Again.

Gathering up his bag and his increasingly meagre belongings, he turned his attention to the slatted shutter covering the window at the back of the room. Originally designed to lift out in an emergency, it was swollen from rain and exposure to the relentless environment on the Levels and despite his considerable strength Derek could not make it budge. He grimaced as a flash of pain shot through his hand and up into his elbow, making the whole arm throb. The tapping was getting closer and it was only a matter of minutes before the searchers found the hollow section covering his room. Gritting his teeth against the pain, Derek shoved as hard as he could, forcing a section of the shutters to splinter noisily. There was silence in the main building behind him, the searchers presumably looking around for the source of the sound. Using his shoulder to push a big enough hole in the ruined window, Derek scrambled out into the cool morning air, hauling his bag behind him.

Not waiting for the intruders to locate him, he stumbled across the strip of yard to the back hedge, pushed his way through and plunged on towards the surrounding marsh. Derek was a Leveller, born in a small hamlet and raised in the watery landscape. From the moment he could walk he had picked his way through the water meadows and canals, and the treacherous land held no fears for him. Risking a glance behind him, he spotted the flash of a uniform and cursed softly. Police or the bloody plastic security men – either would be bad news. Distracted by the threat behind him, stiff and a little dizzy from lack of sleep, he slid down the incline from the old factory keeping the surrounding shrubs between him and the pursuers. Splashing round the edge of the marsh, he edged out towards a thick clump of reeds that offered firm ground and cover knowing if he could get out of sight they were unlikely to chance coming after him. The muddy ground sucked at his feet, slowing progress and making it impossible to move silently. A shout from behind indicated he'd been seen but his best option was to continue, pressing on through the swamp of the West Waste and hoping they were too afraid to follow. As the two uniformed men halted at the start of the mud, their voices fading into the distance, Derek pushed on across the treacherous landscape, a feral grin on his face. This was his land, his home and he had little to fear.

Suddenly his foot slipped and he lurched to the left, sliding towards a pool of stagnant water. The bag swung round off his shoulder, threatening to pull him over and, instinctively, Derek put out a hand to steady himself. His arm slid beneath the surface, up to his elbow, before Derek could throw his weight in the opposite direction. Moving as slowly as he could he tried to extricate his arm from the mud but his left foot was firmly mired and sinking, pulling him over, face down towards the marsh. As the cold struck through his soaked clothes, Derek tried not to panic. Thrashing about was a sure way to get yourself killed out on the Levels. His only hope was to distribute his weight and work his left side free without breaking the surface mud – unless he was going to call for help from the police. Not an option, he thought, wriggling his way out of the strap holding his bag. Loath to lose his remaining few possessions, he shrugged it away to the right where it landed in another puddle of water.

Relieved of the additional weight, Derek turned his full attention to freeing himself from the marsh but despite all his care, all his knowledge and experience his left side continued to slide down into the infinity of mud below him. Trying to keep himself flat, level with the surface, Derek reached out towards the reeds on the small rise, hoping somehow to use them as leverage. It was very cold in the water and he could feel the start of the shivers, the beginning of the end if he did not free himself in the next few minutes. Mentally he cursed the police, all the people who had driven him to this desperate life on the run, and himself for a clumsy, arrogant fool.

'No-one knows the marshes', his late father had told him. 'A safe path one day is gone the next. Just you learn the signs and treat 'um with some respect unless you want to end up rotting in the peat!'

The smell rising from the icy water filled his senses, the scent of earth and rotting vegetation overlaid by the smell of grasses from the new growth. As the water rose around his prone body Derek abandoned caution, lunging for the false hope of the reeds. The sudden movement disturbed his fragile balance and his right leg sank below the surface, sucked down into the mud, taking all hope with it. As the realization of his fate struck him, Derek ceased to be a rational, thinking person. Reduced to a creature trapped and dying, his instincts took over as he struggled in the mire, hands and feet snatching and clawing for some support, anything to keep him above the rising water. Suddenly his right arm struck something solid, just a few inches under the surface. Ignoring the pain in his festering hand Derek reached out, scrabbling through the mud until he felt something – wooden, solid and blessedly stable.

As his strength began to fade he grabbed the structure and hauled himself towards it, fighting the mud around his other limbs. After an agonizing time when it seemed he was too late to save himself there was a stirring around his left leg and his body moved an inch or two towards the security of the underwater framework. Slowly and painfully he pulled his frozen body towards the mysterious structure until he was able to haul himself up, almost clear of the marsh. For a minute he just lay there, trembling from cold and shock, his breath coming in ragged gasps. He was lying on some sort of wooden platform that ran a few inches under the surface of the water. Feeling around with numb fingers he came to the conclusion it stretched across the liquid mud, running from the clump of reeds behind him to more solid ground where the land rose to form the low hillock where the cider factory stood. Confusingly, however, he could not feel any supports underneath. It didn't seem to have any legs but something had to be holding it up. After a few minutes he felt a little better and began to move backwards towards the shelter of the reeds. A hundred yards or so away he could see the figures of the two men – police he reckoned – who were walking back and forth, examining the broken window and occasionally turning to peer out over the marsh. Squirming slowly through the thin layer of water to safety, he timed his movements carefully, lying flat when they were looking, trusting the mud and debris that soaked his clothes to camouflage his bulk.

As he reached the small section of firmer ground his foot hit something hard and he bit his lip to stop a curse at the jolting his knee had taken. Twisting round cautiously, making sure his weight was still supported by whatever it was he was lying on, he saw two low wooden uprights hidden in the undergrowth and a slow grin replaced the scowl on his face. He had stumbled on one of the Levels' oldest secrets, something he had searched for in vain throughout his youth. Safe in the shelter of the reed bank he examined the curved supports that held one end of the wooden pathway. Made of alder wood sourced from the surrounding wetlands, the uprights were set into the ground forming an 'x' with the boards of the path running through the middle. The recent rain and flooding had raised the water level to cover the bridge rendering it invisible to anyone who didn't know it was there. Derek peered out across the water, searching for the other supports. Now he knew what he was looking for, he identified the rest of the path hidden in the mud. The bridges and pathways offered a secret way across the supposedly inaccessible stretches of the Levels and stories of this hidden network had circulated the area for many years. Originally devised by settlers in Neolithic times, the tracks had been recreated and used for smuggling, illegal peat cutting and a wide range of nefarious activities over recent years. Derek lay on the small rise and considered the positioning of this particular path. Thinking about his recent sighting of Tom Monarch, he doubted very much it was coincidence.

Chapter Fourteen

It was difficult, Alex thought, trying to balance the two roles making up her job. The social worker in her wanted to sit down with Simon and talk through the issues surrounding his new 'job', looking at the wider implications and perhaps even making some sense of his obsession with 'driving' everywhere. She was sure that, given a bit of time, she could help him overcome his fixation. If she could do that, she might be able to find him a job, or training scheme or something that allowed him to earn some money – and then he wouldn't need to carry drugs for unknown dealers like Max from Bristol. So many of her clients ended up in trouble with the law because they solved their problems by committing offences. Alex still considered the most important part of her job was helping them find other, legal solutions round their difficulties. It seemed very simple in theory but in an economy with rising unemployment, limited opportunities and a system that demonized those dependant on the dole, it was sometimes almost impossible to achieve.

She picked up her diary with a sigh, going through the sessions she had planned and blocking in the other commitments that made up her professional life. By the time she had finished there was hardly any white space left on the pages, leaving her to reflect how the growing popularity of the day centre was fast becoming something of a mixed blessing. She'd taken a unilateral decision and sacked the workshop instructor, a decision high on moral grounds but low on practicality, as Gordon had pointed out when he found her struggling to put a bike chain back in place for one client.

'You can't do everything,' he'd scolded at the last supervision session.

'He just went out and left them,' Alex protested. 'You don't leave that bunch alone, especially in a workshop full of tools!'

Gordon agreed but suggested she might wait until they procured a suitable replacement should the situation arise in future. He was right, of course, though finding suitable replacements was proving difficult, unexpectedly so given the reported level of unemployment.

'Who wants to work with a bunch of criminals?' said Sue. 'Let's face it, the money isn't great and the level of hassle can be pretty horrendous sometimes. Besides, a lot of people are scared of them.'

Alex would have liked a bit more sympathy and a bit less logic as she wrestled with a rising case load and diminished staff to help run the groups Garry had promised at his original briefings. She was now getting referrals for courses and sessions she'd not had time to plan, let alone deliver. Life skills, she thought, should be a priority, like how to budget, shop and cook simple cheap meals as well as some first aid and health sessions. Perhaps some work on applying for a job and putting a letter together. One request that appeared almost every week was for an alcohol education course, hardly surprising considering the number of offences committed 'under the influence'. She flicked through her reference library, pulled out a couple of books and settled down to an evening of planning at her desk.

Around eight, Bert, the evening janitor, looked in to say good night.

'Got a big skittles match tonight,' he said. 'Is us against them bastards at the Iron Beehive. Reckon should be exciting evening if you want to come along.'

Whilst Alex generally avoided the local pubs in general and the Iron Beehive in particular, she was tempted. It was a big thing, to be invited out by someone in the office, even if it was for a skittles match, and she'd wanted to see how the game was played in Somerset. A lot of the pubs had old-fashioned skittle alleys and the rivalry between them was almost as fierce as it was at Carnival time. Looking at her outline for the alcohol course, still just headings and a few notes, she declined rather regretfully.

'Well, maybe next time,' said Bert. I'll be putting the door alarms on so don't you open no windows. You know how to set it when you is done?'

Alex assured him she did and then wasted a quarter of an hour wondering if she could change her mind and run after him, but finally she settled down again.

She was making some progress when the door alarm began to beep faintly across in the main office, indicating that someone had come in through the front entrance. Setting her pen down, she stepped over to her door and listened. The sound stopped without setting off the full alarm system. That meant whoever had come in knew the code. Alex cast around the room, looking for something she could use to defend herself if it came to a confrontation. The office was depressingly cluttered but offered nothing obvious in the way of a weapon unless she was going to creep up behind the intruder and hit them over the head with one of her many textbooks. She paused to listen again at the door, turning off the main light before pushing it open a fraction more. All was still and she decided to risk a quick foray into the main room where the pool cues rested temptingly on the table.

Before making a move, Alex glanced at the telephone. The obvious course of action, the most sensible thing to do, was to call the police but she could not get a direct line without going through the main switchboard in the office. If the intruder was in there, the lights would pinpoint her location the moment she dialled for a line out and they would either be gone by the time help arrived or – she didn't want to think about the alternative. Taking a deep breath she opened the door and slipped out into the darkness. Keeping close to the wall in the corridor, she felt her way towards the day centre. The connecting door was stiff, the wire-laced glass adding to the weight pressing back on her as she slid though the gap, pausing for a moment to let her eyes adjust to the gloom.

A trickle of light bled through the windows running along the top of the back wall, a sickly yellow from the sodium lamps on the road outside. Falling at an angle, it cast shadows at random across the floor, patches of darkness between her and the pool table where the cues nestled invitingly but just out of reach. As she stepped forward into the room there was a rustling from the direction of the reception area and she froze, sure her thundering heartbeat had betrayed her. She heard a soft footfall from through the main door and a shadow flicked across the reinforced glass. Fighting complete panic, Alex took two steps and grabbed the nearest cue, turning to flee for the dubious sanctuary of her office. There was a clatter as the cue, unexpectedly heavy in her weakened hand, caught the edge of the table disturbing the eight-ball that lurked, unnoticed by the centre pocket. As she dashed for the back door she heard the ball fall, running noisily down the central channel before hitting the rest of the set with a loud thud.

Bloody hell, she thought as she struggled with the fire door, why not announce your presence with a brass band? The door from reception banged open and she squeaked through and ran into her room, slamming the door and hauling the heaviest chair in front of it. Whoever it was certainly knew where she was now so she grabbed the phone, dialling as fast as her shaking fingers would allow. The handle rattled and twisted at her door and the intruder pushed, trying to force their way in.

'Police please, emergency!' she gabbled as the operator answered and began her scripted introduction.

'I'm in the probation offices at Highpoint,' she yelled, cutting across the smooth, calm voice. 'There's an intruder – they're trying to break down my door right now! Get someone out here – for God's sake hurry!'

The chair, wedged under the handle, moved a few inches and Alex dropped the phone on the desk and threw her weight against it. Whoever was outside gave a grunt as the door slammed shut again, then pushed back, twisting the handle furiously. As the two of them wrestled with the door the person outside hammered on the woodwork, beating a tattoo that echoed around the small office. Alex screwed up her face, holding on to the arms of the chair as she braced her feet against the desk, ready for another assault but suddenly all was still. In the unexpected silence she could hear the voice of the emergency operator, an incomprehensible squawking that issued from the phone, now out of reach on the far side of the desk. Too afraid to move she yelled towards the receiver.

'I'm holding the door closed! They're outside my room – I can't reach the phone without moving – just send someone, will you?'

There was a rather peevish sounding squawk in reply to this and then the line fell silent. Alex waited – let the 'phone off' tone come on, please let the 'phone off' tone come on she thought. Nothing. The line was completely dead. Either the intruder had disconnected it from the office, in which case they were no longer outside the door and she could try to make a dash for safety, or they'd cut the line outside her room – in which case they were still out there and she was trapped in here, hoping the police got the message, hoping someone was coming. With no phone she couldn't call anyone else. She was on her own.

Leaning her ear against the door she listened, ready to brace herself against the desk again at the first sound, but all was silence. Had they gone? She was trembling, more from shock than fear, and her legs felt as if they had turned to rubber. Tempting as it was, she doubted she could outrun the intruder at the moment, which left her exactly where she was, stuck in the office with only her hopes of rescue to hang on to. As the minutes dragged on, she felt a mixture of hope – maybe they really had gone – and despair – where the hell were the police? Still she waited, the silence and the darkness all around causing her to doubt her own senses. Her eyes seemed to see flickers of movement outside the office's small, barred window, her ears were filled with faint sounds that were probably the result of the blood pounding in her head but just might be the stealthy footsteps of the stalker returning to the barred door. She risked leaving the chair for a moment to put the phone back on, lifting it again in the hope of hearing the dialling tone, but it was completely dead. Replacing the receiver with something close to despair, she hefted the pool cue, relishing the weight in the handle. It was too long for her to wield comfortably and for a moment she considered breaking off the end before remembering the cues unscrewed in the middle. That would have really endeared her to Garry, she thought with a wry smile. Armed with the heavy end of the cue she returned to her post by the door. Nothing stirred outside and when she finally got up the nerve to open the door a fraction all was still in the corridor. Clutching her make-shift weapon she slipped out into the hallway, creeping one agonizing step at a time towards the closed door that led to the main room.

As she reached out to push it open she saw the exit into reception open slowly and the outline of a figure look round the door. The face was in shadow and she could only see the shape of a head turning towards her as she turned and bolted for the office once more. She could hear footsteps behind her, coming closer as she stumbled in the dark, tripping over her own feet and just making it to the door as a hand grabbed at her shoulder. Tearing herself free, she swung blindly with the weighted pool cue. There was a grunt of pain and then her assailant tore it from her hand.

'Now then, careful Miss Hastings. You could hurt someone with that,' said a familiar voice. The lights in the corridor came on and as she blinked against the unexpected glare Alex found herself staring into the welcome face of Sergeant Willis. To her shame and embarrassment she burst into tears as the policeman guided her gently back down the hallway, through the day centre and out in to the reception area. Here there were uniformed officers hurrying back and forth, securing the area whilst waiting for the photographer and crime scene team.

'What's going on?' she asked, bewildered by the activity after the eerie quiet of the last half hour. 'Did you catch them?'

Sergeant Willis nodded, his face grim.

'Oh yes, Miss. We got him alright. He's out in the van now, all covered up again. Don't you worry.'

Alex frowned at him. 'What do you mean – all covered up?'

Sergeant Willis dropped his gaze, squinting out through the front door to the police car parked outside. He cleared his throat before speaking.

'Well, when we got here he was . . . he'd, er . . .'

Just then a young constable hurried over holding out a pile of clothes.

'Should I put these in the car with him or are they evidence, Sarge?' he asked.

Alex stared at the bundle for a moment.

'I recognize that jacket,' she said. 'And that shirt. Those are Garry's clothes.'

The next morning officers and staff arrived at work to find it was a crime scene. Gordon was already in attendance when Lauren rolled up in her adapted car and hurried to intervene when she tore into the police who were parked in her disabled space.

'Just 'cos they's coppers they think they can do what they like,' she grumbled as an apologetic Gordon hustled her inside and upstairs to the common room. In the yard, several constables looked at one another in frank disbelief at her fluent and inventive language.

'Reckon he's got his work cut out there,' said one, shaking his head. In response to his colleague's puzzled look he explained. 'Dave Brown – you know, the smart fast-track one, working with the Saggers at the moment over that thing on the Levels. Well, *that*,' he pointed to Lauren's car, parked at an angle near the door where she'd left it, 'is his girl-friend.'

'Bloody hell,' muttered his colleague.

Lauren settled herself in her chair and waited, still fuming. Pauline and Gordon had their heads together over in a corner, she noted. Lots of muttering and occasional anxious glances towards the door as each new member of the team made their entrance.

When Alex, looking very pale and tired, arrived Gordon hurried over, taking her arm and leading her to a chair away from the rest of the group. Sue followed her in and Lauren beckoned her over, judging that she might know what was going on. From the look of her drawn face, Sue had a pretty good idea of the night's events but she was reluctant to share them.

'We need to wait,' she said. 'Gordon needs to talk to everyone – that's why he's called us all together. *No*, Lauren!' she finished, turning away when Lauren became insistent. Just then Ricky trailed in, half-asleep as always and looking as if he'd been up half the night as well. For a wild moment Lauren thought maybe he'd been caught breaking in to the office but the continuing police presence made this unlikely. They were not going to let him wander about the scene of his own crime so, sadly from her perspective, he was not the mystery prowler. She settled back in her seat and waited as the last of the staff arrived and the babble of speculation rose around her.

Gordon finally managed to restore order and begin his announcement closer to ten o'clock than the official start time. He was brief, factual and as neutral as possible but it was difficult to present the previous night's events in anything but a scandalous light. Garry Nugent, their senior probation officer, had suffered a spectacular nervous breakdown and was responsible for the recent break-ins at the office. The police, he said, were trying to unravel the motive behind some of his actions but were hampered by the fact he refused to speak to them. Or refused to speak intelligibly, anyway. Garry, it seemed, had been visited by God himself and had been granted the gift of tongues. When he was being questioned, all the police got was an incomprehensible babble.

'Well shit,' muttered Sue. 'Messiah complex do you think?'

Alex shrugged, too tired to really care. She had been unable to sleep last night when finally getting home and despite several strong cups of coffee this morning felt like curling up in a corner and just drifting away for the day. She forced her attention back to Gordon who was outlining the arrangements in place whilst the police still occupied parts of the building. The top floor, he told them, was sealed off for the moment whilst they searched Garry's office. A locked cupboard at the back of his room had been found, along with a paper shredder and a large pile of client files, many of them current. The floor was ankle-deep in shredded paper and cardboard.

'So that solves the mystery of the missing paperwork,' he concluded. 'I have requested a list of all the surviving cases so we can begin the task of restoring what is missing, as far as we can. Some notes may still be on your dictaphone tapes.' He nodded towards to the officers. 'Take a moment to check before reusing anything as that may be the only copy.'

It was a sombre little group that left for their offices as the meeting broke up. Lauren sidled over to Alex who gave her a stern look.

'I can't talk about it,' she said. 'I'm probably going to be a witness so I can't discuss it with you.'

Lauren managed to look both hurt and indignant simultaneously. 'Just wondered what the exact outcome might be,' she said. 'Reckon he's not coming back so we'll need to sort out the bets, won't we.'

Alex didn't know whether to laugh or yell at her. Everything she had gone through last night, all the disruption, suspicions, extra work they had put in – and Lauren seemed most concerned about settling the bets. Sometimes, she thought, as she tramped down the stairs and made her way to her office, sometimes she was sure she would never understand these strange and unpredictable people.

Phil Watson was nervous. It showed in his rigid posture, the tiny trembling of his hands as he tidied the bar, repeatedly wiping down the same patch in front of him. It showed, especially, in the slight sheen across his forehead. He jumped each time the door opened and a customer came in and he replied to the greetings and orders in a vague way as if listening to something far away, something only he could hear. In truth, he was hearing the tearful voice of his wife as she whispered in protest at Max's treatment of little Charlie Dodds. He was hearing his mother scolding him for his cowardice, for standing by as a bully picked on someone weaker. And most clearly of all he could hear his own voice railing at the stupidity of allowing these sorts of people to buy his loyalty – or at least his silence.

His train of thought was interrupted by the abrupt arrival of two new customers – new in the sense he'd never seen them in the Royal Arms before. He knew who they were, of course. Everyone on the Levels knew Ada Mallory, and his nephew had been a school friend of Charlie Dodds. Phil and Marie had often helped collect the boys from school and drive them over to football matches or to Glastonbury for an afternoon out. Phil had a deep respect for Lily Dodds, the way she had stepped in and looked after Charlie when his parents had abandoned him. Now he found it hard to look her in the face.

'What can I get you ladies?' he said rather gruffly.

Ada looked around at the half-empty bar, taking in the dusty tables, the unwashed windows and the cobwebs hanging from the picture frames.

'Nothing for me,' she said firmly. 'Just a word in private if you don't mind.'

Her tone left Phil in no doubt she didn't care if he minded or not really. Calling for Marie to take over the bar, he lifted the flap in the counter and beckoned the two women through to the back. Marie had been preparing today's lunch-time special and the rich aroma of chicken and bacon stew filled the kitchen. As she stepped through the door, Lily peered around and gave a sharp hiss as she spotted the pot bubbling away on the stove. Ada laid her hand on her friend's arm gently before turning to the landlord who stood in the centre of the room, looking thoroughly miserable.

'I guess you know why we is here,' Ada continued. 'That was right shocking, what happened to Charlie. Now!' She held up her hand to stall any protest. 'I know was not your doing and you was out the back when it happened.' Ada paused, glancing towards the door leading to the bar. The clinking of glasses was clearly audible along with a low hum of conversation. It was obvious to them all that, despite Phil being in the next room, he must have heard everything that went on that afternoon.

'I know,' said Phil. 'I've been thinking about it – can't get it out of my head to be honest.' He turned to Lily, holding his hands out in supplication.

'If I could, I'd go back and change it but is too late now. I was a right coward and if there's anything I can do to put it right, you just say.'

Ada nodded her head vigorously. 'Reckon there is,' she said. 'He 'ent working down here on his own say-so, right?'

Phil sighed, hesitating before shaking his head. He had an idea of where this was going and he didn't like it at all.

'You know I can't say,' he mumbled. 'More than my life's worth – and more important, I'll not do anything to bring trouble on Marie.'

Ada pursed her lips together and gave him her best hard stare.

'Seems to me you already brought trouble here. Invited it in and gave it a drink too. Seems to me you need to sort this out afore the police gets it into their heads to come round

231

looking to talk to all them as was here the night poor old Micky Franks died.'

Phil felt the corner of his eye twitch as he tried to face down his formidable visitor. He was sure Ada was bluffing – but could he take the chance? As he struggled for composure there was a call from Marie at the bar.

'Phil, can you come out? Someone to see you – says it's urgent.'

Beating a hasty retreat, Phil slid through the door and found himself face to face with possibly the second to last person he wanted to see at this exact moment.

'Now then Phil,' said Tom Monarch pleasantly. 'A word in private, if you please.'

Before Phil could stop him, he had brushed past and opened the kitchen door.

'Ladies,' he said as he found himself facing Ada and Lily.

'Tom Monarch. Well now, I should have guessed.' Ada's voice dripped scorn as she squinted up at the big gang leader. Tom blinked at her for a moment and then a great grin split his face.

'Ada – is that you then? My, it's been – how long now?' He stepped over and lifted her off her feet in a great hug.

'Put me down you great oaf!' said Ada, trying to wriggle free.

Tom was laughing as he let her go.

'That's no way to treat an old friend,' he protested. 'You're looking good Ada. Sorry to hear about Frank by the way. Nasty business that.'

Ada's husband, Frank Mallory, had been one of Derek Johns' victims and the discovery of his mangled remains in a freezer formed the basis of many nightmares for the policemen who had found him. Ada had buried what was left of Frank but sizeable portions had not been recovered, including his head and hands. Local legend already had Derek Johns marked down as a cannibal and despite the estrangement from her weak and ineffectual husband, Ada still found it difficult to talk about what had happened to him.

'Thank you,' she said softly. There was an uncomfortable silence in the room and Phil hovered in the doorway trying not to draw attention to himself.

'So Phil,' said Tom before the landlord could slip out again, 'seems to me you've got some explaining to do.'

'I 'ent said nothing,' said Phil. 'They come here to ask about Lily's lad. Seems he was picked on by some bloke from Bristol, in the bar last week, it was. They'm hoping I might know who he was. I was just explaining I can't help 'um. Lots of people come in – don't mean I know who they is.'

Lily, who had been hovering at the back watching proceedings with interest chimed in.

'Maybe you didn't give no names but I reckon we know enough to see something wrong is going on around here and when it starts hurting my boy I'll not stand for it. I want to know who this Max is and where I can find him.'

Tom and Phil looked at Lily in astonishment but she folded her arms, pulled herself up to her full height and stared them down.

'I mean it,' she added.

Tom threw his head back and burst out laughing.

'I can see you do,' he said as he recovered his composure a little. 'However,' his face grew serious, 'I would not recommend you go looking for him yourselves. Max is a rather impetuous young man and he has a lot of equally unrestrained friends. I'm sorry I ever introduced him to the Levels. That was my mistake and I apologize for it, but I think I should be the one to set things straight. Perhaps you could spare a few moments to tell me exactly what happened to – your son is it?'

'My grandson, Charlie,' said Lily.

'Surely you're not old enough . . .' began Tom, but Ada interrupted him.

'That's enough of your smooth talk, Tom. You and your fancy long words too. We'll not be fobbed off by a few promises so you listen and then you tell us what you intends to do. And if we don't like it then we'll just sort it out ourselves.'

Tom cast Phil a helpless look. He had forgotten just how determined (some said bloody-minded) Ada could be and there was no reasoning with her when she was in this mood.

'Perhaps we could avail ourselves of the upstairs room?' he asked. 'I would be happy to order you ladies some lunch and we could sit and discuss this in a civilized manner.'

Ada hesitated for an instant before following a relieved Phil towards the door.

'I don't see why not,' she said. 'But don't think we're going to agree to whatever you say just 'cos you's buying lunch.'

Tom smiled rather fondly at her and shook his head. 'The thought never entered my head, Ada,' he said.

Returning to work at the Highpoint station that Monday, Dave was both amused and alarmed by the stories of the break-in at the probation office.

'So why did he take his clothes off?' he asked Sergeant Willis, who shot him a sour look.

'You're the one with a degree lad, you tell me,' he replied. 'Never mind that for now, come over here and give me a hand. I'm right worn out, been up half the night and I can't make head nor tail of this'

He led the way through the crowded main room to a semi-private corner. Here Willis had his desk, phone and filing cabinet but today the table was taken up by what seemed to be a large plastic television with a keyboard sticking out from the front.

'Wow, you've got a computer!' said Dave, throwing both professional reserve and protocol away in his enthusiasm.

'Glad you recognized it. Most of that lot didn't even know what it was when it arrived.' Willis sat down at the desk and stared at the blank screen glumly.

'What have you got on it?' Dave asked. 'What about the operating system – has it got DOS? Do you know what version?'

Sergeant Willis shrugged his shoulders and sighed heavily.

'I thought you might know something about them,' he said. 'Do you think you can possibly explain how it works and why it's supposed to help us without lapsing into a foreign language?'

Dave opened his mouth, caught sight of the suspicious expression on his sergeant's face and closed it again.

'I'll do my best,' he said. 'Have you ever used a computer before, Sir?'

'We went on a training day, last year it was. I think they looked like this but they were all lined up in a room and turned on ready for us. The stuff we did, it wasn't much different from using the typewriters. Except it was a bit easier to correct a mistake, I remember that. When they said we'd be getting machines this year I thought it would be just the same, but this . . .' He banged on the case in frustration. 'This just sits here and don't do nothing. Just takes up the whole bloody desk. Weighs a ton too.'

Dave looked alarmed.

'You didn't move it while it was switched on, did you?' he asked.

Sergeant Willis laughed, a short, barking sound.

'Might have done,' he said. 'Might have done if I'd the faintest idea how to switch it on in the first place.'

Dave nodded, relieved and frustrated in equal parts. He was itching to get his hands on the computer but the only way that was going to happen was if he showed his sergeant how it worked.

'Okay, may I sit down?' he said, drawing up a chair. Sergeant Willis nodded, shuffling his own seat over to one side in the cramped space.

'First we check there's no disk in the drive,' said Dave, peering around the front of the computer for the slot. 'Ah, here you are. Wow, this is a really modern model. Look – it takes 3½ inch floppies.' He reached out and lifted the lock on the gate to the disk drive. Beside him Sergeant Willis rolled his eyes and gave a soft groan.

'Sorry, sorry. Look – the slot is 3½ inches wide. This means it takes a newer, better sort of disk. They're stronger because they've got a rigid plastic cover and they take a lot more stuff. You should have one with the start-up program on it somewhere. Maybe in the plastic bag there . . .' He pointed to a sealed bag containing closely printed sheets of paper, some cables and a very thick, complicated looking book.

Reluctantly, Sergeant Willis broke the seal and tipped the contents out on the desk. He picked up the manual and flipped through it before he spotted a much smaller flyer labelled "Start Here!" in bold letters. Abandoning the manual he began to read out the instructions that, in theory, would take him step by step through setting up and using his new computer. Dave waited, curbing his impatience although he knew from the cables lying around loose what the next few steps should be. His hands twitched as he watched Willis picking up each item, matching it to the pictures in the booklet and setting it back on the desk.

'Oh come on, Sarge,' he said finally. 'I bet you count all the screws and bits from your MFI furniture before you start!'

Sergeant Willis laid the booklet on the desk and turned to look at him.

'Of course,' he said. 'Makes no sense, just jumping in. You need to be careful, do it right the first time.'

Dave slumped back in his chair trying not to grit his teeth in frustration as one of the men across the room called his name.

'Dave – Dave? Phone call for you.'

Sergeant Willis was on his feet, reaching around the computer to plug in the mains cable and he waved a hand at his constable.

'Go on. I'm okay here for a bit. You go and do some real work now.'

Feeling slightly hurt by this dismissal Dave trooped over to the phone but the voice on the other end snapped him out of his sulk in an instant.

'Are you sure?' he asked. There was a stunned look on his face as he replaced the receiver.

'What?' asked the owner of the phone.

'Oh bloody hell,' Dave whispered and hurried back over to Sergeant Willis.

'Sir,' Dave swallowed, his mouth suddenly dry with anxiety. 'Sir, that was Taunton on the phone. They've had a report from Dr Higgins at the lab. That piece of glass from the torch . . .'

Sergeant Willis twisted his head round and dropped the cable on the desk. 'Spit it out Constable. What about the glass?'

Dave took a deep breath before continuing.

'It had fingerprints on it,' he said. 'Most of them were from Andrew Cairns, obviously, but there was one from someone else. They matched it with the records – Sir, it's from Derek Johns.'

Chapter Fifteen

Alex rounded up her gang of attendees who were clustering in the far corner of the car park, eyeing the continuing police presence with suspicion. There was very little she could do with them as the day centre was still being photographed and would need cleaning of fingerprint powder before it was fit to be used again. Reluctantly she told them to go home, checking their names against the register and handing out bus money before reminding them they were booked in for the workshop later in the week and were expected to attend regardless of what was going on in the main building.

'So we's free to go then?' said Brian hopefully.

Alex nodded, her frustration at yet another break in the routine evident on her face.

'Try to use the time constructively, Brian,' she said wearily. 'Perhaps a trip to the Job Centre, as you're in town.'

Brian screwed up his face in disgust. 'They got no real jobs in there no more,' he said. 'Lots of this "Community Programme" bollocks but 'tis all.'

Alex wasn't sure she approved of the Community Programme herself but anything legal would be an improvement where most of her charges were concerned.

'It would give you some experience,' she said. 'A chance to earn a bit of money too.'

'Most of 'em, they pays the dole and maybe a tenner more,' Brian protested. 'Cost more'n that gettin' in to town for a week. Reckon I'm going to work for nothin' – not likely.'

'Yeah,' chipped in Charlie from the back of the group, 'there's no decent jobs left now. Everyone calls 'em "Community Programme" so they can get us to work for pennies. Same jobs as used to have decent wages, just made cheaper. 'Tis a con.'

There was a general murmur of agreement as most of the lads nodded their heads, hands in their pockets. Alex was struck by how few of them seemed to be smoking nowadays. That was a good thing, obviously, but she suspected it was down to lack of money rather than common sense or a proper regard for their health. In the distance the clock on the Cornhill Exchange rang the hour and Brian was off, heading for the gate.

'Got to see a man about some stuff,' he yelled over his shoulder and was gone off up the road before Alex could react.

'Is not stuff like that,' said Charlie softly, seeing her anxious face. 'He's getting some things from a mate. Nothin' illegal. Well, not really. I mean . . .'

He stopped, looking flustered as Rob kicked him on the ankle. 'Well, I'll be off then,' he finished with a rather sickly grin.

Alex picked up the register and made her way across the yard, running her eye down the list of names before stopping and yelling at the group as they drifted off.

'Simon! He's on the list – anyone know where he is?'

There was a general shaking of heads and several youths made 'cuckoo' gestures, swirling their fingers round beside their heads.

'Probably off on the Levels again,' came an anonymous voice as the last of the group disappeared.

Alex ground her teeth in frustration. 'Off on the Levels again' – bad news with the increased police presence, not to mention an unknown predator stalking people seemingly at random. She hurried back inside and hounded Sue until she produced the file again.

'Where the hell is Lower Godney?' she demanded, poring over the faded carbons.

'Oh, you don't want to go out there,' said Sue airily. 'Horrid little house with a baby crawling around with no nappy on. Honestly, I'm sure I picked up something nasty last time. Anyway, Simon's not there most of the time. Shows he's got some sense I suppose.'

'If he's not there then where does he live?' demanded Alex. 'Come on Sue, he could be heading for a whole world of trouble if the police pick him up and he's carrying those horrible drugs. They won't care if he doesn't understand or even if he doesn't know about them. They'll just lock him up and you and I both know that will probably kill him.'

'You're frightfully melodramatic today,' Sue observed.

'So would you be if you'd had the week I have,' Alex snapped.

Sue refrained from pointing out that, although she hadn't been hunted through the day centre in the dark she had been woken by Alex's return and sat with her friend for several hours whilst the police took statements, fingerprints for elimination and consumed a considerable quantity of coffee. Consequently she was feeling pretty worn down herself.

'Look, what can you do?' she said, trying to be conciliatory. 'You can hardly watch him every moment of the day. If he's not here tomorrow, well you'll have to chase him but give yourself a break today.'

Alex remembered Gordon's words of wisdom, felt her heart rate fluttering with all the caffeine she had consumed in an effort to keep herself going and finally allowed common sense to prevail. A quick word with Gordon and she was off home for some much needed rest.

That evening Sue let herself in to the house and was greeted by the aroma of roast chicken. Alex was up and feeling better, she thought with a grin.

Determined to enjoy a good meal at home, she refused to discuss the day's events with her friend until they had eaten, but once the dishes were cleared away Alex could not be deterred.

'We could ask the police to drop by . . .' Sue had suggested hopefully. Alex didn't even grace this idea with a reply. There was nothing like a sudden visit from the police to send Simon racing out in to the night, even if he hadn't done anything wrong.

'Well, I'll come with you,' said Sue, trying not to let her reluctance show.

Alex smiled and shook her head. 'No, you don't need to put up with my obsessive ideas,' she said. 'I'll be fine – probably only gone for an hour or so. Don't worry, I'm feeling fine now. I got to sleep all afternoon, remember?'

Sue watched through the window as Alex pulled away in her battered old Citroën. Sometimes she wondered just how safe the car was. It seemed to keep going, but in bad weather often needed a jump-start and the eccentric hydraulic suspension gave her the shivers. Anything that could fail and take the brakes out at the same time was a really bad idea in her view. Suppressing a twinge of guilt at abandoning her friend, she returned to the comfort of the back room and the dubious joys of evening television. Just as she pressed the on button the phone rang and she answered it with a sigh. It was the police. They were sorry they hadn't called earlier, said the desk sergeant. Just to warn Miss Hastings, Derek Johns was still alive and out on the Levels. Nothing to be alarmed about – they were hunting him right now. Just sit tight, continued the patronizing voice on the end of the line. Let the police handle this. Sue replaced the receiver, her hand shaking. Drawing back the curtain, she peered out at the night. Oh

Alex, she thought. Where the hell are you? And what the hell do I do now?

Simon Adams loved to run. He relished the freedom it gave him, the breeze in his hair and the sense of control over himself and his body. Wrapped in his fantasy lorry, he pounded the streets and footpaths of the area in all weathers (after all, he had a cab to keep him dry and warm), alone with his thoughts. Simon's mind could best be described as 'fuzzy', and he had serious issues with the gap between himself and the real world, but he was nevertheless talented in his own way. With an instinct for the terrain, the ability to find his way without maps or signs, and tremendous stamina, Simon could run for hours at a steady pace, burning up the miles, without even getting out of breath.

This evening he was running for pleasure, out across the Levels without worrying about being stopped by the police or arriving too late for his delivery. It had been several months since he'd been able to choose his own routes and he gloried in the cool evening air, admiring the moon as it rose in the dark sky. His bare feet rustled in the grass and the mild air felt good against his body. He settled in to a steady rhythm, moving with a curious grace across the broken landscape of the Levels. Shifting marshes and hidden bogs held no fears for him as he cut across the reeds and peatlands, hopping over small ditches and jumping larger rhynes. As he ran he hummed a strange and wordless song to himself, the music he heard as he travelled through the countryside.

Suddenly he stopped humming and listened, straining his ears as he ran. Above the sound of his feet and deep, regular breathing was a different kind of music. A soft, hypnotic swirl, like a flute piping gently but insistently in the distance. Without realizing it, Simon slowed, his running falling into the slower cadence of the ghostly sound. As it faded away he slowed to a halt, confused and a little afraid as he peered around in the evening gloom. A memory stirred, long buried in his early childhood, the legacy of an imaginative babysitter telling stories to frighten her charges into compliance. Shifting from foot to foot he waited, holding his breath as he waited for the music to resume. There was a slow swirling from his left and Simon started, leaning forwards as he strained to make out the sound. Then it seemed to get louder, as if the invisible musician were approaching through the twilight. Simon was off like a startled rabbit, bounding over the rough ground, leaping the narrow channels and splashing around the pools of water that seeped across the wetland.

All grace, all rhythm gone, Simon fled in panic, his childhood terrors filling his mind and blinding him to the more immediate dangers. Stumbling in the growing gloom, Simon tripped on a concealed dip, his feet sliding away from under him as he crashed headfirst into a shallow stream. Spluttering and coughing, he tried to haul himself out only to slide further in the mud, his arms sinking deep into the slurry lining the bottom of the ditch. The music swirled around him mockingly as the terrified youth struggled to free himself from the treacherous mire that seemed to suck at him, threatening to pull him back every time he managed to grab for support from the surrounding foliage.

After what felt like an age Simon finally succeeded in hauling himself out of the ditch and he lay gasping for breath on firmer ground, shivering as the breeze struck through his soaked clothing. As his breathing settled a little he was relieved to hear only silence around him. The haunting music was gone and he began to feel a bit better as he got to his knees and then up on his feet. Even Simon realized he needed to get home and out of his wet clothes before he got any colder so he took a moment to look around, seeking the quickest and safest route. In the distance, ahead of him, came the murmur of voices. Indistinct but clearly male and coming closer, they carried on the light breeze. Simon's heart began to pound as he twisted round, frantically trying to decide which direction to choose. Ahead were unknown people, almost certainly up to no good all the way out here but he could not bring himself to retrace his steps for behind him was the terrible, ghostly music and all it stood for. Trapped like a hunted animal, Simon dropped to his knees and curled up into a ball, shaking and trying not to cry as the voices approached. Perhaps, he thought, perhaps they wouldn't see him. Perhaps they would pass by and he could escape. He curled up as small as he could and waited.

Tom had been reluctant to show the secret bridges to Max but it was necessary, a vital part of the plan he and Ada had put together in the upstairs room of the Royal Arms. It wasn't exactly the sort of thing he would normally come up with, which was probably a good thing. Max was a nasty, violent piece of work but he was not stupid and he had a gift for reading other people. Tom was sure if he had tried to deal with the problem alone, Max would have seen through him in an instant. Ada, however, had reserves of cunning and imagination he had not previously appreciated. He doubted very much that Max could anticipate what she had in mind. He just wished he could contact his brother and let him know why he was breaking the promise he had made. If Milosh discovered what he'd done, he would see it as the final betrayal and despite their long estrangement, or perhaps because of it, Tom had begun to yearn for his brother's approval. He sighed and rose to his feet, looking around the clean, empty little cottage he called home. There was no more time to brood. He straightened up and headed out of the door to meet Max and his little gang of Bristol boys.

Max was parked up in a lay-by off the Glastonbury Road, his shiny new Sierra blending in as well as a giraffe on a bicycle. Tom pulled his shabby old Vauxhall in behind the oddly styled silver car and tried not to let his exasperation show on his face. Max's Ford might be the car of choice for hoodlums in the city but out on the Levels there were few better ways to get the attention of the local constabulary. He moved round to the driver's side and tapped on the window, making sure his face was visible to the occupants. There were four young men in the car and the couple in the back looked jumpy, twitching round and glaring at his appearance. Amateurs, Tom thought. Any one of *his* boys would have already noted his arrival, jotted down the registration and been ready for just about anything. Max wound down the window and stared up at him.

'What ho, Max,' said Tom as cheerfully as he could. 'Ready for a bit of a walk then?'

There was some muttering from the other occupants and one lad said, 'Didn't say nothing about no walking. Got my new boots on. I 'ent plodding through no mud nor nothing.'

Max snapped his head around and snarled, 'Well you can bloody well stay here then. Need someone watchin' the car and reckon that's about all you's good for.' He pushed open the car's door, narrowly missing Tom, and stepped out, stretching his heavy frame.

'Right, the rest of you, on your feet,' he shouted, and the other two young men scrambled to obey, leaving New Boots in the back looking decidedly mutinous. Max leaned through the open window and removed the keys from the ignition.

'Just in case,' he said with a smirk. 'And no smokin' in the back neither. You want a fag, you get out the car. And don't be leaning on my paintwork.'

Well, thought Tom, who would have thought tough-guy Max was so precious about his car. He turned his back and stared out over the darkened landscape. A cool wind began to pick up, swirling the debris in the lay-by in miniature whirlpools and the new leaves on the surrounding trees hissed against one another. Tom felt a chill run up his spine and suppressed a shiver. He was not a superstitious man. Any apprehension he felt was easily explained by the risky business he was planning. Shoving his hands in his pockets he turned back to the bunch of Bristol boys who were still squabbling by the car.

'Reckon we'd better be moving if you'm wanting to get there and back afore midnight,' he said pleasantly. Ignoring the group, he felt in his bag to check the equipment was all there, slung it over his shoulder and set off along the narrow grass verge towards a gap in the hedge. The shuffling of feet from behind him indicated the bunch had at least started off. Moving softly and easily around the hedges and across ditches, he led his little band of followers along a footpath before turning off and seeming to follow a faint trail in the grass. After several minutes this too faded away and Tom struck out into the heart of the marshes, his confident movements a stark contrast to the tripping and swearing that followed him. He suppressed a grin as he listened to the sounds of the lads from Bristol slipping and splashing around the edge of the marshes and took great delight in leading them further into the boggy wasteland before stopping and gesturing for silence. Max ploughed over to him, teeth gritted in fury.

'What the bloody hell you think you'm playing at?' he demanded. 'What we doin' out here? 'Ent nothing for miles so why is we in this . . . this bloody swamp then?'

Ignoring his hostility, Tom waited for quiet before answering.

'That's rather the point, 'ent it,' he said. 'A few farms, see – over there – so you need to tell them,' he nodded towards Max's two followers, now looking thoroughly wretched, 'to pipe down a bit. Lot of water around here and sound carries real well over water. Wouldn't want to be attracting too much attention now, would we?'

Max stared at Tom, holding himself very still before swivelling round and barking at the other two.

'Shut the fuck up! You don't like it out here – maybe you can just bugger off back to the car an' wait there. 'Ent like you's any use anyway.'

Tom tried not to let the satisfaction show as he said, 'Maybe they should stick with us Max. Is a bit tricky, getting back 'less you knows the way.'

This was just the type of thing to bring out the latent arrogance of Max's gang and, just as he'd hoped, the two stragglers shrugged their shoulders and exchanged a grin.

'Just a bit of mud,' said one. 'Don't frighten me none. Now St Pauls, Saturday night, that's something to be scared of.'

His mate nodded like an eager donkey.

'Well, you just watch your step,' said Tom feigning reluctance. 'You see that line of trees over there?' He pointed back the way they'd come. 'Just head for the centre of that, then keep on the grass, single file mind, and you should make it back.'

He watched as they set out, veering off the indicated route almost immediately as they shoved one another and sniggered over their shoulders. Max screwed up his eyes as he peered into the gloom. 'Am I gonna need a couple of new lads?' he asked, a touch anxiously.

Tom, who had deliberately chosen a route with the maximum of mud but no really dangerous areas, hastened to reassure him.

'No, should be all right. Not too much rain around recently. Is further in you might need to watch your step. Wouldn't want to ruin them nice shoes, eh?'

Max gave him a hard stare but seemed reassured by the sounds of wrangling and grumbling coming from his mates, which gradually faded as they became more distant.

'Well, lead on then,' he said. 'Don't know what all the secrecy is about though. Is easy enough to find, this path. And easy enough to see at night for miles if'n we'd use torches.'

Tom turned away to hide a smile, setting a steady pace across the Levels.

It was almost full dark by the time they reached the first of the bridges and Tom was grateful for the pale silver of the moonlight. To an uneducated eye the land looked no different from the slightly boggy ground they had been covering, but even at night Tom could tell they were approaching the centre of the marshes. The air was cooler and there was a sense of dankness as the excess moisture filled the air. It was quiet too, a deeper, heavier quiet that came from a lack of wildlife, for few animals lived in the deep marsh. The land turned to liquid mud at the lightest rainfall and even amphibians struggled to survive the treacherous conditions.

Impatient at the delay, Max elbowed Tom aside and made to step out onto what looked like a path. Grabbing his shoulder, Tom pulled him back on solid ground and held up a hand as Max turned to remonstrate.

'Watch,' Tom said and broke a piece off a nearby, pathetic apology for a bush. He leaned forwards, making sure his feet were firmly on solid ground and pushed the branch into the path ahead. It slid below the surface smoothly and Tom let go when it was almost half submerged. Max watched as the rest of the stick continued to slip forwards until only an inch or so was visible. Then, with the tiniest of popping sounds it vanished.

'Bloody hell,' said the man from Bristol stepping back and looking around anxiously.

Tom laid a reassuring hand on his arm. 'Is quite safe if you knows what you'm doing,' he said softly. 'And think, who's goin' to follow you into that? Is the perfect safe place for carting and hiding.'

Max swallowed hard as he continued to stare at the place where the branch had disappeared.

'So . . . so how far down is it then?' he said.

'Oh, well now, no-one knows, rightly,' said Tom, who was beginning to enjoy himself. 'Leastways, no-one ain't ever come back to tell us.'

Max was holding himself very still, as if a step, any step, might lead him into the nightmare of mud around him.

'So how's that any use,' he said angrily. 'Middle of the Levels is impossible to pass – well, I knows that. Everyone knows that.'

Tom knelt by the side of the path and felt around in the stubby reeds. For one panicky moment he thought it was gone, that Milosh had decided to abandon him after all. Then he found it and could barely keep the relief out of his voice as he stood and faced the reluctant young man.

'Not for those as have access to the secret paths it 'ent,' he said and pulled on the rope.

For a moment nothing happened, then Tom felt something give and the rope moved up and back in response to his efforts. There was a ripple in the mud before them, then a gurgling noise as thick bubbles of dark mud rose to the surface, leaving dips in the liquid when they burst. Before Max's eyes, a slatted pathway made of timber pushed its way out of the marsh, rising above the surface before Tom lowered it carefully on to the top of the mud. Carefully tying the rope off on to a peg set at a sharp angle to the bridge and hidden in the undergrowth, Tom stepped forwards and set foot on the track. Max took another step back, watching with wide eyes to see if Tom was going to go the way of the branch but the slender pathway held, dipping a little but still supporting his weight.

'Bloody hell,' said Max again.

It took a few minutes to coax him on to the pathway, and then only by trotting along it to the end and back again.

'You sure will take us both?' Max asked, his eyes darting from side to side as he lowered his weight out on the fragile-looking track.

'Long as we keep a couple of feet b'tween us will be fine,' Tom reassured him.

Foot by foot, they stepped across the great marsh, the pathway bending and swaying occasionally but never dipping more then an inch or so below the surface. The bridge led them to a low mound, tufts of thick grass crowning the top and a halo of reeds around the base. There was just room for the two of them standing shoulder to shoulder on this tiny piece of firm ground. Max cast around for a peg or rope but Tom changed direction and stepped confidently out on the mud to the left. Again Max waited to see if he was going to sink but Tom laughed softly and held out his hand.

'Only the entrances is sunk,' he said. 'Others is well-hidden see, and 'ent no-one can reach 'um without knowing where the first bridge is so 'ent no need to be pullin' 'um up and down all the time. Come on – them's fixed right good – look.'

He pointed to the reeds next to Max's left foot where the cross braces were hidden. With some reluctance, Max stepped out onto the trackway. His foot sank a couple of inches into the ooze but just as he was about to jerk himself free he felt a solid path beneath him once more. Leaning forwards and shifting his weight, he stepped gingerly along the path, following in Tom's footsteps whilst keeping a few feet between them. Moving from one inconspicuous mound to another the two men crossed the wasteland of the great marsh, looking from a distance as if they could walk on the water.

Casting a surreptitious glance at his watch, Tom was pleased to see they were keeping to his schedule. He slowed his pace a little, using his experience to time his arrival at the final set of bridges. As they approached the area leading to the closed peat works Max froze behind him. On the breeze came a series of sounds, the same eerie flute music mingled with a strange, rhythmic moaning. Even Tom, who had experienced the music before, felt the hairs on his neck rise and his breathing shortened to a gasp.

'What's that?' demanded Max. 'Hey, you – who's there?'

'Shut up you girt fool!' Tom snapped. 'You want to just tell the whole world we's here then?'

Max was staring out into the surrounding wasteland and for an instant Tom was reminded of something his grandmother had said. 'Eyes like chapel hat-pegs, mouth flopping open catching flies', she had snapped at him on more than one occasion. That was exactly what Max looked like, standing up to his ankles in mud in the cool, blue moonlight. Mind you, Tom wasn't sure he looked any better himself. The secret of any plan was to anticipate the unexpected, but no-one could plan for the supernatural.

Bugger the supernatural, he thought angrily. The only ghosties on the Levels were the Drowners and they were just a story, a staged accident set up by his men. Other folk might believe all that crap but he had spent his childhood watching his elders manipulate the *Gadjo*, playing on their superstitions and fears, sometimes for profit but often for survival. Appearance, he'd learned, the impression of confidence or innocence, was as important as the reality. That and saving face – and he was certainly not going to show any fear in front of this arrogant, vulgar lad from the city. Ignoring the squirm of apprehension inside, he grinned at Max and pulled on another hidden rope, making sure to secure it properly before he stepped across on to the next section of the track. Feigning a confidence he did not fully possess, he headed towards the moaning sounds. Max hesitated, eyes searching around for a way off this nightmare of a path and Tom was certain that if he knew a safe way back he'd be off like a frightened rabbit. The walk was having the desired effect – Max was truly, deeply scared, frightened out of his wits in this hostile and lethal environment. Not long, Tom thought. Soon he'll be keeping to the roads, off my patch and the coppers'll have him.

He almost trod on Simon as he reached the last point on the track. The boy was lying on his side, curled up into a tight ball with his hands over his ears and his eyes closed. He was shivering on the cold, damp ground and he gave an involuntary moan as Tom tripped and kicked him whilst trying to stay upright. Recovering his balance he turned back towards Max, trying to shield Simon from the Bristol man, who was now edging across the bridge. Pretending to check his boot laces, Tom risked a quick warning.

'Shut up now, don't make no sound, you hear? Don't mean you no harm so you just lie quiet.' He risked a glance in the direction of Max, who was still hovering, and added, 'Wait till we's gone and then scarper. And don't be coming this way again, neither.'

He had no idea whether Simon had understood but at least the moaning stopped. Tom stood up and stepped forwards, waving Max across, straight up the bank and off to his left. Max was decidedly wobbly when he reached firm ground and scrambled along the bank with alacrity.

'Where's we now then,' he demanded, peering around and squinting into the darkness. The moon was up but it cast a pale, blue-tinted light, giving the landscape a strange glow as if it were shimmering, a mirage that might vanish in an instant. It was almost impossible to distinguish safe ground from deadly marsh, for the undergrowth and occasional trees threw shadows across the landscape, blurring the outlines of the canals and hiding tell-tale reeds and mosses. At night the Levels became a monochrome world, cast from a horror film and twice as frightening. Tom hurriedly dropped the bridge out of sight into the marsh and straightened up, resisting the temptation to glance down at Simon, who was still rolled up, trembling on the wet earth.

'Now we got an easy bit,' said Tom, stepping ahead and striding towards a narrow footpath that snaked away out of sight behind a stand of trees. Simon waited, his breath coming in short gasps as he struggled to keep absolutely silent. He didn't know who the man was who had spoken to him but he had a good idea who Max was and he had no desire become more closely acquainted. Simon might not understand a lot about the world outside his own head but he had experienced more than a fair share of malice in his life and he could almost feel the anger and malevolence oozing from the Bristol man. The last time someone had scared him that much had been his close encounter with Derek Johns, a meeting that left him kicked unconscious and left by the side of the main road outside Highpoint.

He waited until the footsteps faded away and then longer still, counting to one hundred in his head before finally risking a glimpse over the reeds that kept him hidden. Slowly and painfully he began to unfold his stiff limbs, biting his bottom lip as pins and needles ran through his feet and one leg threatened to spasm with cramp. Taking his weight on one arm, he levered himself up onto his knees, all the time watching the area in front of him. Suddenly a shadow flitted between two trees and Simon froze in place before slowly, silently lowering himself back behind the safety of the covering reeds. Peering through the plants he watched as a figure emerged from the edge of the wood and took a step towards the footpath before stopping and then turning in his direction. After a long, long moment the figure looked down the footpath once more and began to follow the two men. Simon realized he had been holding his breath and let it out in a ragged gasp. He was shaking, really shaking not just shivering from the cold. Scrambling to his feet he scuttled over to the path, checked the coast was clear and set off as fast as his stiff legs would go. He didn't know how it had happened, he didn't care to ask any questions – in a brief flash of bright moonlight Simon had seen enough of the figure's ragged face to recognize Derek Johns.

Alex bumped her way across the Levels, cursing every rut in the road, every hidden ditch and blind corner as she marvelled at how such a flat landscape could be so impenetrable once you were actually on it. In the short time between nightfall and the rising of the moon she was forced to slow to a crawl as the twisting road seemed to throw unexpected obstacles in her path, the numerous canals and rhynes threatening disaster to the unwary motorist at every junction. Finally, the moon rose above the surrounding land and she was able to navigate her way towards Lower Godney, home of Simon – or at least of his remaining family. Several times she was forced to pull over, a manoeuvre that consisted mainly of running the car a foot or so to the left, up against the hedge and putting on the handbrake, so narrow was the road she was following. In the dimness of the interior light she peered hopefully at the map of the Levels thoughtfully provided by the office staff back at Highpoint. Referred to as the 'Edgar' by everyone who had tried to actually navigate by it, it was indeed composed of 'mystery and imagination' and bore less resemblance to the surrounding reality than any map she had ever used. Finally, she threw it back in the glove compartment with a snarl, put the car into gear and lurched off in what she thought might possibly be the right direction.

After some fairly futile zigging and zagging through a series of apparently endless and identical country lanes, she emerged at a junction with the main road. At least she thought it was probably the main road. It had a white line down the middle rather than a strip of grass and that, she thought, could only be a good thing. After peering out of the side windows at the moon whilst trying to remember which direction it rose and therefore which direction Lower Godney might lie relative to that, Alex resorted to the time-honoured method of guessing. Turning right out of the junction she headed off between the flat, watery plains of the Levels and hoped some lights might appear soon to give her a village or hamlet by which to navigate. Now she was off the rough, barely metalled road she was more aware of her car and she realized with some alarm it seemed to be making a strange grinding sound. Alex's car was something of a joke amongst friends and clients. An aging Citroën DS with the hallmark hydraulic suspension, which made the car look like a hen settling on her eggs when being parked, and numerous dents now adorning the bodywork, it was instantly recognizable over an area of some fifty square miles. Alex hoped every month she might be able to replace it with something a bit more modern, or practical, or just a bit more reliable, but by the end of the month she was merely grateful it was still running. Despite being in her second year as a 'salaried professional', money was incredibly tight and a new car was still the stuff of dreams. The mortgage rate on her treasured little house had risen by about five times the rate at which her salary was increasing. Now, as she eased the car round a long, slow bend and the grinding got louder, she suspected her dreams were about to be reduced to something like a new exhaust.

There was a lay-by up ahead on the right by some trees and she decided it would be sensible to pull over and have a look. If the exhaust was loose, she thought, she could always tie it up with something until she got home. As she indicated and began to turn in, she realized the lay-by was occupied – a shiny silver car with three occupants was parked at the far end. For a moment she hesitated but then common sense overcame the moment of concern. This was rural Somerset, a long way from her previous patch in the slums of South London. Life was very different here and people were more likely to help each other out than prey on a stranger. She pulled up about ten feet behind the silver car and turned off the engine, relieved to have got it this far in one piece. The Citroën seemed to sigh to itself and the car body sank slowly and gracefully down as the suspension relaxed, a sight that never failed to fascinate her clients, who had often gathered in the car park to watch her leave of an evening. Alex grinned at the memory and opened the door, stepping out into the night. Despite the moonlight it was very, very dark and as her eyes tried to adjust she wondered if she still had a torch in the boot. A quick rummage around in the debris revealed that although she had a torch, it didn't have batteries. She threw it back into the car and slammed the lid, cursing her own idiocy. Checking the underside of the deflated vehicle was difficult enough without trying to do it in pitch darkness, she thought.

The sound of the boot attracted the attention of the silver car's occupants and the interior light came on as the driver opened the door and stepped out on to the damp grass verge, followed a moment later by the front seat passenger. A pale face pressed against the slightly steamed-up back window and Alex felt a faint qualm, wondering if she had interrupted something private – and possibly unsavoury. She stood to face the newcomers and realized as they walked up to her that at least one of them was only too familiar.

'Well now, looks like you is in a bit of bother,' said the driver, but Alex ignored him, staring instead at the figure hovering just behind his right shoulder. The silence stretched out between them until the driver realized something was wrong and glanced over at his companion.

'What?' he demanded.

The passenger shoved his hands into his pockets, hunched his shoulders and glared down at the ground.

'Nothing,' he muttered.

The driver was not to be deterred.

'What?' he repeated, this time in Alex's direction.

It would have been wise, perhaps, to follow the lead offered her. It was possible these lads might have been persuaded she was no more than a woman in a broken-down car, who needed a bit of a hand. It was even possible they might have helped her on her way – but before this sage advice could filter through her tired brain Alex opened her mouth and heard herself say, 'Nick – Nick Stevens. What are you doing out here? Your curfew doesn't end until the last day of July.'

A look of confusion washed over the driver's face as he turned from one to another.

'What?' he said again, rather plaintively this time.

'Oh, shut up Jason,' said Nick.

The damage done, Alex decided to go for a frontal assault in the hope she could scare Jason away – ideally taking Nick with him.

'Didn't he tell you?' she asked, her voice sounding convincingly casual. 'He's not long out of Pucklechurch and he's supposed to be living at the Probation Hostel up in Highpoint. Only he's obviously not because all residents have to be in by nine, don't they Nick.'

'How would you know that then?' asked Jason. 'How would she know?' he repeated as he turned to look at his companion.

''Cos she's my bloody probation officer, is why,' said Nick. He removed his hands from his pockets and was leaning forwards towards Alex. There was no doubting the menace in his voice and now she recognized the jerky movements and rapid breathing she'd first seen in Brian, back in the Highpoint day centre. Alex realized she had miscalculated badly.

'I hate bloody probation officers,' said Jason conversationally. 'Bunch of interfering do-gooders as don't know nothin' about what 'tis like tryin' to make a living in the real world. Reckon they's as bad a coppers.'

Oh great, thought Alex. Middle of the night, broken down car and a couple of yobs with a grudge against the probation service. So this was what you got for trying to look after your clients.

Flight, she knew, was the very last resort, especially as she would be going on foot. The only chance of getting away would be over the fields, on to the Levels proper, a prospect that frightened her almost as much as the two lads now advancing with feral grins on their faces. For a second she hesitated and then she spun around and took off down the verge, scrambling over the stile and fleeing across the boggy ground as fast as her shaking legs could take her. Her eyes were fairly well adjusted to the gloom and she could just make out a faint path running away across the marsh. Hoping for some cover to disguise her route, Alex veered to the left and almost tripped over the edge of a small canal. Lurching backwards she set off again, spurred on by the sound of her pursuers, puffing and panting behind her. Thank goodness Nick hadn't been sentenced to the 'short, sharp shock' initiative, she thought, as she stumbled along next to the canal. The only thing *that* achieved was to take pathetic weedy little no-goodniks like him and turn them into super-fit, muscled no-goodniks who could do a lot more damage and then run away. Nick, by contrast, had smoked his way through several months on remand and now could be found lounging in front of the television at the hostel most days. She was surprised he had found the energy to clamber into a car in the first place.

She slowed her pace and then stopped, listening for sounds of the chase. Some distance behind her, she caught the faint sound of voices arguing. Moving as quietly as she could, Alex edged towards a stand of willows on the bank between two canals. The whole area was thick with reeds that rustled as she approached and she bent down, wary of treading on some animal or nesting bird. She almost screamed aloud when Simon's head popped up, finger to his lips as he gestured her down in to the safety of the undergrowth. Alex flung herself on the ground and wriggled out of sight, fighting for calm as the bickering came closer. She looked at Simon who was laying completely still, his eyes glinting in the moonlight as he peered out from the reeds. After a minute she heard footsteps coming along the path and then a curse as one of them, Jason she thought, trod in a muddy patch.

'They's new, these boots. I told Max I weren't tramping through no bog. You want her – you go 'n' get her. I ain't going out there.'

Jason spun on his elegant Cuban heels and splashed his way back towards the main road, now a long way out of sight. Nick hesitated, dithering first one way and then the other before following.

'Is alright for you,' he whined as he disappeared round the trees, 'she 'ent your probation officer. 'Tis I is going to get sent back to Pucklechurch now, 'cos of that bitch . . .'

Despite her position, crouched in a ditch with a client, with no idea where she was and a broken-down car, Alex still felt a surge of indignation. It wasn't her fault if the little moron got sent down. She hadn't made him break the curfew and spend the night roaming the Levels with his undesirable friends. He'd screwed up his one chance all by himself and, come the morning, she was going to tell him so to his face. She went to get up but Simon laid a restraining hand on her shoulder.

'No,' he said.

'Why can't . . .'

Simon shook his head and laid a finger on his lips.

'Reckon You'd better stay here,' he whispered. 'He's out there. I seen 'um and I don't reckon you's safe.'

'Seen who?' asked Alex, confused and alarmed at the same time.

'Was Derek Johns,' said Simon softly. 'All torn up he was, an' like a big dent in his head, but I knows 'um. Was real too, not like a ghost. Derek Johns out here, an' he'll be after summ'et.'

Alex felt sick. Of all the names Simon could have conjured up, Derek Johns represented her worst nightmare. She, like the rest of the Levels, had been convinced he was dead. Truth told, most people were pleased he was gone; that he had been swept out to sea and now was nothing more than food for marine life. A fitting end for a human predator such as him. She swallowed, aware her mouth was suddenly dry, and when she answered she had to fight to keep the trembling from her voice.

'Are you quite sure it was . . .?' She despised herself, hearing the hope in her voice.

In the dim light she saw a scowl flit across Simon's face. 'Reckon,' he said shortly, and slid over the edge of the reed bed, rising to his feet cautiously.

Alex felt a surge of panic at the thought of being left alone, stranded and lost out in the muddy wilderness.

'I'll come too,' she whispered, and began to get up but Simon knelt next to her and pressed her back into the sheltering undergrowth.

'I know the way around,' he replied softly. 'Knows where's safe an' where's not. I'll go get some help for 'un. 'Sides,' he added with crushing honesty, 'I seen you run and frankly you is rubbish.'

With that he was gone into the cool night, without a sound. Alex stared after his fading outline and shivered. It was getting cold, she was wet and muddy and around her the mist began to form on the sodden ground. Skulking in the reeds she wished that, just for once, she had listened to Sue's advice.

Chapter Sixteen

Derek moved as carefully as he could around the broken landscape, skirting puddles and hopping over ditches, his eyes never leaving the two figures ahead of him. After the shock of hearing the strange music he had almost lost them as they moved off towards the last patch of marsh before the peat works, but Derek had thought things through. Tom was planning to use the works for something and he wouldn't want to draw attention to himself or his men by using the road, especially with the continuing police presence in the area. No, he would have another way in, a secret way – a track that Derek had traced and followed over the last few nights; a track with a couple of little surprises waiting for him. He hadn't expected the young bloke from Bristol but actually it saved him the problem of dealing with the man later. Derek was eager to finish up and get off the Levels as fast as he could. Just break up this new gang of infiltrators to leave the field clear for Newt on his release, then a bit of domestic housekeeping and he would be away. Somewhere warm, he thought. Somewhere out of the reach of the British coppers too. He paused, looking around at the flat, open way ahead of him and decided it was getting too risky, tailing them. One glimpse and Tom Monarch would realize something was up and Derek had waited too long for that to happen. Reluctantly he turned back, making his way to the narrow road where he could follow at a distance, hidden behind the scrubby hedgerow.

Despite travelling at no more than a trot he was soon feeling breathless, a light sweat breaking out all over his body. A slow throbbing in his injured hand grew in intensity until he was forced to stop and massage the arm, muttering impatiently to himself at the delay. When he set off again he stumbled a little, feeling surprisingly light-headed. Under his grimy jacket the tell-tale red streaks of blood-poisoning were snaking their way up his arm, raising his temperature and heart rate. Focussed on his final act of revenge, Derek ploughed on regardless into the night.

Despite his rising anxiety, Tom forced himself to walk confidently out across the final elevated bridge, leading an increasingly jumpy Max towards the ambush he and Ada had planned. In his head he visualized the route, counting the walkways down as they approached the area of the peat works. Behind him Max shambled along, all trace of the arrogance gone as he struggled with the uneven terrain and layers of slick mud, now icy cold as the wet seeped through his boots. Four more, thought Tom. Across to this hump, then a right towards that stand of withies, stop and face to the west . . . He realized he could no longer hear footsteps and turned to peer into the darkness behind him.

'Max?' he called softly. There was an answering grunt and a faint splash followed by a curse.

'Max – keep up. Is not safe, getting too far behind. Easy to miss your way out here 'less you knows the paths.'

'Bugger this,' snarled Max looming out of the night. 'Don't care – I'm goin' back. Sick of this bloody wasteland, I is. Not like there's even a decent profit to be made with all this carry-on anyway. You can stuff your secret paths, you can stuff your Levels and you can stuff all your bloody yokels. Make more in a night out 'n St Paul's than I can with all this shit.' And he turned on his heels and began to feel his way back to solid ground, inching forwards one step at a time.

Tom stared after him, mouth open with astonishment. Well now, who knew he was such a softy, he thought. They'd not even needed Ada and the gun . . . Oh crap. For a moment he was torn between shepherding Max off the pathways and alerting his little band of conspirators, but Max was only one track away from solid ground and the thought of Ada lying in wait with her semi-legal shotgun had been preying on his mind all evening. After a few seconds he turned and plunged further into the marsh to warn them Max wasn't coming. Would be just like Ada to shoot at some innocent poacher, he thought as he splashed through the water. Suddenly it seemed very important he reached them before anything went wrong.

Lauren twinkled at her reflection in the mirror, turning her head from side to side as she admired her new ear-rings. Discrete and distinctly classy, the tiny rubies gleamed in the lamplight, sparkling almost as brightly as Lauren's eyes. She loved them, not least because they were a gift from Dave, a small apology for his recent neglect. It was going to be difficult, giving him a suitably hard time tonight, she thought. Maybe she should just forgive him now. She slid off the stool and headed for the bedroom door, heart as light as her steps. No-one gave girl rubies unless they were really interested, she thought happily.

The evening began well and just got better as it went on. Dave had booked a table at the Pear Tree and Partridge, a surprisingly good restaurant on the road out past Nether Stowey. The food was excellent, the wine list impressive and the prices matched the quality of the meal but Dave didn't blink when presented with the bill. Instead he sent a glass of wine through to thank the chef, left a substantial tip and swept Lauren off in his car to the car park on top of the

Quantock Hills where they sat in companionable silence, holding hands and watching the stars burning across the deep, navy sky.

'I'm so sorry about the past months,' said Dave finally. 'I know I've been busy – all the extra shifts and night work. It's just, with these murders, well we have to catch whoever's responsible. And, well, I've been given a bit more responsibility, working with the big boys in Taunton. You see . . .,' he shifted round and took Lauren's hands in his, staring at her earnestly, '. . . I'm hoping I can make detective. That's what I wanted when I joined the force and I think they are testing me out. You don't apply, you know – you get invited. Only most coppers don't. I want to be one who does, and I know I can do a good job. It's a decent wage too, a bit of seniority – a really important career move if I can impress the right people.'

Lauren nodded to show she understood but waited, hoping there was more.

Dave swallowed nervously and glanced out over the soft, dark hillside before continuing

'Just, I hope I impress the right person too. I don't want to wind up detective if it means I lose you.'

Slow, warm tears filled Lauren's eyes, trickling down her cheeks as she stared up at this wonderful, kind man who for some reason liked *her*. She'd been under no illusions about her chances of marrying. A lot of people like her didn't even live long enough to get married – she'd already beaten one lot of odds. What with her reasonably robust health and a real job, Lauren counted herself extremely lucky. And now there was Dave, lovely, gentle, handsome Dave who gave her rubies and apologized for letting her down when he was up to his eyes in the biggest case of his life. She shook her head, not trusting her voice, trying to communicate her feelings through her hands as they squeezed his, clinging on to this moment of fragile happiness.

'May I?' Dave asked and kissed her gently.

Lauren thought her heart would burst with happiness.

Despite his anxiety, Tom still moved with caution along the track. He knew the way of course, every inch of it, and the bridges were safer and a lot more stable than the surrounding land. In the winter and on through spring, the high tides and rainfall raised the water table and despite the maze of channels and sluices the water seeped into the surrounding land, making treacherous what had been safe a few days previously. Tom had been taught well by his father many years ago, before he met his beloved Bella and suffered the humiliation of banishment from the *Roma*.

As he edged his way towards the peat works he muttered the directions softly, following his own instructions but always aware of the feel of the track, the smell of the surrounding marsh, the look of the next few feet in front of him. It was this that saved him as he turned to the left and stepped out onto the penultimate section of the alder track. He felt a tiny movement where the footing should have been firm and, ahead a couple of paces, he spotted the broken stems of reeds where there should have been straight plants – Tom shifted his weight backwards and felt the track slide away from under his feet. One leg went through what felt like a hole in the hidden decking, twisting his foot almost backwards and he let out a cry at the sudden pain. Jerking futilely in an effort to free himself, he fell backwards, landing spread-eagled in the mud. For a moment he thought he had landed on a solid section but then the support to his shoulders and hips seemed to melt away and he felt his body settle into the mire.

The immediate instinct was to panic, of course. Panic and you're dead, Tom thought. Don't move, don't struggle, keep breathing slowly and carefully. The cold water seeped through his clothes, wrapping him in its icy fists and he fought to keep himself from gasping, snatching at the precious air in the few inches between his mouth and the surrounding marsh. He leg had come free from the gap in the boards but was now sinking deeper into the mud, where it pulled at his lower body, inch by inch, as it was sucked under. One part of Tom's mind focussed on the reason for the breakdown of the track. Despite his predicament he could not understand how the walkway, so carefully constructed and scrupulously maintained by the *Roma*, could collapse under him.

The thought that his brother – or some other member of the *kumpania* – had arranged this little accident haunted him. Were they so angry with him still? He couldn't believe Milosh, his own brother, would have any part in this, but who else knew about the secret bridges? The rest of his mind was struggling with the realization he was probably going to die, horribly and alone, out here in the dirt and the mud of the marsh. There would be no funeral; no proper marking of his life's passing. No-one would know where he had gone or what had happened to him. Soon, if he was lucky, he would sink into unconsciousness from the cold and then he would simply slip below the surface and vanish. He didn't want to think about his last few minutes if he was not lucky.

He decided he had nothing to lose now. Opening his mouth he gave a great yell, a shout of despair and anguish that echoed across the watery landscape, carrying his last hope with it. The effort caused his body to shift slightly, dipping a fraction lower in the mud. Tom took a deep breath and cried out again. Either he would be heard and perhaps saved or he would hasten his end. Given his current situation, he reckoned it was worth the risk.

Derek stopped on the verge by the side of the tiny road and a slow grin spread over his mutilated face. The trap was sprung and the arrogant intruders into his empire were in full retreat. At the second shout, Derek nodded to himself and turned round, heading back towards the main path to Middlezoy. Despite his weakened condition he picked up the pace, eager to finish up and be off the Levels as soon as possible. He stumbled on the road, his feet tripping over themselves as he swayed slightly from side to side. Probably picked up a bit of a chill, he thought wiping away the sweat that trickled into his eyes. Half a mile down the road he was forced to stop, leaning over and gasping for breath, a stitch in his side. Definitely getting a chill, he thought, propping himself up against a tree to rest for a moment. On the other side of the hedge, Simon crept past, his head down as he fought the terror that threatened to paralyse him. As Derek hauled his feverish body upright and resumed his shambling trot down the road, Simon settled back into his natural pace. He moved with a fluid grace, feet kept low as they skimmed the smooth surface of the footpath, each stride even and controlled. Years of 'driving' his phantom lorry everywhere had turned Simon into a natural long-distance runner. Undaunted by the distance he still had to travel, Simon pushed on, the yards and miles falling away behind him.

Ada waited impatiently by the side of the abandoned peat works, shivering as the temperature dropped and the mist began to rise from the old workings. Lily Dodds was hunched up next to her, a bag full of fireworks, most of extremely dubious provenance, clutched in her hands.

'How much longer?' she hissed through chattering teeth.

Ada shifted her precious shot-gun, a weapon of equally dubious provenance, from one hand to another, peering up at the night sky before answering.

'Not long now I reckon,' she said finally. 'Said to listen for a signal when he was getting close. Maybe is time you was getting off – get yerself in position.'

Lily scowled at her. 'Why is I havin' to move?' she asked crossly. 'Why not you, then?'

Ada sighed and shook her head. 'We talked this through,' she said. 'Loudest noises and stuff behind him so's he'll run this way. That way he'll not go haring off into the marsh and drownin' hisself.'

'After what he done to my Charlie, reckon he deserves to drown hisself,' Lily muttered.

'No,' said Ada firmly. 'We ain't having no killing. I don't hold with that and is asking for trouble anyway. We scare 'um off so they all go running back to Bristol and that's an end to it.'

Lily looked as if she was tempted to argue, but at that moment there came that sound again, the soft, almost-tuneless music that had haunted the Levels since the start of the year. Lily squeaked in terror, dropping her bag of fireworks as she looked around frantically for the source of the sound. It was close, very close. Just behind them in fact. Ada spun round and lifted the shot-gun, pointing it towards the direction of the music, which drifted away again leaving only an uneasy silence. With shaking hands, Ada lowered the shot-gun and flicked the safety catch back on.

'Wha . . . what was that?' asked Lily, eyes wide with fright.

Ada stared out into the night, searching for signs of movement. Whoever it was – and Ada was determined it was a person, not a *thing* – they were very close. Supernatural scare aside, she didn't want any witnesses to the evening's planned events. All was still, with only a slight breeze moving the fronds of the surrounding willows. Letting out her breath slowly, Ada felt her shoulders relax.

'Reckon they's gone,' she said, sounding more convinced than she really felt. Where could they have gone, after all? Perhaps they floated away on the breeze . . .

A sudden thought struck her and Ada suppressed a chuckle. Taking a few steps back towards the yard she peered at the layout of the workings. Nodding to herself, she hurried back to where Lily was scuffling around in the mud, retrieving her fireworks.

'Don't be worrying about that,' said Ada firmly. 'Just keep them fuses dry, you hear?'

Muttering beneath her breath, Lily fished the last of the brown paper wrapped cylinders from a rut in the road and straightened up with a soft groan.

'I'm getting too old for all this,' she grumbled. 'Running around the Levels in the middle of the night. Don't know why I agreed to all this.'

Ada held up a warning hand, cutting off the flow of complaint as a faint cry, a desperate call for help floated across the Levels from the direction of the hidden track. Lily opened her mouth to speak but Ada's gesture cut her off.

'Hush now!'

They stood in silence, straining their ears as the shout came again.

'This way,' said Ada and set off towards the bank that led down to the edge of the marsh. Lily followed behind, dragging her illicit load and wondering just what, exactly, she'd got herself into.

Ada stood at the very edge of the mud, leaning forwards as she strained to pick up the slightest sound, but all was still once more.

'Maybe a fox or summat?' ventured Lily hopefully.

Ada fixed her with her best withering glare. 'A fox?' she said. 'A *fox*? 'Ent nothing like no fox. Is someone out in the marsh. Someone caught out there, in trouble. Give me that now.' She held her hand out for the bag of fireworks. 'And go break some of them withies off. Get a dozen or so and bring 'um back. Go on, look sharp will yer? If some poor bugger's in the marsh they've only got a few minutes.'

Lily trotted back up the bank and began twisting at the young branches on the trees. A number were already snapped and hanging down, marking Derek Johns' escape through the window a few days previously, and she was able to twist them free quite easily. The new growth was another matter as the twigs were smooth and supple but extremely tough, and she cut her hands a couple of times before Ada's urgent voice sent her stumbling down to the water's edge. She stared in astonishment at her friend who was, miraculously, walking on the liquid surface out towards a large clump of reeds some twenty feet away.

'Don't stand there gawping,' Ada snapped. 'See that bit of a stump there? No, over a bit, there – right, now just keep facing me and walk out towards us. Slow now, feel with yer feet. Come on woman!'

In the biggest leap of faith in her entire life, Lily stepped out onto the slick, liquid surface and made her way towards where Ada was standing, sure in her heart this was either suicide or a miracle.

From the little mound on which she stood, Ada reached back, helping Lily to the dubious safety of relatively solid ground. In silence they switched loads, Lily happy to pass over the bundle of cumbersome withies. Peering around the edge of the reeds, Ada located what she hoped was the next track. Selecting a branch from the bundle, she poked through the slime before stepping gingerly out on to the second section. Lily hovered behind her, uncertain whether to follow.

Desperately cold in the darkness of the marsh, Tom was sinking very, very slowly into the mud, his body almost entirely encased in the slime. He still had one hand on the surface and his shoulders were not fully submerged but he could feel the tickling of the water as it flowed around his neck. As the first trickle flowed into his ears he almost jerked his head away, desperate to clear them, but the tiny reflex flickered through his body, losing him another inch as the mud flowed around him. Why, he wondered, why was he prolonging the agony? There was no-one coming and there would be no miracle. His shoulders and neck were aching abominably as the tension of his rigid muscles pulled at his spine. It would be easier just to relax, let his hips go and sink down into the marsh, but the horror of that final moment kept him fighting even though he knew it was hopeless. The water continued its inexorable rise up around his face and he decided to give one last shout, a yell of defiance before it reached his mouth.

Ada almost fell off the track as the shout rang out.

'Who's there?' she called, hurrying towards the voice. 'Hold on – we'm coming.'

Tom heard her above the sounds of his own breathing, a roaring in his ears as the surrounding water rendered him close to deaf. He was gripped by conflicting emotions. Hope, impossible hope was followed in an instant by fear for Ada and Lily. They didn't know the track was down and unless he could alert them, they too would be lured into the marsh, floundering and dying in the mud. He didn't hesitate and used the last of his breath to shout a warning.

'No! The track is broken – don't come any closer – please.'

'Tom?' came Ada's voice. 'Tom, that you out there?'

Each time he called out, he slipped a tiny bit further into the mud and the water rose a fraction towards his mouth and nose. He knew it was close to the end now but he had to make sure Ada and Lily were safe.

'You stay away,' he shouted. ''Ent nothin' you can do, not from that side any road. You get outa here Ada.'

Ada swung round and beckoned Lily towards her.

'You follow me now and we'll see if'n we can keep 'um afloat for a bit,' she said.

Lily trotted after her, across to the central hump that lay just a few scant yards from where Tom was stranded, spread-eagled in the marsh.

'Gimme one of them fireworks,' Ada said, placing it carefully on the ground and as far away from them both as the tiny island allowed.

'Close yer eyes Tom,' she ordered, as she lit the waxed string that acted as a fuse. For a moment it seemed the firework was a dud, but then with a brilliant flash and a bang that left their ears ringing it exploded, lighting up the surrounding area.

'Bloody hell, woman, what you doin'?' shouted Tom, blinking and trying not to flinch as he struggled to maintain the delicate balance that just kept him above the water. Bereft of his night vision, he had a horrible feeling he was rocking from side to side. Ada had only a brief glimpse of his face, white and tense as it just protruded from the surrounding mire but the sight filled her with horror.

'Don't you move now, Tom,' she called. 'We's going to get you out. Just stay still!'

'Well now, woman,' muttered Tom to himself, 'Why didn't I think of that. Just stay still eh?'

'You watch it, Tom Monarch,' came Ada's voice. 'Don't you be bad-mouthing me. Specially considering the predicament you's in right now.'

Despite the predicament he was in, Tom managed a grin. He'd forgotten just how much he liked Ada over the years. He wished now he'd tried to keep in touch with her. It was a bit late now – such a waste, he thought sadly. He was startled out of his fleeting moment of self-pity by something nudging his arm as it lay just on the surface of the mud. Fighting every instinct to flinch, to lift his head to see what was crawling towards him through the ooze, Tom kept his body rigid.

'You got that then?' Ada's voice floated over to him.

'Got what?' he managed. His breath was coming in short, harsh gasps now and the cold was so intense he could no longer feel his legs. The first ripples of a shiver ran through him and he knew any moment he would start to shake, disturbing the fragile surface tension that held him just clear of the water.

'Just slide yer arms on this, use it to keep yer head up, man,' snapped Ada, pushing a hastily woven raft of withies across the swampy surface. As his vision cleared, Tom focussed his eyes on the frail-looking mat. It was inconceivable such a weak looking thing could save him but Tom inched his arm over and carefully slid it across the rough surface. Despite its futility, Tom was overwhelmed with gratitude. He would not die alone, nor would the marsh be his final, unmarked resting place. Someone cared about him, cared enough to risk their own life for his.

'I got it,' he called. 'Now, you get clear. And – Ada?' There was a pause.

'What?' came the reply.

'Thank you, girl. I wish . . .'

'Don't you start getting soft on me now,' hissed Ada. 'We 'ent done yet. You just stay still till we get round your side.' And with that she was gone, leaving him to float in the cold, dank water, clutching at the little mat of willow, alone in the dark.

Sue felt guilty. It was not an emotion she indulged in very often and quite frankly she didn't much like it, but as the

271

hours passed and there was no sign of Alex she was starting to think perhaps she should have insisted on accompanying her friend. She flicked through the offerings on the television but none of the four stations held any appeal. Getting up to turn off the set she glanced out of the window at the night. It was clear, with no sign of the heavy rain that had made the last few weeks miserable, but it was still unseasonably cold and Sue suspected Alex was too tired to drive safely, especially at night. Her brush with meningitis had done something to her eyes and she still struggled to focus properly in dim light.

Sue thought of the bottle of wine on the side and cast an eye longingly at her half-finished book lying open on the little table, but she could not shake a nagging feeling something was wrong. With a sigh she fished in her bag for her car keys and then picked up the phone. There was a pause as she waited to be connected to the Highpoint police station and then a five-minute wrangle with the constable at the other end of the line before she slammed the receiver down in frustration.

'Not a missing person until they've been gone over 24 hours. What the hell use is that?' she muttered, tapping her foot angrily. After a moment she picked up the phone again and dialled another number.

'Hi, Lauren? It's Sue. Look, sorry to interrupt your evening but is Dave there?'

Lauren's answer was muffled by the sound of the phone being dropped at that end but Sue made out enough to leave her blinking in surprise. She didn't realize Lauren even knew some of those words. The sound of raised voices came down the line before a decidedly testy Dave said, 'Yes?'

Sue explained her problem as clearly as she could, trying to inject some of her anxiety into her voice. There was a pause when she had finished.

'Look,' said Dave finally, 'she's an adult and the rules are quite clear – and actually quite sensible. Virtually all adults just come back in less than 24 hours. It's a total waste of police time looking for them when they're not lost or missing at all.'

'Dave, please – this is Alex we're talking about. Alex, out on the Levels in the dark, trying to find her way? She could drive in circles for hours and run out of petrol without ever finding a village or even a farm. You know what she's like.'

There was another silence before Dave asked, 'What's she doing out on the Levels anyway? It's not safe until we find Derek Johns – she must know that.'

Sue felt her mouth go dry.

'We phoned through a warning this afternoon,' said Dave, anxiety now echoing through his voice. 'The station should have called to let you know we have evidence Johns is still alive and possibly implicated in at least one of the recent deaths.'

'Well, she didn't get the bloody message!' Sue snapped back. 'She doesn't know anything about this and now Alex is out there, alone, with a mad stalker on the loose!'

At the other end of the line Dave was torn between concern for Alex and his almost overwhelming desire to stay with Lauren. He could hear her in the next room, slamming the fridge door and banging the crockery on the side. 'Dave?' came Sue's voice, and he took a deep breath. He owed Alex and Sue a lot for their support and friendship over the past year and, besides, he was a policeman. He had dedicated himself to the job, promising to protect and serve the public. There was no way he could refuse and still look himself in the eye tomorrow.

'I'll be over in about twenty minutes,' he said softly. 'Don't do anything silly –- you wait for me. See if you can dig out a torch or two and some decent shoes as well. You'll need something a bit more substantial than those sandals if you're heading out on to the Levels.'

He replaced the receiver softly and turned to meet Lauren's angry stare.

'I have to go,' he pleaded. 'Look, they're your friends too. I can't leave Alex out there, on her own. She's not been well and after everything she went through last night . . .'

His voice trailed off as Lauren just glared at him without speaking.

This was not how he had imagined his evening, Dave thought, as he climbed into his car, fastened his seatbelt and drove off down the road towards Highpoint. Although he tried to concentrate on his driving, Lauren's voice kept echoing in his head.

'This is how it's going to be 'ent it?' she had asked.

Unable and unwilling to lie, Dave had just nodded.

'Well, I reckon is goodbye then,' said Lauren, closing the door before he could offer anything in the way of a defence. He had stood there for a moment, cold with shock. Reaching out he touched the bell but withdrew his hand without ringing. Maybe she just meant for the evening, he thought. That must be it. She couldn't really mean . . . For the first time in a number of years Dave found himself questioning his own ambitions but, despite that, he knew he had to go to Alex's aid. He had a nasty feeling, a sense of foreboding that he could not shake off as he sped through the night.

Alex waited in the ditch, cold and wet, with no real way of telling how long she had been there. She tried judging the time by the pale moon as it crept across the sky but that was only likely to be successful if she knew how fast it moved – or even what the time had been when Simon left. She squinted at her watch but it was too dark to make out the hands, even if she could have focussed on it without her glasses which were currently lying beside the useless map on the front seat of her car. She clenched her teeth, partly in frustration and partly in an attempt to stop them chattering with the chill that was creeping through her body. She didn't know exactly how long Simon had been gone but it was surely longer than necessary if he had just been going to fetch help. There was always the possibility he had forgotten about her, or lost where she was. She had to admit she really didn't know an awful lot about how Simon's mind worked and she was worried she might freeze to death out here, waiting for help that never arrived.

She forced herself to crouch absolutely still, straining to hear the slightest sound from the direction of the road, but everything was silent out on the Levels. Slowly and painfully she uncoiled her stiff body and clambered out of her hiding place. Peering into the darkness, Alex crept through the misty landscape, edging her way towards the car. It might not be fit to drive but she did at least have a blanket in the back and it was a sight more comfortable than her bed amongst the tree roots and reeds. She stopped to listen every few yards but there was nothing. They've gone, she thought with relief. She was starting to shiver in earnest by the time she made out the roof of the car over the hedge. Fumbling in the pocket of her sodden jeans she pulled out her car key, then dropped it as her frozen fingers refused to grip properly. Cursing softly, Alex dropped to her knees and felt around her on the path. It has to be here somewhere, she thought, sliding her hands across the slick grass. Then there was a rustle from off to the right and she froze in place, heart pounding.

'Well now, look what we got here then,' came a mocking voice as strong hands grabbed her from behind and hauled her to her feet. Instinctively she lashed out, catching whoever was behind her a nasty crack on the shin. Following this up with an elbow to the gut, she felt his grip loosen for a moment and wriggled free, heading off towards the road at a speed that might have caused Simon to revise his opinion of her running ability. From the sound of grunting and puffing behind her, they were giving chase and she abandoned all caution, swinging her body over the stile and leaping as far as she could towards the road before landing hard and stumbling on the tarmac. Pushing herself upright once more she set off down the road, glancing behind as she approached the first bend. If she could just get out of sight she might lose them . . .

The force with which she cannoned into Max as he hurried round the corner knocked the breath out of them both but it was Max who recovered first.

'What the bloody hell . . .' he gasped as he grabbed her, swinging her round with a tight grip around her neck. Alex was too winded to struggle as the rest of Max's little band stumbled round the bend and stopped, staring at their boss in surprise.

'What's you doin' back?' asked Jason.

'Never mind that,' Max growled. 'What's goin' on here? And who is this?' He pushed Alex towards them before hauling her off her feet and dragging her towards the cars in the lay-by. 'Anyone want to answer me?'

'Is my probation officer,' muttered Nick who was shuffling along at the back. Max swung round to face him, keeping a firm grip on Alex.

'Your probation officer? Well, what the hell's she doin' here? Paying a visit maybe, to make sure you's behaving or summ'et?'

'Don't know why she's out here,' Nick mumbled. 'She just drove up and seen us. Now I's in real trouble on account of I'm in the hostel, see. 'Ent supposed to be out.'

Max reached Alex's car and dumped her down next to it, glaring at the sorry bunch surrounding him. There was a moment when Alex thought she might be able to talk her way out of her predicament but a swift kick from Max laid her groaning on the ground. This is bad, she thought. This is really bad. Closing her eyes for a moment she tried to remember all her training, desperate to dredge up something, anything that might help, but all the work they'd done at college had been designed to help her avoid this sort of situation in the first place. From what she had seen of Max, from his actions and the tone of his voice, she had little hope of appealing to his better nature. This young man was dangerous, a little psychopath in the making.

'Reckon we've no choice,' said Max to his followers. 'Can't be having you sent back to prison, can we now?' He chuckled, a humourless sound that made Alex want to shudder. 'No, I say we put her to good use. Got all these accidents set up as drownings – well, let's do it properly this time.'

There was a gasp from someone in the group but no-one protested as Max went on.

'Is sick of all this anyway. We'm clearing off after this, boys. More profit to be made in Bristol any night of the week. Don't know about you lot but I'm sick of all them yokels. Sick of Old Man Monarch and his stupid secrets an' all. I say we leave her in the marsh, make it look like all the others and make sure Tom Monarch's lot get done for it.'

'How we gonna do that then?' demanded someone – Jason, Alex thought.

'Easy,' said Max. I got a couple of notes from him – just rip off who they's sent to and leave 'um scattered around. Mr Plod'll maybe think he lured her out here. And look,' Max fished in his pocket and pulled out the torch he'd been using out on the marsh, 'he give us this. Now, it maybe has my prints on the outside so I'll have to wipe it, but sure as eggs his prints is on the batteries, inside. So that's getting left too.'

Nice, thought Alex. Cunning – and it just might work. She felt a twinge of pity for 'Old Man Monarch', whoever he might be. Sounds like an old river legend, she thought. A venerable fish or maybe a frog . . . Focus, she told herself fiercely. This is not the time for stupid flights of fancy. Max stood over her and stared at the slumped form.

'So lads,' he said, his voice turning sly and suggestive, 'anyone fancy a bit of fun before we do her?'

Alex went cold with horror, then felt a rush of fury that made her head swim. She forced herself to lie still, waiting for one of them to get within range. As a man, Max's followers stepped back and Alex was relieved to hear Nick Stevens' voice.

'That's out of order, just wrong that is. 'Ent having nothing to do with that sort of thing.' There were murmurs of agreement from the others but Max rounded on them angrily.

'What, you's not worried about wasting her then? Pretty sick set of values you lot has.'

''Ent so sure about that neither,' muttered someone, and Alex could sense the fear in them now. Max was not about to let any reluctant witnesses leave the scene and they knew it.

'Well, let's just get rid of her and be off,' said Max, and he leaned over to haul her apparently senseless body up.

Despite the desire to flinch away from him, Alex lay heavy and still, her full weight forcing him over towards her. As Max heaved her upright she brought her knee up as fast as she could, slamming it between his legs. Max went down as if he'd been slugged round the back of his head and Alex stepped backwards, looking down at him as he writhed in agony in the mud. She risked a quick glance around and froze in shock as she realized that not three but seven or eight men were now surrounding her. Nick stood a few yards away, his posture rigid, his eyes staring at her in terror and she realized he had something pressed up against his throat, a knife – the stranger behind him was holding a knife to his throat. Moving very slowly she stepped out of reach, searching frantically for a way out of the situation.

'Do not be afraid,' said a soft voice, and a tall, muscular figure with greying hair stepped forwards. 'We don't mean you harm,' he continued. 'We were about to intervene but it seems you's more than capable of taking care of yourself.'

The unknown man grinned at her, flashing a gold tooth before gesturing to several henchmen to pick up the still-writhing Max. They dragged him away and dumped him unceremoniously beside the other car, leaving Alex in the centre of a group of men, all but one total strangers. She looked at Nick and realized he seemed close to fainting.

'I don't think these three were going to go through with anything,' she said, addressing the man with the gold tooth. 'Anyway, he's one of mine and I'll be in real trouble if he gets killed when he's supposed to be in the hostel.' There was an uncertain pause before the man threw back his head and laughed. The others raised a few chuckles but kept tight hold of Max's gang, watching their leader for any indication of his wishes.

'You have spirit,' said the leader nodding with approval. 'I like that in a woman.'

Now was not the time to protest at being patronized, Alex decided. Anyway, she owed this man and his collection of ruffians a huge debt. Providing they were going to let her go, of course. She wasn't sure she trusted them and she didn't like the glint in Gold-tooth's eyes as he watched her, standing still but poised like a cat wondering whether to pounce.

'What will you do, to teach him a lesson, if I release him?' he asked.

Bloody good question, thought Alex. Take him back to court and have him sent down? He wouldn't like it but he'd not learn much from it either.

'I want to make sure he learns from this,' she said, tilting her head defiantly and meeting his stare with a confidence she was far from feeling. 'If I take him back to court I can get an extended residency order . . .' She was losing them. A look of impatience flitted over the leader's face at the jargon. She took a deep breath and began again. 'I'm his probation officer and I can make it so he lives where I say, works where I say he can, comes to my centre and does anything I want him to. He will learn a proper trade and I'll not let him go until he shows he's fit to mix with decent people. His life will be mine until then.' At least, that's the theory, she added silently.

Gold-tooth nodded and a slow grin spread over his face. 'That is quite a lesson,' he said. 'And also quite a task. What makes you think you can do this?'

'I think it is harder to live under constant supervision for two years than do a short time inside,' said Alex. 'If lads like Nick break the law then they give me the right to stick my nose into their lives and tell them what to do until they learn how to behave.' Or until the probation order ends, she added mentally.

Gold-tooth flicked his fingers and the man holding Nick let him go, stepping away as the young man slumped forwards, almost falling over.

Staring at him, Gold-tooth said, 'You are fortunate you have someone who cares enough to argue for you. Remember this and learn your lesson. Now go – get off the Levels and stay away.'

Nick needed no encouragement. Taking to the road, he raced out of sight, arms and legs pumping frantically as he tore through the night to the dubious welcome of the hostel in Highpoint.

'So,' the man continued, 'we need to decide what to do with the rest of you.'

Chapter 17

After a short but brutal argument, Dave drove off towards the Levels with Sue following in her own car. Despite his misgivings, her argument that with two vehicles they could cover twice the ground did make sense, though he had insisted she take a torch, some chocolate, a flask of hot tea and several blankets. He had also set out her area for the search.

'Don't go outside this part,' he said, marking Sue's copy of the 'Edgar' with a red pen. Sue considered this unnecessarily melodramatic but agreed, somewhat reluctantly, when he added, 'I don't want to be looking for you as well. If we meet up at this point here,' he indicated the road running past Kings Sedgemoor, close to the peat works, 'say every forty-five minutes, then no-one's going to be searching for someone who has already been found.'

Slightly reassured by his show of confidence, Sue set off, heading for Godney, where Simon's mother and two brothers lived with occasional additions from unspecified relatives. Although she had done the journey several times for home visits, she discovered driving on the Levels at night was a whole different game from popping out during the day. Even in winter it was possible to orientate yourself by looking out over the landscape, but in the dark every road, every hedge and ditch looked the same. She found herself resorting to Alex's method of route finding – reciting landmarks and turns to herself in an effort to keep on track.

'Right on to gravelly bit, big hedge on my left,' she sang softly as she bowled through the night. 'Then left at the willows, watch out for the rocks.' She swerved round the broken stones in the centre of the track and headed up the slow, low hill towards her destination. Suddenly there was a bright, white flash followed by an explosion behind her and off to the left. Sue slammed on her brakes and leapt from the car, peering out over the marsh and blinking to clear the faint spots from her vision. All was still and she was just about to dismiss the incident as kids playing with fireworks when the faintest sounds reached her. Tiny, plaintive voices were coming from the same direction as the explosion. Gritting her teeth as she wrestled with the heavy steering, Sue fought the car into a multiple-point turn and headed down towards the source of the noise. It was close to the meeting point and only a bit off her designated area, she thought. It wasn't like she was going to get lost on the marsh.

Simon had also seen the flash and was heading towards it as fast as his tired legs could carry him. He didn't like fireworks and the bang had caused him to stop in his tracks, frozen for a moment as he shivered in the cold air, but Alex was relying on him: he had promised to get help and Simon always tried to keep his word. Rounding a long, slow bend in the road he slowed when he saw several figures hurrying towards him. Slipping in amongst the stunted willows, Simon shuffled forwards, alert and ready to bolt past if necessary.

'Who's that then?' came a voice ahead of him and he stepped out into the road with a sense of relief.

'Mrs Mallory?' he managed, though his breath was coming in short gasps. He was an accomplished runner but steady, long distances were his great strength. In his anxiety over Alex he had upped his pace too high and had been fading fast.

'Oh – 'tis you lad. Just in time too. Come on – 'ent no time to waste, else he'll be gone. Come *on*!' Ada grabbed Simon's arm and began hauling him towards the path leading to the first hidden bridge. Simon flinched, pulling his hand away and scuttling out of reach.

'No, you's gotta come with I,' he said. 'She's out there, and they's looking for her and I promised.' He was almost crying in his desperation.

Ada grabbed him again and held on more firmly this time.

'I don't know what you is on about, boy, but unless your friend is up to their neck in the marsh I reckon we got more of an emergency situation right here. Now come on!'

Swerving round the bend, Sue almost took them all out. Responding instinctively to their shocked, white faces she slammed on the brakes, swerving over to the other side of the road and just missing Lily by a few feet.

'Simon!' she shouted as she flung open the door and hurried across the road. Simon took one look at her and tried to bolt but Ada still had him firmly by the arm, determined he was not going anywhere.

'Where the bloody hell have you been?' Sue demanded, then paused as she took in the motley little group. 'And just what is going on?'

Stepping into the silence, Ada gestured urgently.

'There's a man fallen in the marsh. He's sinking – could even be gone if we'm going to stand around here gabbing. You got to help, both of you.' Still gripping Simon's arm she dragged him towards a narrow gap in the hedge.

'I got to go,' wailed Simon. 'I left her and they was looking for her. 'Ent safe – and I promised.'

Sue leaned forwards and took hold of his other arm.

'Promised who? Who's not safe? Come *on* Simon!'

'You'm hurting,' said Simon. 'You's pulling me in two. Let go or I 'ent going nowhere.'

Sue let go of him and gestured to Ada who reluctantly released the distressed young man. Simon groaned and rubbed at his wrists and elbows, turning his back on the others before speaking over his shoulder.

'Is Alex, out there, up along she is. Was a couple of lads from Bristol an' one from hostel and they was chasing but I hid her. So I got to get back with help and soon 'cos I reckon she 'ent safe there. Not for long.'

'We can go after,' said Ada. 'You got to help – he's drowning out there!'

Sue laid her hand gently on Simon's shoulder and spoke to him softly.

'We have to help Ada's friend,' she said. 'Then we'll go and get Alex, I promise. Come on – Ada, you lead the way.'

Ada was off across the fringes of the marsh, bounding from one tuft of reeds to another with a speed and grace that belied her years. Lily, who had been silent throughout this exchange, gave Sue a hard look and set off after Ada, her face grim as she hopped carefully across the worst of the mud.

Reluctantly, Simon followed with Sue bringing up the rear, her feet still encased in light sandals despite Dave's good advice. The dank water oozed around her feet, trickling between her toes, and she fought the temptation to rip off the useless shoes and scrub her feet clean on the drier grass. Some 'night in' this was turning out to be, she thought, as with gritted teeth she ploughed after the others.

Out in the marsh, Tom still clung to the fragile mat of withies but he could feel his strength failing and it was getting harder to grip with every passing minute. It would be so much easier just to let go and slip beneath the surface but his will to live was strong and he tilted his head back, thinking of Ada. How would she feel, he thought, coming all this way round to find him gone. She'd had enough grief this past year without having to carry that as well. Despite appearances, Tom was at heart a kind man and he had always nursed an affection for Ada. He rather wished he had hung around when they were both young and free but he had followed the *kumpania*, still being the dutiful son, and by the time they had returned to the Levels Ada was walking out with Frank Mallory. He closed his eyes, remembering Ada as she had been all those years ago, but forced them open again as he felt himself drifting, in danger of falling asleep as the cold wormed its way through his body, slowing his heart and making each breath a little shorter than the last.

It would not be long now, he thought. There were lights dancing in front of his eyes and he was beginning to hallucinate, soft voices whispering his name out in the dark.

'Tom? Tom! Don't you go dying on me now! I 'ent been ploughing through all this muck just to see you give up.'

He wasn't hallucinating and the lights were reflections from the torches held by Ada and her friend. Friends, he corrected himself as he saw the shadowy figures out of the corner of his eye. Oh, she was a real miracle worker. He smiled and felt the surrounding water slip up around his mouth. Too late, he realized, just a few minutes too late . . .

There was a flash of agony from his head and he felt his face rise an inch or two out of the water. Not daring to open his mouth to protest, he stifled a moan as Ada, leaning far out across the mud, held on to him by his hair. Behind her, Lily held her by the belt of her coat with Simon and Sue hovering on the little mound, unsure what they should do.

'Gimme your belt,' Ada puffed. 'Come on Lily, we needs something for a rope here.'

Tom, his head pulled back by Ada's fierce grip, wondered briefly if she was going to lasso him around the neck and try to pull him out that way. He wasn't sure he wouldn't prefer that – quick strangulation would be preferable to scalping. Then he heard another voice in the distance, a man, and he had a horrible vision of Max returning to gloat over his plight.

'Sue? Sue – I saw your car. What the hell are you doing out there?' called Dave Brown, hovering on the solid ground and peering out over the mud.

'Dave? Dave, stay where you are!' yelled Sue, turning to Ada for help.

'I don't know the way – can you show him?'

'And how do you suggest I do that then?' puffed Ada from her prone position holding on to Tom. 'Lily, gimme the belt – hurry up woman. Now go and get that lad. 'Nother pair of strong arms is what we need.'

Lily slid down the side of the mound and began to retrace her steps across the little causeway towards Dave.

'Ask him if he's got anything useful in that car of his,' Ada shouted after her, 'like a rope or summat.'

Dave watched in astonishment as Lily appeared to walk on the water towards him, her feet hidden by the low layer of mist that clung to the landscape, coiling around the willows and snaking through the reeds.

'Stop looking like that,' she said, reaching the bank beside him. 'Like a guppy, with yer mouth all flapping open. Now, you got anything useful in yer car? I'm assuming you is in a car, unless you's another crazy runner like young Simon.' She blinked up at him, eyes bright in the moonlight. Like a curious little bird, he thought.

'Do you know Simon?' he asked, still trying to understand what was going on.

'Course,' said Lily pushing past him. 'Everyone knows Simon. Now – have you got a rope or summat useful or not? A man's drownin' out there. Hurry up, will you?'

Dave opened his mouth to ask another question but she seized his arm and shook him impatiently.

'What part of "drowning out there" is you having trouble with? Stir yerself will you? Don't know how long Ada can hold him up.'

Galvanized by her tone, Dave ran to his car which was pulled up on the road just behind Sue's vehicle and flung open the boot, rummaging amongst the contents for his tow-rope.

'How far away is he?' he asked over his shoulder.

'Too far to use the car so is up to us to get him out,' snapped Lily. She nodded her approval as he returned, tow-rope, torch and a blanket in his arms.

'Just you be careful and don't go wandering off,' she said stepping on to the hidden track. Dave followed her, stepping gingerly on to the mud and jerking his foot back as the walkway swayed a little under their combined weight.

'Give us a bit of space, boy,' Lily snapped. 'You stay about three, four paces back and we'll be fine.'

Out on the marsh Ada had succeeded in looping the belt around Tom's shoulder where his arm was still supported by the make-shift mat. As Simon and Sue took the strain, she released Tom's hair and together they hauled his head a bit higher. Tom spluttered and spat as his mouth came clear of the dank water.

'Damn you woman,' he said, 'I reckon I'm nearly bald now!'

'Just be grateful you 'ent,' snapped Ada. 'Don't know what I'da hung on to otherwise.'

The arrival of Lily with Dave in tow was too much for the small mound on which they were all balanced. Simon felt his feet slip as he tried to stay on solid ground and he was only saved by Sue grabbing his shoulder and spinning him round to the track way. As they loosened their grip, Tom felt himself begin to sink again but Dave, alerted by his frantic shout, grabbed the belt and took the strain, lifting his head clear once more. Swiftly organizing the group into a line to take the strain, Dave began the difficult and muddy task of securing the tow rope around Tom's upper body. Ideally he wanted to get it around his chest, under his arms but after several attempts and a face full of marsh mud he was beginning to wonder if that were possible.

'We could tie it on to the belt,' suggested Ada but Dave shook his head.

'We're going to dislocate his shoulder if we try to pull him out that way,' he said.

'Don't care,' came Tom's voice from the marsh. 'Just get us out will yer? Reckon that's better than drowning.'

Dave hesitated, but a look at the group showed him they were tiring. It was late, it was getting much colder and the moon was waning. If they were going to save Tom, he thought, it would have to be soon. He lined them up again and settled on the edge of the mound.

'Wait,' he said. 'Don't pull until I tell you, then slowly and as smoothly as you can. I'm going to try and get the rope around him but we need to raise him up a bit first, okay?'

The group nodded wearily, shifting their feet on the damp ground and flexing their shoulders. Dave called to Tom.

'Can you turn round at all?' he asked. If you can move that arm a bit I can use the mat to support me and get this around you.'

Tom groaned softly but began to twist his upper body, inching the withies towards the kneeling policeman. As the mat came within reach, Dave reached out and grabbed Tom's arm, pulling as hard as he could.

'Now!' he called.

On the mound, Ada, Lily, Sue and Simon gripped the belt and pulled. They were crammed up close together, hands almost touching, and it was difficult to get a proper pull going, but slowly, inch by painful inch, Tom's body moved closer to the mound and safety. The pain in his shoulder was awful. It felt as if his arm was about to be ripped off and Tom stifled a groan. Then he felt the mat dip as Dave slid forwards and reached under the water, struggling to get the rope around him. Tom moved his floating arm, ready to help but Dave hissed at him to stay still.

'If that goes,' he panted, 'we'll never get you out. Hold on – nearly there . . .'

Choking and spitting, Dave pulled his face free and sat back, the muddy end of the rope in his hands. Swiftly knotting it into a loop he passed it along the line of followers.

'Don't just drop the belt,' he yelled as Lily grabbed for the rope. 'Hang on – Ada, you and me, we'll take the strain on the rope first, then the rest of you let go of the belt and get the rope. Can you move back a bit – space yourselves out so you can get a good pull going?'

For a long, back-breaking time nothing happened. Like the world's most unlikely tug-of-war team, the mismatched little group set their heels into the mound and hauled as hard as they could. At the end of the line Simon wrapped the end of the rope around his body and leaned backwards, using his bodyweight to steady them. Then, so slowly they barely noticed, Tom began to move through the mud towards the safety of the hillock. There was a judder as his shoulders were pulled clear and he wrestled to free his other arm, before reaching out to touch the mound with his fingertips. The feel of solid ground filled him with hope and he felt his energy returning, despite the bitter cold and the tearing pains in his head and shoulder. Forcing himself to stretch his arms further than he thought possible, he grabbed on to the nearest clump of reeds, hauling himself a further few inches before they came away in his hand. Dave dropped to his knees again and reached out, catching hold of Tom's wrists. Suddenly it was all over. With a drawn-out sucking noise, Tom's upper body popped clear of the mud and he slid along the mat to land on the mound. Wriggling and kicking he freed his legs before collapsing exhausted, soaked and barely conscious, all his energy burnt away in the last desperate few minutes.

Dave sat down heavily, drawing a deep breath before feeling around for the torch he had abandoned in the reeds, and was nearly pushed into the water himself as Ada shoved him out of the way to kneel beside Tom, lifting his head and checking his breathing.

'Tom? TOM! You alright then?' She shook the semi-conscious man by both shoulders until he coughed, took a great breath and let it out in a groan.

'Let me be, woman,' he said, 'you're killing me. Let go my shoulder will you?' He rolled over and tried to get to his knees, flopping back on to the ground with a cry as he put his weight on his damaged arm, his ankle turning over beneath him.

'Think maybe it's broken,' he said, clutching his right leg.

Dave scrambled to his feet and took control, ushering Sue, Lily and Simon off the marsh and wrapping the blanket around Tom.

'Can you stay with him?' he asked Ada. 'I've got a police radio in my car – I'll call for an ambulance.'

'Don't you leave me alone with her,' grumbled Tom. 'She's a mad woman. Nearly killed me, she did.'

'Oh stop yer grumbling,' said Ada fondly. 'Was your stupid idea in the first place, remember? And you said you didn't care – said was better than drowning.'

'That,' said Tom, 'was before I knew how bloody much it would hurt.'

On the bank beside the hedge Dave found Sue and Simon in animated conversation.

'I'm going to take him off to find Alex,' said Sue. 'He knows where she is – says there's something wrong with her car so I need to go and get her . . .'

'Before them men find her,' added Simon. 'Is from Bristol, most of 'em and I know they's up to no good.' A faint smile flitted over his face and he added, 'When I was hiding, this Tom, he seen us but he never let on. Told us to wait until him an' the other lad was past. Was then I saw Derek Johns and I figured I'd better be getting off the Levels myself.'

Dave grabbed Simon's shoulder and pulled him round.

'You say you've seen Derek Johns? You're sure it was him?'

Simon tried to wriggle free, frowning at the young policeman.

'I know what I seen and I knows Derek Johns. Went over that way.' He pointed across the fields towards Glastonbury and Lily drew her breath in sharply.

'What?' Dave demanded, turning on his heel.

'Middlezoy is over that way,' Lily replied. 'There's this footpath, see. Cuts out a whole mess of roads so is an easy distance.' Dave looked at her, waiting for some information that made sense of her concern. 'Lawks, boy, Iris lives there!'

Dave found himself in a situation with three emergencies all needing urgent action but he was stuck out on the Levels on his own. To make matters worse, he didn't know where Alex was so he couldn't send a car to her aid, even if he could get the radio working. Reception all the way out here was patchy, to say the least. Tom was the most urgent case, he decided. He needed to get to hospital as soon as possible. Apart from his shoulder injury and broken ankle, he was almost certainly suffering from hypothermia and shock.

'I'm going to call for an ambulance for Mr – Tom. You wait here until it arrives and make sure he gets to hospital. Then you, Simon, are coming with me. I need you to show me where Alex is hidden. No,' he cut off Sue's protest, 'I'm a police officer and if she's in any kind of trouble then I need to handle it. I'll try to get some back-up sent to Iris Johns' place just in case Derek turns up.'

'What do we do after the ambulance arrives?' demanded Sue.

'You go home,' said Dave firmly. 'You go home and wait until I bring Alex back. Make tea or hot water bottles or – well, you know.'

Sue glared at his retreating back. 'Of all the insufferable, patronizing, sexist little shits . . .' she muttered.

Lily watched her anxiously. 'I really does think we should be warning Iris,' she said touching Sue's arm. 'Maybe we could go when Tom's in the ambulance. Take that nice car of your'n and just check all's fine.'

Sue's eyes followed Dave as he pulled open the door to his car and tried to raise the control room on his radio.

'That's exactly what I'm thinking too,' she said softly.

Derek could not believe how hot it was. Despite the drizzle that fell and soaked his worn clothes, he was wet through from the inside out. A pulse beat in time through his hand and arm up to his head and his vision was blurring as he scrambled and slid his way across the fields and ditches towards the house in Middlezoy that had until recently been his home. Despite his discomfort, Derek was feeling optimistic, buoyed by the success of his recent plans. Tom Monarch was out of the picture – right out by now, probably. The Great Marsh was unforgiving and few men fell foul of that bleak landscape and survived. That left the way clear for his lad, Newt, to take over when he was released from Dartmoor because there was little chance the rest of the gang would hold together without Tom's guiding hand.

Derek was tired – tired from running, tired from hiding and tired from worrying about the constant danger of being seen, recognized and captured by the police. By his own standards he'd worked long and hard for his position and the money he had squirreled away in a couple of places and he reckoned he'd earned a decent rest. His idea was to escape abroad, somewhere there was no extradition and with a halfway decent climate. He wasn't worried about getting out of the country. Derek had 'friends', and more importantly he had people who owed him a favour or two. They might think they had escaped their obligations but for the unlucky few there was a nasty surprise coming.

He rounded the last bend in the footpath and trotted along the hedge that bordered the road heading into the village. Most houses had their curtains closed against the cold night, he noted. A few street lamps cast a feeble trickle of yellow light but apart from the village pub, a beacon of warmth at the end of the main street, all was still. Derek crept out from behind the hedge and made his way to the footpath running down through the allotments. This had often been his escape route in a tight situation and tonight it was the key to the back of his house. Stealthily he edged past the garden gate and moved slowly up the path.

A harsh, white light came on, blinding him with its intensity and he stumbled, knocking over the rubbish bin and setting a dog several doors up barking frantically. Damn the woman, he thought savagely. What the hell was she playing at, setting traps like this? He grabbed the door handle and pushed but it refused to budge, either locked or bolted. Furious at this thwarting of his plans he wrenched the worn bag off his shoulder, buried his uninjured hand in it and punched out the glass. The pieces had scarcely hit the floor before he had his arm through and the latch undone. The door flew back, hitting the wall with a resounding thud and he stepped into the familiar kitchen, coming face to face with Iris.

There was a moment's stillness as she stared at him before opening her mouth to scream.

'Now then,' Derek said in what he hoped was a calm voice, 'no need for that. 'Tis only I.' He smiled, oblivious to the hideous gargoyle features he presented to the woman before him.

Iris stepped away from him, feeling behind her for the knife drawer. She managed to get it open and grabbed the handle of one before Derek seized her arms, causing the make-shift weapon to clatter on to the counter.

'What kind of a welcome d'yer call this?' he said. 'You was waiting for this, weren't yer? Else why not have no funeral, nor nothing – reckon you knew I was still around. Never said nothing, neither. Good girl.'

He tried to pull her close but Iris wrenched herself free and stood a few feet away, shaking from the shock of his appearance.

'I need to get a message to Newt,' said Derek. 'Is all clear on the Levels again, I seen to that so he can pick up again when he's out. Just, I need 'um to pull a few decent deals a bit sharpish. I'll be needing some money where I'm going and a boy should look after his father.'

Something snapped inside Iris. All her caution, all the little tricks she had employed over the years to help her survive a marriage to this man deserted her. Her one instinct was to protect her remaining son from this man and his evil influence.

'I told you before,' she said. 'You 'ent having nothing to do with Billy. Inside or when he's out, makes no difference. He's no son of your'n. You'm not even his father so you just get out of here and leave us alone.'

At last it was said, out in the open and to hell with the consequences. A fierce joy filled Iris as she watched Derek's face, what there was of it, crumple as the meaning of her words struck him.

'What d'you mean, I'm not his father?' he asked finally.

Iris watched him, poised like an animal ready to flee.

'I asked you – what do you mean?' Derek yelled, lunging towards her.

Iris made a dash for the kitchen door, slamming it in his face and leaning her full weight on it before he could react. Derek swayed back and forth, blinking his eyes to clear his sight. Damn lights, he was getting black spots what with the light bulbs flashing at him and him being so tired. Hungry too. He'd better get his wife to make him something and then they could sit down while he sorted all this out. He reached for the door handle, grasping it with his injured hand. A fierce pain burned through his arm and he let out a cry, almost falling as the dizziness threatened to overwhelm him.

Behind the door Iris bit her lip, shaking in terror and close to fainting herself. The shock of seeing her dead husband was matched by the horror of his appearance. That once handsome face was torn and ragged with the great scar across one cheek. His eye, clawed by Andrew Cairns as he fought for his life, was bloodshot and swollen and there was that awful dip in his skull, evidence of the collision with the lock-gate last November. He was ragged, filthy and he stank of the marsh, of sweat and a sickly overlay of infected flesh.

She took a deep breath, trying to clear the smell from her nostrils, and cast around the room for something to jam the door shut whilst she called for help. Perhaps she should just run, she thought. Get out of there, appeal to a neighbour for help. No, she could not bring that horror to anyone else's door. Still shaking she risked leaving the door for an instant, seizing an armchair and pushing it across the doorframe. There was silence from the kitchen and she wondered if he'd gone, but she knew Derek too well. He wasn't going anywhere before he got what he wanted, whatever that was.

Her suspicions were confirmed by a knocking on the door, quiet at first but accompanied by the rattling of the door handle as he tried to force his way through. The phone, she thought. Call for help, get the police. As she scuttled across the room there came a hammering on the front door and her knees buckled in terror. What if Derek was not alone? What was she going to do now?

'They're on their way,' Dave said. 'As soon as he's been picked up I want you all to go home, understand?'

Ada stared at him sullenly and then turned back to Tom who was laid out on the mound, still swathed in Dave's car blanket. Sue shrugged and muttered something.

'I guess,' she said.

Simon was frantic, hopping from one foot to another in desperation. In his head he could see Alex as he had left her, small and helpless, her large eyes watching him as he disappeared, leaving her alone with only his promise to sustain her. Simon was an excellent runner but not much of a judge of character. In his imagination he was supposed to return like an avenging knight of old, saving her from an unspecified but deeply unpleasant fate and she would smile at him, thank him and tell her colleagues how brave he was. He was so busy with this wonderful outcome he didn't hear Dave's voice.

'Come on Simon, stop dreaming will you? Get in the car – you know where Alex is so we don't need to be driving around the rest of the night looking for her.' Glancing over his shoulder at Ada and Tom, Simon trotted off and settled himself in the front seat of the car.

'Buckle up,' said Dave turning the key. Simon blinked at him uncomprehending.

'Seat belt,' said Dave, 'Put the damn belt on!'

When the young man started pulling at his waistband, Dave leaned over and tugged the seatbelt around him, fastening him in safely. Simon squeaked and pulled at the fabric and Dave realized he'd probably never ridden in a modern car before.

'It's all right,' he said, trying to sound patient and calm. 'That's just to hold you safe while we're moving. Look, you can move it slowly but a sudden jerk holds you in the seat.' He gave a tug on the belt to demonstrate before turning his attention to driving. Simon sat beside him, pulling the belt back and forth, a grin spreading over his face. Glancing at him out of the corner of his eye, Dave wondered how reliable he was as a witness – or a guide. He seemed a bit simple minded sometimes – a lot of the time, actually.

''Tis there,' said Simon abruptly as they swept round a bend and flashed past the lay-by. Dave caught a glimpse of several figures huddled around two cars, one of which was Alex's Citroën and he braked hard, swinging the car around and causing the belts to lock as he did so.

'Ooof!' breathed Simon.

'Now you know what they're for,' said Dave grimly, skidding to a halt in front of a silver car. The glare from his headlamps showed a scene resembling something from a crime film. One young man was slumped on the ground clutching at himself and moaning whilst two others knelt near him, heads bowed. Behind them several figures prowled, heavy sticks or something similar in their hands. Flinging the door open, Dave leaped out of the car.

'Police!' he shouted. 'No one move. Stay where you are.' There was a moment's silence, broken by the rough breathing from the man on the ground and then another figure stepped into the circle of light.

'A timely arrival,' said the newcomer, smiling at Dave. The man was tall with dark hair, a sprinkling of grey at the temples. Dave stared at him in astonishment, lost for words.

'But – I've just pulled you out of the marsh,' he managed finally. No – it was not this man, he realized. A gold tooth glinted at him in the light from the car. Not this man but surely his twin . . .

'You must mean my brother Tamas,' said the man. 'I trust he is safe. You say he has had an accident?'

'He's fine,' said Dave. 'Never mind about that – what's going on here?'

'It's a good job they were around,' said a familiar voice, and Alex stepped forward. 'Hello Dave. I see Simon found you in the end.' She nodded at Simon who was wrestling with the seat belt, nearly choking himself in his efforts to get out of the car. 'Stay there Simon. Wait in the car. Everything's alright.'

Dave began to feel he was losing control of the situation, though in truth he had never had control in the first place.

'Alex, I'm glad you're safe,' he said. 'Can you go over and wait by the car with Simon please.'

Alex walked over to stand beside the gold-toothed man, Milosh.

'These men came to my aid,' she said softly. 'I don't know what they were doing out here but I think I have been very, very lucky. It's these little toe-rags you should be questioning.' She indicated Max and his gang.

'Especially him!' She pointed to Max. 'He was going to kill me. Leave me out here as a warning, I think. To their credit, the lads didn't seem too keen to do anything much. It's only him,' she pointed to Max again, 'who thought it was a good idea.'

'Now Alex, you know that's for the courts to decide,' said Dave. 'Perhaps we could start with a few names?'

He looked around and realized that most of the surrounding figures had vanished, slipping away into the rising mist. He felt a moment of anxiety, remembering his instructor from Hendon.

'Never rely on the badge, lad. There's some that respect your authority and a darn sight more who won't. You need to make them know you are in charge and, if necessary, have the means to back it up.' Here he was, alone, outnumbered and very much struggling to stamp his authority on events. In fact he was having trouble understanding events, never mind controlling them. There was a footstep behind him and he whirled round to see Simon, who had finally succeeded in freeing himself from the car.

'We were out around here, checking on, shall we say, our assets,' said Milosh calmly. 'There have been reports of trespassers and some who seem intent on damage or harm. It is indeed fortunate we happened on this group and were able to assist in our small way. Now, it is late and I think I would like to see how my brother is after his misadventures, so I bid you farewell . . .'

'Not without answering a few questions first,' said Dave, stepping forward to grab his arm. 'For a start, there's the matter of this man.' He gestured towards Max, who was still slumped in a heap by the car. Milosh laughed and shook his head.

'Sadly we cannot claim any credit for him,' he said. 'Your friend here did that all on her own.' And with that he was gone, slipping away into the night with the last of his men.

Dave opened his mouth to protest but it was too late. Jason, who had been listening with interest to the exchange, began to sidle round the car, hoping to emulate Milosh and his men, but Dave grabbed his arm and pulled him back towards his own car.

'Alex, can you reach into the glove compartment and get my cuffs please?' he said, hanging on to Jason, who started wriggling frantically until Dave pulled his arm behind his back. Dave swiftly handcuffed the two accomplices together, looping the chain through the handle of Max's car. There was a faint protest over this as Max dragged himself up into a sitting position, his face white with pain.

'They scratch my paintwork an' I'll have you, copper,' he said, speaking through gritted teeth. 'And you', he pointed a shaking finger at Alex, 'I'll have you for assault, bitch.'

Dave stood over Max and stared at him thoughtfully.

'Reckon you're in enough trouble already,' he said. 'I could add threatening behaviour to the charges if you carry on.'

Max sneered up at him. 'You got nothing,' he said. 'I'm the one is hurt and you just got her word about what happened. Crazy bitch assaulted me on account of nothing. 'Ent that right lads?'

The two young men both looked away, heads down as they stared into the distance. Dave grinned and shook his head, then beckoned Alex over.

'You want another go at him, be my guest. I'm going to call for a wagon, get them taken in to Highpoint.' He walked away leaving Alex staring down into Max's red-rimmed eyes. She hovered over him for a minute before turning her back and walking a few feet towards Simon.

'Keep an eye on him with me,' she said. Simon glanced over at Max who was still struggling to stay upright.

'No,' said Alex in response to his unspoken question. 'That would make me almost as bad as him.'

Simon felt a flicker of disappointment. He was wondering how Alex had managed to fell Max in the first place and had rather hoped for a repeat performance.

'Iris? Iris! Open up, is just I,' came a familiar voice through the wooden panels of the front door. Iris gave a sob of relief on recognizing Ada's voice, casting an anxious eye at the kitchen door before she hurried down the hallway to let her in. Her eyes widened with surprise at the sight of Sue and Lily but she stepped back and gestured them inside, glancing around the street before closing and locking the door again. Ada pulled a face as she heard the thumping coming from the back room.

'We was coming to warn you,' she said. 'Sounds as if we'm a bit too late.'

'You knew?' Iris said.

Ada shook her head, reaching inside her coat for something. 'Only just found out,' she said, pulling out her shotgun.

Sue was horrified. 'You brought a gun!' she said. 'You brought a gun along with you – and you had it in my car?'

'Weren't going to leave it behind on the river bank, now was I?' said Ada reasonably. 'All that damp – would ruin it.'

'No, you don't understand,' said Sue. 'You can't wander around the countryside with a concealed weapon. It's illegal – and not safe either. What the *fuck* were you *thinking*?'

''Ent no need for that,' said Ada disapprovingly. 'Is only a rook startler anyway. Was to make a decent noise, scare that little punk Max off.'

Both Lily and Iris looked at Ada in surprise. They knew the difference between a shotgun and a rook startler and the weapon in Ada's hands was most certainly an example of the former.

There was a crash from the back room, cutting short further protests from Sue, and Iris lunged towards the chair, now moving in jerks across the floor as Derek flung his weight against the door. Lily and Sue hurried to the chair, flinging their weight on it and forcing the barrier back in place.

'Phone the police!' panted Sue. 'Now, Iris – get the police here now. Is he armed?' she added as an afterthought.

Iris stopped half-way to the phone. 'I don't rightly know,' she said.

'Best step away in that case,' said Ada lifting the gun.

There was one final shove from inside the kitchen and then an eerie silence before they heard a muffled thump. The women froze in place, forming a loose semi-circle around the kitchen door. A minute passed, then another with no sound from the kitchen.

'Maybe he's gone,' Sue whispered. She looked over at Ada and added, 'This in no way means I approve of that,' she pointed to the shotgun, 'but perhaps we could risk a quick look.'

Ada stepped forward, taking up position to the left as Sue and Lily wrestled the chair out from under the handle. Despite the noise they were making there was still no response from the kitchen.

'Give me the gun,' said Iris suddenly.

'What for?' asked Ada, backing away from her.

Iris darted forwards and held out her hand. 'If we need to shoot I can get away with it,' she said softly. 'Is my house he's broken into. Is me he's threatening. I can plead self-defence and there'll be few questions asked. Now, give me the gun.'

Ada handed the shotgun over in silence and they took up positions around the splintered door.

'Okay,' said Sue, and Ada reached out and opened the door a few inches, stepping back swiftly into the group. Iris moved forward, shotgun at the ready and nudged the door open a foot or so, then stopped and stared.

Raising the gun to her shoulder she called out.

'Put yer hands up, Derek. Come on – let's have you.'

Derek lay on the floor, his eyes closed. Iris waved Ada back and stepped over the threshold, approaching him with the wariness of a cat creeping around a dog.

'Derek?' she whispered. There was no response. 'Derek? What's happened to him?' She turned to face the women who crowded into the confined space.

'He don't look too good,' commented Lily, screwing up her face at the ripe aroma surrounding the comatose man. Ada leaned over and poked him gingerly with her foot. When there was no reaction Iris, emboldened by her husband's stillness, reached out and felt for a pulse in his wrist.

'I think he's dead,' she said.

Chapter 18

Alex had gone home with PC Brown, dozing off in the car from exhaustion. She was surprised to find Sue was missing but she was so tired she collapsed into bed and slept until half-way down the next morning. Dragged from a deep slumber laced with dark dreams of chases and hidden dangers, she finally stumbled down the stairs at around 11 o'clock, just missing a telephone call. Swearing with frustration, she was brewing coffee and planning a call to the office to explain her absence when the phone rang again.

'Yes?' she growled, snatching up the receiver on the second ring.

'Hi, is that you, Alex?' said Hector, sounding decidedly tentative.

Alex sighed heavily. Just what she needed after the last few weeks, she thought.

'Yeah. Who were you expecting?'

'Sorry, sorry – just I tried you a couple of times last night and there was no answer.'

Alex flirted with the idea it was brotherly concern that had led to this unusual level of communication but was rapidly disabused of the notion.

'There's a bit of a problem down here,' Hector continued. 'It's Mother. Er, she's been arrested again and they want to send her to prison.'

Alex raised her eyebrows at this. It was not unheard of for retired school teachers to be jailed but it certainly wasn't an everyday occurrence.

'It's that bloody protest group,' said Hector. 'She went back and was arrested again but this time she had to go to court and she stood up and refused to pay the fine. I've spoken to Archie and Dad but they said she threatened to walk out and never come back this time if we pay up. What should we do?'

He sounded so plaintive, Alex thought, like a little lost boy. So her mother had stood up to them all, had she? Despite her concern, Alex felt a stab of pride. It was not easy facing down the bullies. She knew that, probably better than anyone in her family. Still, this would cause a scandal in the circles in which her family moved and she wondered if her mother was really aware of how unpleasant a spell in prison could be.

'How long did she get?' she asked.

'Thirty days,' said Hector miserably. 'In . . .' There was a rustling of papers.

'Please don't let it be Holloway,' Alex muttered to herself.

'. . . somewhere called "East Sutton Park". Where is that?'

Alex let out a sigh of relief. At least it wasn't Holloway – or Styal or 'Grisly Risley', possibly the worst of all.

'Right, listen, Hector. Firstly, she'll probably only serve about twenty days if she behaves. East Sutton Park's down in Kent, by the Weald. It's not too bad as prisons go, actually, though there are a lot of silly rules. She'll be in with the "tellies" most likely, not with too many long-term inmates, and her sentence is so short she'll mainly be bored.'

'Who are the "tellies", Alex?' came Hector's plaintive voice.

'All those poor women who get caught without a TV licence,' said Alex. 'It's mainly women because they can't afford the licence, so they certainly can't afford the huge fine. And they're the ones stuck at home looking after the kids, all of whom spend their waking hours clamouring for a television. Not exactly hardened criminals anyway.'

There was the sound of a key scraping in the lock of the front door.

'Look, I've got to go. I'll call tonight and we can talk about what to do. Just make sure you get the court to confirm where she's been sent. Sometimes they send prisoners off in a different direction. Don't worry, Hector – it will be all right.'

She slammed the receiver down as Sue came through the door looking decidedly worn and tired.

'God, what a night.'

Sue flopped into a chair and dropped her keys on the table. Her eyes were red-rimmed with fatigue, her long hair tangled across her shoulders in a series of snarls and her feet, Alex noted with interest, were caked with mud.

'Yomping with Eddie?' Alex asked sweetly. Sue had stubbornly refused all Eddie's attempts to get her involved in his improving and energetic programme of activities.

'Fuck off,' said Sue wearily.

'Charming. And a good morning to you, too. Coffee?'

'Please. Anyway, it's your fault I've been up all night.'

Alex returned with a mug of coffee that Sue accepted gratefully. She sat at the table, waiting for her friend to recover a little before challenging her last statement.

'You buggered off last night and I waited but you didn't come back,' Sue continued after downing half the mug in three large gulps. 'I phoned Dave Brown in the end because the muppets at the police station wouldn't do anything. The next thing I know I'm out on the Levels up to my knees in mud helping Ada haul someone out of the marsh before rushing off to warn Iris about Derek who's been on the loose.'

'Yeah, I know about Derek,' said Alex. 'Simon told me. God, I hope they catch him soon. He gives me the creeps, that man. I think he's unhinged.'

Sue finished her coffee and put the mug on the table with a satisfied sigh.

'I don't think you need worry about him any more,' she said. 'He collapsed in Iris's house and they shipped him off to hospital but I heard he's in a really bad way. He's got blood poisoning and gangrene in one hand and they thought he might have septic shock. He'll certainly lose his hand, maybe an arm if he survives.'

Alex felt sick. Despite her loathing of the man, she felt a twinge of pity for him: he had lost so much in the last year – one son dead, one son in prison and rejected by his wife. He might have brought a lot of this on himself but even so . . .

'Don't start feeling sorry for him,' said Sue, who was watching Alex closely. 'He broke into Iris's house and threatened her. And the police reckon they have evidence it was him who killed that river warden and the security guard out on the Levels. He was a bit more than unhinged, believe me.'

Alex leaned her elbows on the table and screwed up her eyes.

'Even so . . .,' she began.

'No,' said Sue pointing at her. 'Not your fault. Anyway, after the police arrived and shipped him off we had several jolly hours answering questions before I was finally allowed to drive Ada and Lily home. Only Ada made me take them both back to the old peat works first.'

Alex frowned and shook her head. 'What was that for?'

Sue grinned broadly. 'She's got this theory. You know the weird music – like a flute – that's been driving everyone crazy out there? Well, Ada reckons it's from those new railings they're putting up all over the place, fencing a lot of it off. They're made from a sort of kit, squared-off metal with holes drilled for the bolts but where there are no bolts, the holes are just left open. Then the wind gets up and – flute music. Now, I'm for the shower. I can't stand all this icky stuff all over me.'

PC Dave Brown stood to attention, sweating in his tightly buttoned uniform whilst his station Inspector prowled around him, stopping occasionally to look out of the window. Dave was expecting the dressing down of his life and it looked as if he was not going to be disappointed.

'Well now,' said the Inspector finally. 'It seems you have been acting with considerable initiative.'

Somehow he made the word 'initiative' sound as bad as 'hooliganism'. Dave considered responding but chose the wiser, silent course.

'Let me see.' The Inspector rifled through some papers on his desk. "Um, a-ha, right. So.' He looked up again. 'Quite a good result under the circumstances. Looks like we've cleared up three murders on the Levels, broken up a major drug-smuggling operation and finally nailed that bastard Derek Johns.'

He seemed to be waiting for something, so Dave swallowed nervously before managing, 'Yes Sir.'

'Yes,' continued the Inspector, 'not a bad night's work. It will look very good in this month's crime figures. However . . .' And here he paused theatrically. 'However, there is the small matter of your actions. Rather than contacting the station you set out on your own, accompanied by a *civilian*, and engaged a number of dangerous criminals without authority or back-up. You placed yourself and several *civilians* at risk in the process. You also used an unauthorized police band radio which I understand is fitted to your personal vehicle, endangering our wireless security.'

Dave thought he was stretching a bit here. Any kid with a short-wave could pick up the police radio and a lot of them probably did. A swift glance at his Inspector's face, however, convinced him that it was better to maintain a discreet silence.

'In addition, we have several complaints,' the Inspector went on. 'Criminal damage to a motor vehicle, assault and wrongful arrest. Would you care to comment, Constable?'

'I cuffed two suspects to the car to prevent them fleeing the scene, Sir. Any damage was done by them. The wrongful arrest – well, I have witnesses to the suspect's threats towards Miss Hastings. And he has been identified as the supplier of the amphetamines we've been finding around town. I can't comment on the assault as I wasn't there when it occurred but I have good reason to believe it was an act of self-defence.'

There was a long silence broken by the sounds of the office next door seeping through the walls. Finally, the Inspector spoke.

'Bloody impressive piece of "self-defence" on her part – off the record mind. Wish some of the lads could handle themselves that well. Well, you will be relieved to hear we will be charging him with drug dealing as well as anything else we can make stick. That leaves me with the problem of what to do with you, Constable.'

This is it, thought Dave. All my hard work, down the drain. A solid lump of misery formed in his chest. What a week this had been. He'd lost Lauren, who was refusing to answer his increasingly frantic calls, and now he was about to lose his job. He realized the Inspector was still talking, delivering his fate in measured tones, and he turned his attention back to his superior officer.

'In light of recent events and your persistent tendency to act in what could be viewed by some as a reckless manner, I do not think you are suited to life in uniform. I am therefore recommending you to the detective branch, on three months' initial appraisal. I understand they take a slightly different view of initiative and independent action over there.'

Dave froze on the spot, not believing what he had just heard. Then he took a long, deep breath and tried to keep his voice steady as he said, 'Thank you Sir.'

'Dismissed,' said the Inspector, hiding a smile as the young constable left the office. Outside, Dave felt a great, silly grin creeping over his face. He'd made it! He was going to try out for detective. Then his smile faded as his next thought was – if only he could share this moment with Lauren.

Things began to settle down at the probation office and slowly life returned to normal – or at least as 'normal' as it ever was. Relieved to be free of Garry's ever-critical presence, Alex flung herself into her work with enthusiasm. Under Gordon's approving supervision she set out plans for several new groups including one on alcohol education.

'That seems to be the underlying problem for an awful lot our clients, especially the younger lads,' she said earnestly. 'They get really drunk and go off and do stupid things. Stuff they probably wouldn't have dreamed of doing when sober.'

Gordon sat in her tiny office, the light from the desk lamp glinting off his glasses, nodding and making notes.

'Is that your opinion as a probation officer or a psychologist,' he said finally.

Alex looked up at him, heart sinking. 'Look, I'm not a psychologist,' she said wearily. 'I did psychology at university – and philosophy before you ask. I couldn't choose between them and actually they went together rather well. Just, don't tell everyone will you? People get really stupid when they hear the word. Someone asked me once if I could read their mind. As if I'd want to!'

Gordon smiled at her reassuringly.

'I think it is a useful asset actually and I'd like to be able to use your knowledge for the good of the team but I can understand your reluctance under the circumstances. Still, perhaps our new senior will be – shall we say a little more open to new ideas.'

'They've appointed a new senior?' Alex said, startled by this news.

Gordon rose and gathered up his notes.

'Starting at the beginning of May,' he said. 'A woman, apparently. Ricky knows her, I think – you could ask him. He speaks quite highly of her.'

With that bombshell he was gone, leaving Alex to wonder whether there might be something – or someone – out there worse than Garry.

There was a timid scratching at her door and the tousled head of Simon Adams peered round. Alex's smile was genuine as she beckoned him inside.

'Thank you for coming in,' she said. 'And a very big thank you for everything you did last week. You were tremendous and I don't know what I would have done without you.' She resisted the temptation to add that she wouldn't have been out on the Levels at night if it hadn't been for him in the first place. This was a rare opportunity to bolster Simon's confidence and she had a couple of ideas on how to help him escape his hopeless and pointless existence.

'I've been talking to some people over in Frome,' she said. 'They were really impressed by how well you run.'

Simon wriggled with embarrassment, hands clutched together and head down.

'Seriously Simon, you are good. You could win races, long hard races. You have a genuine talent for this and they would like to help you.'

Simon squinted at her through his floppy hair.

'Why do anyone want to help? Don't even know I, do they?'

'They know about you,' said Alex. 'They want to offer you a place at the local college. Now, don't panic.' Simon was twitching and starting to hyperventilate. 'Listen to what I'm saying and then we can talk about it. No-one is going to make you do anything you don't want to, all right?'

Simon nodded, dropping his head on to his chest once more.

Slowly and clearly, Alex explained about the college, the running tracks and the gym and the accommodation they were offering him. Gradually, Simon lifted his head, his eyes growing wider and wider as she spoke.

'Would be a room just for me?' he asked finally.

Alex nodded. 'All your meals cooked for you and a place of your own to live in,' she said. 'There'll be other lads there but you will be the best runner in the whole college, I promise. No-one will pick on you and there are special teachers to help you get even better. You will need to do some classes as well but they will help you with them too.'

Simon waved a dismissive hand at this.

'Don't worry I none about that,' he said. 'Can read and stuff, not like Kevin Mallory or some others.'

Alex hid her surprise at this, annoyed with herself at assuming Simon might be illiterate. She studied him discreetly as he considered the proposal. Not simple, she thought, more obsessed. He had a distinct lack of social skills and very little awareness of other people, but a lot of this could be put down to his dreadful family situation and the almost total neglect that had marred his childhood.

'Really get a room all to myself?' said Simon.

Alex nodded.

A slow grin spread across Simon's face. 'Reckon I could manage that,' he said happily.

Lauren was utterly wretched. It was harder and harder to resist answering Dave's calls but she was determined not to cave in. The way he had rushed off even though he wasn't on duty had really upset her and she clung to her anger despite her misery. All that week she had struggled to focus on her job and several times Pauline had taken her into the little side office to discuss her work. Still on trial as the primary support for first-year officers, Lauren was slipping. Her work was not helped by the fact she still felt a deep dislike of Ricky. The news that the new senior was a friend of his did nothing to improve her mood.

'Reckon I might look for something else later in the year,' she confided to Sue on Friday lunchtime. 'Don't fancy another Garry in charge. Maybe worse than Garry if *he* rates them.' She nodded in Ricky's direction.

Sue was only partly listening, her attention focussed on the tea room door.

''Um, well we must wait to see,' she said, giving a bright and utterly unconvincing smile. Lauren threw her sandwich papers in the bin in disgust, sliding off her chair and stamping across to the exit.

'Forget it,' she called over her shoulder, nearly bumping into Alex on the way out.

'Lauren, come with me,' said Alex, reaching out to steer her by the shoulder. 'There's something I want to show you.'

Lauren shook her off angrily and continued down the stairs.

'Lauren!' Alex ran after her, catching up by the door into the reception area. 'Please, just a minute. It's important.'

Lauren glared at her but allowed herself to be ushered out of the main door out onto the steps. Blinking in the bright sunlight, she looked down to see Dave in the courtyard with a bicycle. Not an ordinary bicycle. Hopping down the stairs she walked over and stared at the strange looking machine.

'It's a tandem,' said Dave, a big smile on his face.

'Oh yeah?' Lauren walked slowly around Dave and his machine. 'So what?'

Dave swallowed nervously.

'Well, Sue and Alex told me you always wanted to ride a bike so . . .'

'What makes you think I would get on that great thing to be ridden around by you then?' Lauren rounded on him furiously. 'Can't even get up on that saddle, let alone pedal. Girt fool.'

She turned her back on him and headed for the steps.

'This one's specially built for you,' said Dave.

Lauren stopped and turned slowly to look at him, squinting in the glare. Dave bent over the bike to demonstrate.

'There's a proper stand to hold it steady, and here,' he tugged at the side of the bike, 'there's a folding step. You put your foot here and grab this support.' He demonstrated, pointing to a metal handle fixed to the rear handlebar. 'And the pedals are reset so you can reach them.'

Lauren walked back over and stared at the bike for a moment, a slow smile spreading across her face.

'You's making a big assumption though,' she said.

Dave rested the bike on its stand and held his arms out imploringly.

'Lauren, please. I'm so sorry about the last few months. I've hardly slept since I last saw you and even making detective doesn't seem to matter . . .'

'You made detective?' Lauren asked.

Dave nodded. 'Last week,' he said. 'But it doesn't matter.'

'Oh, I think it does,' said Lauren. 'Anyway, was not that I was thinking of. Why's you assuming I won't want to ride on the front?'

Dave flung his head back and laughed, relief and delight combined in his happy face.

Alex was joined by Sue and the rest of the office on the steps and together they watched as Dave and Lauren took their first wobbly ride around the car park, the joy on Lauren's face plain for all to see.

'Now he has to teach Brian to ride a bike,' said Alex, after they had waved the pair off onto the road and made their way back inside. 'I promised I'd help him get Lauren back – but that was the price.'

Sue shook her head in admiration. 'You are a bad woman,' she observed.

On the train to Dartmoor, Iris sat by herself, staring out of the window. Early the day before she had taken a call from the hospital telling her Derek had finally succumbed to multiple infections. She had sat, numb, for a long time. It was difficult to mourn a man who had threatened her and destroyed her family. It was even harder to mourn him a second time, for she had been convinced he was dead back in November. But, despite all the events of the past months, she still felt the need to cry. Derek had been a fine man once and even with all his criminal ways and violent past he had loved her, looked after her and in his own way treated her well. Biff, her younger son, was gone and now it was just her and Newt.

She watched the scenery flicker past the window and considered the forthcoming visit. Newt was expecting her but she had asked the prison authorities not to tell him her news. There was so much she needed to say and she had been silent for too long. A sense of desperate sadness swept over her as she thought of her eldest son, waiting for her arrival and probably wondering why she was coming. However she tried to say it, Newt was losing two fathers today.